To Theresa Menefee

PART I

CHAPTER 1

JAYNE: AUGUST 24, 2012

I'd been at the dig site since dawn, heart pounding as I watched a big yellow backhoe roar into life and begin eating away layers of modern concrete until it exposed the makeshift grave. By noon, the August heat beating down on the hot asphalt of the Leicester City Council car park had rivers of sweat trickling down my back and armpits. My face must have been crimson, because one of the archeology students I met in the pub last night had mercy on me and handed me an old hat and a damp rag to tie around my neck. I helped bring in some sandwiches for the crew, and when we returned to the grave, two of the older archeologists from the University of Leicester climbed down into the trench and began brushing away the medieval dirt by hand, moving with glacial caution. As the volunteer water girl, I was supposed to hand out Gatorade, and snacks, but most of the time I stood transfixed, as close to the narrow pit as the crowd of scientists and students would allow me. My hands were clasped behind my back so no one would see them shaking. Finally, to the morbid delight of the crowd, the corner of his left hip and a length of thigh were revealed, but darkness started to fall, so one of the crew covered him with a plastic tarp and they stopped the excavation for the night.

I wanted to beg them to bring in some lights and get on with it, for

God's sake, but they hurried over to the waiting reporters, leaving me alone beside the trench. The likely discovery of Richard III's lost grave was international news, but they phrased their claims judiciously, since it would take DNA testing to prove for certain that the bones belonged to Richard. But I already knew. Maybe I should have told them that Richard was my ancestor, and I sensed his presence beneath the concrete as soon as I set foot in the car park. But if his bones revealed that he was a hunchback, he'd be labeled ruthless and deadly as well, and capable of the murder of those two innocent boys. If I couldn't be proud of his blood in my veins, at least I would finally know the truth, and maybe the nightmares that had wrecked my sleep since I read Shakespeare's play would finally cease.

I inched closer to Richard's bones. The air from the trench carried a graveyard chill up into the warm August evening, taking my elation at their discovery with it into the twilight. The scientists and the clamoring press had moved away towards the front of the council building, but I could still hear them congratulating themselves, calling him a "find" and a "discovery." Did no one but me see him as a man?

When the soft breeze blew a corner of the tarp loose from its fastening, and left his slender white bones exposed, their nakedness brought tears of shame to my eyes. Tomorrow's headlines would probably be vile: "The King in the Car Park," or whatever tacky phrase the British press concocted, and a warrior, struck down in battle, and thrown in an unmarked grave by his enemies, would be humiliated anew, and there was nothing I could do about it.

So far I'd done a rotten job of proving Richard's innocence, but maybe I could offer him one small service. If I reattached the tarp, at least I could protect him from prying eyes of strangers for one more night.

I glanced again at the crowd of archeologists and my fellow volunteers, all hoping for their fifteen minutes of fame. No one was looking my way. I put my hand on the edge of the narrow chasm, and the smell of dank earth, last disturbed over five hundred years ago, filled my nostrils. I aimed for a safe landing spot before I braved the five-foot drop, but when my feet hit the rocky floor they slipped out from under me, and I landed with my back against the side of the trench, my Nikes only inches from his fragile hip bone. I jerked them back; maybe this hadn't been the best idea after all. I could easily cause more harm than good, and the sides of the pit were pretty steep. How the hell would I get out of here? But first, I had to do what I set out to do. I reached for the plastic edge of the tarp, just as the last ray of sunset revealed the seductive white glint of silver in the sandy rubble that my feet had scraped away. The archeologists hadn't mentioned finding anything beside his bones. A discovery of my own? Whatever it was, it must have belonged to Richard.

I closed my fingers around a hard, thin object, and before I could get a good look at it I felt a dizzying sensation that went straight to my gut. The bile rose in my throat, so I shut my eyes. When I opened them, the grey and brown sides of the trench, along with the fading light of the summer evening, had disappeared.

In their place was the crisp radiance of an early morning sun, shining on a village of canvas tents topped with bright heraldic pennants that snapped in a brisk wind.

Did I hit my head on the way down? I put a hand to my hot forehead, and took a deep breath, but instead of the graveyard scent of the trench, I inhaled the aromas of dew-soaked meadow grass and the dying embers of cook fires.

Men in polished armor, astride massive, caparisoned horses, gathered in a green field just below where I sat. I squeezed my eyes shut again, but when I opened them the knights were still there! One of them stroked the glossy neck of his restless mount before putting his metal-clad foot into the stirrup and swinging into the saddle to join the others as they formed into battle ranks. Another of them carried a banner in his shining mailed fist, and when the wind unfurled it, a white boar gleamed against a field of red and blue: the battle standard of King Richard III. It was as familiar to me as my own name.

I heard the rallying sounds of drums and trumpets, then the spectacle was gone, and I saw only the rocky floor of the trench, and the white gleam of Richard's bones. Panting, I slipped the metal object into the pocket of my jacket.

"Jayne! What are you doing down there? Are you hurt?"

Duncan, the archeology student I met last night at The Green Lion, peered over the edge of the trench.

"I'm fine. I just wanted to get a look at him, but my foot slipped."

"Here, let me help you out of there before one of my professors sees you."

He grinned and held out his hands. He didn't look angry, just drunk with triumph at being part of the greatest find of the decade.

"Want to go grab a pint with us?" he asked, after he assisted my scramble out of the trench and reattached the wayward tarp.

"No thanks, I think I'll head back to my room."

He raised his eyebrows. "You sure you didn't hit your head down there?"

"No, I'm fine. I'm just tired. Not used to getting up before dawn."

I wanted to run away from the dig site, clutching my treasure, but thieves shouldn't call attention to themselves, so I said my goodbyes and forced my pace down to a brisk walk, my sneakers silent on the pavement of the dark Leicester street. I checked my pocket, and through my thin nylon jacket I could feel the hard metal shape of Richard's white boar.

I passed a couple holding hands, headed in the other direction. It was Saturday night, and the pubs were just cranking up in the old part of the city, but tonight I didn't feel the familiar pang of loneliness. I headed straight for the door of my rented room, but my hands trembled so that it took several attempts before I could work the simple lock.

I put the object on the table, next to the chair, which along with the single bed comprised the full inventory of my furniture. I wasn't sure what caused my hallucination in the trench, but my body still trembled at the memory, so I kept the fabric of my jacket between the silver and my flesh. I needed a drink.

I opened a bottle of wine and jumped into the shower to rinse off the sandy grime that permeated the air around the dig. Should I call my mother? No, it was two a.m. in the States, and besides, what would I tell her? That I'd stolen a valuable relic that was technically the property of the British government, and that the dreams of Richard that had plagued me for years were now invading my days as well?

No way. She was worried enough about me already.

THE MEDIEVALIST | 7

The Brits didn't believe in A/C, so my room was like an oven. I threw on a thin cotton nightgown and sat down with my wine to contemplate my prize. While paging through Yale's vast collection of musty history books as I researched the fifteenth century and the Wars of the Roses for my dissertation, I'd seen dozens of drawings of the white boar Richard adopted as his emblem when he was in his teens, but they didn't prepare me for the beauty of this grotesquely exquisite item. Some long-dead artisan had lovingly rendered every monstrous detail: its coarse hairy hackles were raised and bristling, and its vicious tusks, long and sharp, were curiously untarnished, considering it had lain in the ground for half a millennium. Richard's motto, "Loyalty Binds Me," was inscribed at its feet. The motto his detractors said he repudiated when he killed his nephews and made himself king in their place.

I sipped my wine and looked back down at it, shining preternaturally white in the dim glow of my table lamp. A small ring at the base of its neck must have once held a strap of fabric or leather. I guessed it had long ago succumbed back to dust, like the flesh it had adorned.

Richard's flesh. I shivered in spite of the heat.

I thought of the striking, dark-haired man in the royal portraits, and imagined the boar against the skin of his battle-hardened young body. I put my hand out to touch the metal, but I stopped myself. Tomorrow was August 25th, the anniversary of the Battle of Bosworth Field, and if what I had glimpsed in the trench was the morning of the conflict, that inspiring scene of martial pageantry would quickly transform into a living hell of desperate sweat and bloody leather.

Not a week went by that I didn't dream of his last moments, in tear-stained nightmares filled with the dying screams of the men and the animals, the clank of steel on steel, the thud of steel on bone. Is that what I would see if I touched the boar again with my bare hand?

I'd spent hours with my head down over my laptop, searching for some tidbit that every other historian had missed, some clue that would prove Richard innocent of murder. I'd maxed out my credit cards and put my teaching fellowship at Yale on hold just to be at the dig in case they found his bones, and I couldn't afford the luxury of flying in a day early so that I could adjust to the time change. Jet lag and anticipation must have me half-crazy. But after all my fruitless research, what if I'd accidentally found a way to confront Richard face to face? What if the boar had some magic that would allow me to see him in the flesh? I had to find out.

You can do this, Jayne! I pushed the back of my chair against the wall and planted my feet squarely on the floor before I snatched the silver boar off the table. A jolt traveled up through arm to my stomach, and my head snapped back, and then forward, and for a dizzy moment, it was all I could do not to vomit. I swallowed a mouthful of sour bile and put my hands out beside me. My eyes flew open, but all I saw was darkness. What on Earth had I done?

~

I put my hands out beside me. Damp grass felt cool and slick under my fingers, and the air was a heady brew of sweat and dung, both animal and human, along with a liberal dose of stale wine and greasy wood smoke. Pale smudges dotted the darkness in front of me, and as my eyes adjusted to the dim light, I realized I was looking at a cluster of canvas tents, some with torches flickering beside them. I looked up into the night sky, and the constellations were as clear as if I were in a planetarium. The torches burning bravely in their holders were not merely for effect; their light alone kept total blackness at bay.

I heard low, brief exchanges, as if men spoke to each other in passing, along with the soft whinnies and restless stomping of horses somewhere in the darkness. A dog snarled, and let out a bark before a stern male voice silenced it.

One of the tents stood right behind me, so close my ass almost bumped the canvas. The back of my night gown was getting soaked from sitting in the wet grass, so, barely breathing, I eased up into a low crouch. I glanced down, and to my horror, saw the outline of my cold nipples through the thin white cotton. What the hell was I doing out here dressed like this? And where the hell was "here" anyway?

I heard voices coming from the other side of the canvas.

"Mayhap there will be an honorable reason why Stanley failed to heed the summons. And all this bother will be for naught."

"Only if you call greed and self-interest honorable reasons," said another man. He sounded older, and more confident than the first.

There were dry chuckles of laughter, and more voices joined in.

"Shouldn't one of us stay here with you tonight, Your Grace?" said one of them.

"He's right, Your Grace," said another. "I would be glad to stay. I know you've had trouble sleeping of late, after all that's happened these last few weeks." The voice trailed off.

"I know you mean well, and I thank you for it," another man said, his voice a deep baritone, with a rich, musical timber that could have narrated documentaries, or commanded armies. "But if I don't sleep, I can't afford to keep my two best men awake as well. Go on to your beds. If I need you, I'll send for you. I promise."

I sat back down in the cold damp grass, my chest heaving. I heard someone murmuring "my God, my God," realized it was me, and forced myself to shut up. Now I remembered it all: finding the boar in the trench, and the "vision" of an army that I saw when I picked it up. And now I was sure I had at last heard the voice of my ancestor, Richard III.

I tried to will my heartbeat back to its normal pace. The search for Richard's lost grave had been widely publicized, especially around Leicester and the University. Could a group of medieval cosplayers be staging a reenactment of his last battle? That made perfect sense. I took another deep breath. No. I hadn't stumbled on some harmless gathering where the greatest danger lay in drinking too much homemade mead. Even the most intrepid 21st century reenactor would never have tolerated the stench, and besides, I didn't hear music, or laughter, or any other sound of people enjoying themselves. A thrill of fear and excitement ran through my body. Hadn't I secretly wished for this?

I rubbed my hands on my freezing arms and decided to risk standing up. Conversation had resumed inside the tent, and this time I heard a new voice, a precise, clipped tenor. It sounded as if two men spoke at the same time. Were they arguing? No. They were praying.

My heart ached from the eerie beauty of the two dissimilar voices chanting in such perfect unison. Could I be listening to Richard III praying for victory the night before the Battle of Bosworth Field? When the chanting ceased, and the voices in the tent resumed normal patterns of conversation, I closed my eyes and listened for the one that I was convinced belonged to the last English king to die in battle.

I had to find some way to get a glimpse of him. "Deformed and rudely stamp'd" was how Shakespeare described him, and Professor Strickland, my thesis adviser at Yale, insisted he was correct. He was none too happy that I chose to use my dissertation to go against popular opinion and defend Richard from Shakespeare's unjust portrayal.

"You're wasting your time and mine, Jayne," he said. "Richard was the main benefactor of his nephews' death, and the boys went missing while they were in his care. If there was evidence to the contrary, a more experienced historian would have already discovered it."

I should have just told him that it was part of our family lore, that we were descended from the last Plantagenet king. My grandmother, Mimi, told me about it when I was still young enough to revel in the fantastic images the idea spawned in my mind, and it seemed to me that our tiny, struggling family was suddenly increased by a bevy of glittering kings and queens. The other kids in Greenville had brothers and sisters, and fathers, of course. So what if I didn't? I was a descendant of the House of York.

Then I read Shakespeare's wretched play. I wanted to believe the Bard deliberately made a fierce young warrior into a ruthless, hunchbacked monster as a dishonest tactic to sell theater tickets and curry political favor. When Richard's side lost the Battle of Bosworth Field, the Tudor victors rewrote history, and I'd been betting his bones would prove at least part of the accepted account was false. Once the seeds of doubt about Shakespeare's version had been planted, I could tackle the rest of the slander. And just maybe, the nightmares that had disturbed my sleep for years would finally stop.

But if the man on the other side of the canvas was a twisted hunchback, would that mean he was also a coldblooded murderer?

I was creeping closer to the tent when someone yanked me to my feet by the back of my nightgown, and jerked me around to face him. He was dressed in the rough garb of a medieval foot soldier, with a badge emblazoned with a bird's talon on his leather brigandine. There was another soldier beside him, holding a blazing torch.

"You brazen trull!" said the man. He put his broad face close to mine.

"What do you think you're doing up here in your chemise? Did you think to peddle your greasy cunny to the King? Get back down to the soldiers camp with the rest of the whores!"

"Let go of me!" I said.

The second soldier let out a muffled bark of laughter as his companion spun me around and shoved me forward. I put my hands out to catch myself, but the side of my face and my right shoulder hit the ground. The pain took my breath.

"There! I let go a' you! Now get up and take yourself back down the hill where your sort belongs."

"See here, Talbott!" said the other man. "Don't spoil her fair face! I've a notion to be her king myself!"

I heard them snicker as I scuttled away on all fours, my long damp nightgown catching against my knees and toes. I had no idea where I was headed, except as far away from the two of them as I could get.

"Say now, what's this? So she's not just a whore, but a thievin' whore! Where'd you get this badge, wench?"

My heart seized. The damn boar! I must have dropped it in the grass! Its magic brought me here; maybe it was my way home, to safety. But the soldier had it now.

I got to my feet and glanced back, like I'd shouted at a dozen horror movie heroines not to do. He had me by the arm in one stride, his huge hand closing around my bicep. I wanted to struggle, but the sickening disparity in our size paralyzed me, so the back of his hand caught me across the left side of my face and blood burst out of my nose.

"I told you not to ruin her face!"

"Bollix, Redmond! She'll do well enough for you as she is. And you better have her quick if you mean to do it afore she's got stripes on her back as well as a bloody nose!"

Talbott grabbed me by the front of my gown and pulled me towards him. He reeked of ale and garlic, and musty flesh.

"I believe it's you as fancies the slut," said Redmond.

"I do, and I mean to make her my sweetheart!"

He held out a round leather case towards Redmond. "Here, you can take this in to old Dick."

"Sure I will, but don't you want to see the surprise on his face when he hears Stanley's come to his aid at last?"

Talbott guffawed. "I'd rather give this whore a farewell tupping 'afore they cast her out of the camp."

He hesitated a beat. "And you can give me the hog. I'll see it gets to Lord Stanley. He can decide what to do with it."

"I can take it in to the King with the dispatch," said Redmond. He'll surely know its owner. They don't give 'em out like tuppence."

Talbott shook his head. "I wouldn't trust 'em. He might think you stole it yourself. It's a cold-blooded sod that kills his own brother's babes! Give it to me, and I'll see Lord Stanley gets it. Best let him deal with the likes of kings."

Redmond shrugged and handed it over.

My silver boar looked tiny in Talbott's wide palm. If only I'd left it in the grave, as I should have done, I'd be safe in my room. I reached for it, but he grabbed my wrist and twisted my arm behind my back. When I squealed, he clamped his hand over my mouth and nose.

"You're a foolish one, aren't you?"

He squeezed my aching nose between his finger and thumb. "I'll not let you have a breath until you quiet down!"

I did my best to nod at him, and he let go. As I gulped for air, he grabbed my arm again, pressing his thumb into the bones of my wrist.

"We've wasted enough time with this whore," he said. "You'd best get Stanley's message delivered. Let me know if old Dick smiles at you."

Redmond grunted, and turned away towards the tent.

"Don't you move," said Talbott. He let go of my wrist, and put the torch in his left hand while he put my boar into his leather jerkin with his right. He took up my wrist again and we started down the hill.

I did my best to stay upright, but my bare feet slipped in the slick grass, and each time I faltered, he yanked my arm, and my sore shoulder screamed.

How sheltered my life had been! New Haven wasn't the safest city, so if I left the campus at night, I always made sure to take a friend. There was no one to protect me now.

"Who'd you steal this fine trinket from anyway?"

When I didn't answer, he yanked my sore arm, harder this time.

"Tell me!"

My brain reeled. If I told him the truth I'd be burned at the stake, or branded a lunatic. Keep it simple, stupid...

"I found it."

"Ha! Took if off some man's cloak after he'd done with you, more like! Now who was it?"

"I don't know...I..."

He snorted. "Didn't tell you his name, did he? That's just as well."

He shoved me onward. My heart clenched like a fist in my chest; the lights from the lower camp were nowhere in sight. Where was he was he taking me?

We went on, further from the camp, and Richard, and hope. I stepped on a sharp rock, and it cut deep into the soft instep of my right foot, and I cried out. He tossed the torch into the wet grass where it sputtered and dimmed as he yanked me off my feet and held me suspended with his arm around my waist like a mother with a misbehaving toddler. He slapped his hand over my mouth again, and this time, when I felt the skin of his dirty hand, I curled my lips away from my teeth and bit a big chunk out of his meaty thumb.

But instead of letting go, he tightened his hand until my lip tore against my teeth and my blood mixed with his. He hoisted me higher under his arm and started off again, his leather boots swishing a steady rhythm through the wet grass.

There must be a vulnerable spot somewhere on this monster! I clawed at his crotch, but my nails only tore against his hard leather codpiece. He suppressed a laugh and flung me to the ground. I gagged on the blood and flesh in my mouth, and then he was on me.

I squeezed my eyes shut so I wouldn't see his ugly face over mine. The weight of his body on my chest drove the air from my lungs, and I expected to feel my nightgown ripped and my knees pushed apart, but he put his hands around my throat.

His knees pinned my arms to the wet ground, so I shoved my knee between his legs. But it was no use. I only managed one scream before he pushed his thumbs into my windpipe, and the world went black.

CHAPTER 2

JAYNE: OCTOBER 18, 1483

I sucked a burning lungful of air and struggled against Talbott's weight pressed against my chest. My eyes flew open. There was a brown beard close to my chin. I coughed out a scream before I realized it was not Talbott, but a huge, rough-coated dog.

"Fergus! What do you there? Come back to me at once!" said someone. The dog ignored him, and licked me.

"Fergus! Leave her be!"

The light of a torch floated before my eyes, and I struggled to focus. When my vision cleared, I was looking up into the face of a round little man, who stared down at me with his bald head cocked to one side and a concerned look in his small brown eyes. After administering another lick, the wolfhound jumped up and sat beside him, with much the same expression on his scruffy face.

"You've nothing to fear from him, except a wet nose," said the man, who wore the grey robes of a Franciscan friar. "It must have been your scream I heard."

The kindness in his voice brought tears to my eyes. I tried to answer him, but the sound that came out was a cross between a gasp and a croak. My throat felt like it had been sandpapered.

"You poor maid! Can you stand? We must get you back to the camp so I can see to your hurts. Can you tell me who did this to you?"

I was not going back to that camp.

I tried to back away from him, but my right arm refused to cooperate, and the pain made my head swim. He knelt down beside me and placed a warm hand on my shoulder.

"I believe your arm's been pulled from its socket. I can replace it, but I warn you it will hurt mightily for a moment."

I'd seen strong athletes cry out from the pain of a dislocated shoulder, and my whole body already ached. I couldn't endure much more, but I nodded and closed my eyes. Despite his gentle touch, it still hurt like hell, and I had to put my other hand over my mouth to muffle my scream. But it was over quickly, and the ache in my shoulder ceased immediately. I sat panting in relief, too overcome to thank him.

"Let's get you to your feet," he said, and carefully hoisted me up. I staggered against his arm, shivering in my damp gown as the soft, grey light of morning showed me we were standing in a vast open field of muddy grass.

"Do you think you can walk? It's quite a way to my tent, but I'll help you, and once we're there I can see to your cuts and bruises. I'm sorry I haven't a cloak."

I was not going back to that camp! I cringed and tried to pull away from him but I almost fell without his support. He set me upright again and peered into my face, and I saw understanding dawn.

"Did someone from the camp do this? He must have run from the light of my torch. But I'll see you come to no more harm."

He wouldn't stand a chance against Talbott. I shook my head, and to my surprise he laughed.

"I assure you I can protect you, no matter who it was that hurt you. I am King Richard's own chaplain, and his friend since boyhood. He even trusts me with his favorite animal."

He gestured towards Fergus, who was in the grass nearby, wagging his long curving tail, head down, sniffing for a rabbit or a mouse.

Richard! Pain and fear had driven him from my mind. He'd always kept wolfhounds, or so the books said. But wasn't this the day of his last battle?

He was there in the camp somewhere, living out his last hours. I leaned on the friar's solid shoulder. There was something comforting about the grey wool habit, and the matter-of fact demeanor of the man who wore it. Maybe he could protect me after all. And maybe I could get a glimpse of Richard.

"We'll be breaking camp soon, now that the rebellion is over," said the friar. He looked up at the sky and smiled.

"The rain washed away Buckingham's luck, and his few adherents. But His Grace will never be the same after his own cousin dealt him such a blow." His calm face clouded over as he shook his head.

Buckingham? Could I have been wrong in my assumption about the date? Early in Richard's short reign, his cousin, the Duke of Buckingham, rebelled against him, some said because he refused to follow the King after the disappearance of his two young nephews. It was one of the many things Professor Strickland threw in my face when he bashed my dissertation.

When we reached the edge of the camp, I trembled, and the friar wrapped my good arm around his and gave it a pat.

"No one will harm you, my child, you'll see. I'm called Brother Cynneth. Can you speak well enough to tell me your name?"

"Jayne Lyons," I said, and coughed so hard that I had to bend over and support myself with my hands on my knees.

"Come, let's get you a cup of ale! I'm sorry I asked you to speak," said the friar. "I'll warrant His Grace will see that the man who did this to you is punished."

Fergus put his rough grey head under my hand. He was as tall as my hip, and although it hurt my cut lip to smile, I couldn't suppress it. Here was protection I could believe in.

The dog stayed beside us as the friar led me through the camp, which was beginning to bustle with activity, even though the sun hadn't fully risen. Men sat on stools in front of their tents polishing armor or sharpening weapons, and there were more horses than I had ever seen in one place. One of them stepped on its handler's boot, and whatever he had been holding hit the ground with a metallic clatter. He hopped around for a moment before giving the animal a kick with the other toe in its wide belly, and someone nearby laughed and called him a "careless sod." There were whistles and catcalls as we passed, and I cowered against the friar. Finally someone had the nerve to speak up.

"What do you with the whore, Brother? We thought you'd sworn off the likes of her!"

The others laughed, but the friar ignored him. It was the second time in as many days that I'd been mistaken for a prostitute, but I understood their assumption. My nightgown must have looked to them like a chemise, the undergarment worn by all medieval women regardless of their station. And what else would a half-dressed woman be doing in an army camp, except selling the one thing she had of value? I kept my eyes lowered until we encountered a young boy with a leather case slung over his shoulder, similar to the one I'd seen Talbott and Redmond carrying last night. Fergus leapt on him, putting his wide paws on his shoulders, and in his enthusiasm, knocking the boy's soft velvet cap from his head. It landed on the muddy ground.

"Stop, Fergus!" said the boy in a stern little voice that hadn't changed yet. But he grinned as he picked up his cap and replaced it on his dark blond curls.

"Where are you off to, Johnnie?" asked the friar.

"Oh, I'm sent to Lord Stanley's camp. Last night he sent some after-ling with the grand news that he'd arrived with a hundred men, so today His Grace thought he would return the compliment by sending his 'thank you' by his page!"

"You take care around Stanley. I must see to this maid."

The boy had been averting his eyes from me as if he thought he shouldn't be looking, but now he regarded me directly for the first time.

"What happened to you, mistress?"

The friar answered for me. "She was attacked by one of our soldiers."

The boy stood up a little taller. "His Grace the King will see the man is punished."

"Come, Fergus," he said, and the dog followed him.

Their comments jogged my memory, and the conversation between Talbott and the other soldier came back to me. Redman and Talbott weren't Richard's men! They were messengers from Lord Stanley, the traitorous nobleman who would betray Richard to his death at Bosworth. If Talbott left Lord Stanley's camp with the boar, I would never get home.

We stopped at one of the smallest tents and he let go of my arm.

"Here, Rose, come and help me see to this lass." His sharp tenor cut through the noise.

A plump, freckled hand pulled back the tent flap, and a young woman peered out at us. Her hair frizzed out like an orange cloud, and her woolen gown was unlaced over her bodice. She looked half-asleep until she saw me. Her wide blue eyes shot open.

"Brother Cynneth! What in the good Lord's creation?"

She moved aside so the friar could help me into the tent. There was nothing inside except a low cot and a small wooden table that held a candle holder, a jug, and a cup. I sat down on the cot, and even though the rough linen bedclothes were stained and twisted, I would have loved to lie down and cover my head with them.

"Rose, this is Jayne. Fergus and I found her in the meadow outside the camp. I believe we saved her life. It's a good thing I was there, giving Fergus his walk." He smiled. "It's not uncommon for St. Francis to use animals to work the will of our Lord."

"You poor dear!" said Rose. She handed me a cup of liquid out of the jug, and sat down beside me. She smelled of sweat and sex, but I was so grateful for her compassion that I wanted to hug her anyway. I took a deep swallow of the ale, and for the first time felt like I might survive.

"I must get my casket of medicines, Jayne. Where are your clothes?"

"I have no other clothes." My voice still sounded like my throat was full of gravel, and the effort to speak made me cough again.

I turned up the cup and drank it dry while they stared at me. I had to get the boar. I had to get home.

"Friar, the man who attacked me isn't Richard's soldier," I said. "His name is Talbott." I closed my eyes against the pain, and forced myself to go on. "He was a messenger from Lord Stanley."

"Oh dear," said the friar. "I'm not surprised a man belonging to Stanley would be a vicious brute, but it may present a difficulty. You see, Lord Stanley is His Grace's ally, but their friendship is tenuous at best.

Lord Stanley arrived with his men to support the King only last night. But don't lets worry about that now."

Rose placed a hand on my arm. "Did you try to fight for your coin, sister?"

No one had ever called me that, and it endeared her to me immediately. Despite the protest from my torn lip, I did my best to smile at her before I shook my head and held out my cup. She poured me more of the sweet ale and I downed a swallow before I continued.

"Talbott stole a silver boar that belongs to the King."

Brother Cynneth's eyebrows shot up towards his tonsure.

"You must be mistaken. King Richard oftimes gives his badge to his retainers who have proven their loyalty, so it must belong to one of them. Why would you think it belongs to the King?"

There was no time to concoct a lie.

"Because I took it from him myself," I said.

~

*I*t was Rose who broke the silence.

"Do you mean you've lain with the King?" she asked, in an awed voice. I croaked out a laugh, and though it hurt my throat, it made me feel better.

The friar smiled, but his healthy pink face had turned white. He looked like he needed to join us on the little cot.

"Jayne, you must explain yourself. Such an accusation could be deadly," he said. "The king rarely lets his own sigil out of his sight. It was the first of its kind ever made, and it's very precious to him."

When I didn't answer, he glanced at Rose.

"Rose, would you please go and fetch Jayne some suitable clothes? A clean chemise and a warm wool gown, and some shoes, if you can find any."

"Yes, Brother, but there's not many wenches with a pair to give away, if you understand my meaning."

He reached into his voluminous robes and pulled out a small leather pouch. He took three coins out of it and handed them to her.

"I can find her something fine with this, even if I need to go into the village," she said. "Jayne, when I come back, will you tell me all about the King? I've been told he never touches the whores. But you're so young and so comely, I suppose he couldn't resist you."

She smiled. Despite the gaps in her teeth and her weathered skin, she was probably years younger than me. I knew from my studies that the life of any medieval woman was full of hardship. But a camp follower? Hers would be much worse than most. What sickness and poverty she must have endured! For a moment I felt ashamed that I'd ever resented my own penurious circumstances. But if I didn't find a way to get home, I might be struggling to survive right beside her.

After she left, the friar sat down beside me.

"I know your throat still pains you, but you must have another swallow of ale and tell me how it's possible that you could have stolen anything from His Grace."

So he didn't assume I'd been in Richard's bed.

I took another swig of the ale, and a deep breath. A half-truth would have to do.

"I found it. I knew it belonged to him but I took it anyway. When Talbot came up behind me, I dropped it. He picked it up. I guess he wanted it for himself. He must have thought I would tell someone..."

I remembered Talbott's eyes, and my voice caught in my throat. He'd enjoyed hurting me, enjoyed watching me struggle. New tears dampened my face, and I wiped them away with Rose's dirty linens.

"I'm sorry to question you, but I must," said the friar. "Where did you find it? And why do you think it belongs to the King? Please, Jayne, I have my own reasons for wanting to know."

His hands shook on his plump grey lap, and he pulled a linen handkerchief out of his cassock and wiped his brow.

He'd been kind to me, but I didn't dare tell him more or he'd think I was a lunatic, or worse, a witch, and they'd have a bonfire roaring before I could finish the cup of ale.

"I'm sorry," I said.

"Very well, you've just survived a very trying experience, so I won't press you about it now. But I must go to the king."

What else had I expected? Did I think he'd go to Talbott, demand the boar, and bring it back to me? Before he left I had to find out one thing.

"What day is today, friar? I don't remember."

"It is the eighteenth day of October."

"And the year?"

"You poor child!" He looked at me as if I were an abandoned kitten. "It is the year of our Lord fourteen hundred and eighty-three. Rest now, Jayne. You'll be safe here, and Rose will be back soon."

I lay down on the cot and tried to steady my breathing. My throat felt like it had been scraped with a razor and the rest of my body was one sore ache. But at least I knew I'd been generally correct about when, and where, I'd landed in Richard's life.

Buckingham's Rebellion, in the autumn of 1483, was almost two years before Bosworth, and that fatal stroke of a Welsh battle ax. He had almost two years left to live. Could I say the same about myself? If only I could wake up safe in my dorm room! There was no A/C in the building, so I left my window open in the summer, and the garbage truck always woke me up at five a.m. Between the noise and the heat, I never got any sleep, and when I did, I dreamed of Richard...

"*J*ayne! Jayne!" Someone was shaking me.

"Stop it!" I croaked. The pain in my throat caught me by surprise.

I wiped my eyes and sat up. Everything hurt. I'd only felt this stiff and tender one other time, after I pulled out in front of a farmer driving his ancient pickup truck.

"You must get up," said the friar. "The king wishes to question you."

So this time, the nightmare was real.

"Oh no, no I can't. I don't feel well. I'm not ready. Can't we at least wait until Rose comes back?"

"The king's sigil is indeed missing, and he demands to know its whereabouts. I couldn't very well tell him that he must wait upon a gown."

He looked into my eyes and his tone changed. "Jayne, you can still tell me your true tale, you know."

I shook my head. He sighed and helped me to my feet.

I must have slept for most of the day, because the light was already fading again. He hustled me through the camp, and this time the men were too busy loading up leather satchels and wooden coffers to pay us any mind.

"Where are they going, friar?" I asked.

"Most will head back to their homes at first light on the morrow, and the members of the king's household, and those of his closest retainers, will begin making their way back to London."

"What about the battle?"

"There won't be another battle, praise God. Buckingham has been captured, and his supporters have scattered. The rebellion is over."

Damn! Talbott could already be halfway to who knew where, whatever unfortunate village he called home, with the boar tucked safely in his saddlebag, on its way to be melted down or sold. In the warmth and safety of my favorite carrel in the Sterling library, I'd dreamed of visiting Richard's world, but now I only wanted to be back in my own.

Despite the chill, I felt beads of sweat rolling from my armpits. My curiosity about my ancestor was about to be satisfied. What if he was a monster, inside and out? Why couldn't I have been more careful what I wished for?

Two guards in full armor stood at the entrance, their pole axes gleaming sharp and deadly in the morning light. Their bright colored tabards were quartered with the lions and lilies of England, and the white boar of Richard Plantagenet.

"Your Grace, may I enter?" said the friar.

"You may."

It was the voice I'd attributed to Richard last night when I crouched outside this very tent and imagined the man inside it. One of the guards stepped in front of us to raise the canvas flap and Brother Cynneth led me forward.

The space was larger than it appeared from outside, and despite dozens of flickering candles, the corners remained dim. A gigantic wooden table stood in the center of the room, encircled by a trio of iron candelabra. A map took up almost its entire surface, and was in turn strewn with stacks of documents and rolled-up papers, many of which were dirty and worn around the edges, as if they'd traveled far, and been consulted often. As we entered, a man stepped out of the shadows and placed another on top of the pile with a long-fingered brown hand.

"Kneel!" hissed the friar in my ear, and pushed me to my knees.

My chest was so tight that I had to fight for every shallow breath. Richard III had been dead over five hundred years, and I'd seen his dusty bones only yesterday. I kept my gaze on the woven rug in front of me until I could compose myself before I raised my eyes and looked at him.

He had a hard, care-worn face, with thin, curving lips and a strong, square chin that could have used a shave. His thick brown hair hung in waves down to his shoulders. He could have been an ordinary man I might meet in the halls at Yale or on the train to New York, except for his remarkable eyes, the likes of which I'd never seen in my life. They were a clear, pale grey, as bright as diamonds in his tanned face.

They were so compelling, that for a moment I was lost in them, and forgot my interest in his body. I was afraid to look down; afraid I would see a cruel deformity that would have earned him the world's sympathy if he hadn't been greedy and heartless, like Shakespeare and Professor Strickland both claimed. I screwed up my courage and lowered my gaze. His broad shoulders were as straight and level as my own. I knew it! And if they were wrong about his body, they were wrong about his soul. I was looking at an innocent man. A huge burden lifted.

When I glanced back up at his face, his brows were raised over those remarkable eyes, and I realized I'd been staring at him for some time. I felt myself flush, and looked back at the carpet. I hoped he took my stare as nothing more than the fascination any poor peasant girl would have for a king. He would never know how much the sight of him, alive and whole, meant to me. Maybe now the nightmares would stop.

"Help her to her feet, Brother Cynneth," he said, and turned away. I chanced another look before he sat down at the table, and caught a glimpse of tall leather boots that came mid-way up his thighs, and a green velvet tunic that was cinched at his slender waist and showed several inches of dark-colored hose.

"It grieves me that a man with business in my camp mistreated you, no matter whose colors he wears," he said. "I have sent a messenger to Lord Stanley and asked that the man you accused be brought to me at once."

My brain was still reeling from the sight of him, so it took a moment for me to realize that he was speaking to me, and another for me to understand what he'd said.

"No, please don't..." I started.

The friar gave my good arm a warning tug, and Richard continued as if I hadn't spoken.

"Brother Cynneth tells me the man took a silver badge from you, a badge that you claim belongs to me. And most curiously, my own sigil is missing from around my neck."

He pulled a thin leather thong from the front of his tunic. "Mostimes, the badge hangs from this cord, and rests against my heart. I noticed it missing only last night, but I've not left this tent."

He put his elbow on the table, rested his chin upon his fist, and regarded me with those eyes, eyes no artist had ever captured.

"So, maid?"

How could I possibly tell this living, breathing king that I'd seen him in his grave? I was preparing to deliver the same half-truth I'd given the friar, when two soldiers in the king's livery burst in, dragging Talbott between them. His hands were secured behind his back, and his face had lost its ruddy color, but his eyes were hard. I jumped back and put the friar's generous bulk between us, but I knew Talbott saw me. And he could probably hear my breathing.

"On your knees, varlet," said one of the men, and shoved him to the ground.

"Your Grace, I found this in his satchel." The king's man held the silver boar reverently, like a gift in his gloved palm.

There it was: the object that could take me home. What was its power? And why was I the only one affected by it? I wanted to disappear back to the safety of my own world, and leave them all gaping behind me. I let go of the friar's arm and tried to pull away but he tightened his grip. Then Richard had the boar in his hand and my chance was gone.

I squeezed my eyes shut and tears rolled down my face. When I could see clearly again, Richard's mouth was set in a thin line, and his grey eyes had turned stony. Thank God the look wasn't meant for me.

"Did you assault this woman? She has accused you by name."

I peered around the friar's shoulder. Talbott was trembling. Apparently "Old Dick" was not so funny now.

"She's naught but a whore, Your Grace," he said.

Richard made a noise like a laugh, but there was no humor in it. "So you think that means her life is yours to take?"

"She's a thief, Your Grace. She stole the badge. I saw her drop it in the grass."

Richard turned to me. "Is that true?"

"I dropped it, yes," I said.

He looked back at Talbott. "So am I to understand you assumed you were acting as judge and jury in a case of theft? And the badge was your reward for your good deed?"

"I never thought it belonged to you..."

"But it didn't belong to you, of that you could have had no doubt. Why didn't you give it to one of my men, or to Lord Stanley?"

"I swear I planned to, Your Grace, but I had no chance. Lord Stanley thought it proper to wait until your party moved out before we headed back to London. I'm to accompany him. I planned to give it to him, next I saw him..."

Richard held up his hand and one of the guards gave Talbott a warning shove.

"I don't believe you. You hadn't the right to assault this woman, regardless of her crime, or her station. But it's your master's place to punish you, not mine."

He took up a quill pen and a crackling parchment.

"I am sending you back to Lord Stanley under guard, with my judgment that you are a liar, a thief, and a would-be murderer, but he may do with you as he likes," he said.

What? He was letting him go? And I'd insisted to Professor Strickland that Richard was the last of the chivalrous knights!

Talbott grunted and his shoulders sagged. The guards yanked him to his feet, and as he stood up he looked me in the face. I turned my head as quickly as I could, but not before I saw the triumph, and hatred in his eyes.

The guards hustled him out of the tent with his hands still tied, but now his shoulders were square and his head held high. I had made an enemy who would neither forgive nor forget, and my only way home was back in the hands of its rightful owner.

~

 hen I looked back at Richard, he was regarding me with his thick dark eyebrows raised.

"You think I should have punished him myself?"

"I do," I said, my voice still sounding rough and strange from the pressure of that monster's hands around my windpipe. The friar gasped.

I knew so much I could never tell them. I knew Lord Stanley was a fickle ally; I even knew where and when the king sitting in front of me would die. But I didn't know how my own story ended, and Richard had left me exposed to danger in a cool way that made me furious. Maybe he would find it easier to punish a whore than a member of a nobleman's household. But God, what would that punishment be? With just a word, he had the power to have me beaten, or killed.

He drew back in his chair and his face darkened.

"I lost the privilege of doing as I wished the day the crown was set upon my head. A king must do what is best for his subjects."

He glared at me as if he expected me to bow my head. I could feel my shoulders rising and falling with every breath, but I kept my eyes locked on his. I tried to see into his soul, to read the mysteries behind his bright eyes, but they gave up none of his secrets. A thrill of recognition flashed between us, and for that stolen instant, we were no longer strangers. But the moment passed, and the world was back as it was.

"I have no intention of punishing you, after I let that ruffian walk out of this tent alive," he said. "Brother Cynneth told me that you found the badge in the grass, and I have it back now, so..." His voice trailed off, but he continued to look at me.

"Brother Cynneth, please see that this young woman is returned safely to her home."

It was a dismissal – from the tent, from the camp and from the man who held the boar. And I had nowhere to go.

"Your Grace, I have no home, and no defense from the man you just released."

He twisted the gold signet ring that he wore on the small finger of his left hand, but he didn't reply.

"If you would give me your protection, I will consider myself to be forever in your debt," I said.

The corners of his mouth turned up just a tad, and I could have sworn he almost smiled. Before he answered me, Brother Cynneth stepped forward.

"Your Grace, the maid was most grievously treated last night. Would you allow me to minister to her until she is healed? Then perhaps we can find a place for her where she can be made safe from Stanley's soldier."

"When have I ever denied you, Brother? Take care of her as you wish, and help her to find a suitable situation," said Richard.

"Johnnie?" The boy I'd met earlier appeared at Richard's elbow.

"Yes, Your Grace?"

"Get this woman something to cover herself with."

The boy scurried back into the recesses of the tent, and I glanced down. My thin nightgown was streaked with mud and grass and splattered with drops of blood. The cuts on my face still burned and my eyes were swollen from crying. The bruises on my face and neck must be good and purple by now, and my braid, so neat the morning of the dig, was frizzed and beginning to unravel. No wonder Richard wanted me covered up.

The boy trotted back to us carrying a red wool blanket that he draped over my shoulders. It was large enough to cover me from head to toe, so I wrapped it tight and smiled at the boy, who grinned back, pleased with himself.

He turned towards his master. "Will that do, sir?"

For a moment Richard's face clouded, but then he smiled. The expression was so fleeting I would have thought I imagined it, if it hadn't completely transformed his appearance. When the care and sadness left his face, he was handsome.

"Yes, that will do very well," he said to the boy, in a tone much different than I'd heard him use towards anyone else.

He returned to his former sober attitude and spoke to me. "I shall remember your promise, maid. You may go."

He looked down at his work, and the friar ushered me out of the tent and back out into the chilly morning.

CHAPTER 3

RICHARD: OCTOBER 18, 1483

"*F*ather, was I wrong to give the woman the blanket? You frowned at me at first. I saw you. Are you displeased?

I hadn't noticed Johnnie standing beside me until he put a small hand on my shoulder. I put my arm around him.

"I wasn't angry, Johnnie, just surprised. Surely you could have found something more suitable to give her than the blanket off my own bed."

He stared at me with his mother's sad dark eyes.

"But there was nothing else to hand! She looked so cold, and I could tell she was trying hard not to cry."

"It's all right, son. I know you were only being kind."

I pulled him close to me. He didn't understand that the world changed when I became king, that now any kindness either of us bestowed on a fellow creature would be the topic of endless speculation. Perhaps I should have waited until he was older before I made him my page, and let him enjoy a few more years of guileless childhood. But I wanted him near me now, while I could savor the simplicity of our bond, before even he looked to me with greedy eyes.

"She was fair, wasn't she?"

"She was that," I said, thinking of the wild russet curls escaping from her braid.

Before long, I'd have to be warning him about the consequences of seduction. He must be careful, more careful than I'd been. I looked down at his shining head. Would I truly change anything?

"Do you think Lord Stanley will punish that man, Talbott? Maybe he'll dismiss him from his service."

God's bones, he was so innocent.

"You must understand that not everyone sees the world as you and I do. Brother Cynneth says the woman is a refugee from the rebellion, and has no family to protect her, and Talbott is Stanley's favored henchman, so I doubt he'll face much in the way of consequences."

"But she asked for your protection, Father! And she looks so much like my Mother."

I'd hoped the boy would miss the resemblance; he'd been so young when she died.

"She'll have my protection until we find a suitable place for her," I said.

But where would that be? Cynneth said she was homeless, but her grass-stained chemise, and her bloody nose, didn't stop her from arguing with her king. She'd fixed me with a stare as bold as that of any man, and made it clear she thought me a coward. Leave it to Cynneth to bring me a refugee with the countenance of a queen! Her proud face completely undid me, but I couldn't let her change my mind. I was no longer Duke of Gloucester, and free to dispense justice as I saw it.

"Fergus likes her quite well," said Johnnie. "Couldn't we find room for her in your household? She'll not be safe if you don't. Talbott hates her, I could tell."

"You argue like a lawyer. When we get back to London I shall tell Catesby I've put you in his place as King's Counsel. But we can't keep this woman like a stray hound. I give you my solemn promise I'll keep her from harm until I've found her a safe position. Talbott will doubtless return to London with Lord Stanley, and we'll find her a home far away from there."

"Do you swear on the boar?"

I sighed, but I pulled the sigil out from under my tunic and clasped my hand around it before I spoke my motto.

"Loyalty binds me."

I heard a familiar voice outside my tent.

"Your Grace, we must speak! May I enter?"

"You may, Lord Norfolk."

Jocky Howard, Lord Norfolk, came in like a whirlwind, as always. It still felt strange to call him Duke of Norfolk; I'd given him the title only a few months ago.

"The commission found Buckingham guilty."

My heart stopped for an instant.

"Johnnie, go and check on Surrey for me," I said. "I think he may have gotten a stone in his hoof when I last rode him. Will you make sure the smith has seen to it?"

"Of course, Your Grace, but can I ask what you..."

"You must do your duty as my page, without asking questions, or I'll send you back to Yorkshire."

He bowed low, and walked out of the tent with his head held high.

After he was out of earshot, Norfolk laughed.

"He's so much like you were at that age. It warms my heart to see it," he said.

"You're not that old, Jocky, to remember me when I was but eleven."

"Well, you weren't much older, when you were hovering around Edward, asking too many questions and generally getting underfoot."

I couldn't deny it. I'd wanted to be with my brother every minute, regardless of the fact that a child had no place in a king's business. He frequently told me to scat, but not because he wanted to protect me. He knew our family's battle with the House of Lancaster had already shown me more killings and betrayals by the time I was eleven than most men see in a lifetime.

"So tell me about the trial," I said. I motioned for a manservant to pour us each a cup of wine. The fine Rhenish went down smooth and sweet.

"He confessed, without cross-examination. The plot was much as we surmised, with Margaret Stanley in the thick of it. The Tudor's ships were ready to land at Plymouth when she found a way to warn him that Buckingham was captured."

Had any mother ever been more ambitious for her son than Lady Margaret? She would never rest until Henry Tudor was King of England.

"And was there any mention of my sister-in-law Elizabeth's part in all this?"

"None. Do you think she's still pulling strings from her lair in Westminster Abbey?"

I almost spit out my wine.

"You know she is! My spies tell me she and Lady Stanley are in constant communication. They must have planned this wretched rebellion between them, and Buckingham's ego, and greed, led him right into their scheming little hands."

"Bring the jug, and leave us," I told the manservant. He left the tent and I poured another for myself, and wiped my forehead.

"What of Stanley? Does he have the impudence to face you?" asked Jocky.

"He has no shame, as usual. He disavows any knowledge of his wife's involvement in Buckingham's treason, and swears his undying allegiance. My head spins when I think how quickly he'd desert me if Henry himself attempts a rebellion, instead of using a cat's paw like Buckingham to do his dirty work."

"Buckingham is a fool."

He took a long pull from his cup, and we sat together in silence for a time.

"The commission sentenced him to death," he said, at last, and pulled a rolled sheaf of parchment out of a case he had suspended from his belt.

I'd known all along it would come to this. After I'd given him every boon and favor, Buckingham raised an army against me, and tried to put a Lancastrian on my throne. If I let him live, he would kill me, or give aid to someone who would do it for him. He was a traitor. But he was also my cousin.

"Did he ask about the boys?"

Jocky shook his head. "No. He must have guessed what you did. But he did ask to see you."

"No," I said.

Jocky finished his wine in one swallow and stood up.

"I don't suppose you need sign the order at once. I'll leave it with you."

He patted me on the shoulder before he left.

Already the nights came early, and the servants were lighting the cressets in the tent around me. The girl, Jayne — where was she now? She reminded me of desires long past, and if she hadn't been injured, perhaps...but no, I couldn't bear to see the warmth in her eyes change to revulsion. It had been too many years since I last craved a female's good opinion. And besides, I'd be damned if I'd follow in my brother's footsteps. Edward's whoring brought us all only grief.

Once I'd longed to be like him: a confident cocksman who took his pleasures as he found them and harbored no regrets. He'd not been on the throne but a year when he asked me to accompany him to a Southwark stew. We took an unadorned wooden barge down the Thames to that stinking, filthy part of the city, both of us dressed in drab woolen hose and plain doublets, so that the whores would never suspect they were servicing the King of England and his youngest brother. Was he ashamed of seeking pleasure in such lowly places, or was he protecting the royal purse from the threat of inflated prices? He clearly enjoyed the ruse so well that I never had the heart to ask him.

He proudly introduced me to Big Sal, the round, pale-faced bawd he favored that week. "You must try this, Dickon," he said, as another man would recommend a mutton chop or a slice of Lombardy custard. I never refused him anything, so I didn't let on that I saw other wenches in the place that better suited my tastes. Big Sal with her huge, flopping teats put me in mind of the Yorkshire cows the Middleham stable boys claimed to enjoy. But I guess I got past my revulsion well enough, for I spilt in her hand before I even got her on her back. I was only fourteen.

Where would I be now, if not for Edward's follies? At home, at Middleham, watching Ned and Johnnie grow up in the clean Yorkshire air, and settling disputes between the locals. Fighting the Scots, keeping the northern borders safe for my king, and living the life of a soldier, a life I loved.

I put my head in my hands. I'd lived in a fool's paradise all those years, just close enough to the crown to harness its power when I needed it. I'd no inkling of its awesome burden. But I'd brought my misery on myself.

I looked down at the order Jocky brought me.

"Henry Stafford, Duke of Buckingham, is hereby condemned to execution..."

It only awaited my signature, and the return delivery by my messenger.

I took up my quill, but laid it down again before I put it to the ink.

He'd made me laugh, even during the worst of it all, when I found out what Edward had done. If only we hadn't disagreed so violently about my nephews.

God's bones, what a fool I was to hesitate! He'd returned my love by plotting my death, and risked innocent men's lives to try to cast me from the very throne he'd encouraged me to take. Yet I'd grown so accustomed to consulting him that it seemed peculiar not to seek his counsel even now, when the decision to be made was his own fate.

Mayhap I should grant his last request, meet with him one last time.

No. He was so like the lost ones: Edward, George, even my father. All my family, gone now. If I saw his face again, I could never sentence him to death. And die he must.

I took up the quill again.

"It is hereby ordered that the head of the Traitor Buckingham be severed from his body..."

I penned my signature and pressed my seal into the wax beneath it before pushing it aside and pulling the jug of wine closer to my cup. I would spend this night, like so many others, alone.

CHAPTER 4

JAYNE: OCTOBER 19, 1483

I craned my neck for a glimpse of Rose, or Johnnie. We rode behind the horsemen and the foot soldiers, and in front of the wagons that the friar said carried the heavier furnishings, and the arms and armor. Our rickety two-wheeled cart was loaded down with sloshing containers of wine and ale, and Brother Cynneth seemed to be an expert driver, but the wooden wheels hit dips on one side, and clumps or rocks on the other, and I felt every jostle in my aching shoulder.

When I stuck my head out of Rose's tent this morning, the camp appeared much different than when Brother Cynneth rushed me through it in my nightgown. Most of the tents had disappeared, leaving only flattened grass behind, and many of the men had gone with them. There must have been around a thousand a day ago, and their numbers had probably decreased by half, but the king's traveling household was still impressive. The mounted men-at-arms rode far ahead of us, in a column two horses wide, and occasionally the sun reflected off the polished steel of their armor and blinded me for a moment. One of my high school classmates had had a horse, and I'd ridden it a few times and thought I had the hang of it, but these men sat their mounts as easily and naturally as I could walk.

I'd known better than to ask Mom for a horse of my own. Was she missing me yet? We hadn't talked that often since I'd been in Leicester anyway, because of the time difference. And last time hadn't been pretty.

"You've made me wish Mimi had never told you that old story about Richard in the first place," she said. I could hear the ice clinking against the glass of what was probably her third Scotch.

But it was way too late to put that genie back in its proverbial bottle. I knew she was worried that defending Richard in my dissertation would ruin my chances to be a full professor, but I had to prove to myself that I wasn't descended from an infamous murderer. Even now, each time one of the students in my Early English Lit class talked about how Richard had killed his nephews and stolen their throne, I was tempted to tell them they were insulting me.

At least I'd agreed with popular opinion about one thing: if his skeleton was deformed, the rest of Shakespeare's negative portrayal was probably true as well. And by now the excavation was in its second day, so the whole world must know what I'd already seen in the flesh: Richard III was no hunchback.

I shaded my eyes and looked towards the front of the group for the glint of a gilded crown. But the only sign of his presence in the procession was the waving red and blue banner with its lion and lilies, and the ubiquitous white boar.

The friar sat beside me on the hard wooden bench that served us both as a seat, holding the reins in his wide, capable hands. He occasionally clucked to the two giant draft horses that pulled the cart, but was otherwise silent.

"Where are we going, Friar? London?"

My throat still felt tender, but I'd never been so happy to use the word "we." What would have I done for food or shelter if they'd left me behind?

"We will reach London eventually, yes. Before Christmas, for certes. But the king wishes to make his way there slowly. It's important to let his subjects see him, victorious in putting down Buckingham's rebellion. We're to make a sweep down through the southern shires, and be to London in time for him to hold his Christmas court."

Christmas? Was time still passing in the normal way back home? If so, God let me be back home before then! I couldn't fathom Christmas here. My poor mother, and Mimi, what would they do? I pictured them, miserable and worried in our apartment, minus the tree they always waited until I got home from school to decorate. We had good Christmases, quiet Christmases, with the best gifts we could scrape up the money to afford, almost always books (historical fiction for me, mysteries for Mom), and some kitchen gadget or other for Mimi.

Our best Christmas had been the one where I surprised them with the news of my scholarship to Yale, even though Mom cried off and on for two solid weeks. Finally I was starting to make her sacrifices worth their effort, the private school and the piano lessons, and she didn't say it, but for the first time I felt like I wasn't such a burden. I'd ruined her own chances, coming along as I did before she finished high school. She'd pinned all her hopes on my success; what had she done when I disappeared without a trace? Thanks to the friar, I was at least safe for the moment.

"I appreciate your intercession for me with the king yesterday," I said.

He smiled. "In my oath to St. Francis, I swore to help those in need. And I admired your courage in treating with His Grace as you did. He is no longer used to having his judgments questioned."

My courage was merely desperation, but I let the compliment lie. He spoke of the king as if he were just an old friend and not a monarch.

"Why don't you ride in the front of the procession with the rest of the king's privy household?" I asked.

"My vow of poverty makes luxury and pride of place sinful for me," he said. "Driving this cart, with its cargo of ale, is a way for me to serve all of those who travel with us, and not just His Grace and his knights. Would you prefer to ride in greater state?"

I felt myself redden, before I saw his eyes were twinkling.

"I am very content where I am," I said, and I meant it. The clothes that Rose brought back for me made me happier than I would have believed possible a mere forty-eight hours ago. Thanks to her, instead of my flimsy nightgown I was wearing a clean chemise made of soft, creamy linen, and a long-sleeved gown of warm blue wool that laced up the front with a thin leather cord. A heavy cloak in a darker blue, with a cozy hood, completed my ensemble. I was lucky to be sitting on the cart next to Friar Cynneth and not wandering down the road alone, looking for a handout.

Our family always seemed poor compared to those of my friends, although I'd been too little during the years my mother slung French fries at the local McDonald's to remember how bad it must have been for them. Only Mimi's teaching salary kept us afloat during those days. But now I had a new empathy for those who were without sufficient clothing, or the guarantee of a roof over their heads.

"And Rose? Where is she?" I asked. I wanted all my newfound friends around me.

"She is part of Lord Norfolk's household, a scullery maid I believe. They travel somewhere behind us."

"But I thought she was..."

"She serves more than one useful function." His eyes twinkled again.

I liked him more by the moment.

I pushed my hood back and basked in the warmth of the October sun. The open fields on either side of the road spread out in greys and browns, with the occasional bright spot of tenacious green that made me wish for a moment that I could see them in their summer glory. We were in wool country; I'd seen more sheep than people. A few of them turned their delicate black faces our way, but most were just blobs of dirty white, with their noses down among the sparse autumn grasses. Around midmorning, giant hedgerows appeared on either side of the track, so high and dense they shaded us from the warm sunlight while we passed beside them. I'd never been so long without seeing a cell tower, or a light pole, or a single speck of paved surface, and the sounds I'd always taken for granted were glaringly absent. There were no irritating cell phone beeps, no angry car horns or revving engines, and no throbbing snippets of someone else's music to disturb the atmosphere. Despite the masculine banter of the soldiers, and the barks and squeals of their dogs and horses, the quiet was like a living presence, hovering just beneath the surface of the noise.

I glanced over at the friar. How did this simple, forthright man become a confidant of the King of England?

"Brother Cynneth, you said you and Rich...His Grace were childhood friends?"

He gave me a sideways glance, and I hoped I hadn't made a misstep. But he returned his gaze to the road and answered me.

"We met at Middleham Castle, where His Grace was training for knighthood. My position was somewhat less exalted. I was there out of Warwick's charity."

I remembered Middleham Castle, and Lord Warwick. He'd been Richard's mentor, until he had a bloody falling-out with King Edward, over Edward's decision to marry a commoner. Edward eventually killed Warwick in battle, but Richard was forced to choose between them. It must have been a wretched way to grow up.

"And yet you have chosen to be here, with His Grace," I said. I hoped he would tell me why he chose Edward, and Richard, over Warwick.

"Yes," he answered. "Warwick gave me a home, out of respect for one of his knights, who bred me on the daughter of a Welsh shepherd. She died at my birth. My father claimed me as his son, but he was killed at Wakefield, along with Richard's father, when I was but nine years old. The Earl of Warwick took me in, and I was trained, or not, and taught, or not, and even fed, or not, according to the whims of his Master of Henchman, until Richard of Gloucester arrived at Middleham Castle, and befriended me. Things were rather better after that. I feel most fortunate to be his personal chaplain."

Here was another poor soul whose natural loyalties had been torn apart by the Wars of the Roses, that thirty-year struggle for power between the House of Lancaster and the House of York. But unlike that of Richard, and many others, this man's struggle had not made it into the history books.

"And now you must tell me about yourself," he said.

And to think I'd actually been enjoying the novelty of the day. I should have known better than to ask questions.

"I never knew my father, either. My mother raised me on her own, with help from my grandmother."

"She didn't remarry?"

"She was never married. We had a hard time of it."

Small towns in the South didn't welcome bastards, not in the Reagan years.

"And how did you come to be in His Grace's camp?" He scrutinized me with his small, clever eyes.

"I was lost."

He pursed his lips. He'd hoped for more and I'd disappointed him.

He returned his gaze to the road ahead.

He didn't seem anxious to question me any further, but I knew he must have concocted some story for Richard. Why was he protecting me? I didn't dare ask.

My stomach started to burble, from nerves and the jerky motion of the cart. I undid the ties of my cloak and pushed it away from my shoulders.

"Brother Cynneth, I'm feeling..." I started but that was as far as I got before Johnnie galloped up to us and yanked his horse to a cowboy stop beside the cart.

"Hello, Friar. His Grace says we need to have our dinner now, and that we must be quick about it. The men have stopped just ahead so he asks that you trot up and bring the ale, and ask a prayer before we're fed."

"Tell the king that I will be there as swiftly as I can. And Johnnie, stop hauling on that horse's poor mouth."

"Yes, Friar," said Johnnie, and after giving me a grin, he cantered off down the supply line, clearly enjoying himself.

The smile reminded me of someone.

Could he be Richard's son? It would explain the look of indulgent amusement he gave the boy yesterday, instead of telling him off for giving a peasant girl the king's blanket. I'd slept under the warm red wool last night, and inhaled its unique aroma, a mixture of some spice, clove maybe, and leather.

Johnnie had Richard's firm chin and aquiline nose, and thick dark hair. But his eyes were brown. Maybe his mother was dark-eyed. Was she one of his court ladies? I pictured a beautiful girl, her tall pointed headdress trailing yards of gauze. Or was she someone more like Rose? My chest tightened. Would I ever see him again, except from a distance? Even though the medieval kings were far more approachable than the Tudor monarchs that came after them (Richard's brother King Edward married a commoner he met while out hunting), chances of me

THE MEDIEVALIST | 41

getting close enough to steal the boar again were slim. I was stuck here.

My forehead broke out in a cold sweat. The friar clucked to the ambling horses, and the cart lurched forward, taking my stomach with it.

"I'm feeling sick," I said. "Can we please stop for a moment?"

He glanced over at me. "Poor maid, you're quite pale. It isn't much farther. Try to hold on and I'll give you something for it as soon as we stop. "He was as good as his word. When we reached the spot where the procession had halted, he pulled his casket of medicines out from where it nestled among the casks of ale. It was filled with vials of liquids, in various dark shades from green to black, and rows of cloth packets filled with what looked like dried herbs. My stomach roiled. From now on, this cook's collection of spices might be all that stood between me and illness, or death.

We left the cart and settled down in the shade of an ancient oak tree, with the soldiers and noblemen milling about us. I was glad to be on a surface that wasn't moving, and I found a giant curl of tree root that was blocked from view by the cart. It made the most comfortable seat I'd had since we'd left the camp, so I hunkered down and pulled my hood low over my face and hoped to go unnoticed. The fewer people who asked me questions, the better.

But my attempt to hide proved to be a waste of time. A long-limbed man in a leather jerkin strode up to the cart and lifted down one of the heavy casks like it was a can of beans. When he saw me, he set it down and, without hesitating, lifted my hood and peered into my face.

He was older than most of the men I'd seen so far. His dark, wiry hair had touches of grey, and his forehead and cheeks were tanned and lined. He looked at me with merry blue eyes and such honest and non-threatening admiration that I couldn't help but smile back at him. The expression hurt my torn lip, so I put my hand up to touch it.

"No need to hide your face, lass! With a shape as comely as yours, no man's apt to raise his eyes that high anyway!"

He roared at his own joke.

"Leave this one alone, John Milewater," said Brother Cynneth. "Come here, Jayne, and drink this. That is, if your stomach is still dretched."

I'd been silly to think I could avoid interacting with anyone other than the friar and Rose. I pushed my hood back and abandoned my seat under the oak tree. He handed me a little pewter cup full of something that looked like dirty brown dishwater. I started to tell him never mind, I was already feeling better, but last night he'd rubbed an equally foul-looking paste on my shoulder that had eased the soreness more than I would have thought possible. So I took a sniff of his concoction, and found it smelled pleasantly of ginger. Thinking to get the misery over with as quickly as possible, I turned up the cup and swallowed the stuff like a shot of tequila. It went straight up my nose and sent me into a coughing fit.

Both men laughed. The man Brother Cynneth had called John Milewater tapped the keg and refilled the little pewter cup, this time with frothy golden ale.

"What are you trying to do to the poor wench, Friar? You've already bruised her pretty face!"

"Not I. She was assaulted by one of Lord Stanley's henchmen."

John stood up taller. "Bones of the Saints! The servant is no better than the master! You look to be on the mend, lass, and I'm glad of it. But what's a friar doing with a toothsome piece like that, may I ask? She should be back with me and my men, I'm thinking."

"The king gave her into my care until she is completely well again, and until we can find her a suitable husband. He has one of his pikemen in mind for her, I believe. Not that it's any of your affair, you old smellsmock," said the friar.

"Me? A smellsmock? I'm sure I don't know why you'd call me that."

John and the friar went on with their joking, but I barely heard them.

So this was the result of my asking for Richard's protection! He would "give" me to some man, as if I was a rescued dog in need of an owner. And in the fifteenth century, a husband could treat his wife no better than a dog. What if he gave me to some brute like Talbott? I pressed my fingers against my eyes to stop the tears. I had to find a way to get home.

"Your Grace!" said the friar. "How do you fare on this lovely day?"

He and Milewater bowed low. My eyes flew open, and I quickly ducked my head.

Richard was sitting perfectly still and balanced on his energetic horse, and though his hands were light on the reins, it was obvious he was in control of the fractious animal. He wore no helm, just a black velvet cap that sat at an angle on his head, and his wavy brown hair hung loose down to his shoulders. Somewhere under his velvet doublet, with its fur collar and slashed sleeves, was the boar.

He nodded to the friar, and John Milewater, before turning to me.

"How is our foundling this noon? Better?"

Before I could answer, Fergus bounded over to me and put his huge grey head in my lap. He lifted his bearded chin and gave my face an enthusiastic lick.

"Well, Mistress Lyons, it seems you've made a conquest," Richard said.

He looked down at us while his horse danced beneath him, and smiled at me for the first time, and again, I saw a fleeting spark of intimacy in his eyes. He wanted me, despite what he thought of my origins.

He hurriedly resumed his usual somber expression, but not before I realized what I had to do. He wore the boar next to his heart, and ancestor or not, I must get there.

CHAPTER 5

RICHARD: OCTOBER 29, 1483

I swung my sword towards Lovell's shoulder, but he blocked me just in time, and our wooden practice swords crashed together with a satisfying whack. He moved in for a tight grapple, and our faces were so close that I could see his nostrils flaring with every breath. The bright October day had us both perspiring in our helms and brigandines.

The small courtyard of the inn wasn't the perfect spot for our sparring; there were chickens to be avoided, and the crowd that had gathered to watch us had to be warned back more than once. But we'd been on the road more than a week, and I practiced every day, no matter the inconvenience. I refused to let the pain defeat me.

Our practice swords weren't as deadly-sharp as our battle weapons, but they were near twice as heavy, and could deal a mighty blow. I had a bruise on my thigh from Thursday's bout that would be there for a fortnight. Now, I used the flat side of my blade to push Lovell stumbling backwards. He was tiring. Good. He'd given me a sound beating yesterday.

But he came back strong, with a swipe towards my gut that almost hit home. I lowered my blade and countered what would have been a nasty clout. He stepped backwards and raised his sword again.

"Well done, Your Grace!"

It was Stanley's voice; I didn't know he'd arrived. I looked back over my shoulder to where he stood watching, and I caught sight of his face just before Lovell's sword caught me square in the chest.

When my back hit the ground, the wind left my lungs and I gasped like a landed salmon. I lay there blinking until Lovell grabbed my arm and pulled me to my feet, a sheepish look on his face.

Stanley stood beside him.

"Many pardons, Your Grace. I do hope I didn't put you off your game."

I pulled off my helm and wiped my brow with my glove before I smiled at him.

"Certainly not. Lovell is a worthy opponent. That's why I choose to fight him."

Stanley's chinless firstborn lurked a few feet behind his father.

"Ah, Lord Strange. How nice to see you. I didn't know you'd accompanied your father from Latham."

"Pleasure's mine, Your Grace," he mumbled, looking at the ground.

"I understand the traitor Buckingham has met with a suitable end," said Stanley. "I congratulate you on your wise decision. I know it must have been a difficult one."

It was a skillful thrust, but I'd be damned if I'd let him see he'd nicked me. I handed my helm and my sword to a squire, but Johnnie rushed to take them from him.

"Are you hurt, Fa – Your Grace?"

"No, I'm quite well. But I've business with Lord Stanley. I'll even the score with Lovell on the morrow."

Lovell grinned and bowed, and Johnnie hoisted the heavy sword over his shoulder and ran off across the courtyard to give my belongings to my armorer. Stanley looked after him.

"What a fine strong lad," he said.

His eyes met mine, and for an instant I saw the hatred he took such pains to conceal. Then he smiled.

"You must be so proud of him."

"Yes, yes, of course," I said. "Let's go inside, I had a particular reason for asking you to meet with me. Lord Strange may join us if you wish."

The crowd that had gathered during our practice had mostly

dispersed, but Brother Cynneth and his orphan, Jayne, stood talking with Francis, who still held his helm under his arm. The ugly bruises on her slender throat had faded now, and Francis seemed in no hurry to leave. She looked up into my face as she curtseyed, instead of bowing her head, as was proper, and the tail end of a light brown braid hung down from under her veil. I wished Johnnie hadn't taken such a shine to her. I would have to have a talk with Cynneth; it was time we found her a husband.

"Good day to you, Friar," said Stanley.

Brother Cynneth nodded. "And to you, Lord Stanley."

The maid's face blanched. Poor girl. I'd almost forgotten it was one of Stanley's henchmen that had injured her. He'd never responded to the message I sent back with the brute.

As we walked away, Lord Strange loitered behind until his father gave him an ugly look. He trotted to catch up with us.

"Who's the wench with Brother Cynneth?" he asked me.

The cheeky brat. I spoke to Stanley instead of him.

"She is a refugee from the recent rebellion, and Brother Cynneth has taken her under his care until she recovers from her injuries. I wrote to you about her, if you recall."

He gave me a blank look.

"Your man Talbott tried to kill her when he stole a silver sigil that belonged to me."

"Oh, yes, Your Grace! I do recall. Very unfortunate. But he assured me that he intended to return the sigil. It was she who'd stolen it."

"So you didn't punish him? I thought you might dismiss him from your service."

He drew back like I'd slapped him.

"Certainly not. He's one of my most trusted servants. I'd not see him flag-fallen because of a thief, even one with a pretty face. I'm somewhat surprised you would suggest it, Your Grace."

Why had I? I'd known better.

They followed me into the private chamber the innkeeper had given me in which to conduct the business of the realm. It was his best, and although it was small, the wide mullioned windows opened onto of a view of the courtyard below made it seem less confining. My secretary,

John Kendall, was hard at work, as always, opening dispatch cases and placing documents in order for my signature.

I went behind the table that served me as a desk and pulled out a parchment.

"I want to thank you and your brother Sir William for supporting me in the rebellion."

He brought so few troops I could count them without difficulty, and he waited until even those were no longer needed, but at least he'd gone through the motions of loyalty. It was more than I'd expected, given he was the Tudor's stepfather.

"I hope my constancy was never in doubt, Your Grace," he said.

"I am granting you the castle and lordship of Kymbellton, formerly held by the traitor Buckingham, and you may tell Sir William that I intend to appoint him Chief Justice of North Wales."

He bowed low. His son stood there staring until he grunted at him to follow suit.

"How can I thank you, Your Grace?" he said.

By showing up in a timely manner, next I send for you, and controlling your conniving wife.

"It is I who thank you for your efforts on my behalf. But there is the matter of Lady Stanley. I cannot punish the others who aided in the rebellion without dealing with her involvement. I intend to ask Parliament to strip her of her titles, and her lands."

The shocked expression on his arrogant face made the risk almost worth taking. He was slack-jawed for a moment before he found his voice.

"But I have told you, when we last met, that I had no inkling..."

"I understand that, so I also intend to ask that you be given the enjoyment of her property for your lifetime."

Stanley nodded, and his shoulders dropped, but he was still white with fury, and his son's eyes stood out on stems. What did he think of his stepmother and her schemes?

"That is all, Lord Stanley," I said.

He bowed his way out of the room, with Lord Strange rushing to follow him.

As soon as Kendall shut the door behind them, I sat down and took a deep breath.

"Bravo," he said.

"We'll see."

Suddenly the ache was more than I could bear.

"Send for Brother Cynneth, and tell him to bring his casket of physic," I said.

CHAPTER 6

JAYNE: OCTOBER 29, 1483

"$\mathcal{I}$ wish you'd take me with you," I said to Brother Cynneth.

Our little cart appeared strange and empty without its usual cargo of ale, but we'd consumed most of it during our ten days on the road. He said we'd load up another supply before we left Avebury. Now he was taking his medicines, and his prayer book, to minister to the family of shepherds we'd passed on our way into the village. King's chaplain or not, he always remembered his oath.

"You'll be fine, Jayne. I shan't be more than a couple of hours. You're known to be my charge now. Even if Talbott is here with Stanley, he won't harm you. And I can't have you dozing while I say mass. You'll be a poor example."

The medievals scheduled their days around prayers, and my pretended piety hadn't fooled him. More than once he'd caught me daydreaming, or worse yet, drifting off to sleep, but it wasn't just from boredom. Even though I was so tired from traveling that I always went right to sleep, I often woke up in the middle of the night, mouth dry and heart pounding. The nightmares of Bosworth Field I'd endured for so long had been replaced with dreams of Talbott's hands around my throat. I listened to the soft, comforting puffs of Rose's snores, and wrapped myself tighter in Richard's blanket until my breathing returned to normal, but I was afraid to go back to sleep.

Now just the thought of seeing Talbott's hateful face made me tremble; he wouldn't be far from his master. But I didn't want to exasperate Brother Cynneth.

"Trust me, nothing will happen to you here," he said, before flicking the reins and clucking to the horses.

I watched him drive out of the courtyard. I had to get back home before they married me off to some farmer and I never saw Richard, or the boar, again. I'd taken every opportunity to place myself in his path (I followed the friar when he said mass every morning, and helped him brush down the big cart horses, which I'd named Slow and Slower), but my attempts to get more than a nod from the king had failed dismally so far. No surprises there. What did I know about seduction? Nothing but what I'd read in books. A freshman year friend-with-benefits and random hookups that never went past the first night didn't really count. But only the loose atmosphere of what was essentially a traveling army made even limited contact with the king possible. Once we reached London, and the more formal social setting of the court, my chance would be over, and I would be stuck here forever. On the nights I didn't dream of Talbott, I dreamed of home, and I was back on the old green couch in our living room, reading *A Game of Thrones* and listening to the music of the croaking frogs that wafted through the screen door.

With the friar gone, I would have to find something to do with myself, maybe look for Rose; she made me feel almost as safe as he did. I crossed the busy courtyard, where Richard fell this morning. I'd taken a step towards him before Brother Cynneth grabbed my arm and shook his head. Didn't anyone else see that Stanley's shout was a deliberate attempt to distract the king at a crucial moment? He'd wiped a satisfied smile off his face before he strolled to Richard's side.

What had caused the palpable tension between the two men? Lord Stanley would betray Richard at Bosworth Field, and some accounts went so far as to say Stanley's treachery probably caused his death, but no historian had ever discovered the original source of their enmity. No wonder Richard hadn't wanted to anger him; now I was ashamed that in our one and only interview I'd implied Richard was a coward.

Since Stanley's arrival, the inn crawled with servants wearing his nauseating orange and green livery. Even his sigil was repulsive: an eagle about to hook its talons into a swaddled baby.

"Watch where you're going, wench!"

A rider barely slowed from a gallop as he tore into the courtyard. His poor horse was lathered with sweat, and the man wore Lord Stanley's colors. Of course.

He jumped down from the saddle, athletic for a man of his size. He gave his horse's reins to a groom and headed for the front door of the inn. Once I scooted out of his way, he didn't give me another look, but I recognized him. James Talbott.

I put my hands up to cool my burning face.

"Mistress Lyons, are you ill?"

Johnnie grasped my arm with his firm little hand.

I took a deep breath. "No, I'm all right."

"Well maybe you should sit down, you look peaked. Have you seen the friar? The king has need of him."

"He's gone out to minister to a family who lives just outside the village somewhere. He won't be back for awhile, over an hour at least."

Johnnie shook his head. "I don't think the King's Grace will want to wait that long."

"You might be able to catch him. He hasn't been gone long. And he took the cart." Everyone knew about the friar's leisurely draft horses.

He brightened. "That's just what I'll do, mistress. I'll go inform the king of the delay." He turned back towards the inn.

This was my chance.

I called after him. "Johnnie, why don't I go tell His Grace what the delay is, so you can go ahead after the friar?"

He could easily send one of the other pages who milled around, waiting to serve the king. I held my breath while he considered my offer.

"Sure, go on if you want to. Thank you, mistress! He's upstairs."

I hated to take advantage of him, but I was desperate. I straightened my veil as best I could and bit my lips to make them red, like I'd seen a girl in a movie do when she'd been caught without lipstick. But when I reached the big oaken door, I froze. The last person I'd seen crossing the threshold was Talbott.

*H*e was inside somewhere. But so was Richard, with my way home dangling from a cord around his neck.

I used my sleeve to wipe the sweat from my forehead. I'd been lucky in the courtyard. Talbott hadn't been close enough to recognize me. Maybe my luck would hold, and even if he saw me, he wouldn't equate the girl in the respectable blue gown with the whore he'd tried to kill.

I steadied my breathing as best I could, and grabbed the door handle, my perspiring hands slick on the iron. The warmth and the funk of dozens of bodies hit me at once, like the garlic reek of Talbott's breath in my face. I held my arms close by my sides. If only I could shrink to the size of one of the mice that probably swarmed over the place!

A serving woman balancing a tray piled with loaves of bread and hunks of cheese passed me without a glance. I peeked into the common room, where a fire blazed in a huge open hearth, and the throng, made up mostly of men, sat on benches at long low tables, eating and drinking and shouting over one another. I didn't spot Talbott among them.

My whole body went limp with relief, and as I sagged against the wall, a man with an apron around his waist elbowed his way around me.

"Sir, excuse me, but where might I find King Richard? I have a message for him."

He looked me up and down and didn't answer.

"It's a message from his chaplain, Brother Cynneth." It was almost true.

He shrugged a shoulder. "His rooms are upstairs, is all I know." He pointed to a door on the other side of the room before he hurried away.

I would have to walk through the crowded common room.

I lowered my head and kept my gaze straight in front of me. I was almost halfway to the door when I felt a tug on my sleeve.

"Have a cup with us, lovely!"

I pulled my arm away and kept moving. I held my breath, ready to run the rest of the distance if I had to, but the man didn't try to follow I grabbed the door. The noise and the smell of the common room faded as soon as it was shut behind me. I gathered the front of my skirts up in my fists. The steep narrow staircase made a sharp right after just a few steps.

My heart raced like I'd been sprinting. What if Richard refused to see me?

I'd just reached the first landing when I heard a heavy tread above me.

"Pardon, mistress," said Talbott.

I nodded and turned my head away, hoping he would go ahead of me down the stairs, but he held his arm out, indicating that I should pass him.

I pressed close to the wall opposite him, and I'd gone two steps before he followed me.

He grabbed my wrist, his touch as familiar as a lover's. He took my chin in his other hand and looked down into my face.

"Jayne! So you've come out from behind the skirts of that fat little friar at last!"

I gasped. So he'd been watching me.

"I haven't forgotten you, nor will I. You can't stay with him forever; he's married to the Church, remember? Mayhap I should take you off his hands. I'm in need of a bride!"

He licked his fleshy lips and put them close to mine.

"Richard would never make me marry you!" The words flew out of my mouth before I could stop them.

He let go of my chin and backed up an inch, but it was all the space I needed to snatch my skirts up in one hand and start back up the stairs as fast as I could. I heard him laughing behind me.

"Richard, is it? Is old Dick swivvin' you, then?"

The staircase opened onto a wide landing with four doors, all of them closed. I stood there, chest heaving. I couldn't let that monster keep me from doing what I had to do. It only made me more determined to get the boar, and get home.

But which door was Richard's? I blotted my face with the edge of my veil and waited. I could hear voices coming from more than one of the rooms, but none of them were his rich baritone. I'd been waiting there for at least ten minutes when one of the doors opened, and the redheaded man who'd been sparring with Richard in the courtyard came out.

"I'll tell Kendall to finish his lunch and check on Johnnie and Cynneth," he said over his shoulder.

Francis Lovell, one of Richard's boon companions. Richard must be just on the other side of that open door.

"Hello, what's this? Mistress Lyons, isn't it?"

He gave me a look that was friendly, but quizzical.

I nodded, and brushed past him before my courage failed me.

Richard was standing by the casement window, bending forward with his hands against the sill. When he saw me his eyes flew open and he abruptly straightened as if I'd interrupted him. There was no welcome in his eyes. Thank goodness for Lovell; his presence made me feel a little less of a fool. I'd give Richard the message and go. But I heard the door shut behind me. I looked back, and Lovell was gone.

The silence made my ears ring. Then I remembered to curtsey.

"I wanted to tell you..." I stammered like an idiot.

"Good morrow, Mistress Lyons. Would you happen to know the whereabouts of our good friar?"

I exhaled, and pasted a smile on my face.

"Yes, Your Grace. I came to tell you that he's gone to visit a farm family, just outside the village. Johnnie went to bring him back."

"Thank you. I was beginning to wonder where he'd gotten to. He oftimes gets distracted, especially when there are other lads his age about. And how are you? On the mend, I hope."

"I'm much better now, thanks to Brother Cynneth."

He nodded, his face pale. "I find I can't do without him." He put his hand on the sill again, and waited for me to excuse myself.

Okay. Out with it, Jayne. You can do this.

"Your Grace, I don't feel that I've properly thanked you for helping me."

He hesitated for a moment before he smiled, teeth white and even in his wide mouth. "You're most welcome. And I haven't forgotten that we need to find a suitable place for you."

A suitable place? He meant marry me off to some brute, and I'd never get home.

"That is kind of you, but...before I'm sent away I wanted to...to let you know that...if you would like...I'm willing to..." Oh, God.

His eyes flew open, and his face turned as crimson as mine felt. He turned and looked back out the window.

"You've thanked me quite sufficiently, Mistress Lyons."

I dropped a useless curtsey, and made for the door as fast as I could without running.

CHAPTER 7

RICHARD: OCTOBER 29, 1483

*W*hat did she want from me?

Noblemen oftimes found splendid marriages for their lemans once they ceased to take their fancy, but it was just as likely I'd cast her off after one swive. She was clearly willing to gamble on her cunny.

But her offer was awkward in the extreme. She stumbled over her words like a terrified child.

It would have been so easy to tell her I'd send for her, to at least leave the possibility open, instead of dismissing her so abruptly. What was wrong with me? Could I blame my rudeness on the pain?

I sat back down at the table. God's bones! Make haste, Cynneth!

A serving man came in, placed a tray on the trestle table and began laying out my lunch. Lovell followed close behind.

"What did she want?" he asked.

"To tell me that Cynneth was off somewhere, and that Johnnie'd gone to fetch him back. Are any of your tenants at Minster Lovell in need of a wife?" His family manor was far away from Lord Stanley's estates. And London.

He grinned at me, blue eyes twinkling. "Truly, I'd be happy to take her off Cynneth's hands for awhile."

"I'd just as soon see her permanently placed, so I can cease being concerned about her welfare. Johnnie's taken with her, and I promised him I would find her a good husband. And Cynneth seems to be fond of her."

Lovell held up his hand. "I'll not interfere, if you're interested yourself."

He wandered over to the table and grabbed a chicken leg. "I doubt it would send you to hell, Richard." He cleaned the meat off of the bone in three bites and tossed it on the table.

"We've been through this before, more times that I care to count. I have no intention of running my court like a Southwark stew, as Edward did. He was a poor example for his nobles."

"But we aren't at court. We're in the middle of nowhere."

Was that God's will, working in some contrary, unexpected way? Edward would have seen our circumstances as fortuitous, while I supposed the wench was placed in my path as a test of my resolve. Was that why he was always the happy one?

Johnnie burst in, red-cheeked and grinning.

"The friar will be right along now. Sorry for the delay. I had to follow him halfway to Atworth. Did Mistress Lyons tell you where I'd gone?"

"She did, although I'd prefer you didn't use her as an errand boy in the future."

"Why do you dislike her so much, Your Grace?"

"I don't dislike her. I don't have any opinion about her at all," I said. "But we've pages we feed and clothe lounging around with naught to do but our bidding."

"She offered," he said with a shrug. "I'll go and see what's keeping Brother Cynneth." He ran back out the door.

Yes indeed, she'd offered. So it wasn't my imagination. She must see her sudden nearness to power as quite the opportunity, and perhaps she was wise.

"So how went the meeting with the Stanley?" asked Lovell.

"He was shocked that I had the temerity to bring up his wife's treason, but he didn't deny her involvement in the rebellion."

"How honest of him. Do you ever discuss the Tudor?"

My dealings with Stanley were fascinating to Lovell. I knew that in my place, he wouldn't have tolerated the endless dance of ambiguity that defined our relationship.

"We mostly pretend he doesn't exist, or at the very least that he isn't the scion of the House of Lancaster."

He sighed. "I don't know why you don't just make a clean breast of things. Surely it would be better. I know you feel guilty about what happened, but what's done is done. Can't you just apologize?"

"To apologize would be to imply I'd beaten him, and would merely add insult to injury."

I winced. The pain was worsening by the moment and the conversation wasn't helping matters. When Cynneth opened the door, with Johnnie behind him carrying the casket full of relief, I'd never been gladder to see him.

CHAPTER 8

JAYNE: OCTOBER 31, 1483

"Cluck to them, Jayne, and flick the reins! There! You are doing quite well, my dear," said the friar.

I'd been reluctant to reveal my lack of skill with horses, but when I told him my mother and I had been too poor to own one, and asked him to teach me to drive the cart, he didn't seem at all suspicious. At first, Slow and Slower ignored my requests to go forward, but we'd had several lessons, and now they trotted along briskly, their resistance worn down by my repeated clucking and flapping the reins across their wide brown backs. There was a plaited leather whip by my left hand, but I never used it. I refused to hit any animal, even these stubborn creatures.

"Do you think I'm ready to drive them by myself?"

The friar pursed his lips, as he often did when considering my questions. "No, not yet. But perhaps if you continue to improve, and they continue to behave for you, I may let you drive them into Salisbury."

He glanced at me sideways, a mischievous glint in his eyes. Salisbury was the first large city on our route to London, and Rose and I were excited to see it. Rose had never been to any place larger than the village where she'd been born, beside the Duke of Norfolk's manor house, and of course I'd never seen a medieval city that was not "under preservation" and crowded with tourists.

Since Avebury, where I'd encountered Talbott, the villages we'd passed through had been too small to house Richard's entire household. While Richard and his knights stayed in the nearest castle, or in the local inn if there wasn't one, Rose and I slept under canvas that Sir John Milewater and his men erected for us. I'd barely glimpsed Richard since my pathetic attempt to seduce him. I hadn't been able to look anyone in the eye for three days afterward, not even the friar. So I was doing my best to fit in; I had no idea when, or if, I'd ever get home. Was time continuing to pass there as before? Was my picture on a milk carton back in the States, or did they only do that with little kids?

"Jayne, would you like for me to take the reins? We're almost to Great Chalfield House, and we'll pass through Atworth village before we reach the manor. It's sure to be crowded today."

"No, unless you don't think I'm up to the challenge."

He raised his brows in his "we shall see" look that was now familiar to me, so I sat up straighter and tried to look capable. I heard the shouts and cheers long before our part of the procession reached the little village. From the sound of things, the entire population of the place had turned out to welcome their king.

By the time we passed through, the people were back in their smithies and shops, and all that was left of their tribute were the dozens of white roses that littered the street. I could smell their sweet fragrance as they were crushed beneath our wheels, and I wondered how many cottagers had plundered their gardens of the last of summer's roses to harvest these symbols of the House of York.

"Look where you wish to go, Jayne," said the friar, as a hay wagon pulled by a lazy bullock stopped in front of us on the narrow street. I pulled hard on the reins. Slow and Slower sat back on their haunches and Brother Cynneth gave me a stern look. It hadn't rained a drop in weeks, so when the cloud of dust raised by the hay cart made me cough, I put my hand over my mouth and pretended to ignore him.

In about ten minutes we were out of the village and back on a country lane; I estimated time now, with no cell phone to tell me the date, or the time. I had only the prayers the friar insisted on saying to tell me the hour.

We drove through a pair of tall stone gates and down a long curving drive, until a grey stone manor appeared around one of the turns. It was built around a generous central courtyard, and the kitchen and other outbuildings formed a square around it. A large stone chapel stood to one side, and a half-timbered building that must be the stables stood slightly back from the other outbuildings under a copse of trees. Great Chalfield belonged to Sir John Milewater, so he had ridden at the head of the procession with Richard today, and now he joined his wife at the wide oaken door.

The courtyard was swarming with both Richard's entourage and the denizens of the manor who'd turned out to see him. From my vantage point on the cart I watched Richard leap down from his horse to greet Mistress Milewater, who sank into a deep curtsey, her gown in a graceful puddle at her feet. Richard took her hand to raise her back up, before leaning forward to give her a quick peck on the cheek. I'd never seen him close to a woman, and the sight made the heat rise in my face. She pushed aside the trailing veil of her tall pointed hennin to receive his kiss; I could tell I wasn't going to like her.

Rose hurried up to the cart and turned her plump face up to show me her gap-toothed smile. "Jayne, I've the best news! We're to have a proper bed tonight, over the stables. Sir John has seen to it. He says it's turning cold, and there'll be a frost in the morning, but we'll be dry and warm."

Sir John was a good man; he'd been kind and friendly to both of us during our journey. I reminded myself to seek him out and thank him. I'd not slept in a "proper bed" since Leicester, and the dig. It seemed so long ago.

"I thought you'd be happy!" said Rose.

"I'm beyond happy. I'm thrilled," I said. "I'm just tired, and this hard seat hurts my back."

I held up my skirts as Brother Cynneth helped me climb down on the wooden step. Life was so much more difficult now that yards of fabric complicated everything I did, but I was getting used to it. The armpits of my one dress were stained with perspiration, and the hem was brown from the dust of the road. Rose had showed me how to brush the dirt out of my skirts each day, but I was never able to remove all of it. Thank God we were able to wash our chemises at least once a week. I'd thought my wardrobe back home was limited, but now what I wouldn't give for all those sweaters and jeans. Here I would be luckier than most women of my station if I had even one change of clothes, but the friar promised to help find me a second gown when we reached Salisbury.

"If you're tired, you must rest up before the revels!" said Rose. There won't be time for us to find guises, but we can watch the mummers."

Guises? Did she mean costumes? Hell, I was already wearing one. When I didn't reply soon enough to satisfy her, she grabbed my arm.

"Don't you know tonight's All Hallows Eve, you featherhead? After sundown there'll be bonfires in the courtyard and all through the village and mummers dressed as ghosts and such-like. We'll most of us stay up 'til sunrise. D'you think the king will join in the revels?" She gave me a knowing look. She'd never quite ceased believing that I'd stolen the boar from around Richard's neck while we were naked together.

I looked over my shoulder at the friar. The church had tried to stamp out the old pagan ways, but apparently hadn't been too successful.

"Rose, I will pray for your soul!" he said. Then he shrugged. "You're a kind girl, and you've a heart full of God's patience. I suppose a little fun will do no harm. Jayne, you watch over her now. I'll be blessing the house, and the barn, and praying for the souls of the departed. And I doubt the king will be playing at mumming and bonfires."

I supposed he and Richard would be sitting at supper inside the manor house, listening to the lute players or watching jugglers, while Rose and I ate in the kitchen and ran amok among the villagers. The idea filled me with dread.

Sir John Milewater again proved himself a better weatherman than the ones back home with their maps and radar. As soon as the sun went down, the temperature dropped, and I was grateful to him for our cozy room above the stalls full of horses, whose body heat rose to warm the upper story. The bed Rose and I would share took up almost the entire room, and the window gave a direct view of the courtyard below.

The bright golden flames of the bonfire threw shadows on the surrounding buildings, and gave the innocent kitchen and smithy, that had seemed so welcoming that morning, an eerie, sinister appearance. I was tired, and my head ached. I wanted to crawl into the soft bed and stay there.

"Let's go down, Jayne!" said Rose. "The mummers have come in from the village. We're missing the best of it!"

The sounds of revelry were growing louder, and an eerie parade of the dead danced towards the courtyard from the village nearby. I shivered, as skeletons, ghosts, and evil spirits advanced in a queer supernatural procession. Moving in a halting, jerky rhythm, they followed the cadence of a drum and the tune of a lute. Their lurid shadows cavorted in the firelight.

"I think I'll stay here, Rose. You go down, and have a good time."

"What's that? I'll not go without you."

She plopped down on the bed and stared at me, with arms crossed.

I sighed. "Come on, then."

We made our way down the narrow staircase that led down into the stable. I envied the horses dozing in their stalls, unconcerned about the activity just outside. Then we were out into the night, and the chilly air felt refreshing against my hot face.

Rose pulled me by the hand up closer to the fire, and a man thrust a wooden cup into my hand.

"Here you go! We've tapped a fresh cask!" I took a delicious swallow, and its sweetness warmed my throat, and cheered my soul.

He handed one to Rose as well, and she grinned at me.

"Better?" she asked, and I nodded. The music and the firelight were not eerie at all now that I was down amongst them. My head still ached but the ale made the pain feel numbed and distant, almost as if it was someone else's head that throbbed.

I looked on as two young men vied for Rose's attention. One of the mummers, dressed in the crude guise of a ghost, jumped up behind her, and her exaggerated screams made them all laugh. One of the men grabbed her around the waist, and she gave him a coy look and pushed his arm away. Their natural, playful interaction with one another made me miss my friends at Yale, and our nights at the bars in New Haven. How long had it been since I talked to anyone without pretending to be something I was not?

I stood back from the fire and watched her enjoy herself, until the man who'd been so generous with the ale came over to pour me another cup. He wore the rough wool jerkin of a miller, or a blacksmith, and he had a friendly, open face that was red from the heat of the bonfire, and multiple cups of the free-flowing booze.

"I've not seen your pretty self a'fore," he said. "Are you part of the king's household?"

"In a way," I said, after swallowing a gulp. "I'm Jayne." Out of habit, I held out my hand for him to shake, but he gave it a long kiss instead.

"I'm called Robert. I'm glad to have you here, though your master and his knights'll no doubt eat us out of house and home. And us with winter comin' on."

"I'll bet Sir John won't let you starve. And surely it's a great honor to have King Richard here."

He shrugged. "I s'pose it's an honor for Sir John. It's just a hardship on us as works here. But I am grateful that the king let us have our celebration without puttin' his royal foot down and stoppin' it. They say he's not one for revels and suchlike, keepin' his head down an prayin' he is."

"Ummmm," I said. I looked away from him, and stared into the fire. I crossed my arms over my chest, but apparently he'd had too much ale to get the hint. He moved closer and put his arm around my shoulders.

"Course, he's one as needs to pray. If you're part of his household I'm sure you know more about it than us."

I stiffened. His breath reeked of onions, and his closeness made my stomach churn, but it was what he said that made me wary. I was torn between indignation and curiosity. Like a foolish cat I chose the latter.

"What do you mean? Why would the king need to pray? To thank God for helping him put down the rebellion?"

He guffawed. "To ask forgiveness, is what. They say those two little boys looked like angels, and now they're with them. But he's got a crown on 'is head, like he wanted..."

I tried to pull away from him, but he tightened his arm around my shoulders.

"Here! I didn't mean to start a brangle! Have another cup and give us a kiss!"

I pushed him off and turned away from the bonfire, and the people. I looked for Rose, but the sweating faces in their hoods and caps were all unfamiliar. A skeleton jumped from out of the shadows behind me and threw his hands up in front of my face.

"Repent, maid! Repent!" he shouted. I felt my gorge rise. I put my hands up to cover my eyes, and heard yowls and squeals of laughter. I reached out to steady myself against the walls of one of the outbuildings, and vomited up the ale that had been so delicious a moment before.

"Don't give that one another cup!" someone yelled, and another round of laughter roared in my ears.

I felt my way along the wall. I had to get away from the heat and noise. I threw my hood back to try to cool my face, but I was still roasting. After a moment, I found the wooden handle of a doorway. Here was some remote corner of the manor, where I could hide until my stomach settled, and my head quit pounding.

The door was heavier than I expected, but inside it was wonderfully still and cool. I took a few steps across a stone floor before I realized I was in the chapel. Ahead of me candles burned beside the altar, their steady light calm and peaceful in contrast to the wildness of the bonfire. I crossed the nave, knelt before the altar, and put my burning forehead down on the cold stone. The quiet soothed me, and after a while, my blood no longer pounded in my ears. My mouth still felt sour, but my breathing steadied, and I relaxed. I must have been dozing when I felt a light hand upon my shoulder.

I gasped. Oh, God, that man, what was his name? Robert. He must have followed me into the chapel.

"Are you quite well, Mistress Lyons?" he asked. The rich, low voice sent my heart into my throat. I looked up into the concerned grey eyes of the king.

I'd never been this close to him, and I could see the lines just beginning to form in his forehead, and around his mouth. My head swam.

"Here, let's get you to the friar." He put an arm around my waist and raised me to my feet. I could feel his lean muscles through his velvet tunic, and smell the clean clove scent of his body, familiar to me from my nights under his blanket.

"Can you walk?"

I took a deep breath. "I think so."

He kept his arm around my waist until we reached the door. We skirted the edges of the courtyard, away from the bonfire and the celebration.

Why was he alone in the chapel, with no one to attend him? What was it Robert said to me, about the king praying for forgiveness for murdering his nephews, and stealing their throne?

I stopped, and put a hand to my hot forehead.

"I'm sorry I..."

He stooped down and slipped his arm behind my knees just before I lost consciousness.

CHAPTER 9

JAYNE: NOVEMBER 3, 1483

The next few days passed in a blur of faces. First Rose, then the friar, then both of them together, staring down and me and mouthing garbled words I couldn't understand and didn't care about. I wanted them to be quiet, and leave me alone, and after a while they did.

When I woke up, Rose was sitting on the foot of the bed, holding a rosary and gazing off into the distance.

"Hello there," I said.

She hopped up and took my hand. "The friar said it would be today you'd 'waken! I didn't believe him."

"Today?"

"Yes! You've been ill with a fever these three days."

"Three days? Is there anything to drink? My throat is so dry..."

I pushed myself up on the pillows, and she handed me a cup of water.

"Not ale? Thank God."

"Sir John has a fine well."

I drank all of it and lay back down. I must have sweat like a marathon runner because my chemise was stiff as cardboard under my arms and down my sides. I was weak, and a little dizzy, but I would live. It seemed the friar could do as well with a handful of herbs as a modern physician could do with an unlimited list of antibiotics.

"I know more about you now, you that won't tell me a thing about yourself," said Rose.

Oh, God. What had I babbled?

"What did I say, Rose? I was probably dreaming."

"Oh, you didn't make a pocket full of sense, but you kept asking for Richard. I'm guessing you meant our king, the one you say you don't know from Adam's cat."

I shook my head, and immediately wished I hadn't. But I was glad she was so interested in my love life. She probably didn't care if I mentioned the dig, or Yale, or anything else, unless it involved a man. The friar, on the other hand, would have picked up on anything unusual. What had else had I said?

"When will Brother Cynneth be back? I want to thank him for helping me."

"Oh, he said to tell you he would come down from London to visit you after you were all settled."

"What? Settled where?"

"With your new husband! You're to be married to one of Lord Lovell's own pikemen! I'm to take you to him in Salisbury, and he's to meet us there next week. By then you'll be strong enough for the journey. It's only a day's ride. I'm trying my best not to be jealous. He has his own farm, a bit of land close by Minster Lovell, I don't know how much, but you're so lucky. I was asking the friar if he thought he had any brothers, or other men kinfolk."

I jumped out of the bed, and almost fell on my face. She grabbed me by my elbow before I hit the floor.

"Stop that! There's no hurry. We're not expected in Salisbury for days yet."

I leaned on the bed until the room quit spinning.

"Help me dress."

"You're not hearing me. We've no cause to rush. Now get back in bed, and I'll bring you a bite of breakfast."

"How are we supposed to get to Salisbury?"

"Brother Cynneth left us a cart and one of the horses. But don't worry about that right now. I'll get you to your new master. He'll wait for us if need be."

My blue gown was lying folded neatly on a chest in the corner. I was too dizzy to bend down for it.

"You've got to help me. I've got to follow them. How long have they been gone?"

"They left just after matins this morning, but you can't follow him! He don't want you again. It was him as found you this fine match. He's the king! You can't disobey him, and why would you?"

"Please just give me my gown!"

She grabbed it, and helped me pull it over my head. I struggled with the laces while she tied up my sleeves. She stopped and gripped my shoulders.

"Jayne, you must tell me what you're doing."

"I can't get married, Rose. I just can't."

"If he's not asked for you again, then you're better off without him."

"Please just help me. I'll explain it all to you someday, I promise."

I couldn't worry about white lies right now. She muttered under her breath, but she helped me pack up my few belongings, one of which was Richard's blanket.

"I can't believe I'm disobeying King Richard," she said, as she tied the strings of her cloak. "At least do let's have a bite, and get them to pack us some food for the road."

"Have them pack up the breakfast, too. We'll eat it on the way."

I sat on a wooden stool in the barn while a groom hitched Slower to a two-wheeled cart that made the ale wagon look luxurious. Brother Cynneth must be riding the faster of the two horses to Salisbury; I cursed him under my breath.

"Even the groom thinks we've lost our wits, Jayne, and I'm not arguing with him. Heavy weather's coming, too. Please, let's go back upstairs and at least wait until tomorrow."

I shook my head. I had to get to Richard, and the friar, and talk them out of marrying me off to some man I'd never met, and would probably hate. And I had to try one last time to get close to Richard. Sick or not, I had to follow the white boar.

While we were waiting, another groom led a sleek mare out and saddled her. She looked like she could fly, and it was all I could do not to steal her, but a man in Lord Norfolk's livery rushed out to mount her before I could so much as get off the stool.

Rose whispered with him, before coming back to stand over me with her hands on her wide hips.

"There's another one as thinks we're daft, going out like this and you barely alive. I shouldn't let you sway me."

I took her hand. "Rose, please. We'll be fine, and I've got to get to Salisbury as soon as possible. You said yourself it's only a day's ride."

"Not with that blonk, it's not."

Slower's eyes were half-closed and his lower lip hung down like it was made of rubber.

"Cart's ready, mistress," said the groom.

Rose took the reins and clucked to Slower, who woke up after she cursed him and flicked the reins, and we headed through the gates of Great Chalfield House and out onto the road to Salisbury.

*T*he first sprinkles of rain felt good on my hot cheeks. I threw back my hood, and held my face up so that they cooled my forehead, and dampened my hair. The sky wasn't all that dark; the expression on Rose's face was blacker. She'd said little to me in the past three hours, even when we stopped to eat the cold meat pies she brought for our lunch. The quiet suited me fine. My mind was occupied with trying to noodle out some new strategy to get to Richard. I couldn't believe I'd been so close to him; it felt like one of the dreams brought on by the fever. I recalled the smell of his body and the warmth of his arm around my waist; Rose said he'd carried me to the friar. If only I could remember more.

The first bolt of lightening sounded like a pistol shot. I jumped, and glanced at Rose, who glared at me before pulling her hood close around her face. The thunder came soon after, and with it the downpour.

I yanked my hood down as far as it would go, but within minutes every ounce of wool and linen on my body was soaked through. My cloak began to have an oily, gamey smell, like a wet sheep.

The rain was loud and steady as it struck the wooden bed of the cart. I could feel the hard cold drops through my clothes. Poor Slower, it must have felt like needles pricking his poor hide. We rode along in silent misery, until Rose finally spoke.

"Well, this ought to help you get over your fever," she shouted over the din. She looked straight out at the road, her round face grim.

I didn't feel up to yelling an answer. The wind was blowing the rain sideways, and the cart threatened to pitch over on its side if we leaned our weight in either direction.

I hadn't glimpsed the sun for hours, but it must be getting close to four o'clock. I'd been toasting in my long skirts just that morning, but now the wind cut though the sopping wool. As the surface of the road turned the sticky consistency of overcooked oatmeal, the struggling horse needed more and more encouragement from Rose. After a while, it ignored her clucks – if it could even hear them over the rain - and she had to slap the reins sharply against its back every few feet to keep it moving. Finally, one of its hooves caught in the mud and it stumbled. When it recovered its footing, it just stood there, sides heaving.

Rose reached down beside her and brought out the long leather whip. Somehow I had my hand on it before she could lash it down on their backs.

"You're not going to beat him?"

She tightened her grip on the whip and looked at me, rain dripping off of her face. "A' course I am! How else will I make him move?"

"I can't stand to see an innocent animal beaten!"

"Then don't look, Jayne! We have to get out of this mud. Do you want to sit here until the wheels sink so deep we can't never get 'em out?

"No of c-c-course not! But can't you lead him?"

"Lead him? Do you mean drag him? Did the fever affect your wits? I can't lead him and I won't try. Now let go of my whip."

I jumped down off the cart. My feet, in my only shoes, sank down three inches into the sticky mud. It was a useless sacrifice, because as soon as I let go of the whip, Rose lashed the horse across his broad back with two sideways cracks of the leather whip that I felt sure could be heard a mile away in spite of the rain.

But it did no good. The horse strained forward with all of its remaining strength, but the wheels didn't budge. I gathered my heavy wet skirts and struggled up to its head. I put my hand on the slick leather beside its cheek and clucked and pulled, but the animal just rolled its huge terrified eyes, and tried to yank its head back out of my reach.

I looked up, expecting to see Rose's furious face, but she was looking back over her shoulder.

"Praise the Lord and all his Saints! There's a whole line of soldiers coming. They'll be able to help us for sure."

I let go of the horse, wiped my wet face with my wet sleeve. Thank God, indeed. She would still never forgive me for getting her into this rotten mess, but at least we could get unstuck and go on to Salisbury, maybe even make it there before full darkness set in.

I looked back the way we'd come. There were more mounted men than I could count. One of them detached from the group and rode up to us at a clumsy canter, his horse's hooves digging into the muck and flinging a slurry of mud and water in all directions before he pulled it to a stop beside me.

"We're so glad to see you!" I exclaimed, before I looked up into the grinning face of James Talbott.

"I'm right glad to see you again, too," he said.

CHAPTER 10

RICHARD: NOVEMBER 3, 1483

*T*he rain drumming down on the metal helms and miserable faces of my men made conversation impossible. The road turned into a thick soup beneath our horses' churning hooves, and the only sounds, besides the constant din of the raindrops, were the men yelling and growling at their tired horses, even the staunchest of which stumbled and balked.

My knights were no happier than their mounts. Even Jocky Howard, an inveterate malapert who could always be depended upon for a jest, was grim and silent. Francis Lovell's nag went lame in the muck, and he was forced to dismount and lead the poor animal as it struggled along, favoring its right foreleg. Thankfully, we were in sight of the first household on the outskirts of Salisbury, and he promised to beg lodging for some of my foot soldiers as he turned in at the front gates.

Only Johnnie was enjoying himself. He splashed happily through the puddles on his stout cob, which flattened its ears when he kicked it but kept the pace without wavering. It was a hateful, ill-tempered beast that no one else would have chosen to ride, but it was as strong as an acre of garlic, and usually he gave it a whack when it disobeyed. But today, even the worst horse had no energy to spare on disobedience.

As much as I loved him, his fearless strength never failed to remind me of his brother's weakness. This morning I had a letter from Anne. Ned was ill again and under Dr. Cranston's care for the second time since All Saints' Day. My heir, my only legitimate child, would never ride at my side in the pouring rain and live to tell of it. I raised my face to the deluge and begged our Lord to let him live; even that was a blessing of which there was no guarantee. I vowed to light candles in Salisbury's fine cathedral this very night.

Only days ago I'd gone to the chapel at Great Chalfield, meaning to take advantage of a rare moment to ask for heavenly mercy for my child. Any time I had alone was precious now; even my prayers were attended like public events. But the nut-brown maid was there before me, and so ill I thought she might die in my arms. Her slim young body had been limp, and hot with fever, and I cringed to think how badly I'd wanted her. Even now, even in this freezing, miserable rain, I stiffened at the memory. But she was a problem I'd finally dealt with: I had Cynneth tend her illness, and left her at Great Chalfield in the capable hands of one of Jocky's scullions. As soon as she was well, she would be sent to Minster Lovell, and have one of Francis' strong pikemen for a husband. I hoped never to see her beautiful face again.

When at last we made it to through the high stone gates of Salisbury, White Surrey was faltering. I swung down from my wet saddle in The Bear's muddy stable yard, and handed him to the waiting groom with orders that he be given a hot bran mash and a thorough rubbing with a dry cloth. My boots squelched in the churned-up barnyard, and I felt renewed sympathy for my foot soldiers. Jockey dismounted right behind me, just as the innkeeper threw open the stout oaken door and bowed so low over his round gut that I thought he might fall over.

"We are honored to host you again, Your Grace. We've your favorite Rhenish ready to pour, and a fine supper laid upstairs."

The smell of roasted lamb wafted after him through the doorway and my mouth watered. A warm hearth and dry clothing awaited me; it was all I could do not to sigh aloud.

Johnnie crossed the churned-up stable yard, dragging his horse by the reins. Its head hung almost to the mud.

"Your Grace, is there aught for me to do for you now? If not, may I see to Towton myself? He did his best for me today, and I've never before seen him tired."

"I've no need of you just now, Johnnie. You may do as you wish with your mount," I said. "Afterwards do join me at table."

He turned towards the stables, and almost collided with a horseman in livery, whose tunic was so darkly wet that it took me a moment to identify Jocky Howard's silver lion.

He bowed to us both and handed Jocky a leather case.

"Bones of the Saints, what can be so important?" said Jocky. He took the case from the lad as if it were sizzling. I suppressed a smile. He must fear some business would interfere with his immediate consumption of lamb and ale.

The lad turned to me with another bow.

"I passed Lord Stanley and his men on the road, Your Grace. He asked me to tell you that the weather had delayed him but that he was making all haste to join you."

"Very good," I said. I handed him a groat and he gave me a gap-toothed grin. He'd gone halfway to the stables when he turned back to Jocky.

"Lord Norfolk, I did also see your serving wench Rose in the court-yard at Great Chalfield. She and the woman Jayne were loading a cart and setting out on the Salisbury road just afore noon this morning. She asked me special to tell you."

"Without an escort?" I said. God's blood! When would this woman cease to plague me?

"Stanley and his men can't be far behind," said Jocky. "They'll not be alone for long."

Stanley and his men. Stanley and James Talbot.

I turned to Johnnie. "Give Towton to a groom and run to find Sir Ralph Bannister. If his horse is done in, tell him to take a hireling back down the Salisbury Road, and escort those women into town."

"Will you go back for her, Your Grace? Along with Sir Ralph?"

"Certainly not. It's bother enough that I'm sending Sir Ralph, after the ride he's just endured. She should have done as she was told. And you should do as you are told as well."

"You promised her your protection!" he said. The scorn and disappointment on his face reminded me of hers, when I'd let the man who'd tried to kill her go back unpunished to his master.

"You swore it on the white boar, Father! Remember?"

I took off my cap, squeezed what water I could out of the velvet and replaced it on my head. The innkeeper had shut the door behind him and was watching the proceedings with a dumbfounded look on his face.

"Saddle your three fastest hirelings," I said.

"What in the name of the Virgin are you doing, Dickon?" said Jocky. He rarely trotted out my boyhood nickname, and never in public.

"I promised the lad."

He took a weary breath. "Saddle a nag for me as well," he said, and within minutes we four were headed west, back down the Salisbury Road. Johnnie gave the hireling a kick as it struggled to keep pace with mine. The determination on my child's face pierced me to the heart. Jockey had said he was like me, and it was true. I'd once been as idealistic as he.

As we cantered through the city gates and back over the stone bridge that spanned the tumbling waters of the River Avon, we met five of my knights, who turned back and joined us, a display of loyalty I felt I hardly deserved. For a time the rain seemed to slacken a bit, but the reprieve was only momentary. We'd not gotten far down the road, which now was near impassable, when the deluge resumed again in earnest. The autumn darkness was almost complete, and no torch would have held in the torrent, so we trusted to our horses to pick their way. The hireling proved a good one, game as could be expected in the wretched circum-stances, and I was thanking the Almighty for that small blessing when I saw figures gathered immediately ahead. I gave my horse a kick and in five or six strides we were within hailing distance of a group of mounted men-at-arms.

My chest tightened and it was difficult to get my breath. I forced myself to inhale deeply, and to relax my clenched jaw. Would Stanley remember that other night, so like this one, when we'd met one another on the road between Carmarthen and Shrewsbury? It had been raining then too.

We reined our horses to a walk. Stanley motioned to his knights and sat taller in the saddle. He must have had no inkling who I was. His bannerman moved up close to him, as if he could display the eagle's claws even in the darkness. His mouth opened when he recognized me; he shut it quickly and jumped down from his mount. His confused men did likewise, and after giving me a low bow he looked up at me with a bright smile on his bearded face that stopped short of his chill blue eyes.

"Your Grace! I hope all is well?"

I nodded, and put my hand out behind me to restrain Johnnie, who was craning his neck to look for Jayne.

"Lord Norfolk's messenger brought us news of your delay, and as we were not far ahead of you, I thought to drop back and to ride with you into Salisbury."

He widened his smile. "Your concern amazes and honors me! Do lead us, Your Grace."

I pulled my hireling in beside his fine mount, and we turned back towards the river bridge. Jockey and the rest of my escort fell in behind, and I gave Johnnie a glare that I hoped would ensure his good behavior. The night had come on clear and cold, and I could see Stanley's arrogant profile distinctly in the glow of his men's torches.

"But where is Surrey?" he said, without turning his gaze from the road. "Not lamed in this mud I hope?" He'd traded his grin for a small, tight smirk.

"It does no good to ride a battle charger in such weather," I said. "He will be fine." I cleared my throat. "Lord Norfolk's messenger also gave us word of one of his household women who'd foolishly traveled without escort from Great Chalfield."

Jockey pulled his nag up on Stanley's other side.

"Yes, that Rose, what a trouble she is," he said. "But her intended husband is a miller on my best estate. I'd just as soon not see her come to any harm. Did you happen to see a pair of wenches driving a cart on the road? They'd have been ahead of you just a bit."

Jockey Howard, you are clever, as well as true.

Johnnie trotted up close. I could feel his frustration. Again, I put my hand out behind me.

Stanley pursed his lips, and made a goodly show of considering Jockey's question.

"I do believe we encountered a pair of whores, just a few hours ago.

We'd no idea they belonged to a noble household, in fact I told my men to make free with them. My apologies to you, Lord Norfolk."

Johnnie choked off a squeal. I was proud of his restraint. I could no longer guarantee my own.

"Lord Stanley, I do hope to find both women unmolested."

He lowered his head, as if considering the generous act of a saint. "Your Grace's concern for fallen women does you great justice."

I felt the insult in my chest. I deserved it.

"Thank you, Lord Stanley. Now please have both of the women brought to us at once. As Lord Norfolk said, he's promised one of them to a miller, and I have settled the other on a Wiltshire pikeman."

He motioned to his squire, who turned his horse and trotted back down the line of men. After a few moments, a soldier drove a two-wheeled horse pulled by a draught I recognized as one of Cynneth's. A plump freckled girl sat beside him.

"And the other maid?"

Stanley shrugged his shoulders. "As I said before, I'd no idea these females were of any particular importance, especially not to you, Your Grace."

Then James Talbott approached us from the back of Stanley's lines, holding Jayne in front of him on his saddle. Rain, or tears, ran down her cheeks, but the relief and gratitude on her face when she saw me sent my heart into my throat. Happiness, so long a stranger, paid me a visit at last.

CHAPTER 11

JAYNE: NOVEMBER 3, 1483

Seeing Richard, waiting there, looking grim and weary, when Talbott brought me to the front of Stanley's troop line, was almost as astounding as finding myself in the fifteenth century in the first place. I hadn't tried to struggle with Talbot this time. I'd been too tired and weak to do anything but hope the sour smell of his body didn't make me sick again. I was just sorry I'd gotten Rose into such a mess.

She'd pled for us both, even told them we were under the king's protection, but another of Stanley's men shoved her aside and took the reins of the cart. Their laughter made her cry furious tears; I would carry the miserable look she gave me for what was left of my life.

She snuck a look at me now, her blue eyes bright with glad mischief. All her suspicions about Richard and me were confirmed, and she could tell her awe-struck grandchildren an enthralling tale about being rescued by the King of England. She'd gone from terrified to preening in an instant, and assured Richard's men that she was fine to drive the cart into Salisbury. Johnnie helped me aboard, after putting his gallant little face close to mine.

"Are you unharmed, mistress?" he whispered.

"Yes Johnnie, I'm fine now, just tired," I said, and he nodded proudly, as if our rescue was all his doing.

Rose clucked to the poor horse and he strained forward again. Richard and his men rode ahead of us, but two armed knights slowed their pace to ours and stayed beside us.

"There, there, sweet one, lean against me. I know you're that worn out," Rose said. I did as she asked, and her warm round shoulder felt as good as any pillow.

"I knew we'd be took care of. I knew he'd come back for his sweetheart."

I decided not to remind her of the way she'd looked at me when Stanley's soldier snatched the reins out of her hand.

But why had he come back for me? I was too tired to consider it long. The next thing I knew Rose was shaking me awake, and we were stopped in front of an inn with a carved wooden sign marked with a dancing bear. I had missed my ride into Salisbury after all.

Richard jumped down from his horse and handed its reins to one of the boys that ran out of the inn to meet our party. But instead of going inside, he walked over to the cart and reached up. I would have taken his hand to help me clamber down in my heavy wet skirts, but he grabbed my waist and swung me to the ground. We stood there for a moment, eye to eye. He had taken off his leather gloves and tucked them into his belt, and he pushed a damp strand of hair from my cheek with a bare, brown hand.

John Howard pushed open the huge carved wooden door for him, and he turned away from me without a word and went inside. The rest of his party ignored me and followed behind him, but Johnnie looked back and smiled at me. I'd never had much interaction with children. In high school I'd worked at the indy bookstore on the courthouse square instead of baby-sitting. Why did the child like me so well?

After a groom took the cart, Rose and I stepped inside the inn, and the warm, dry atmosphere was such a relief I thanked God for it. The big room was crowded with people, and I smelled the now-familiar animal stink of tallow candles, along with sour ale and unwashed human bodies. The fireplace was so enormous I could have stood inside it if it hadn't been filled with bright, hot, wonderful flames. I headed towards its crackling warmth until I felt a hand grip my arm.

"Jayne, do let's go straight upstairs," said Rose. "We both need resting. I'll tell the innkeeper to send us up some supper."

I was too weary to argue. I gathered my skirts and followed her up a narrow staircase to a tiny room. I struggled out of my wet gown and collapsed on the straw mattress before our food arrived, and I was dreaming of warm bread and ale when Rose called my name.

"He's sent for you, Jayne!" Her eyes sparkled like she was the one he wanted.

I was instantly wide awake. I rubbed my eyes, and saw a young man wearing a tunic emblazoned with the lions and lilies of England standing in the crack of the door, holding a candle. I sat there for a moment, heart pounding, and tried to get my breath. I threw back the covers, snatched up my cloak and went with him.

He led me up another flight of curving stairs, and at the top of the landing he opened a door into a much larger room than the one I shared with Rose. There was a fireplace with a well-established fire roaring, and candles on the wooden mantel as well as on the long trestle table that stood against one wall, and the narrow sill below the closed casement window.

The only other furniture was a huge bed with a wooden canopy and heavy linen draperies. Richard stood alone in his shirtsleeves by the window, his hair tied back with a leather thong. He didn't turn around until the man had left us and shut the door behind him with a firm wooden thud.

He turned around and stared at me, and I could see his chest rising and falling with every breath.

"Come and stand by the fire, Jayne," he said, at last. "But first do pour us some wine."

There was a pottery jug and one cup on the trestle table. Did he expect me to serve him? I'd never waited on any man, but he was a king, after all. I moved to obey him but before I could react, he strode over to the table and filled the cup himself.

He took a thirsty swallow that made the stuff look delicious, and handed me the cup. My mouth was dry and cottony, so I drank a big gulp. It tasted worse than cheap merlot that had been open for a week, but it was all that was on offer. I finished it, and went over to the table to pour us a second serving. I handed it to him with a nod of obeisance. We stood looking into the fire together in silence, while he clicked his short dagger up and down in its sheath. He reached out and took my chin in his rough hand. His touch was so gentle that my eyes filled with tears.

"What's the matter, Jayne?" he said softly. "Don't you want to lie with me?"

I tried to look away from him. Why is it that, when we humans finally get our dearest wish, it can be so hard to accept, and enjoy? I did want to lie with him, as he had put it, and I wanted him to know it.

I reached up behind his head and found the thin leather strap that held his hair. He raised his eyebrows, but he bent his head forward to make it easier for me to untie the simple knot.

I pulled the thong away, and the soft brown waves fell forward to frame his face. My fingers ached to touch them, but first I wanted to savor the incredible moment and just look at him. He stared back at me, with a bemused expression, but I couldn't explain to him that the simple routine acts of his breathing, and the blood pumping through his veins, were miraculous to me. So I took his face in my hands and kissed his mouth.

He wrapped his arms around me, his body lean and spare against mine. I felt the hard shape of his erection through his hose, and I wanted him so badly that the ache between my legs was painful. I put my hands into his silky hair and slipped my tongue in his mouth, and felt myself melting.

In one fluid motion he lifted me off my feet, and carried me the short distance to the big bed. He set me on my feet in front of him, and slid his hands slowly up my bare thighs to my hips, raising my nightgown until it gathered midway at my waist. He pulled me forward with my knees spread around his narrow hips.

When he put his hand between my legs, he groaned, and squeezed his eyes shut for a moment, as if it pained him to find me so wet. I leaned back to enjoy the pleasure of his fingers inside me, putting a hand on each of his shoulders for support.

I gasped. It wasn't noticeable under the fullness of his linen shirt, but the right one was higher, and it felt rounder and thicker in my grip. He flinched at my reaction; he must have thought I was callous to be repulsed by a minor deformity. I couldn't tell him that my discovery of his condition was much more damning that he could imagine. But the disappointment on his face was all that mattered now.

"Does it ever hurt?" I asked him.

He looked at me for just a moment with those old-young grey eyes.

"Sometimes," he said. "But not right now."

He gripped my bare buttocks in his hands and set me on my feet. He eased my nightgown over my head and laid me across the bed.

He was still fully clothed, so I put my hand under his tunic to touch his bare skin but he shook his head and moved my hand away. He stood above me and gazed at my naked flesh, before he bent over and with a hand on either side of my waist began to caress the outline of my body. His hands traveled slowly down the curves of my hips, back up again. He spread my knees and stroked the insides of my thighs, until he coaxed a moan from me.

He reached under his tunic to untie his hose, and I realized that sound was what he'd been waiting on. This time when I reached under his shirt, he didn't stop me, and I gripped his smooth silky shaft, and pulled it towards me.

Richard climbed between my open legs and entered me in one smooth, deliberate motion, then lowered his face to mine and kissed me again. He tasted of sour wine and spices, and I put my hands down and gripped his narrow buttocks, pulling him deeper as my pleasure peaked.

He buried his face in my neck and I wrapped my arms around his shoulders, freeing his hips to find their own rhythm. I joined the tempo, until he paused and bore down for one deep final thrust.

I went to sleep with my head cradled on his chest, but when I woke up the next morning I was alone. A fire was laid, and a warm loaf of bread sat waiting for me on the table. I'd almost finished it before I realized I'd forgotten all about the silver boar.

CHAPTER 12

JAYNE: NOVEMBER 6, 1483

*W*e stayed at The Bear for three days, waiting for the weather to moderate and for Richard to conclude his business with the mayor and aldermen of Salisbury. When I got back to our room after my first night with him, Rose was gone out on some business of Lord Norfolk's, and I was thankful to be alone. The last thing I needed was her questions and chatter, however well-meaning. I lay back on our bed. I could still feel the misshapen lump of Richard's shoulder under my hand.

I imagined the little click of Dr. Strickland's teeth against his pipe, and the rasp as he inhaled. He would expel a pungent fog of smoke into the already-claustrophobic atmosphere of The Anchor bar before he started the speech he'd been longing to make ever since I told him the subject of my dissertation.

"You admitted it yourself, Jayne. If there is truth to any part of Shake-speare's story, there's probably more than a little validity to the rest of it as well."

But why had I agreed to such a thing? Richard's deformity, if it could even be called that, was slight. So, employing Dr. Strickland's own logic, Shakespeare's other claims about Richard were probably exaggerated too.

But his nephews couldn't be just slightly dead. The miller at Great Chalfield said they were "with the angels," so even the rustics in the middle of nowhere knew they were missing, and attributed their disappearance to Richard. And, as he'd shrewdly pointed out, Richard was the one to benefit from their death. I'd heard it all before, of course, but from historians, not Richard's own subjects. His crooked shoulder was just another piece in the damning puzzle.

And now I'd slept with him. So what? I'd slept with a complete stranger I picked up at The Toad in New Haven once. But he probably wasn't a murderer, he certainly wasn't my ancestor, and I hadn't enjoyed it nearly so much. It was all for nothing, too; the boar was nowhere to be seen. I curled up on my side and rested my head on my hands, and wished I knew how to pray.

*H*e sent for me after midnight again the second night. I'd planned to grab the boar and be home before I had to worry about the consequences of multiple encounters, but I hadn't seen it anywhere. God, what if I got pregnant? It was Mom's worst fear. She'd put me on the Pill after my second date with my high school boyfriend. She was determined to keep me from following in her footsteps. Even though I tried to tell her the world had changed since the eighties, she would always see unwed mothers through small-town eyes.

But here, I had more to worry me than Southern bigotry, like bleeding to death, or succumbing to a deadly infection. Maybe Brother Cynneth would have some herbal concoction that would be better birth control than nothing.

On the third morning, a new gown made of fine wool the color of cabernet appeared like Christmas on my bed, and that evening I was sitting in my room with Rose, when Johnnie knocked at our door.

"Mistress, His Grace would like for you to join him at table this evening," he said.

My confusion must have shown on my face, because he added, "There's just a small group to dine, only Lord Norfolk, and Lord Lovell, and our friar. Oh, and John Milewater. He's just joined us today from Great Chalfield."

Rose squealed. "Aren't you so pleased, Jayne? It's one thing to lie with the king but it's another to dine with him!"

She buzzed around me, and pulled at the laces that attached my sleeves to my gown, and adjusted the soft linen veil that covered my braid and hung in creamy folds around my shoulders.

Johnnie gave me a smile of encouragement as he led me up the same staircase that I climbed each night to Richard's bed. He knocked on the adjoining door, and the same young servant who'd been fetching me every night opened it for us.

"Ah, Jayne, I'm quite pleased that you could join us," said Brother Cynneth. The familiar calm acceptance in his eyes made me feel as if I had at least one friend in the room, and John Milewater's knowing wink made me feel comfortable instead of insulted.

"Welcome, Mistress Lyons." He bowed over my hand. "It's grand to have a comely maid to grace our table. I grow weary of the ugly mugs on these three."

The man I recognized as John Howard, Lord Norfolk, nodded at me and smiled, and Francis Lovell walked over to kiss my hand. It seemed I was in a position of some respect. Despite myself, I began to relax.

Richard came in by a side door that must connect with the bedroom where my elevation from refugee to king's mistress had taken place. He nodded to the others, but walked directly up to me and took my hand. I felt myself redden, as much with pleasure as embarrassment, and when he led me to sit on the bench by his side, my heart swelled.

The table was at least ten feet long, but hardly an inch of its wooden surface was visible under the platters of food, and jugs of wine and ale. We sat on a wooden bench along one side, facing a bright roaring fire. The two torches set in metal rings in the walls helped too, but they did less to dispel the darkness, and a square-paned window on the wall opposite the fireplace reflected the blackness outside. The warmth and the light were exactly enough to make the small room snug and pleasant.

Francis and Jocky Howard shared one oblong wooden plate. Sir John and Brother Cynneth shared another. Johnnie served us, before sitting on a stool at the end of the table beside Richard to eat his food.

My happiness made me hungry, but at first I confined myself to the delicious white bread that Richard said was a specialty of The

Bear, and the creamy yellow cheese. I would have been content with that, washed down with the frothing ale, which I much preferred to the sweet Rhenish wine he so loved. But he tempted me with a slice of fish he said was called plaice, fresh from the River Avon. It was delicious – white and flaky like flounder, and I could taste onion and vinegar, and brown sugar in the sauce. I tried the pigeon baked in a pastry shell, seasoned with cinnamon. But I drew the line at baby eels.

"Come, Jayne," said John Milewater. "Dugan will be heartsore if he finds out you refused to try the elvers. My dear, they are a delicacy to be found in few places, and none so good as Salisbury!"

I shook my head. The "delicacy" looked like overgrown worms in Jell-O and smelled like canned cat food. I hated to see Richard put them in his mouth.

There were only knives and spoons and fingers to eat with, and I missed having a fork, but I managed, until I was warm and full and drowsily content. No one spoke much during the meal except to ask for more of something, and it was not until Johnnie went downstairs to get dessert that anyone attempted conversation.

"So where do we head on the morrow, Your Grace?" asked Jocky Howard, dipping his fingers in the bowl of water Francis had left beside his plate.

"We'll continue towards Canterbury, and I was thinking of stopping at Dover Castle. That is, if this wretched downpour ever ceases. I'll not force my foot soldiers to suffer another day like the march from Great Chalfield. And even if the sky clears, I intend to send scouts ahead to check on the condition of the roads."

Jocky nodded. "That was a miserable day, for sure. I saw Stanley in the cathedral this morning after matins, and he voiced the same concerns. It was the first time he's spoken to me since we deprived him of his prize on the road the other night."

"Oh, I don't think he holds a grudge over that," said Richard.

Jocky shook his head. "I wouldn't be too sure, Your Grace."

John Milewater leaned forward and looked at Richard.

"What's this? Did that devil get up to some new mischief while I was still home doing my duty by the missus at Great Chalfield?"

"He came across Mistress Lyons and her companion on the Salisbury Road, and detained them, that's all," said Richard.

"You came to no harm, I hope?" Sir John asked me.

"We'd already made it here, to The Bear, but His Grace rode out and asserted his claim on her," said Jocky, before I could answer.

His words were already bumping into one another, but he poured another cup of wine. "Stanley would have harmed her, sure, if he'd had the chance. Vengeance is mine, and all that! But he didn't!"

He raised his full glass in Richard's direction and took a swig. He was drunk, and babbling, but his implications confused me. I spoke up for the first time.

"Lord Stanley wasn't the one who..."

But they ignored me.

Sir John Milewater raised his brows, and grinned down the table at Richard.

"Your taste in wenches may be all you two have in common, Dickon!" he said. Jocky Howard roared, and Francis' mouth turned up at the corners for just a moment. I couldn't see the friar's reaction, but Richard only threw his hand up, as if the conversation bored him.

"Ah, here's our Johnnie, with the custard," said the friar.

Johnnie came in carrying a pewter tray with a dessert that looked like a cheesecake baked in a pastry crust. The manservant followed him, holding another jug and six new cups.

"Do you like Lombardy custard, Jayne? It's my favorite sweet," said Richard, and cut a bite with his knife for me without waiting for my answer.

I was full already, and uneasy after the last conversation, but I couldn't pass up the chance to try his favorite dessert. This was a detail about the man that hadn't made it into a single history book, like the story that must lie behind Jocky Norfolk's comments about Stanley. The custard was delicious, with hints of cinnamon and clove. I could have made a meal out of it.

"You are a dainty eater," he said softly, and I had to smile, remembering how, in my other life, Mimi made fun of me for gobbling down my giant cheeseburger with a book in the other hand.

The stuff in the jug turned out to be hippocras. It was better than the other wine I'd tasted so far, since the spices and sugar counteracted the vinegary sourness, but it was still a far cry from the dry cabernet I adored. I took one swallow for politeness' sake, and soon after Richard stood up, indicating that the dinner was at an end. They all jumped to their feet, and Jocky supported himself on the edge of the table.

"I'm thinking you'll not have further need of us this night, Your Grace."

Richard rolled his eyes. "I'd be rather unlucky if I did," he said, and their laughter followed us out of the room.

I stroked his chest, and laid my ear against his heart. More than anything else in my new world, the sound of its beating brought home to me the miracle of my accidental journey. For bad or ill, Richard III was no longer a character in a play, or the subject of a history book, or a long-dead ancestor. In little more than a year, the rise and fall of his chest, so regular against my cheek, would cease forever. Stanley would betray him, and let him die on Bosworth Field. I clutched him too tightly, and he pulled back and frowned down into my face.

"Rich − Your Grace, what was the story about Lord Stanley, that no one would finish? I didn't understand John Milewater's joke," I said.

I could feel my own heart beating now. What if he jumped out of bed, and sent me back to the room I shared with Rose? But he just lay back and stroked my hair.

"You may call me Richard when you're in my bed, Jayne." He adjusted his arm around my body and took a deep breath.

"About eleven years ago, my brother King Edward gave me my first command. He sent me into Wales with an army, to recover a castle that had been taken by rebel forces. I was just eighteen, barely a man, and although I'd begged him for the honor, I was terrified. More than five hundred men answered my call to muster, many of them veteran soldiers, and my worst fear was being caught out a fool by them, just a babe who was only commanding an army because he was the brother of the king."

"By February, we were ready to move, so I led them on a cold, slog-ging journey along the dog tracks the Welsh call roads, to where a band of rebels had seized the castle of Carmarthen in South Wales. Early on, I made a few blunders, but we recovered the castle."

How intriguing! "Tell me about the blunders," I said.

"It has but little to do with your question."

"Please tell me anyway. I find it hard to imagine you blundering."

He snorted.

"The rebels were led by a notorious Welshman by the name of Morgan ap Thomas ap Griffith," he said, "and he was reputed to be as wild and rugged as the Welsh hills that nurtured him. I meant to waste no time setting him wise to my authority, so as soon as we had set up camp in the snow-covered rocks outside the castle, I sent Robert Percy, one of my household knights, with a small escort to take a written warning addressed to Morgan: surrender the castle or face attack. I remember I was outside my tent with two of my knights, I believe one of them was Thomas Berkeley and the other was Jocky Howard, who was at table with us tonight, when Rob returned less than two hours later, with a rolled paper in his hand. As soon as he dismounted, I ordered him to read it to us. He stared at me with the most baleful expression, but made no move to obey me.

"Berkeley and Howard were both older than I by at least twenty years, and I feared that if I tolerated such defiant behavior from a knight whom they knew was my personal friend, it would invite their scorn, and undermine my authority. So I put on my best commander's face and said to Rob, 'Read it to me, Percy, now!'

"He shook his head. 'Morgan doesn't write, Your Grace. He bade me to recite his message to you instead.'

"I began to feel uneasy, and I almost asked him to step inside the tent and give me the message there, but I had gone too far in front of my captains.

"'Then let us hear it, Percy,' I said. 'And pray do not continue to leave us standing here freezing and awaiting your pleasure.'

"Rob looked as if he wanted to cry. He gestured with the rolled document, which I now recognized as my own. He held it between his gloved fingers as if it bore a curse.

"'Morgan says he can't read a word of this codswallop, but it made a fine rag to wipe his arse with, and now you may have it back to wipe your craven face.'

"I laughed, and he tightened his arms around me. I could feel him smiling in the darkness.

"Thomas Berkeley demonstrated such impressive self-restraint that I vowed I would learn to emulate it someday. Jocky, on the other hand, let go a yelp of laughter, which he attempted to disguise as a fit of coughing, and asked to be excused while he turned his back. I learned a valuable lesson about reading faces, and heeding what they told me, as well as attempting to impress the veteran soldiers under my command."

"What happened? Were you able to save face somehow?"

He nodded.

"I told my squire to saddle my horse, and I rode forthwith up to the castle myself to meet with Morgan. It was the first of many such meetings, all of which came to naught for the first few weeks, but after a month-long siege and an offer of pardon, we restored the castle to safe custody and proper governance and pardoned any rebels willing to take an oath of fealty to my brother. Then we headed home."

He pushed his shoulders up against the massive oak headboard and looked into my face.

"We were tired. The siege had been long and we'd been stuck in snow for most of it. On the way home, we stopped at a manor just outside Shrewsbury. The daughter of the house was close to my age, and beautiful. All soft shades of brown and gold, like a Yorkshire sunset. She looked very much like you."

I looked away, ashamed of how happy the compliment made me.

"I knew she was promised to another. I knew I was committing a political error that would haunt my future and embarrass my brother. But I was so full of my victory, and so proud of my manhood, that I grew greedy for one more conquest. By the time I left her, she was carrying my child."

"Then, on my way into Shrewsbury, I met her intended husband on the road, making his way in the other direction."

"Lord Stanley," I said.

He nodded.

Do you still...I mean, where is she now?"

"She died some years ago. Johnnie is our son."

He stopped there, and sank back down into the pillows, pulling me close to him again. I was glad he couldn't see my face.

The fantastic irony of the situation took my breath. Richard prevented Stanley's marriage to some ordinary young woman, with the ultimate result that Stanley married Margaret Tudor, the mother of Henry Tudor, the man who would take Richard's throne, and his life.

"Thank you for telling me," I said.

He moved down to lie beside me, and slipped his thigh between my knees. For the rest of the night I forgot about Richard the king and gave myself to Richard the man.

CHAPTER 13

RICHARD: NOVEMBER 15, 1483

*M*y secretary's face glistened with sweat, and his shoulders sagged. The ride from London was a long one, and he'd not see forty again.

"Thank you, Kendall. Johnnie will show you your room. Do get yourself a meal, and some rest."

He looked uncertain. He'd traveled with all haste to bring me a satchel full of dispatches, and I knew he thought it both a duty and a right to go through them with me.

"I assure you, I'll take no action without your consultation," I promised him. He cheered a bit, but I could tell he would have preferred to remain, and hover about me like my childhood nurse. Johnnie jumped up from the pile of armor he'd been polishing to lead him out of the anteroom to my chamber, which I was using as a traveling office.

Jockey lounged in a chair in front of my makeshift desk, and Francis took up a greave and began industriously rubbing it with a soft rag.

"That's Johnnie's task, Francis. It's been many a year since you were my squire," I said.

"Oh, I rather enjoy it," he said. "Idle hands, and all that." He looked out of the window instead of down at his work, and I knew he was only biding his time until he could slip back to the yeoman's widow in whose bed he'd spent last night.

"Read this stuff, will you, Dickon?" said Jockey.

I'd put it off as long as I could. I opened the case and pulled out a stack of documents several inches thick.

There was much to do, but little to give me pause. I was almost to the bottom of the pile when I reached a sealed letter from one of my oldest friends, Thomas Paston. I both relished and dreaded his correspondence. He was often entertaining, but always truthful.

"Your swift dispatch of Lord Buckingham and the other rebels has London abuzz with praise for your generalship," he wrote.

"But rumors persist that give me much concern, Your Grace. The fact that your brother's widow, Lady Elizabeth, and her daughters Bess and Cecily, continue to remain in sanctuary in the Abbey does your reputation much injury. It is said that the former Queen only remains in such close and inconvenient quarters because she fears you will do to death her remaining children, as you did her sons."

I closed my eyes. My nephews again. What other decision could I have made under the wretched circumstances? If Edward's sons remained for rebels to rally round, the country would be in civil broils again, just as it was throughout my youth and childhood. Now the very people I sought to protect made me out a villain. My sister-in-law was doing her work of revenge exceedingly well.

I hated to read the rest of the letter.

"And I have it through a most reliable source that the Lady Elizabeth is trading messages with Lady Margaret Stanley through the latter's physician, who allegedly attends one of the Princesses on Margaret's recommendation."

"What now, Your Grace?" asked Jockey.

"The unholy trinity is still conspiring," I replied. "And the rumors abound in London that Elizabeth is still hiding from me because I'm a danger to the Princesses. The Ladies Bess and Cecily, rather."

I was still in the habit of referring to my nieces as princesses, even though they'd been proven bastards, and were no longer permitted the title. Foolish of me, since the bastardy of my brother's children was the reason the weight of the realm now rested on my shoulders.

"You need a spy of your own," said Francis, from his perch by the window.

I rubbed my forehead. "We've been through this before, more times than I care to count. There's no way to introduce a man into that entirely feminine ménage. And if I could, there's no one I could trust except one of you, or Brother Cynneth. Can you picture him, cooped up watching them embroider? He'd probably end up making excellent swordsmen of them."

They laughed.

"No, I must keep Stanley happy. At least happy enough to dissuade Margaret from plotting with her son to try to start another rebellion. I have made him Lord Constable. He will be formally invested when we reach London."

"Tell me you jest!" said Jocky.

"No, I'm in dead earnest. He won't bother trying to replace me with his stepson unless he thinks he'll fare much better under the Tudor's rule."

"But Lord Constable of England? He'll be the most powerful law enforcement in the land," said Francis. "Remember when your brother gave you that office? We were all so proud."

"I remember. But the importance of the post is why it will please him. God knows he's rich enough as it is."

"Well, do what you must, lad," said Jockey.

Instead of offending my dignity, his familiarity brought back fond memories. Not so long ago, my brother Edward ruled and I was merely his favorite soldier. He made the decisions, and I enforced them. What a wonderful world it had been.

Johnnie blew back into the room, and let the heavy door bang shut behind him.

"Is Kendall well settled, son?"

"He is, Father, but I do believe he wanted to stay here with you. We met Mistress Jayne on the stairs, and I introduced them."

Francis smirked. My secretary's well-known prudery always amused him.

"Did the sight of her make him want to unlace his hose for the first time in a twelvemonth?" he asked.

Johnnie blushed. He adored her. "I didn't tell him who she was, exactly. He just bowed over her hand. I could tell he thought her beautiful, if that be your meaning, Lord Lovell."

It was all I could do not to laugh at Francis' expression.

"Your gallantry does you credit, Johnnie. Now do finish my armor, and then start upon your own. We'll ride to Dover Castle tomorrow."

He grinned at me. For the first time, he would ride in the procession in full armor, and although I couldn't have him in Ned's place, at my horse's hip, he would be close by, and I'd never seen any human so thrilled. He rushed over to the greave that Francis was still pretending to polish.

"Oh, but Your Grace," he said. "Mistress Jayne did mention Ipomedon. She wondered if she could have it to read, to pass her time this afternoon."

Jockey raised his eyebrows. "What? The woman reads?"

I handed Johnnie the oldest volume in a stack of others beside my desk. I'd had it since I was not much older than he.

"You may take it to her, but don't linger," I told him. He dashed from the room with the worn-out book in his hand.

"Do you think she just likes the look of the pictures?" asked Jockey.

"No, she's read parts of it aloud to me, when they especially take her fancy. What do you care, Jockey? Did you want to borrow it yourself?"

Francis grinned.

"Certainly not," said Jockey. "I can't see why you bring a romance on your travels. It seems a mite strange to me. But it's even more curious to find a woman of her station able to read, is all. What do you know about her? Can she write as well?"

"They've not been practicing their letters together, Jockey," said Francis.

Jockey rolled his eyes. "Do you trust her?"

"I know very little about her, in truth," I said. "When I've made feints of inquiry, she closes up like a castle under siege, so I saw no reason to press the inquiry. I don't know if she writes. I suppose I could ask her. And yes, I trust her. Does that answer all your questions?"

I did trust her, and the realization made me yearn for her. I wished I could have taken the book to her myself.

He slapped his palm down upon my desk. "That must be your plan, Richard," he said.

"Pardon?"

"Send her to Elizabeth. Let her be your spy. They'll never suspect she can read."

I shook my head.

He stood up, and paced the chamber. "It's perfect, and you well know it. She can get you messages through Cynneth. No one will be suspicious if they meet."

"I'll not put her into that danger. She's been through a great deal already, you might remember. And they'd never accept her anyway."

He sat back down and leaned towards me over the desk. "If you send her to them as a waiting woman, they'll have to accept her. They might not like it, and they'll not speak a word of their plots in her hearing, but she might be able to get a look at their treacherous little missives."

"I've told you, no. I'll not hear another word about it."

"I know she pleases you, but you've the good of the realm to think of, not just your own desires!"

"You go too far, Lord Norfolk. Please leave us."

He bowed and left the room, shutting the door with a thud behind him. The cordial atmosphere that had existed in the room only a few minutes before was banished for the day. I read the rest of the reports in silence, and after a moment, Lovell excused himself too. When Johnnie finished his task and went out to see to our horses, I was alone at last.

I picked up Paston's letter and read it again. How dearly my decision about the boys had cost me! Would Buckingham have betrayed me as he did, but for our disagreement over them?

I got up and poured a cup of wine, went to the window, and looked north towards London.

There was nothing to be done about the gossip Paston said was rampant. Once the boys were no longer seen about the Tower, there was bound to be idle talk about their whereabouts. Buckingham and I agreed that it was inevitable, and that only the passage of time, and my good leadership, would make their fate seem less important. So why did it pain me so severely to hear of the gossip now?

How Elizabeth must be enjoying her stirring of that injurious soup! I had an urgent need for a mole in her lair, just not my Jayne.

Jockey had asked me what I knew about the girl. She could read, she asked more questions than she answered, and when I made love to her she looked up at my face as if the very sight of me was a great boon she'd been granted. I had never, to my knowledge, been the author of such contentment. I daresay looks of similar adoration from a female might have been common for Edward, but for me it was a novel experience. If it was naught but mummery, Jayne had a fine career waiting for her with the next troupe of traveling players who crossed our path.

I told him I trusted her. But why should I? Mayhap it was her concern for my disfigured shoulder that made me feel peaceful when she was near me. I'd talked of it before with few people, and none of them outside of my family except Brother Cynneth. I asked him to examine it once, years ago, when it first began to pain me. He ran his hands over the joints of my neck and back, and bade me raise and lower both of my arms.

"It won't hamper your use of a sword as long as you keep it limber," he told me. "But it won't be going away."

I felt that verdict like a knife in the gut, although somehow I was not surprised. The recurrent, nagging ache already had a hideous feeling of permanence.

"But will it worsen?" I asked.

He looked at me with those intelligent little eyes of his, and I knew the answer before he spoke.

"I'm sorry. I think that it probably will. But slowly."

He'd been truthful, and accurate, as always. By now, it seemed something shameful, that I would do well to hide. Jayne touched it when first we lay together, but although her question about whether it pained me was impertinent, somehow it didn't insult me. Perhaps because her face was full of honest concern, rather than the revulsion I expected, and I found the sentiment pleasing in someone who had no cause to care about my comfort. Her soft hands soothed the ache of it, and her gentle touch made it seem less like a curse.

No, Jayne would stay at my side, where she belonged.

CHAPTER 14

JAYNE: NOVEMBER 16, 1483

Since the deluge in Salisbury weeks ago, the late autumn breezes had kept a chill in the moist air, so I snuggled the fur-lined cloak, a present from Richard, tighter around my shoulders as our horses trotted under the archway between the round stone towers that formed the gatehouse of Dover Castle. The eighty-foot walls of the keep rose as if by magic out of the flat coastal plain, and its eastern side lay only feet from the English Channel. Brother Cynneth assured me that the massive Kentish stronghold was the largest in England, and dwarfed even gigantic fortresses like Warwick Castle and Pontefract. I believed him; when the heavy black edge of the iron drawbridge fell across the moat with a reverberating boom, and clanged into place against the metal lip beside us, it was all I could do not to gape, open-mouthed, like the tourist that I was.

They raised the portcullis, and Richard and his escort clattered ahead of us over the drawbridge. His rich red banner with its gleaming white boar caught the wind and streamed out beside them. As he passed under the stone archway into the keep, the heralds blew a fanfare, and on the parapet, some fifty soldiers in mail shirts and kettle-shaped metal hats stood at attention as he passed. Johnnie had dressed him with great care that morning, and in place of his usual somber velvet, he wore a bright silk tabard over a polished metal breastplate, and his gleaming sword dangled from a belt at his waist. Instead of a helm, he wore a crown.

Despite myself I was proud in his reflected glory. But grand as he was today, I preferred him in his plain linen shirtsleeves, teaching Johnnie to play chess by candlelight, while I sat by the fire and tried to decipher the Gothic script of one of his beautiful books. Or, better yet, the way I saw him this morning, his bare chest slick with sweat above mine, my legs wrapped around his hips and his beautiful grey eyes half-closed in pleasure.

The irregularity of his shoulders wasn't apparent when he was in armor, or wearing one of the heavy tunics, gathered at the shoulders, which were the style of the time. But I felt the difference when I held him, and I'd seen the curve of his spine when he sprawled on his stomach in our bed. There could no longer be any doubt that, at least on that point, Shakespeare was right. But he was so patient with Johnnie, and spoke with such tenderness of Ned, the legitimate son he had with Queen Anne, that I found it hard to believe that he'd killed his nephews. Although when I saw him with the heavy gold crown on his head, I wondered what he'd done to be king, and how he justified taking a throne that should have belonged to his brother's eldest son. But I didn't dare broach the subject, for fear of disrupting the delicate balance of our relationship.

He reined White Surrey to a halt and saluted Sir Dunbarton, the constable of the castle. The sun gleamed on the gorgeous enamel collar alternating with white roses and golden suns, symbols of the House of York, which spread out over his shoulders. Dangling from its center, so that it lay over his heart, was the silver boar.

Before our first night together in Salisbury, I'd envisioned grabbing it as soon as I was close enough. But he hadn't worn it except on ceremonial occasions since he took it from the soldier's hand on the day we met. When I heard him tell Johnnie that he was afraid of misplacing it, as he'd done the night I found it, the irony wasn't lost on me. Now it was kept in a silver coffer that traveled everywhere in his squire's saddlebag. But it was only a matter of time before I got my hands on it.

"Dreaming, Jayne?" asked the friar. He rode beside me on Slow. He said Slower was fine for me, and besides, I'd bonded with the horse after that dreadful night in the rain.

"I suppose," I said. "And dreading the hours of dancing and lute playing that we'll have to endure tonight."

He laughed. "You shouldn't waste your time dreading what you can't change," he said. But I knew he understood.

I'd grown comfortable with the intimate suppers at the inns or taverns, where the only other diners were the members of Richard's closest circle. Jocky Howard, John Milewater, and Francis Lovell were now warm acquaintances of mine. But tonight, I would dine in the Great Hall at Dover Castle. Even though I would be seated far down at the end of the table, and the friar would be beside me, I was still unsure of myself, but I looked forward to the pageantry of a royal dinner in a medieval castle.

We dismounted, and Rose helped me carry my belongings into the small chamber, which was to be our bedroom. I looked around the cozy little room, and felt a foolish sense of dread. Richard assured me we wouldn't be truly separated, and that he would send for me when he could. Still I didn't like to think of sleeping without his lean body wrapped around mine.

Rose spread my clothes out on the little bed. I had a wardrobe of three dresses now – the one the friar brought me on that first morning, that never quite fit, and two that were made for me while we were in Salisbury. One was fine, heavy wool, and I was glad for the inspiration I'd had to select murrey, the dark reddish purple, of the House of York. I usually wore it as it was over my chemise. But the tailor insisted I have a pair of extra sleeves made up for it in brocade, which could be pinned into place for ceremonial occasions. I almost told him that there would be few of those in the short time I would be staying here, but now I was glad to have the sleeves, which he had sagely suggested I have made up in blue. I would dine in the castle wearing the colors of Richard's house.

Rose helped me to dress, and soon excitement won out over anxiety. Although she was technically part of Jockey Norfolk's household, he allowed her to stay with me all the time now, like a lady's maid. But I thought of her as my friend, and my equal, so I usually refused to have her dress me. It was a custom of the age that I found intrusive and unsettling. But it would be impossible for me to attach the sleeves on my own, so today I was glad of the help.

I'd been surprised to find she was only eighteen, but guessing ages here was difficult; everyone was much younger than they looked, or behaved. Her plump good cheer and careful fingers soothed my nerves, as always. She saw me looking at her and smiled at me.

"Are you looking forward to the celebrations, mistress?" she asked.

"I am, but I'm nervous too," I said.

She nodded, pins in her mouth.

When both sleeves were attached, she said, "You'll not be nervous after you see the goose, and the fine beef you'll be eatin' on this Martinmas. They're to have three removes, and seven courses in each of them so I'm told. And even the servants are to have a bit of the goose. Lord and Lady Dunbarton are that flattered by your lover's visit." She winked at me.

The holiday marked the end of autumn, and celebrated the harvest, and in wealthy households fattened geese and cattle were slaughtered and served up in lavish style. No wonder Lord Dunbarton was being so generous; the feast would have been extravagant even without the presence of the king.

Rose brushed out my hair, and pinned my veil to a small strip of linen called a barbette, that went under my chin. Some type of head covering was mandatory, but at least an unmarried woman was allowed to wear her hair loose. So she skillfully arranged my unruly mop, pulling a curl out here, and tucking one there. My hair had been a constant source of irritation to me back home, where smooth, obedient locks a la Kate Middleton were the rage. Here it seemed my curly hair was finally appreciated.

She gave my veil a final pat. "You be lovely in your murrey and blue, mistress. His Grace will be right proud."

How I hoped she was right.

Lady Eleanor Dunbarton looked like a drawing from a medieval Book of Hours. Her bright blue silk gown had a black velvet collar that made a deep V across her narrow chest, and she wore a black velvet belt fastened high on her tiny waist. A tall steeple hennin perched on the back of her head, with an airy white gauze veil suspended from its point. When it was her turn to greet Richard, I could see she was trembling.

When she successfully executed her curtsey and got a quick kiss, she looked as pleased as an Oscar-winner. Richard clasped the men's hands, or slapped them on the shoulder, and nodded to the women, or bowed over their hands. When he passed in front of me, I dipped my knee as low as I dared and looked down at the rushes on the floor. He moved on without a word and continued into the Great Hall. Then he glanced back over his shoulder and smiled at me. I had passed muster.

I waited beside the doorway, not sure exactly how to proceed, when the friar called my name.

He wore a clean grey cassock, and his round face looked freshly scrubbed. I followed him into the Hall, grateful yet again for his understanding presence, and we sat down together midway down one of the tables that spanned both sides of the hall. They were covered in snowy white linen, and formed a "U" shape, with benches along its outer sides. Darkness had fallen outside, but the torches suspended every few feet along the walls, and the dozens of wax candles placed down the center of the tables, gave the place a warm, golden glow. Richard sat in a carved wooden chair at the top of the room, with the Dunbartons on either side of him. I'd felt a flush of glory at his approval, but it left me as quickly as came, and I was a stranger again, watching a beautiful scene that didn't involve me. I usually sat beside Richard at supper myself, and shared his trencher and his cup, and although I'd known that would be impossible tonight, I hadn't expected it to make me feel so forlorn.

The friar and I shared a pewter plate with a bread trencher to soak up juices from the meat, and we each had a pewter cup for our wine. The servants brought out the first courses, and held out platters of goose. I took a little, to be polite, but I was too overwhelmed to be hungry. Apparently the friar suffered no such emotions, because he took a generous portion and immediately began to pull it apart with his fingers.

"Well, Jayne, what do you think of your king tonight?" I smiled at his choice of words.

"I think he looks very handsome, and is a very shrewd politician," I said, recalling his entrance into the Hall.

"I do think he is learning to emulate his brother King Edward, God rest his soul," said the friar. "Though it's not his nature to be so friendly among strangers. He was happier as a soldier."

The food kept coming. At the end of each course there was a sweet made into some meaningful shape, called a "subtlety," and after the first course we had a white, fluffy cake shaped like a goose, which was apparently a symbol of St. Martin. It seemed sacrilegious, but I glanced at the friar and he was munching contentedly.

Johnnie served Richard on bended knee, proud and resplendent in his red and blue livery embroidered with the lions and lilies of England. His red cap was decorated with a white boar, and the one that had brought me here was pinned on the shoulder of Richard's black velvet doublet. When its owner, darkly handsome in the torchlight, saw me looking at him, he nodded. I wanted him; I hoped I was not too far away for him to see it on my face.

"You are staring at the king, Jayne. It might be considered rude," said the friar.

"Everyone's staring at him for one reason or another. He must be used to it by now. I'm just thinking about how bored he looks."

He winked at me. He knew better.

"You must not expect him to send for you tonight. He'll be occupied until well after midnight with his host, and the other noble guests. He must put his duty first."

He was right, of course. Lord and Lady Dunbarton, no doubt thinking to impress the king, had arranged numerous entertainments, including a lute player who sang twelve verses about St. Martin. I could see Richard's eyes glazing over from where I sat far down the hall, but he continued to smile and nod, and to drink copious quantities of wine. He kept filling his own silver cup, and it was all Johnnie could do to keep a full jug on the table for him.

At last he stood, and the benches screeched backwards across the floor in unison as everyone rushed to their feet. He left the Hall, trailed by Lord Dunbarton and a dozen men in silk and velvet.

*A*fter Richard disappeared with his host, Brother Cynneth showed me to the curving stone staircase that led up to the wall walk, which ran around the perimeter of the keep.

"Go up and enjoy the view, Jayne," he said. I was agog over the castle, and apparently my fascination was typical for a commoner not used to such grandeur.

Once I was at the top I leaned against the parapet, and looked down on the thatched roofs of the village below. I suspected that on most nights it would be nearly invisible, but tonight rush lights burned brightly at intervals on the battlements, and torches and bonfires lit up the narrow streets. The sounds of celebration that wafted up on the cool air made me smile. The medievals loved to celebrate, and tonight marked the last day of autumn. The harvest was in, and winter started tomorrow. It was a good excuse for revelry.

I felt like rejoicing myself. I'd gotten through yet another public appearance without making a fool of myself, and I'd seen the magnificent spectacle of King Richard III dining in state. I would never forget the brilliant colors of the silk and velvet gowns, or the way the candlelight glinted on the beringed fingers of the noblemen as they raised their silver chalices. And at the center of it all was a man with a golden crown on his head, and he met my eye just one glorious time as he looked down the table. Even if he didn't send for me tonight, he soon would. I would go back to my room, if I could find it. Maybe Rose would already be there. She would love to hear about the feast.

I heard a noise coming from my left, between the stairs and where I stood. Maybe it was just the soldier on watch, making his rounds, and he would do his appointed duty quickly and go back to his celebrating.

I stayed put, waiting for him to pass. Then I heard voices, one of them female. I huddled closer into a corner made by the stone outcropping of one of the bastions. Lonely as I was for Richard, I was in no mood to disturb a luckier couple at their tryst. I couldn't see them without moving out of my hiding place, but I could hear them, kissing and murmuring. Was I going to have to wait through their entire sexual encounter? I was getting cold, and I hoped they would get on with it. I was about to try to find another way down when I heard a familiar name.

"Well, Rosie, did you get a gander at the nobles? I knowed you was hoping for a sight of their grand feast."

So it was Rose, and her new sweetheart! She said she'd met one of Lord Dunbarton's grooms this afternoon in the castle bailey, and that he'd asked her name and called her "toothsome." She certainly worked fast.

"Aye," she answered him. "I did see the feast, and my own mistress had a seat at the table." She made it sound like such an honor.

"Well, the king's leman ought to have a place there, I suppose. His brother's whores always did. Now there was man as didn't need no jewels nor a crown to look like a king."

Ah, there it was: fresh evidence that Edward IV's fabled charm had worked its magic on both genders.

"He was day to night different from that little brother of his, that be for sure," said the man. "What a dark, sour piece of work that one is, wearing a crown on his head what don't belong there."

I stood there, seething, but I didn't dare rush to his defense.

"Oh, I don't know, Tommy," said Rose. "He's right good to Mistress Jayne. She does come back to me fair done in most mornings."

I grinned. I couldn't deny it.

"Well, if you've a liking for her you better hope she keeps pleasin' him, and don't never get in his way," he said.

I felt my face flush.

"Why, Tommy? He do seem taken with her. And his household wenches have told me he's not tupped a one of the serving maids, not even the fairest of 'em. Not 'til her."

Damn. I was torn between fury at my most personal affairs being discussed so blatantly, and happiness at Richard's constancy.

"You women's tales is all so much fadoodle, Rosie. He'll soon tire of her, with so many maidenheads waiting in line for him to practice his swordplay on. Just see she's careful, and don't make a big stir when it happens. He's one as kills those that gets in his way, 'sall I'm sayin."

"I've heard those tales too, but I'm not believin' 'em."

You go, Rose!

He snorted. "Where do you think those boys be? Hidin' in the Tower, waiting for their uncle to come play with 'em? In their graves is where they are, and that little thief's got no shame, makin' himself a king."

I didn't stay there to listen to any more. I turned away from them and moved out around the bastion and down the wall in the other direction, not caring if I was momentarily exposed. My head was pounding, and my eyes burned, whether from tears or the smoke from the rush lights I didn't know or care.

I kept walking along the wall, and finally came to a gap in the inside wall that turned out to be another staircase. I dragged my heavy skirts down the stairs, and found a page who was still awake in the Great Hall to direct me to my room. I lay in my small bed, alone and miserable, until long after midnight, when he sent for me.

CHAPTER 15

JAYNE: NOVEMBER 19, 1483

A manservant I'd never seen before led me by rushlight through so many turns and twists that I would never find my way back alone. Thank God I'd thrown a heavy wool cloak over my chemise; my little chamber was warm enough, but the wide halls and stone stairwells of Dover Castle were freezing. At last the servant stopped and knocked on a massive wooden door, and I heard Richard's voice tell us to enter.

I only caught a glimpse of bright tapestries and Richard's huge desk set up in a corner before I was in his arms.

"Is this what were you wanting, Jayne? Or did I misinterpret that look you gave me over the bread?"

I kissed his smiling lips and put my hand under his doublet to stroke his slim, muscular thigh. After a moment I reached higher, and found him already hard. I caressed the rigid shaft through his hose, and then I reached to untie the leather points that held them to his doublet.

He lifted me easily off my feet and carried me to the giant bed. Pulling back the red velvet hangings, he laid me sideways across it, climbed in beside me and began unlacing the front of my gown. He reached in and cupped my breast, and slowly traced the nipple, first with his thumb, and then with his tongue. He put his hands on mine, palm to palm, and pushed them up over my head.

Holding me there firmly, he spread my legs with his knee, and entered me slowly and deliberately, up to the hilt. As he kept the pressure on my palms he looked down directly into my eyes.

"Is this what you were asking me for?" he whispered, as he thrust again, and I could tell he was finding it difficult to maintain his game of mastery over me without succumbing to it himself.

"Yes, yes," I cried, and pushed my hips against him. He arched his back in a spasm of pleasure and his face contorted as he forced himself to delay. I found the evidence of his desire for me so arousing that I whimpered his name, and he could wait no longer. He lowered his face and put his lips on mine as he let himself go, and I cried out again as my body responded to his, as it always did.

Afterwards, I snuggled in the cradle of his arm, and soon the regular rise and fall of his chest told me he was sleeping. I was exhausted myself, but I needed to pee, so I slipped out of his arms to look for the privy.

Despite the light from the fireplace and the candles that still burned, it took me a moment to locate the screen that hid the chamber pot. Like everything else in the room, it was beautiful, woven with a scene of forests and unicorns. I was heading back to bed after taking care of business, when a gleam of silver caught my eye. The white glow of the boar was unmistakable.

It lay on a bed of velvet, in an open casket on his desk. In his hurry to make love to me, Richard must have overlooked its usual careful storage. I tiptoed up to the desk. This was the first time I'd gotten a good look at it since I dropped it in the grass outside his tent. Its ferocious beauty was just as I remembered. Now maybe all I had to do was touch it, and I would be back home, in the world of cell phones and electricity.

Where would I land? In my room in Leicester, or back at the dig, in his makeshift grave? I shuddered, and looked back at the man in the bed. His shining hair was spread out on the pillow so that his thin brown cheek was barely visible beneath it. How I'd loved to wrap its curling tendrils around my fingers! He would die before his lithe, battle-scarred body ever grew old. I ached to touch him one more time, but I couldn't risk waking him.

I could never tell anyone what had happened to me, but I would have knowledge no other living person could match. Even if his bones had already revealed his crooked shoulder to the world, only I had seen the living man, and knew how he hid it, and how it shamed him. And only I knew that it sometimes hurt him at night, and how to help ease his pain. I put my hand over my mouth so he wouldn't hear me sob.

The man on the wall walk said Richard would tire of me soon. He was right, of course. Then where would I be, trapped in this ruthless, ignorant time with no way to ever get home? Mom's worried face appeared before my eyes. I had to get back to her.

The man also accused Richard of killing his nephews, and this was the second time I'd heard the rumors from an ordinary citizen. What was that old saw about smoke and fire?

But I didn't know anything for sure. I'd been plopped down in the midst of one of the greatest mysteries in history and didn't have the guts to look for the answer. If I went back before I knew the fate of the Princes, and the guilt or innocence of the man I loved, I would drudge, safe but bitter, in the history department of some college, and curse my own cowardice for the rest of my life. And the nightmares that had ceased entirely since I'd been close to him – would they resume? They'd be more horrific than ever now that I'd held him.

I crept back into the warm bed and left the boar lying in its nest of blue velvet. Richard sighed in his sleep, wrapped both arms around me, and pulled me close against his chest. I listened to the beating of his heart until the sun shone like burnished gold through the huge mullioned window.

The next day I only saw Richard from a distance, strolling in the castle bailey with Lord Dunbarton and some of his other noble subjects, and from the end of the table at supper the next evening. The only attention he gave me was a quick nod from the high seat, but I was fine with that. The longer we were together, the more confident I became in his affection, and my decision to stay in his world, for a least a little while longer, lifted a burden from my shoulders. I shared my chamber with Rose that night, and listened to her chatter about the groom, Tommy, the man with whom I'd heard her talking on the parapet. I tried not to resent her. After all, his feelings about Richard weren't her fault. I did my best not to let her see that she'd disappointed me, but when she asked me coy questions about Richard, I couldn't answer with the same trusting familiarity that I'd felt just a few days before.

The friar was at loose ends, too; the castle had a chaplain, and in observation of some rule of ecclesiastical etiquette, the friar yielded the tending of Richard's spiritual needs to him. So Brother Cynneth showed me around the castle, and I spent a day like a historian's wet dream, touring the buttery where the wine and ale were kept, and the bakery where the bread was baked and the pantry where it was stored. Preparing food for the hundred or so people who usually lived at the castle was a constant process, and the addition of Richard's household had doubled the frenzied activity. I felt safe and unworried for the first time in a great while, and I enjoyed the friar's witty company with pleasure unmitigated by my former uneasiness.

On the afternoon scheduled to be our last at Dover Castle, the friar and I stood together in front of the buttery, while Richard and Francis Lovell practiced with their broadswords on the wide grassy area in the middle of the inner bailey yard. Watching his daily ritual had become my own.

A silent crowd of nobles watched from the other side of the yard as the two men moved in close to each other, their sweating faces close as lovers, before one of them would use the flat side of his blade to push the other staggering backwards.

"It keeps his shoulder limber," said the friar.

I nodded. When the two of us were alone, we talked openly of Richard's physical issues. There were times it was all I could do not to tell him that the problem had a name, scoliosis, and that his recommendation that Richard engage in regular physical activity to keep the pain at bay would still be considered good advice five hundred years later.

"Do you think Francis ever lets him win?" I asked, as Richard gave Francis a shove that sent him flying back towards the kitchen.

"No," said the friar. "On the contrary, he tries all the harder because he knows that is the only way to please him. Francis was Richard's first squire. Seems an age ago."

The swordsmen finished their practice, to the respectful clapping of the nobles who scurried to follow Richard back to the armory.

"Would you care to take a view of the outer bailey, and then walk up to the curtain wall? You'll be able to see the shore of the Channel," asked the friar.

"I would love that."

I pulled the fur-lined hood of my cloak up over my head, and we walked under the stone archway. We were about to climb up to the pinnacle tower when a horseman galloped past us into the yard, scattering chickens and scullions in his wake.

I caught my breath. He reminded me of Talbott, until he wheeled his horse around and I saw that he had on a blue and red livery jacket with leopards and lilies embroidered on it, quartered with a white boar. He dismounted and threw the reins of his lathered horse to a groom and stepped up to Brother Cynneth.

"Good morrow, Friar," he said. He pulled off his helm, and put it under his arm. "Do you know where I might find the King's Grace? I've a message for him."

Unlike most of the medieval men, his dark hair was cut short and close to his head. His biceps strained the sleeves of his leather brigandine, and he was by far the tallest man I'd seen since Talbott. He resembled him, both in size and demeanor.

"Good morrow to you, Sir James," said the friar. "I believe His Grace was headed towards the armory just moments ago. No unpleasantness to report, I hope?"

The man shrugged his shoulders. "I'll only be telling my news to the king himself."

He strode off towards the inner bailey.

The Ffriar sighed. "Ah, Sir James Tyrell! Always so secretive, and always in such a hurry. I'd not be surprised if he galloped that poor horse all the way from London. But he's as loyal as a hound to the king, so it's no wonder he's his most trusted henchman. Shall we continue to the parapet, Jayne?"

I nodded, but I'd lost all interest in pretty views. The calm of the day had been completely shattered, but perhaps it was for the best. I wasn't just playing Middle Ages, like I'd done when I was ten. This was deadly reality, and no one could have reminded me so well as Sir James Tyrell.

"The king's favorite henchman," Brother Cynneth had called him.

The friar was quoting Shakespeare, a hundred years before the man's birth. Although the term "henchman" didn't have the sinister connotation that it would in modern times, according to the play, Sir James Tyrell was the devoted servant to whom Richard assigned the murder of his nephews.

The steps up to the battlements were worn and slippery from the tread of a thousand archers, and there was no handrail to assist the timid. I gathered my skirts in my left hand and the friar took my right.

"Your hand is sweating, my dear. Don't be afraid. I've noted your excellent balance when you're in the saddle."

I did my best to fake a smile, and we continued up.

Did Tyrell dash here from London to tell Richard that the boys were no longer a threat, that he'd done as commanded, and killed them? According to history, the boys disappeared from the Tower at the end of August, but that didn't mean they'd been killed immediately. Maybe they'd been alive until just a few days ago, when Richard finally decided they were too much of a threat, too much of a focus for any rebellious nobleman disgruntled with the king, and he'd given Tyrell the order to dispose of them.

"One can see almost to France today," said the friar, indicating the stunning view as proudly as if he'd built the castle himself. I looked out across the water, and the waves of the English Channel flung themselves again and again against the foot of the wall, only to be dashed apart into millions of freezing droplets. I nodded, pretending to agree with him, but it was too cold and unforgiving to be beautiful.

In the Great Hall that evening, Tyrell sat in a position of honor on the other side of Lady Dunbarton from Richard. I watched him smiling and chatting with her. He would survive Bosworth, only to be executed by the next king, Henry Tudor, some said for his part in the murder of the last Plantagenet princes.

When the servant came to my door with his rushlight sometime in the early hours of the next day, I'd made my decision. But when I saw Richard's face I almost changed my mind. He looked so weary and careworn, almost as haggard as he did the first night I met him, after Buckingham's execution.

"Sweet Jayne, you are like a balm to my soul," he said, as soon as the servant shut the door. Tired as he looked, he carried me to the bed and made love to me without stopping to drink his usual cup of wine or ale, and afterwards he snuggled me under his arm and sat up against the headboard, as he did when he was in the mood to talk.

"Have you enjoyed Dover Castle? We shall leave it behind in the morning."

"Yes, I have. Brother Cynneth showed me the view of the channel today, and I went up on the inner wall walk, the first night, on my own."

I wondered if he could feel my heart beating.

"Richard," I said. "I heard something strange while I was up on the wall walk, our first night here. Two people, a pair of lovers I think, were talking. They didn't know I was there." I took a deep breath. "And I overheard them."

"Ummm? What was strange about that?" He stroked my cheek.

"Well, they were saying things about you. Awful things."

His body went rigid next to mine.

"What were they saying, Jayne? Tell me."

His voice was cold, and measured, but I felt the quick rise and fall of his chest with every breath.

Oh, God, why had I done this? My eyes filled with tears, but it was too late to go back.

"They said that your nephews were missing, and that something terrible had happened to them," I said. "They said it was your doing..."

He slipped out from under me in one smooth motion, and called for the servant who slept outside on a pallet in the hall. He turned his back on me, and went to stare out the window at the blackness. His familiar naked body was clearly visible by the light of the fire; pale against the dark panes, fit and perfect, except for his crooked shoulder.

The servant helped me into my robe and out the door. He hustled me down the cold hallway and back to my room so quickly that when I threw myself down on the bed to cry, my body was still warm from lying beside Richard.

A different servant knocked on my door early the next morning, and waited for me while I dressed myself. Rose was nowhere to be seen, and my hands shook so violently that it took me forever to tie the laces of my bodice.

This time I was escorted to the solar where he met with his nobles, and conducted the business of the realm. Richard sat at a huge wooden desk, and his secretary, a quiet little man named Kendall, waited at his right shoulder as he signed a document and imprinted the wax seal with the signet ring he wore on his little finger. He often fiddled with it when he was nervous, moving it up and down his finger. Today his hands were quiet; every movement was deliberate.

"Leave us, Kendall," he commanded, handing him the rolled parchment.

As soon as the secretary left the room, I started my apology. "Richard..."

He held up his hand, palm facing me, like I'd seen him do so many times to silence someone who was saying something he thought was of no consequence.

"You made a promise to me, not long ago, that in return for my protection, you would be of service to me if ever I needed your help. Do you remember?"

I stared at him. At first I had no clue what he was talking about. He went on, without waiting for my answer.

"I protected you from James Talbott on the Salisbury Road. Do you remember that?"

It seemed a lifetime ago, but I nodded.

"I will continue to see that he does you no harm. But I need to call upon your promise now."

He rubbed his hand across his mouth.

"I am in most urgent need of eyes and ears in Westminster Abbey, in the temporary abode of my sister-in-law, Dame Elizabeth Grey, and her daughters Bess and Cecily. I'm sure you know she claims right of sanctuary there, and has for some months since her children by my brother King Edward were declared to be bastards, and thus banned by the rules of the Church to rule England."

I knew he didn't expect me to answer.

"Now she conspires with Lady Margaret Stanley, the mother of Henry Tudor, the Lancastrian who claims the right to my throne, to make him king in my place. He is currently in exile in France, but I had word yesterday that he is raising money for ships and mercenaries to launch an invasion of England, perhaps as soon as next spring."

Oh no. That must be the news Tyrell rode his horse into the ground to bring him. Not the execution of the Princes.

"Few women of your station have their letters. It is so unusual, in fact, that your ability to read the women's correspondence will go completely unsuspected. You will go to the Abbey, and serve as their waiting-woman, and remain as long as they continue in their false "sanctuary." You must read any communication, no matter how innocuous, that you are able to lay eyes upon, and do your best to remember its contents. Brother Cynneth will meet with you regularly, as your confessor, and through him, you will relay to me any intelligence you are able to gather."

He cleared his throat. "It is inevitable that Dame Grey will leave the Abbey, and she will do so sooner if her schemes come to naught. When she does, I will consider your promise to me fulfilled, and our obligations to one another concluded."

My lungs felt empty of breath, as if there wasn't enough air in the whole castle to fill them again. I could no longer see his face, or the intricate tapestry behind him. I could only look inward; I had never admitted to myself that I thought he loved me, until this moment, when he showed me that he did not.

I left him waiting for an answer, while I tried to comprehend the enormity of my mistake. At first no sounds made it through the bubble of silence and misery that surrounded me. Then I became aware that he was speaking again.

"Will you go willingly, or must I order you to do this for me?" He must have repeated it several times before I remembered he was a king, and I was no one, just a fool.

"I will go," I said.

He snapped his fingers and a squire appeared as if he'd conjured him. He looked down at the pile of documents on his desk, and without further ceremony, I was escorted from his life.

PART II

CHAPTER 16

JAYNE: NOVEMBER 25, 1483

I curtsied as low as I dared, and waited for her to tell me to stand up. She left me in that excruciating pose until my legs shook.

"You may rise, Jayne Lyons," she said, just in time before I collapsed at her feet.

I stood up, and waited another breath before I looked up into the face of Dame Elizabeth Grey, the former Queen of England. She stared at me, her face expressionless except for the disdain in her clear blue eyes. I could not deny she was beautiful, in the same colorless, frozen way the marble carvings of Aphrodite on the walls of the library Mimi and I visited each Sunday when I was a child were beautiful. But even though the room was warm, and I still wore my heavy cloak, the chill she exuded made me shiver. She looked me thoroughly up and down, but if she noticed that my eyes were swollen almost shut from days of crying, she didn't comment, and for that at least I was grateful.

"You must know," she said, "the Royal Princesses and I have no wish for your service, or your company. We are well aware the Usurper has placed you here as his emissary, to cause us yet more unease in our already distressed circumstance."

She sniffed, and raised her perfect chin.

"We only accept your presence out of fear of him, and the pitiless reprisal he might perpetrate on us if we refuse. Your master is a ruthless man."

She turned away from me and paced a few steps in the crowded chamber, head held high. Her heavy silk skirts swirled and trailed behind her, but her theatrics were spoiled by the necessity of dodging the collection of chairs, mirrors, and rolled-up tapestries that gave the place the appearance of a yard sale from the British Museum. Brother Cynneth told me she'd robbed the royal apartments of so many priceless objects that a wall had to be demolished to get them all into the Abbey.

"What my daughters and I can do, however," she continued, "is to prevent you from carrying tales back to him. So your time, and his, will be wasted, and you may tell him that I know who and what you are."

My mouth dropped open for a moment. Did she know I'd been Richard's mistress?

"I know you are a low-born refugee," she continued, "with no family and no one to recommend you except that friar the Usurper so loves. His sending you here is an insult I'll not forget."

She'd been born a commoner herself, and her marriage to King Edward had been a scandal that incited a civil war, but I wasn't about to challenge her opinion of me. Her pacing gave me a chance to glance past her at her two daughters, who were watching her performance, and me, from a corner. The younger, smaller one might have been pretty, but as long as her older sister was in the room, no one would ever look at her long enough to know.

I'd not been lucky enough to see Jennifer Lawrence, or Emma Stone, or any of the celebrated beauties of my day from a distance of only ten feet, but I was certain that they could never have competed with King Edward IV's oldest daughter. Brother Cynneth told me that she was now called Bess Grey, rather than Princess Bess, as she was known before her father's death. But even if the almighty Church, and Richard, and everyone else declared her a bastard unworthy of the title, she was still the living image of a princess from a child's storybook.

"Mother, there's no point in going on so," she said, and her voice suited the rest of her. "We must do as Uncle Richard says, and make the best of it."

Her mother whirled.

"Bess! Don't refer to that demon as your Uncle! He has called you, and your brothers and sisters, all bastards, and me your Father's whore! Don't you dare give him the honor of kinship! And both of you stop staring and get on with your needlework. It's important for you not to remain idle while we endure this imprisonment."

Brother Cynneth said she was staying here of her own volition, out of stubbornness. But I wasn't so sure. Maybe she was truly afraid of Richard; I couldn't deny he was everything she said.

Three chairs out of the many that were stockpiled around the edges of the vast room had been placed in a circle around a fireplace, which took up almost half of one of the long walls. Like pictures of obedience, the girls moved out of their corner, and took up their seats and began plying their needles.

"You may do as you wish, Mistress Lyons," said Elizabeth, indicating the rest of the chamber with a sweep of her arm. Clearly I was not to have a place by the fire.

The one thing I would have liked to do was to read one of the dozens of books that were stacked on the tables, and the floor. But of course that was impossible, since my mission depended upon my supposed ignorance of the written word.

"I am here to serve you, madam. Is there anything I may do for you?" I asked, sensing that she expected only the strictest formality and respect from her servants.

She raised her perfectly arched brows.

"Yes, now that you ask, there is something. In our confinement here, we are forced to share a close stool. You may keep it emptied for us."

I could feel my face blazing.

"It is located there, behind the screen."

I had no choice but to obey her. The girls snickered; the pottery basin that sat under the close stool was full to the brim with their piss. Thank God it had raised handles, so that I didn't have to put my hand down into it. But I still couldn't lift the basin without spilling some of its pungent contents onto the floor.

"Careful! See, daughters, your 'Uncle Richard' has sent a clumsy lack-wit to wait upon us," said Elizabeth.

I struggled out the only door and into the fresh air. Elizabeth's "sanctuary" was actually part of the Abbot of Westminster's house. He'd given her (or she'd taken) the use of a large room called the Jerusalem Chamber, and a smaller gallery that connected with it. I was pretty sure there was a cesspit somewhere that served the living quarters of the Abbey, but it might be a long walk with my nasty burden. There was a small garden outside, and I looked around for witnesses before I poured the piss behind an acanthus bush.

I sat down on a stone bench and tossed the basin onto the dry grass beside me. I couldn't cry again. My eyes were dry and burning, and the tears had been replaced by a consistent dull ache in my chest that blurred my senses. In a way it was helpful; my heart was insulated from even the most piercing insults and humiliations. Still, I hadn't been so homesick since that first week, just after my encounter with James Talbott. The last time I saw Westminster Abbey, I'd worn jeans, and I'd taken photos of the Chapel with my cell phone. Now the picturesque garden full of herbs and roses, enclosed by the stately masonry walls, just depressed me. I closed my eyes and put my head in my hands. I would never see my friends from Yale, or Mom, or my old life, again.

The sliver boar had been within inches of my fingers, but I was too curious, and too enamored of its owner, to pick it up. Fool! If I hadn't looked back at Richard's head on the pillow, I might be home now.

At least I had the solution to the age-old riddle; his reaction to my remarks about the Princes was an eloquent answer to the question of who had killed them. I was lucky he'd found a way to use me; otherwise the servant who came to fetch me that next morning would probably have broken my neck. God, how I needed to hate him! And sometimes I did. But my own body betrayed me. My breasts didn't care that he was a murderer; they ached for his mouth, and the caress of his warm tongue. I'd grown used to the weight of his body on mine, and the sound of his voice in my ear. I got wet thinking of him, even when I thought of what a monster he was. But I didn't have to help him spy on his sister-in-law.

After awhile, the hard bench hurt my back. I took up the basin and went back to do my penance for my stupidity.

*T*hat night I slept on a pallet at the far end of the chamber, as far away from the fire as Elizabeth could put me. She and Bess shared a massive carved wooden bed, festooned with sumptuous velvet hangings and layered with red blankets embroidered with lions and lilies of England. Cecily had a cot beside them. The big bed had probably belonged to King Edward, and Elizabeth must have smuggled it out of the palace on the night she decided to sequester herself here. Her children were probably conceived in it, and I felt a flash of pity for her. What must it be like to fall so far?

But I woke up the next morning stiff, and sore, and anxious to get away from her. I must make a life for myself here now, in this world a where a woman's destiny was determined by how she used her body. I could breed babies, or take holy vows of chastity. Those were my choices.

The days passed slowly, as I brushed hair, tied and untied laces on their gowns, or sat with hands in my lap and waited for someone, usually Elizabeth, to give me an order. I gazed at the spectacular Flemish tapestry from which the chamber got its name, until I memorized every curve of every minaret in the city of Jerusalem. And even when I was helping the girls choose their gowns for the day (they dressed as if they were still at court), or brushing the mud from the garden off of Bess' skirts, my thoughts ran in a continuous loop around Richard. My obvious misery must have prompted Bess to give me an old piece of needlework on which to try my hand, and my attempt to mimic her fine stitches proved a welcome distraction. The pattern was yet more of the ubiquitous lions and lilies worn by the royal family of England. The ladies had by no means given up their claim to royal status.

Sometimes Bess read aloud to us, but instead of entertaining me it just reminded me of those happy nights with Richard, when he would work late at his desk, and I would read my favorite passages to him. He seemed to enjoy it, and I saved the most erotic episodes for when I could see that he was tiring of his documents and ready to come to bed. So far, no messenger had arrived with a note or letter for me to try to read, had I been so inclined, and whatever previous correspondence they'd received must have been hidden, or destroyed. There was nothing for me to do but wait, and nurse my heartache.

More than a week later, we were stitching away when a herald announced the arrival of a Dr. Morton. I kept my head down over my work, and strained my ears. While we were traveling from Dover to London, Brother Cynneth had briefed me on the players in this deadly little drama, and told me that this doctor was the suspected intermediary between Elizabeth and Margaret Stanley, the woman who was both Lord Stanley's wife and Henry Tudor's mother.

He bowed low over Elizabeth's bejeweled hand.

"Good day, my Queen. I hope you are feeling quite well after the tinctures I prescribed for you? And the Princesses? How do they fare?"

"We are all much improved, thank you," she said. "I'm so much better that I was planning to take a turn about the garden this afternoon. Would you care to join me?"

He nodded, and I jumped up to help her with her cloak.

"Thank you, Jayne," she said, and gave me her widest smile. "Dr. Morton, the Usurper had mercy on us, and sent us a waiting-woman. Who among us can say he isn't a kind man?"

The doctor sniffed, and took her arm.

"We'll be back presently, daughters," she said, over her shoulder.

I sat back down and took up my hoop.

"Are you going to tell Uncle Richard that Mother still calls herself Queen?" asked Cecily.

"No," I said. "I don't talk to the likes of kings."

"We know you're here to spy on us."

I sighed. "What is there to spy on? You sew, and read, and fight amongst yourselves. I doubt the king would be interested in the arguments of teenage girls."

I thought I'd gone too far; Elizabeth would have slapped or pinched me, but Bess laughed.

"You speak the truth, Jayne! Mother's convinced you're recording our every word to report it all back to Uncle Richard. We must find something more entertaining to say to one another. Here, do come and comb my hair."

Her laughter made me realize how much I missed Rose. She stayed at Dover Castle to marry her Tommy, and I tried to be happy for her. We'd cried when we parted, and she'd insisted we'd see each other again, but I doubted it.

I dropped my hoop and went to find the brush. I didn't like being a slave, but her golden hair fell below her waist, and was so thick and glossy that I enjoyed brushing it despite myself.

"I don't know what Uncle Richard would find interesting," said Cecily. "I'm sure he'd like any excuse to kill the rest of our family."

So they believed he'd killed the children, too! Did they know when and where the murders took place? That was the last piece of the puzzle.

"We've been over all of that a thousand times, Cecily," said Bess. "Hate him if you must, but Uncle Richard is the only one who can find husbands for us now."

"We can talk about it a thousand times more, but I'll still be surprised that you can even think of cooperating with him."

"If we don't, we'll be locked in here with Mother forever. I'm telling you, he won't hurt us. He doesn't need to."

"You mean like he 'needed' to hurt our brothers? Even if you don't care about them, remember it's his fault you're a bastard, and not a princess. It's his fault you'll never be a queen."

Bess jerked up out of her chair, and the brush went flying out of my hand. She stalked over to one of the wide mullioned windows that looked out over the Abbey lawns.

"Do you ever even think of them, Bess? Edward and Richard, I mean? Remember how delightful we all thought it, them being named for our father, and his youngest brother? The man who would kill them."

"I'll not allow you to torture me, Cecily. Jayne, help me with my cloak. I'll go join Mother and Dr. Morton in the garden."

The cloak was on a chair, where I'd left it, instead of in the wardrobe where it was supposed to be. I tucked her hair under the fur-lined hood and tied the ribbons under her chin. Her wide blue eyes were full of tears.

I ignored my "station" and patted her on the shoulder before she slammed the heavy door behind her. I understood; we both needed to hate Richard, but neither of us could bring ourselves to do it.

I sat back down and picked up my embroidery. As usual, Cecily ignored me, and I didn't care. It was freezing outside, and several inches of snow fell just yesterday. At last Elizabeth and Bess came back, with heavy flakes on their shoulders and clinging to the bottom of their skirts. I was wondering how I would get them clean and dry when Elizabeth walked over to one of the ornate desks she'd hauled out of the palace, and unlocked a small drawer in its front. I put my embroidery hoop in my lap and rubbed my eyes, and snuck a peek. She laid a small parcel in the drawer, shut it, and locked it with the key, which she replaced somewhere in her voluminous skirts.

She glanced in my direction, and I put my arms out and stretched. I wondered about her secrecy; surely she assumed I couldn't read. Then understanding dawned. She wasn't hiding it from me. She was hiding it from her daughters.

CHAPTER 17

RICHARD: DECEMBER 2, 1483

The mayor and aldermen of London, clothed in scarlet velvet, along with five hundred of London's most prominent citizens arrayed in violet, met my party at Kennington to escort me across London Bridge. How many tailors must have worked from matins until midnight since October to create their grand costumes! I knew London had no more love for me than I for it, and so they would have waited until my victory over Buckingham was assured, and Henry Tudor was sailing back to Brittany, before they threaded the first needle.

"Smile, Richard," said Jocky. "Wave! God's bones, pretend you are your brother Edward if you must, but try to look pleased with your subjects!"

Just then, a little girl who was watching the procession from a window in one of the homes whose upper stories overhung the narrow street, threw me a nosegay made out of rough white fabric twisted into the form of a rose. I caught it in my gauntlet, and she clapped her hands and squealed. I made a show of holding it next to my heart, and although I could barely hear her over the din, I saw the happiness in her face, and for a moment I was happy too.

"There you go! Now that was well done," said Jocky.

"That was easy. Her compliment was sincere," I replied.

The real roses of summer were long since blown away; this creation was tied with a length of white ribbon she must have put there herself. I held it up to my nose. It smelled of lavender, and a small child's grubby fingers.

"And I am truly pleased to have this gift. God, how London stinks. I'm sorry to require your attendance upon me here, Jocky. I know you must miss Framlingham as much as I do Middleham."

"I'm not sure I could love any place as well as you do that cold old pile of stone," he said.

"It may be cold, but the air is fresh, and I can ride over the moors for hours before I encounter another human. Unlike this place, where they're packed in on top of one another like pigeons in a poacher's sack."

He gave me a warning look, just as the mayor sidled in close, and put his horse's nose in next to Surrey's bridle.

"Will your lovely Queen be joining us at Blackfriars, Your Grace?"

I nodded. Anne would be there, waiting for us to arrive, and no doubt lovely, as he'd said. The plan was for her to greet me on the steps of the priory, with a curtsey and a kiss for her victorious husband.

"And the little prince?"

"He remains at Middleham, Lord Mayor. The doctors have said that the cold air of the North is beneficial for his lungs just now."

"My good wife and I pray each day for his continued good health," he said.

I nodded, and glanced back over my shoulder through the line of riders. Johnnie was riding somewhere behind the middle, and I missed having him close by. He'd been downcast this morning, and I didn't blame him. He knew his bastardy was only part of the reason he wasn't allowed at my side. He was well aware that his stepmother resented his boisterous good health rather than my liaison with his mother. It hurt him; at his age, knowing how she felt and understanding it were different things. I hated to see him without his customary grin, but he'd smiled far less than usual since Jayne had been gone.

I pasted a smile on my own face. The narrow street was lined with people of all sorts. The laborers in their best worsteds jostled rich merchants in bright velvets and goodwives in their finest veils.

"I could not be more pleased at the attendance of my homecoming," I said. "You have organized it well, Lord Mayor."

He beamed. "Thank you, Your Grace. We did work most diligently to make it successful," he said. "Not that we'd any worries on that account, you understand. To a man, the people of London saw your speedy victory over the traitor Buckingham as a sign from the Good Lord that your reign is to be blessed, despite..."

His face had already grown red before he got the last word out of his mouth. I glared at him, and he turned his head away to stare straight ahead, silent at last.

I looked at the crowd with new eyes. How many of them had he paid to stand there in the winter chill and wave at a murderer with a shining crown on his head? The men and women closest to my horse were bowing and cheering, but weren't those behind them queerly silent and unsmiling? Or was I just seeing accusations and disloyalty everywhere these days?

We reached Blackfriars before sundown, just as planned. Anne stood on the steps, with William Catesby beside her. I'd not realized until that moment how much I'd missed both of them.

I jumped down from my horse, raised my wife out of her curtsey and kissed her cool cheek.

"You're not looking well, Cousin," she murmured.

"So I've been told."

She glanced over my shoulder to where Francis Lovell was dismount-ing. So that hadn't changed.

"Welcome home, Your Grace," said Catesby.

He'd decorated his usual somber garb with the enameled collar he wore as my Esquire of the Body. I'd missed him; I wondered how many people could say that about their lawyer.

The prior of Blackfriars had gone to considerable trouble to make my welcome feast a fine one, but I had little appetite lately. I forced myself to eat a portion of every course to please him, and I found his wine to be as good as it was plentiful. Yet I was glad when the sweets were served and tasted, and I could gracefully leave the table. After thanking him heartily, I stood and left the hall, with Anne behind me. Francis and

Jocky followed, and I knew that after speaking with his fellow clerics, Brother Cynneth would make his way upstairs to join us.

The prior had given me his finest accommodations, and the solar that lay just outside my chamber was already warm, with a wide desk for my use not far from the fireplace.

After waiting for me to sit, Catesby pulled up a chair and unrolled a parchment he'd tucked somewhere in his robes.

"Your Grace, if I may," he began. "I received word just yesterday that a wool fleet bound for Calais was compelled to return here to London for fear of being captured by the Bretons. The merchants are most upset."

"Damn Duke Francis! Jockey, you must see to this. I can't afford to lose the support of the wool interests. And we must show the Duke that his backing of Henry Tudor will come at a cost."

"Perhaps if we put enough pressure on his fleet, the Duke will kick the pretender out of his lair in Brittany," said Jockey, eager to wage his first war as my admiral.

"See to it, my friend," I said. "And any Breton ships you capture must be outfitted with English crews, and their cargo distributed among the merchants who lost money in this debacle."

"Make it part of any treaty that Henry Tudor must be returned to English soil," said Catesby.

"If he's here, can't he plot with his mother and that blasted Stanley all the more easily?" mused Lovell.

"I think I've satisfied Stanley, at least for now. Besides making him Lord Constable, I've given him Kymbelton and made his brother Chief Justice of North Wales. And at any rate, I'd just as soon the Tudor was here, instead of raising funds on the continent. He'd find it harder here, and even Stanley can't be bold enough to back him right before my eyes."

Lovell shook his head and snorted. "Mayhap. But he's bold enough to disavow knowledge of his own wife's schemes, and we all know that's a lie."

A manservant knocked and presented Brother Cynneth.

"Come and have a cup with us, friar," said Jocky, who'd found the jug of ale.

"I believe I will do," said Brother Cynneth. "I must say the prior keeps a fine table."

"Duke Francis' fleet has been attacking our merchant ships, friar. It seems we're to have a naval war on our hands."

"And it's for certain some of the monies from the sale of the goods they steal go directly into funding the Tudor," said the friar.

"Yes!" Jockey agreed. "That's why we must force him to sue for peace. By the by, what do you hear from our little mole? Has she uncovered any of Elizabeth's plots for us yet?"

"No, but she's not been there but a week."

"She'll do right well, I suspect. You must admit I had a good thought there."

Jockey never knew when to stop. He was a fine admiral, and a loyal friend, but I often wanted to clout him. I thought I'd kept my face expressionless, but something must have registered there.

"Oh, don't tell me you're still on about that? Richard Plantagenet, I've never seen you so..."

Francis yanked his arm. Jockey looked about to strike him, until Francis jerked his head towards my wife, who sat reading by the fire, so quiet she'd been forgotten. It was unusual to allow a woman's attendance during such talks, but I trusted her absolutely, and often she shared a comment that showed her intelligence to be as keen as any man's. Her presence had never until now proved inconvenient.

Jockey sputtered a moment before he recovered. "At any rate, I'll see to the Breton fleet, by Christmas, or my name's not John Howard," he said.

"Will we keep a grand Christmas court this year?" asked Brother Cynneth. "'Tis your first as king. It must be memorable."

"I think we shall. What do you say, Anne?"

"My preparations are already well underway," she said. "There's to be a Yule log the like of which none of you've ever seen."

And with that, the conversation turned to mummers, and roasted capons, and all things Christmas. I must bring myself to enjoy it this year, for the sake of my subjects. Soon Jockey and Francis excused themselves; Anne blushed when Francis bowed, and kissed her hand. How I hoped not all love was so enduring!

The friar lingered to bid us good night. "My Lady Queen, how good it is to see your fair face," he said to Anne. They'd known each other for more than half their lives, and been friends from the first moment.

"I trust you with Richard, Cynneth," she said.

"And I do my best by him." He bowed again and took his leave.

She looked at me, for so long that at last I felt compelled to look away.

"Good night, Richard. I can see you're bothered, and by more than just Duke Francis. But I'll not beg you to tell me," she said.

"Good night, Anne. I'll survive, I promise."

She looked as if she doubted me, but went on to her room, which the prior had thoughtfully put next to mine.

I could have told him his courtesy was unnecessary. She conceived our only child dutifully, with her arms held flat against her sides, and almost died giving birth to him, so she wasn't eager for my embrace. And her poor heart lay elsewhere. What would her life have been like, if she could have wed Francis Lovell, slept in his bed, and borne his offspring? Would they have been easy births, and healthy children? But he'd been betrothed by the time they met, despite they were both children themselves. Our own marriage had been of benefit to us both; I became the owner of her father's vast landholdings in the North, and she became a duchess, the wife of the brother of the king. At the time it had seemed like enough.

My squire came in to help me undress. The slashed sleeves of my velvet doublet took some time to unlace and put away, but he bustled about, efficient and cheerful, although I knew he must have been tired as I was.

"Shall I pin this onto your hat for our ride to Westminster tomorrow?" he asked. He was holding my sigil in his palm.

Westminster. The palace, now my principal residence in London, lay side by side with the Abbey. Only a few feet of stone would separate me from Jayne. My chest ached as if I'd been knocked from my horse by an expert lance. I looked at the boar and wanted it out of my sight.

"No," I said. "Lock it in the wardrobe when we get to the palace. I won't be wearing it any longer."

CHAPTER 18

JAYNE: DECEMBER 20, 1483

"It's good to see you, Jayne," said Brother Cynneth.

He slid his grey hood back so that I could see his face. Our footsteps made rhythmic crunching noises on the snowy walkway, and I could see the gusts of our breath for just a moment before they dissipated in the cold air. The wooden pattens I wore over my boots to protect the soft leather kept slipping on the icy patches, so he gave me his solid arm to hold.

We'd met each week since I'd been living in the Abbey, and I looked forward to walking about the grounds with him. His smile reminded me of our daylong rides on the ale cart, and cozy dinners at roadside inns.

"I wish I had more to report," I said. "Elizabeth always speaks with Dr. Morton out of my earshot, of course, but she often brings back folded bits of parchment after their walks. Trouble is, she keeps them locked in a desk, and the key with her every minute. I haven't gotten a look at a single thing."

I didn't tell him I hadn't tried.

He sighed. "That could mean that she's hiding something of great import, or it could just be more of her theatrics. You don't think she is aware that you can read, do you?"

"No, I really don't think so. I think she is hiding whatever it is from the girls, not me. But she's seemed agitated lately, pacing even more than usual, and murmuring to herself. And she's eating less, although the bishop keeps an excellent cook."

We dined on venison pies and fried quail served to us in the small gallery just outside the Jerusalem Chamber, and our meals were all I had to look forward to each day. They didn't offer to let me use their mirrors, but my laces had grown tight across my chest.

"I've heard rumors that the abbot is embarrassed by her presence, not to mention inconvenienced," said the friar. "And he fears displeasing the king. We must find a way to convince her to leave."

We walked awhile in silence. Since I'd been at the Abbey, Richard had sent multiple bishops, and several members of his King's Council, to persuade Elizabeth to bring herself and her daughters out of their seclusion, all to no avail. One afternoon about a week ago, the friar himself spoke with Elizabeth, and tried to convince her that she and her girls had nothing to fear from Richard, and would be safe in his care. She usually left the Chamber to talk to the king's emissaries, but she invited the friar to come stand by the fire while she shouted at him. She called Richard a liar, and a murderer, and asked the friar to tell her what had happened to her children. It almost made me sick to listen to her accusations, after I'd held him in my arms, night after blissful night. And it made it even more difficult to betray her and her daughters.

"Even if I managed to get my hands on the key to the drawer, she rarely leaves me alone. This weather isn't exactly conducive to long walks."

It was beginning to snow again.

"I know you're doing your best, Jayne." He squeezed my hand.

"I am, please believe that. I want to get them out of there, I really do. The Queen's stubbornness is hard on the girls, Bess especially."

"Yes, I suppose so. Most girls her age are wed by now, and with a babe in their arms."

I didn't reply. I'd led a soft life compared to my new contemporaries; no one here dreamed I was twenty-six, but they did know I was past eighteen. The friar must have misread my silence to mean that I was pining for a husband myself.

"You can rest easy that the king will find an excellent match for you," he assured me. "Especially if you are able to help him in this matter."

So we were back to that again. It was more than I could bear.

"That's all I am to him now? A cast-off he needs to find a place for?"

He stopped, and faced me. "Jayne, even if he hadn't needed your help with Elizabeth, I don't know that your union, pleasant as it was, could have continued. How would he have explained your presence at court, if he were so bold as to bring you there? And kings can't sneak about London like commoners to see their lemans." He shook his head. "That's to say, they shouldn't. Edward did, but Richard desires to be nothing like him."

On our ride from Dover it had become obvious that Brother Cynneth didn't know about the argument that caused Richard and me to part. Now it sounded as if our separation had been inevitable anyway.

We were almost back to the abbot's doorstep. The friar stopped, and put his hand on my shoulder.

"God bless you. I pray for your soul, and your heart, every day."

We'd walked far beyond the confines of the abbot's courtyard. I pulled my cloak closer around me and prepared to head back to my three charges, but before I got too far away I turned around.

"How is Fergus?"

He smiled. "Oh, he hates the confinement of London, and the palace, but he makes do. And he misses you dreadfully."

I went back to the Jerusalem Chamber with the burden on my heart lightened by just that little bit.

I found Bess in tears.

"I hope your confession left you absolved of all your sins, Jayne," said Elizabeth. "Thanks to your master, my girls and I must spend our Christmas in this wretched place, while he holds a lavish Christmas court. Why God allows it, I'll never know."

Bess took my hand and pulled me away from her mother and sister. The chamber was huge, and we'd dragged some of the smaller chairs into the corner where we could sit together and chat without them hearing every word.

"What is it, Bess? What's happened?"

"Oh, I know I shouldn't have, but I asked her if we could please not spend the Yuletide cooped up in here. You see how she's going on. She's furious with me. She said I'm impatient, and selfish, and that I don't appreciate what she's trying to do for me."

What did that mean? Did whatever Elizabeth was plotting have something to do with her daughter? I'd assumed whatever she was concocting was related to some new rebellion.

Bess wiped her face with a linen handkerchief.

"Bess, don't cry, dear. You'll get out of here eventually."

"But, Jayne, did you know that before Father died, I was to be a queen? For most of my life, I was called Madame la Dauphine. I was betrothed to the Dauphin of France. I know we would have had such beautiful Christmas celebrations. Instead I'm trapped in here."

I was pretty sure I remembered that some political disagreement between her father and Louis XI of France had put an end to her engagement long before King Edward's death, but I wasn't about to point that out to the poor thing.

Our Christmas was dismal. The abbot gave us a Yule log for our fireplace, and decorated the mantle above it with fresh greenery. He served us roasted capon, with a murrey sauce, that was made with a dark red berry, which complemented the taste of the bird perfectly.

But most of the meal was taken away untouched, even by me. We sewed, and Elizabeth paced, and I brushed the hems of trains and surcoats until not a speck of dust adhered to the velvet. The abbot said a special mass for us, and although I tried to take comfort in the beauty of the ceremony, I found nothing in his Latin phrases to cheer me.

Five days after Christmas, Dr. Morton knocked on the door of the chamber, and as soon as I saw him, I knew something was up. His long narrow faced was as flushed as if he'd run through the halls of Westminster, black robes flapping, and lurched to a stop just outside the door of the Jerusalem Chamber.

Elizabeth took one look at him and shut the door behind her without stopping to put on her cloak, so they wouldn't be venturing far. How I would love to put my ear to the door, instead of sitting quietly by the fire and repairing a tear in Cecily's favorite veil.

After what felt like an age, the former Queen swept back into the room, glowing with triumph. The dour expression she'd worn since I met her had been replaced by a smile that lit up her chiseled face, and her stiff, angry demeanor had changed to the relaxed grace of a conqueror. She seemed taller and grander that I'd ever seen her, and she had a large rolled parchment in her hand.

"Jayne, fetch your cloak, and leave us. Girls, I've joyful tidings to share with you."

I was not allowed to use the carved oak wardrobe where they hung their clothing; my things were folded in small trunk in a corner of the room. I went to it, heart pounding, and pulled out my cloak. I could barely fasten the ties.

She slammed the huge door behind me. It was no use trying to eavesdrop, and I'd been cooped up inside all day, so I went out into the frozen garden, and wandered among the snow-covered rosebushes. What on Earth could have made her so ebullient? She'd looked at me with glittering eyes full of victory. Victory over Richard.

If I gave him a piece of critical information that he wouldn't otherwise have had, would he still die in battle at Bosworth Field, some eighteen months from now? Or would I, by exposing Elizabeth's schemes with Lord Stanley and Henry Tudor, manage to save his life?

I stopped on the path. Could history be changed? I would never have believed it, but I would never have believed this whole experience, until I lived it. My presence here must have some meaning, and some effect on the outcome of the lives I touched.

Elizabeth had rushed me out so fast that I'd left my mittens behind; I rubbed my hands together, and realized they were shaking. If I did nothing, I was sure he would die at Bosworth in little more than a year, outnumbered and fighting for his life against Henry Tudor's Welsh pikemen.

I headed for one of the stone benches, and sat there, frozen, like one of the statutes of the saints that flanked the walkway. My breath came out in rapid gusts that quickly dissipated in the freezing air. He was a ruthless usurper who'd murdered a pair of innocent children. Wasn't his death on that bloody plain just what he deserved?

I was so cold my face had grown numb. I went back into the gallery and knocked on the door to the Chamber.

"You may enter," said Elizabeth.

They were all three giddy, but Bess was holding her skirts out and pretending to dance with an imaginary partner.

"Oh Jayne, Jayne! I'm so happy!" she said.

"Not a word, Elizabeth!" snapped her mother.

"Oh, at least do let me give her a hug!"

Her mother nodded, and she had her arms around me before I could even remove my cloak.

"Oh you're so cold. You'll be ill. Come and sit by the fire."

Usually this kindness would have drawn a hiss from Elizabeth, but she was serenely regarding herself in one of her mirrors.

"My daughters and I are going into the nave to give thanks for recent blessings," she said. "You may remain here by the hearth."

My mouth dropped. She had never ventured so far from the sanctuary she'd established for herself. And her tone towards me was, for once, magnanimous. I took off my cloak and stretched out my cold, red hands towards the flames.

Bess kissed me on the cheek before they swept out of the chamber, heads high, skirts trailing.

Could the lock on the drawer be picked? I had pins in my hair and veil, and if none of them worked, the girls had dozens I could try. I put my hand to my head and yanked out the first pin I touched.

The top of the desk was painted a dark, brilliant green, and accented along its edges with carvings of a hunting scene. The hunters were on horseback, chasing a stag using bows and arrows. A white parchment, still curled at the ends from being rolled and placed in a dispatch case, lay right in the middle, between hunters and prey. She never dreamed I could read it, so she just left it behind.

Although my reading of the ornate Gothic script was still painstaking, the most important passage didn't take long to decipher.

"Henry Tudor, heir of the House of Lancaster and the throne of England, has this day pledged himself in marriage to Elizabeth Plantagenet, true heir of King Edward IV and the House of York."

It was dated December 25, year of our Lord fourteen hundred and eighty-three, and signed by Lord Thomas Stanley.

I sat down on one of the priceless chairs Elizabeth kept for her own use. If Stanley's plan came to fruition, Lancaster and York, the two royal

Houses who'd been fighting over the throne for decades, would finally be united. They shared a common ancestor, John of Gaunt, and had kept the country in civil war for the last fifty years while they argued over which of his sons' descendants should rule England. A marriage uniting the both sides of the family, and ending the argument at last, was a move worthy of the best political strategist in Washington. Tudor, as scion of the House of Lancaster, would automatically have the support of that branch of the family; now those Yorkists who were still loyal to Edward's children, and considered Richard a usurper, would fall in behind them. Richard's reign, and his life, would be doomed.

Henry Tudor would take Richard's crown off of his battered head at Bosworth and make Bess the first Tudor Queen. Unless I stopped him.

CHAPTER 19

RICHARD: MARCH 4, 1484

"May I compliment Your Grace on the swift manner in which you brought the Bretons to heel? I was pleased to hear about your treaty with Duke Francis, and that our ships may once again traverse the Channel freely."

"Thank you, Lord Stanley. The Duke of Norfolk has made a fine admiral."

"Your Grace was wise in choosing him," he said, nodding.

Mayhap the only person he hated more than me was Jockey Howard, and Duke Francis had loaned his stepson the ship he sailed on during his aborted attempt to invade my country, so nothing about Jockey's success could have pleased him. But his smile was calm and bland, and as natural as if we'd been discussing the recent Christmas festivities. It was a grand performance, and I admit I almost envied his skill as a liar.

He crossed his arms, then uncrossed them, and stroked his pointed beard, as if considering some deep question. God, how I wanted this interview to end! I would have loved to send him back to his northern stronghold, but I knew I should keep him, of all my enemies, as close as possible.

"There is one difficulty which continues to concern me, as well as your other noble subjects." He made a concerned face.

Ah, here it came, some thrust of the dagger he couldn't quite bring himself to forego.

"What is that, Lord Stanley?"

"The question of your nephews' whereabouts remains unanswered, Your Grace, and those who love you, and wish to support you, find themselves in the unenviable position of having to defend their allegiance without being able to satisfy their detractors with a proper reply. Why, only yesterday, Northumberland came to me, visibly shaken, because his captains charged him with following the leadership of a man with innocent blood on his hands."

I realized I was twisting my ring up and down on the small finger of my left hand, as I was wont to do when I was nervous. It was a weak and revealing habit. I stopped, and placed both hands down on the desk, but I couldn't force my heart to slow its beating.

Did this arrogant fool think to trap me into an answer I would forever regret?

"It pains me to hear that a man like Harry Percy, to whom I've given every favor, cannot summon the courage to defend his king," I said.

He stared at me expectantly and I forced myself to meet his gaze. The silence hung between us until he cleared his throat and began again.

"But, Your Grace—"

Before he could finish, I heard three rapid knocks on the door to my chamber and Johnnie bowed his way into the room.

"Your Grace, Brother Cynneth waits in the gallery. He says he must speak with you at once," he announced. He glanced up at Lord Stanley and gave me a worried look. The child could sense the tension between us, but had no inkling that his existence was its original cause.

"Fetch him in," I said. " Lord Stanley, I believe our business is concluded."

Stanley gave my son an appraising look before bowing low, as he always did. His eyes met mine just before he turned to leave the room, and there it was again, the raw hatred. He would never forgive me.

Brother Cynneth rushed into the room, his round face pale, and gleaming with sweat.

"Brother, you frighten me!"

"I've just come from Jayne."

"Is she ill?" I was halfway around my desk before he could answer.

"No, no, she's not ill. She's done what we asked of her, but her news is dire. The Tudor is begging Louis of France and every other royal on the continent for funds and provisions so that he may invade England this summer..."

I shook my head. This was hardly news.

"And Richard, he has pledged to marry your niece, Bess, and make her his queen."

I gaped at him like a half-wit.

"Johnnie, go send for Norfolk, and Lovell. Now!"

He ran from the room without a backward glance.

"God's blood, but this has Stanley's mark upon it. Henry Tudor hasn't the head to frame such a plan," I said.

"You're right. The letter Jayne saw proclaiming the engagement was written to Elizabeth by Lord Stanley."

So Jocky's scheme had worked. Jayne had found out a vital piece of intelligence. But I was no closer to breaking my sister-in-law's determination to remain locked away in the Abbey.

"Can Elizabeth think she can stay in the Jerusalem Chamber until Henry Tudor has mustered an army, sailed from Brittany, and taken England from me?"

"Jayne says she is near-delirious with victory."

Jocky strode into the room without waiting to be announced.

"What's happened, Your Grace? Johnnie had to stop to catch his breath before he could tell me I was needed."

My head ached. I pressed my fingers into my burning eyeballs before I answered him.

"We must congratulate Stanley on his cunning this time. He has had that milksop Tudor pledge himself to Bess."

"Bones of the Saints! How do you know?"

"Jayne," I said.

Pride flickered across his face but he didn't remind me he'd been right, and that Jayne had proved more valuable to me in the Abbey than she was in my bed.

"The union of Lancaster and York, at last," he said instead.

We stared at each other. The two houses had been locked in a struggle for the crown since before either of us was born. We'd grown up in it, lost brothers and fathers to it, and believed it to be over and the House of York at last victorious when my brother Edward took the throne after the Battle of Towton. Now it seemed the bloodshed, and the grief, would begin again. With my reign still in its first year, and with rumors abroad like the one Stanley had just used to taunt me, the threat was a very real one.

"I fear even my staunchest supporters would find the marriage a fitting excuse to avoid another civil war," I mused.

"I don't agree. It's a brilliant idea, I grant you," said Jockey, "but you've a dozen battles to your credit, and he's never bloodied his sword. He can't win against you in the field; the nobles from both houses know that. They won't risk their fortunes, or their lives, for such sentimental tripe."

"No, they won't do it for romantic reasons, but because they're tired of war, tired of losing men in combat who could be working on their manors and making them wealthy."

"They'll support whoever will best feather their nests," said Jockey. "And the same goes for Elizabeth. The success or failure of Stanley's scheme lies in her hands."

"I can't make her daughter a queen."

"No, but you can find her a high-born husband, and now, not after some invasion and coup that will likely never take place. You must convince her that she is better off casting her lot with you than with Stanley, and Tudor."

Brother Cynneth had been uncharacteristically silent during Jockey's rant.

"Friar? What say you?"

He shook his head. "You can't afford to alienate any of your more powerful nobles by forcing them to marry a maid that's been declared a bastard. And the promise of some lesser suitor may not suffice."

He paused, and looked away. "And too, Jayne says Elizabeth's professed fear that you may harm her daughters is not merely for effect..."

His words stung, but only because I knew they were true. I'd called her playacting, but I'd lied to myself, and to all who heard me. And could

I blame her? She was conniving, cruel, and ambitious, but she loved her children. Why wouldn't she fear for those that were still in her care? I knew last summer when I made my decision that I was breaking her heart.

"There's naught to be done about that," said Jockey. "What's done is done. Set about finding husbands for the two maids, Your Grace, as soon as you can. And they'll soon remember the old adage about a pheasant in the pot and not wait for Stanley to flush Tudor for them."

By the time Lovell arrived it was time to go in to supper. How I wished I could remain in my chambers! But I had noble guests, including the Lord Mayor of London and his simpering wife. I did my best not to let them see my distraction; a worried king was a weak one. But the effort strained me, and I excused myself as quickly as I could, pleading pressing business that I must tend to, much as I would prefer to remain and enjoy such good company.

Norfolk and Lovell made to follow me up the staircase.

"Friends, I am beyond even your good counsel," I said.

Lovell looked about to protest, but I put up my hand.

"I know your love for me, and I cherish it. But I must have solitude in order to think. And to pray."

"So shall we tell the friar to remain below as well?"

I knew Cynneth would understand. "Yes, tell him I will see him early on the morrow."

When I reached my chambers I dismissed the manservant and went to stand by the fire. For the first time since the friar gave me his news, I let myself think of Jayne. How she must hate me, now. Her trust in me had been shaken by the idle talk of some country groom; Elizabeth and her daughters would have confirmed the suspicions about me that she already harbored. If any spark of love for me remained in her heart, my sister-in-law's lurid tale of treason and murder would surely have doused it forever.

I crossed my arms on the wooden mantelpiece and rested my head upon my hands. It was weak of me to let the opinion of a woman mean more to me than that of my nobles, but in truth, I could have faced the accusations of every Englishman alive if I'd had her unquestioning trust.

But I must soldier on without it, and without her. I must add her lovely face to the long list of others I would never see again, like my brother's son, the boy who would have been king if Bishop Stillington could have kept his silence but a little while longer.

All at once, I knew what I must do. I drew in a deep breath, and a grim and awful burden that had beset my soul lo these many months lifted. I called for the servant who waited just outside the door.

CHAPTER 20

JAYNE: MARCH 4, 1484

our days passed between my discovery of the marriage plot and my next meeting with Brother Cynneth. When I told him what Elizabeth and Stanley were planning, he whirled around and headed for the palace without even saying goodbye. But he'd not gone far before he trotted back to me, and took my hand.

"Thank you, dear Jayne!" he said. "You've done better than any of us could have hoped. He'll be grateful."

Our eyes met for a moment before he turned away again, and shouldered his way through the crowded Westminster streets, for once not stopping to speak to the beggars and alms-seekers that impeded his way.

In the meantime, the atmosphere in the Chamber changed from one of high dudgeon to barely restrained glee. Until now, Elizabeth and her girls had only picked at the excellent meals the abbot provided. Now they ate the fine white bread and savory pigeon pies with gusto, and made sly references to Bess needing to fill out the bosom of her gowns again.

My own secret had the opposite effect on me. I couldn't eat more than a bite of anything. I was distracted from meals, and every other activity, by the thought that what I had done might somehow save

Richard's life. I had made a promise to help him, and I'd kept it. But at what cost?

I could tell Bess was dying to share her clandestine engagement with me. Since she didn't dare anger her mother, she satisfied her desire to include me by putting her arm around my shoulder or patting me on the hand, and even taking the brush from me when I was combing her hair and helping me with my own unruly locks. One day, in a fit of joy, she took both my hands and whirled us around the room, and when my skirts knocked over a chair, I expected Elizabeth to deliver pinch or a slap to us both, but all we got was an indulgent *tisk* and a warning.

One evening, Bess brought out a lute that must have been tucked away in some trunk or other, and the three of them sang ballads in a delightful three-part harmony that would have shamed most professional folk musicians. After a comical tune about a miller, that had us all giggling, Elizabeth insisted we all go to bed.

"Jayne, you may bring your cot in close to the fire, if you wish," she said.

I tried not to look stunned and ran to move my rickety wooden bed. I slipped out of my chemise and between the sheets before she could change her mind. The medievals slept naked, and although the practice made me uncomfortable at first, now I was accustomed to it, and enjoyed the freedom of my nude body against the soft linen.

Bess and her mother whispered together in their big bed, their words too low for me to decipher their meaning, but the contentment of their tone was soft on my ears. I felt less like a spy now that I'd accomplished my mission, and my fear for them surprised me. I was bound by my promise, and my love, to help Richard, but I was destroying their happiness in the process. Had I put their safety in jeopardy as well?

I pushed my rough blanket down away from my face and neck. I wasn't used to being so close to the fire, and usually huddled under every layer of wool I could find. Tonight I was warm, and watched the flames instead of just the shadows they made. Perhaps it would all come right. The friar said that Richard would probably reward me with some independent wealth of my own, maybe even a small manor house with some land around it, which would keep me from needing to marry until I found someone with whom I actually wanted to spend the rest of my life.

But it wouldn't be Richard.

I let the tears come unrestrained, as I often did when I was sure they were asleep. I'd learned to weep in almost complete silence, so now the water ran down my face but the only sounds were the occasional crack of a used-up log falling from the grate into the ashes, and the gentle puff of Cecily's snores.

I burrowed down deeper into the bedclothes and had just closed my eyes when I heard three firm knocks on the stout oak door of the Jerusalem Chamber. I heard Elizabeth gasp, and I sat up, with the blanket around my shoulders.

"Oh, God, he's sent soldiers for us!" she said. The three of them jumped out of bed and scrambled to dress themselves unassisted while I threw my chemise over my head.

Three more knocks sounded, not loud, but insistent.

"Let's ask who it is, since we've nowhere to run," said Bess. Her ability to keep cool and reasonable never failed to astound me.

"Who's there?" said Elizabeth. "Why do you disturb us in the middle of the night?"

There was a brief silence, before I heard his voice. "It's Richard. I'm alone. I'll not harm you. Please open the door."

My mouth fell open and I put both hands to my face.

"Jayne, go and tell him we'll not see him, now or any other time!"

I threw my robe over my chemise and snatched the nearest candle. She'd had the abbot install three locks on the door, and now I fumbled with them, clumsy-fingered.

"Don't let him in this room!" she said, from behind me.

When I pulled the door open he was standing less than three feet away. A manservant stood behind him with a torch, and in its light I could see that his dark, handsome face was thinner than it had been on that miserable day when I'd seen him last, and his soldier's tan had faded. The creases beside his mouth were deeper, and the angle of his left shoulder was a tiny bit higher than I remembered it, but still the difference in the two sides of his body would only be noticeable to one who knew to look for it. Everything about him was as familiar to me as my own heart, and the sadness in his grey eyes made me want to touch him so badly that I gripped the candle in one hand and the edge of the door with the other to keep from giving in to my desire.

He'd thrown his cloak back over his shoulders, and I could see his chest rising and falling with every breath.

"Jayne," he said.

I felt a tear escape from the corner of my eye. He reached out his hand towards my cheek just as Elizabeth stepped up behind me.

"I'll not allow you to enter this room."

He stepped back, but he held my gaze for a long moment before he looked past me to his sister-in-law.

"Please come out, and we can talk here in the gallery. I'll wait for you to dress. Please, Elizabeth! For the sake of Edward, whom we both loved, at least hear me out."

I could feel her behind me, staring at him. I leaned against the door, and stared at him too.

"Jayne, help me dress. Quickly!" she said, and pulled me away by my arm. I took one last look over my shoulder before she slammed the door.

"Why are you going to talk to him?" asked Cecily. "You hate him!"

"Because he's the king, and he can have us brought out of sanctuary by force if she doesn't," replied Bess.

"He would never dare," said Elizabeth, but she was trembling so that I could barely do up the laces of her sleeves. When it took me three tries to fasten the girdle at her waist, she slapped me.

"Mother, really!" said Bess. "She's still half-asleep, she can't help being slow."

Elizabeth slipped out the door, and pulled it closed gently behind her as if someone in the room was still sleeping. I sat down on my cot, and gazed into the fire, just as I'd been doing when I heard his knock on the door. But now everything had changed.

The wound in my chest that had been gushing blood for months had finally been staunched, and the relief was so intense that I was breathless.

"Jayne, is something the matter?" asked Bess.

"I'm fine. Just startled, that's all."

"Is he angry with you?" asked Cecily. "He sent you here to spy on us, and we haven't let you hear anything you could report back to him, so he can't be too pleased. I bet he'll take you away with him tonight, and put you in the Tower."

Bess gasped. "She's not right, is she? He won't take you away from us, will he?"

I shook my head. How I wished he would take me away from here, to some place where I could use every breath in my body to ease the worry I'd seen written on his face! He wasn't angry with me, not any longer. The love, and forgiveness, in his expression had been wrought as clearly as the pain.

If only they would leave me alone, so that I could replay that moment in my mind before I lost a single detail. I might have to live on the memory for the rest of my life.

But Bess was much too excited too let me sit without talking.

"Jayne, what do you think he wants? Why would he come here alone, in the middle of the night?"

"I don't know, Bess. Maybe he's given up on anyone else being able to budge her," I said.

But I knew I'd brought him here myself with my last message, as surely as if I'd conjured him out of the air. The engagement between Bess and Henry Tudor must be as threatening to Richard's reign as I thought. But why did he think he could convince Elizabeth to come out when all of his ambassadors could not?

We waited. The candles we'd lit so hurriedly when the knock sounded still burned in their holders, but the scattered chairs and rolled-up tapestries and other objects cast hulking shadows that looked like an army of merciless soldiers. The girls were frightened for their mother, but Richard wouldn't harm a woman. When we were together, he'd been protective of me, gallant even. But in the flickering gloom, I felt my pulse quicken. Maybe Elizabeth was in danger. Maybe last summer, he'd paid a late-night visit to the Princes, awakened them from their bed in the Tower...

When the door creaked open we all jumped. She shut it behind her, and stood with her back against the oak panels, breathing as if she'd run a marathon. Richard must still be just on the other side, I wanted to push past her and run to him, but I stayed where I was by the fire, and watched her walk slowly to the big bed and sit down. She stared in front of her, with eyes glazed over like those of a person under the influence of some strong narcotic.

Bess and Cecily ran to her side.

"Mother, what did he say? Why are you so upset? Did he threaten us?"

She shook her head, and put a trembling hand to her forehead. "I must think. I must think. Leave me be."

They looked at each other, and then at me, as if I could possibly know what had happened in the gallery.

"But Mother," Bess started. Elizabeth waved her away.

"Douse the candles, and get back in bed."

Her voice had none of its usual brisk authority, but we obeyed her, out of habit, and fear. Over the next few days, her demeanor barely changed. The routine we'd settled into, there in our gilded prison, while hardly exciting, had been pleasant in its way, and the girls and I tried to continue it. We brushed each other's hair, and embroidered, and Bess even tried to give me another dancing lesson. But Elizabeth barely spoke, and pushed me away when I tried to help her smooth her disheveled braid.

More than once, I thought I saw tears glittering in her eyes, but she never cried. She sat, fist against her lips, and gazed at nothing, until finally Bess went to her, and dropped down on her knees in front of her chair.

"Mother, won't you please tell me, so I can help you," I heard, and then their voices dropped to a murmur.

I was dying to hear what Elizabeth would say, but their mother-daughter posture made me feel like the outsider that I was, so I walked over to the window to give them their privacy. Cecily came and stood beside me.

"What can it be, Jayne? She doesn't seem frightened, but she's not changed her gown in three days, and she's not been angry with us even once. Not even with you." Her voice cracked, and I put my arm around her shoulders.

To my surprise, she leaned her head on my shoulder and wrapped her arm around my waist. We were standing together, under a truce at last, when we heard a light knock on the door. I moved to answer it, but Elizabeth jumped up from her chair before I could get there, sending poor Bess, who'd still been kneeling beside her, back onto her ass on the carpet.

When she got to the door, she opened only a quarter of the way, but through the sliver, I saw a servant in a plain woolen cloak hand her a leather pouch. After she took it from him and shut the door, she held the parcel to her chest with her eyes squeezed shut and her lips moving silently as if in prayer. She ran to the window, and tore at the strings of the pouch, and pulled out a folded square of parchment.

The three of us looked at each other but didn't dare speak. Elizabeth was sobbing now, and I could hear the rasp of every breath.

"Leave me, all three of you!" she ordered us between sobs.

"But Mother," said Bess. She looked confused, and worried, and even I hated to go out with Elizabeth in such a state.

"Jayne, fetch their cloaks. Now!"

I helped them tie their laces and then did up my own, before the three of us left her still standing by the window.

"Oh, Jayne, do you think Henry Tudor has changed his mind about our marriage?" asked Bess, as we wandered aimlessly through the abbot's garden.

It was early March, and the sun shone but the air still held winter's chill. Her selfishness surprised me, but I remembered she'd been engaged once before to a prince she'd never met, and been discarded by him. Perhaps her mother's reaction had been much the same, that other time.

"I'm sure he hasn't changed his mind, Bess. It's something else."

We wandered amongst the hedges for almost an hour, and when we returned to the Jerusalem Chamber, Elizabeth was quiet and serene again. There was no sign of the parchment, but the next morning, a messenger in full royal livery brought a second document, this one tied with gilt cord and proudly emblazoned with the king's seal.

The three of us, along with the messenger, watched her read to the bottom of the page, not once, but three times, before she turned to him and nodded.

"This will do," she said. "Have your master send his stoutest servants to assist us in removing our belongings."

He bowed and headed for the door, with its wide oak panels and triple locks. As soon as he shut it behind him, she turned to the three of us with a triumphant smile.

"My daughters, I am sending you to your Uncle's court."

CHAPTER 21

JAYNE: MARCH 17, 1484

I'd seen the Great Hall at Westminster Palace once before, during the several days I spent in London before heading to Leicester. The tour guide said the Great Hall was the only part of the medieval structure to survive into the twenty-first century, and I, along with the fourteen other tourists, had marveled at the vast timbered roof and the pale stone statues of the early kings that lined the second story walls. The guide's voice had echoed against the long, empty expanse of marble floor, and I had shivered in my fleece jacket. Today the stone statutes were still painted their original reds and greens, the immense room was brimming with people, and I was perspiring in my heavy silk skirts.

The yards of fabric worn by the women in the room, and the dozens of colorful banners lining the walls, didn't muffle the fanfare blown by ten trumpeters as they sent their martial notes up into the great timbered ceiling.

I couldn't see over the tall hennin of the woman in front of me until she knelt before the passage of the king and queen. I waited a beat before I bent my knees, and put a hand to my own headdress before sneaking a look at Richard. I only caught a glimpse of his chiseled profile under the golden crown, but it was the closest I'd come to him since that night he'd paid his midnight visit to Elizabeth in the Abbey.

The crowd rose to its feet as he took his seat on the throne at the top of the marble dais at the end of the room. He handed the queen into a smaller chair beside him. The woman next to me gave me a hard look as I forced my way to a better view, but I didn't care. I had to see him. And her.

The herald announced John Howard, Lord Norfolk, and the man I knew as Jockey came forward. I caught his eye as he passed, and he raised his brows in acknowledgment. I wondered if he remembered our days on the road together with Richard as fondly as I did. He knelt before the throne.

"You may rise, Lord Norfolk," said Richard. "My admiral, you have pleased me well. Your swift success against the menace posed to our merchant ships by the Breton navy showed me, and England, your courage, and loyalty. For this your service, I grant you the manors of Preston, Cokefield, Aldham, and Mendham."

How I'd missed the sound of his voice!

Jockey bowed his head again, and murmured something I couldn't quite catch. A page brought out a gilded casket and handed it to Richard, who opened it and removed an enameled collar. He stood up to place the gift around Jockey's shoulders himself, and I had a decent view of him at last.

I'd never seen him in court clothes. Even when he'd dined in state at Dover Castle, he'd looked more like a general than a king. Today he was every inch the monarch, from the jewel-encrusted crown on his head to the long pointed slippers on his feet. His velvet robes were such a rich, dark red that they would have appeared black, except that the doublet he wore beneath them was of true jet, and a perfect contrast for the wide gold collar he wore around his shoulders. He was magnificent, but his expression was fixed, and formal, and I missed his smile.

I took a deep breath and looked at Queen Anne. I immediately wished I hadn't. I'd felt beautiful just a moment before; my green silk gown was a gift from Bess, and it was trimmed with marten fur, the richest adornment a commoner was allowed to wear. It had taken me several days to learn to manage the tall black steeple hennin and its floating gossamer veil, but despite the occasional wobble, I felt comfortable in it now.

But the woman beside Richard looked like a queen from one of the Flemish tapestries that adorned the stone walls of Westminster Palace. She was tiny, probably not much more than five feet tall, with the waist of a twelve-year-old. She wore a gold crown that was a diminutive version of Richard's, and beneath it her small face was exquisite. She looked at Jockey Howard with a kind smile.

I reminded myself that medieval marriages were more business transactions than love affairs, especially among the nobility, who had so much to gain or lose by them, but still, she had a claim on Richard that I could never achieve. And in her own fragile way, she was very attractive. No wonder he'd found me so easy to give up. He had her bed to go back to.

Standing among Richard's courtiers, I felt a fool in my pointed headdress. When Elizabeth made her startling announcement that she was sending her girls to their uncle's court, a tiny spark of hope had sprung up in my heart. I did my best to ignore it, and to prepare to be sent away from him, to the bed of some archer or pikeman. I gave myself pep talks. I told myself I could survive in this world, ruthless as it seemed. But images of lying in his arms again filled my dreams at night, and when I awoke I knew my attempts to be practical were useless. Seeing him now, no longer a soldier on his march home, but a king in his court, he seemed almost as distant from me as he'd been when I was locked away in the Jerusalem Chamber.

"Lord Thomas Stanley," announced the herald.

I recognized the tall, bearded man who'd allowed his henchman to try to kidnap me that night on the Salisbury road. He walked in as if Westminster belonged to him, and bent his knee to Richard with a theatrical flourish that smacked of sarcasm. But however proud he might be, I'd stopped his grandest scheme. Bess was to be officially presented to Richard's court tonight, and her engagement to Henry Tudor was ended. Tudor's chances of uniting the nobles against Richard were slim without Bess at his side, and Louis of France and Francis of Brittany would now be reluctant to help him fund an invasion that had always been a doubtful endeavor. The thought lightened my spirits and I stood up taller. Who, but me, in this crowd of toadies could say they'd changed history?

I watched Richard bestowing some favor or other on Stanley, and smiled. If only I could have seen his face when he found out the Greys were leaving sanctuary and coming to Richard's court so that he could find husbands for them! I was enjoying imagining his shocked expression when the herald announced the Ladies Elizabeth and Cecily Grey.

Bess and her sister wore simple velvet gowns that befitted their youth and status as the king's wards. But the courtiers hadn't seen Bess since her father's death, and there was a collective intake of breath as she approached Richard's throne. She was by far the most beautiful woman in the room, and she smiled at the crowd like a movie star on the red carpet. No one but Cecily and me knew she was confused and hurt by her mother's about-face and the ending of yet another royal engagement.

"I can't understand you, Mother!" she'd cried. "What can Uncle Richard possibly have promised you? Henry Tudor has pledged to make me his queen!"

Elizabeth just shook her head, more like a queen herself than I'd ever seen her. The pinched, victimized look she'd worn since I met her was gone. She looked, not happy, but at peace.

"Henry Tudor is in exile in Brittany," she said. "Before he can be king, he must raise an army to invade England, and defeat your Uncle, a veteran general, on the battlefield. And while we are waiting on a miracle that will surely never happen, you and your sister are growing older and less marriageable by the day. Your Uncle has promised to find noble husbands for you, and to provide you with generous dowries."

"When did you start listening to him? We've spent months in this chamber, ignoring his offers because you said he couldn't be trusted."

"He made me this promise before his Parliament, and has put it in writing," said Elizabeth.

That was the document she'd received, the one brought by a royal messenger, and bearing the king's seal. The document that changed everything. I considered trying to get a look at it, but they were convinced I couldn't read, and it would astonish them to find out otherwise at this point. And I needed them. I had no idea what the future held for me.

We'd been out of the abbot's house and sleeping in a small bedchamber in a corner of the palace for two days, waiting on Richard to formally acknowledge Bess and Cecily. Nothing had been said about my fate.

"Welcome to my lady wards, Elizabeth and Cecily Grey," said Richard. "You are now under my own protection, and care, and if you need for anything, you have but to ask it of me."

Bess rose from her deep curtsey, and the queen stood up and reached her hand out in welcome. Even though Anne remained on one of the dais steps, Bess still towered over her, and overshadowed her dainty, pale prettiness with her golden beauty. But Anne didn't seem to mind. She gave her the same sincere smile she'd bestowed on Jockey Howard.

Bess kissed her hand, and backed away from the royal presence. As soon as the next courtier came forward to claim Richard's attention, she made her way through the crowd to my side.

"Well, that's over," she murmured in my ear. "What did you think of Anne?"

"I thought she looked very kind, and not at all like a queen," I said. Not at all like your proud mother, was what I meant, but Bess heard a different meaning.

"She's always been quite pleasant to me, but I agree she's not fair enough to be a queen. And she's only given Uncle Richard the one sickly child. He can't be too happy with her."

My jealous heart leapt at her words. Could she be right? He'd spoken so fondly of the little Prince of Wales that I found it hard to imagine he resented the child's mother. But Ned was eleven or so, an only child in an era when the families often numbered in the double digits. And Richard needed heirs.

"Jayne? Are you listening?"

"I'm sorry, Bess. This crowd is distracting."

"I said I'm going to see my Uncle as soon as he's through granting rewards and favors, and I want you to come with me."

I wanted to see him, closer than fifty feet away, and surrounded by a hundred people. But I was afraid. The love and forgiveness that I'd been so sure I saw in his eyes as he stood at the door of the Jerusalem Chamber might have been my imagination. The memory of that night, and the night he dismissed me from his life, fought one another for validity in my mind. Which face would he show me now?

"I'm not sure that's a good idea," I said.

But it was too late. Richard and his queen stood and the nobles bowed again as they left the Great Hall, and as soon as they had passed Bess grabbed my hand and pulled me after them.

"Bess! Stop this!" I hissed, but she was used to getting her way

"He'll go into his solar now, and she'll go into hers. I have a favor to ask, and he just said he'd give me anything I need. I know what to do. I'm the daughter of a king, remember."

She dragged me up a curving stone staircase behind a group of noblemen who were stepping cautiously so they wouldn't trip on their long pointed slippers. Bess rolled her eyes. When we reached the landing, they stared at us with incredulous expressions on their faces, whether at our cheek, or her beauty, I couldn't tell.

Richard had already passed through a tall arched doorway, and Johnnie stood outside, wearing his father's white boar livery.

"Good afternoon, Lady Bess," he said. "How good to see you!"

She didn't return his smile, and I wondered if she was remembering that the last time she'd seen him, she was a princess. Now they were both bastards.

He glanced at me, and turned towards the door, and I thought he meant to ignore me. He turned back and looked up into my face.

"Jayne! It's you!"

He ran to me and hugged me so hard I had to pull his arms from around my waist.

"I'm glad to see you too," I said.

"Seems you two are well-acquainted." Bess frowned.

"Jayne was Brother Cynneth's ward," explained Johnnie. "He brought her back with us from the rebellion."

"I must see the king. Announce me, please."

He looked past her at the waiting noblemen, some of whom had documents in their hands.

"You may as well announce me, Johnnie. I'll see him anyway," she said.

I'd never heard her sound so much like her mother.

Johnnie did as he was told, and in a moment I heard Richard's voice, telling us to come in.

He'd taken off his crown, and robes, and was sitting behind his desk in his black velvet doublet. I stayed a step behind his niece.

"Bess!" he said, half rising from his chair. "How delightful it is to see you again so soon!"

But he looked confused, and not especially pleased. Then he saw me, where I was half-hiding behind her.

He clamped his mouth shut, and stared at me. After a moment he nodded.

"Mistress Lyons, I hope you are well."

Bess didn't give me time to answer.

"Uncle, I'd like Jayne to stay here with me, as my lady-in-waiting," she announced.

I gasped. Oh, God, please let him say yes!

He didn't answer her for so long that I thought he was going to refuse. When he spoke, it was to me.

"Mistress Lyons, what say you? Do you wish to remain here at court? I can find any number of ladies who will wait upon my niece."

"I want to stay," I said. "With Bess."

He looked away. "Bess, my steward has prepared a comfortable chamber for you and Cecily, and Jayne may have the smaller one adjoining."

Bess curtsied, and pulled me down beside her.

"Thank you, Uncle," she said, and rewarded him with her most brilliant smile.

"You are most welcome," he replied, and looked down at the papers on his desk. The interview was over.

Johnnie, and the irritated noblemen, were still waiting outside. Bess smiled at them, too, and they forgot their impatience and smiled back.

When I saw our accommodations, my heart felt lighter than it had in months. My little room had a door that connected with Bess' much larger chamber, but I had my own entrance as well. I could come and go as I pleased, and if he sent for me, she would never know. I thought surely that was the reason he'd chosen those particular rooms for us, and that night I barely closed my eyes, listening for a servant's soft knock. It was three weeks before I gave up and slept through the night.

CHAPTER 22

RICHARD: APRIL 15, 1484

*M*y men and I ducked under limbs and branches, and held our arms up to protect our eyes from the ones we couldn't dodge. Up ahead, an ancient ash had succumbed to last winter's storms and lay immediately across our path. White Surrey engaged his powerful hindquarters and leapt the trunk of the fallen tree at a gallop. For a magical moment, we were suspended in the fresh spring air, flying like a winged horse in a Greek myth. I could hear Francis Lovell a few strides behind, cursing his nag, and me. It was our third hunt in two weeks. Nothing in the world distracted me so completely from my cares as a wild gallop in pursuit of a stag.

The hounds tore ahead of us, noses to the ground and tails up, their jubilant cries more beautiful to me than the music of a hundred lutes. Johnnie was a stride or two behind Lovell, with Brother Cynneth somewhere just after. And in front of us all, was the stag. He broke cover just long enough for me to spot the wide, curving rack of antlers that adorned his noble head. He was a king among his kind.

And, like any king worth his crown, he led his enemies a fine dance, and they lost his scent in the river after we'd run for almost an hour. Fergus shook the water from his coat, reared up on his hind legs, and put his wet muzzle on my boot before running back to join the rest of the pack as they splashed across to the opposite bank. My huntsman blew three long notes on his horn to encourage them.

While we waited for them to recover the line, Lovell trotted up to me, and offered me a pull from his flask. He was grinning, and his ginger curls were damp with sweat under his velvet cap.

"Christ's blood, what a run he's given us so far," he said, wiping his shining brow.

I took a long swig of the sweet malmsey before handing it back to him.

"He's a grand creature. Did you view him?" I asked.

"I did, just for a moment. Long enough to see he could feed a whole village with one of his haunches! I'm glad we've been hunting so frequently of late. It does us all good."

The friar rode up on my other side and gave Lovell a significant look.

"Is there a swallow left for me or have you two finished it already?"

Lovell passed me the flask again and I handed it to Cynneth.

"Aren't you toasting in that gown of yours?" asked Lovell.

"Oh, I fare well enough. As well as a courtier in fine velvet, I'll warrant."

Lovell's bright green doublet was torn at the sleeve, and stained with blood from his cheek where he'd failed to timely duck a thorny limb. The friar's grey habit was immaculate by contrast. I looked down at my own garb. My leather jerkin was scratched and scored, but from this hunt or the many others before it I couldn't tell.

"I wonder if the Tudor has the heart to hunt this spring," said Lovell.

The friar shook his head. "The heart mayhap, but the means may be lacking."

We'd had the intelligence from our spies in Duke Francis of Brittany's court that, after the news that Elizabeth had brought her daughters out of sanctuary and put them under my protection, Henry Tudor was finding scant financial support for his schemes. His broken engagement to Elizabeth branded him a poor risk, and without money from the royals on the continent, he couldn't hope to raise an army. But his mother, Lady Stanley, was still one of the richest women in England.

"I'll bet he has the wherewithal to go hunting, even if he can't find the funds to invade my country," I said.

"The Tudor is a babe who's never fought a battle except with the little toy soldiers that his lady mother bought for him," said Johnnie.

We all laughed.

"Your Grace, why do my cousins Bess or Cecily not come out hunting with us? I've asked them more than once, but they always refuse."

Lovell grunted, but for once didn't chime in, for which I was glad.

"Son, you will find there are many different types of ladies in this world. Those that go hunting, and those that are afraid to get a scratch on their pretty faces."

He frowned. "Jayne has a fair face, fairer that either of theirs. But I bet she'd come hunting if we asked her."

"Mistress Lyons' time is taken up by her duties. You forget that she waits upon Bess, who doesn't hunt. So I doubt she would spare her."

"I bet she would if you asked her, Fa... Your Grace."

I sighed. Perhaps I'd been wrong to let him see my relationship with Jayne while we were traveling back from Salisbury. But he adored her, and we three had been happy together. Now he couldn't understand why she kept her eyes down when I passed, like a modest handmaiden too respectful to gaze openly at her king.

Had she forgotten the nights when our sweat had mingled until we could no longer tell the tastes apart? Or did she cringe at the memory of taking pleasure with a murderer?

Even if she hated me, I owed her a better future than playing lady in waiting to my niece. She had helped me, mayhap even saved me from a battle that would have cost many men their lives. And now that concerns about the Tudor no longer beset me, I could at last concentrate on ruling England for my subjects. I should marry her off to some country squire, as I should have done before ever I lay with her.

There was little chance of keeping a liaison secret in a royal court, and I was damned if I would allow myself to follow in Edward's footsteps. He'd taken his pleasure as he chose, and his sons had paid the price. Who knew the cost of having Jayne back in my bed, or who would ultimately have to settle the account? My own son? Anne had had a letter from Dr. Cranston at Middleham just yesterday. Little Ned was mending well from his difficult winter, and should be able to travel to London in just a few weeks. He and Johnnie got on well. If he continued to improve, mayhap this time next year he would be hunting with us.

I looked down at Johnnie's eager face, still waiting for my answer. I was tempted to tell him the truth, that Jayne and I would never be together again, and that it was best for all of us, but the words stuck in my throat. Then we heard the huntsman's horn. The hounds were back on their quarry.

Lovell shoved his flask back in its case and I wrung the sweat out of my cap and thrust it back on my head. Surrey danced and pulled on the bit, so I reached down to stroke the curve of his neck. I could feel the crunch of dried sweat on his coat from our earlier run, but now the tireless beast was eager to be on again.

As soon as we were sure the hounds were well away, we careened through the wood after them. In less than an hour, they had the stag at bay, with no direction to turn but into their teeth. The triumphant huntsman doffed his cap at me as I rode up to watch the kill.

The great stag's heaving sides were foamy with sweat. His shining nostrils flared with every breath, and his long pink tongue fell sideways from his mouth. He was exhausted, and defeated, but he still held his head high and looked directly into my face with wide black eyes, king to king.

He was the largest stag I'd ever seen. How many battles must he have survived to have reached such and age and size?

"Call them off!" I commanded

"What?" asked the huntsman, so surprised he forgot his manners.

"I said call the hounds off the stag, man!"

He swallowed his shock and blew the horn call to tell the hounds to leave their quarry and return to his side, but it was too late. They were too close, and too sure of the kill. Only Fergus looked back, before following the others as they leapt on his neck.

The stag's roars of pain and fury were no different than a hundred I'd heard before. But I yanked my bow from the back of my saddle, nocked an arrow, and shot him through the heart. I'd spared him all I could.

The herald found me in the sunny courtyard of the Abbey. He was trembling, and his clothes and face were covered in dust, except where tears had made streaks down his dirty face. When he handed me the rolled parchment with its cord of braided black silk, my heart seized. It was almost exactly a year ago to the day that another distraught and frightened messenger brought me news of the death of my brother Edward.

In my haste to know the worst I tore open the seal and read it where I stood, without waiting to seek a place where I could sit and wail in private. So the monks and the courtiers, and the servants who attended them heard my scream. The herald crossed his arms over his head to ward off my fist, but instead of striking him, I forced my sorrow back down my throat, clenched my jaw and walked as rapidly as I dared through the blur of humanity that my outburst had summoned.

"Your Grace, how may we help you?" someone asked, but I shook my head and kept walking until I reached St. Stephen's chapel.

Morning mass was long past, and the nave was empty, save for one monk who knelt at his prayers. The warmth of the afternoon had no power here, and I was glad; it was a cold place made for grief. My little son Ned, Edward's namesake and my only heir, was dead.

Dr. Cranston's letter said he died three days ago, when I'd been out hunting, and dreaming of one day having him gallop by my side.

"The Prince complained of a pain in his belly, which I hastened to treat with mint, and chamomile, but it gave him no relief. By that evening he was tossing with fever, and insensible. His soul left his body without his ever awakening."

So this was to be my punishment. So many times this last year I'd knelt on cold stone and begged forgiveness. Each time I rose to my feet sure in the belief that my decision was for the best, and that Almighty God had seen my dilemma, and pardoned me. Now, I knew I had conjured absolution where there was none.

I prayed for Ned's innocent soul. Had he been frightened and called for me, or for his mother? He died without either of us there with him. Anne would never forgive herself, or me.

The last time I saw him, three months ago, he begged me to bring him with me to London.

"Father, I'm much better now," he said. "My chest hardly ever hurts anymore. I know I could ride Tristan all the way to Westminster."

The new pony had been a source of disagreement between his

mother and me, but I'd insisted, and the exercise did him good. He was past his childhood illnesses, or so I'd thought. Now he was gone.

Was I to be the last Plantagenet? A king with no heir was a vulnerable king. If I were to breed another son tomorrow, I would have to reach a greater age than my brothers or my father had done before they died, else I would leave a child to rule England. A child as defenseless as my brother's sons had been.

From above the altar, the image of Jesus' mother looked down on me with sad, knowing eyes, as if she pitied me for a fool who brought down a once-great House. But I didn't deserve her forgiveness. I said one last prayer, and begged that all her mercy, and comfort, go to Anne. I forced myself to my feet, and went to tell the mother of my child that he was dead.

CHAPTER 23

JAYNE: APRIL 21, 1484

"No one's seen him for days, except Brother Cynneth," said Bess.

"Not even the queen?" I asked.

"Not even her. She's still under Dr. Hobby's care."

My former jealousy of Anne now felt like the height of selfishness. Her ladies said that when Richard told her their son was dead, she'd screamed and fallen to her knees.

"My child! My poor child!" she cried. The court gossips repeated the story until it was as if we'd all been there to witness her grief.

The April day was unseasonably warm, and Bess and I walked in the gardens of Westminster Palace. None of the plants were blooming yet except the Lenten roses that clustered beneath the mulberry trees. But the paths between the evergreen hedges made it a pleasant place to stroll, and the bright spring sun felt good on our faces, even though we still needed our wool cloaks. It rained yesterday, so we held our long black skirts up to keep them from dragging the ground. We'd been in mourning for the Prince of Wales for almost a week, and my heart was heavy with pity for Richard, and Anne.

Richard's son had meant the world to him. During our time together, it was a rare day that he didn't mention Ned with obvious pride and concern. He'd pinned all his hopes on the boy's survival.

Whispering courtiers said Ned's death was God's way of punishing Richard for stealing the throne that rightfully belonged to his nephews. Although I didn't share their superstitions, I felt a chill when I realized how close the date of Ned's death was to that of King Edward, just a year earlier. And I understood Richard well enough to know that he would be punishing himself. He wouldn't need the help of any vengeful deity to do it for him.

"What was Ned like?" I asked Bess, as we approached a small bench at the end of a vine arbor. She dusted off the seat before sitting down and indicating that I should join her.

She sighed. "He was a serious little fellow, I think because he was sick so much, and couldn't run and play with other children. He was like a man grown, in a child's tiny weak body. Very like his father was as a child, so I'm told."

I'd never seen Richard sick, or even tired, so the picture she painted was difficult for me to imagine.

Bess continued as if she'd read my mind. "But Uncle Richard rallied from his childhood illnesses. He fought at my father's side at Barnet, and my father gave him his first command when he was only eighteen."

She leaned back against the bench and gazed out at the garden, but she seemed miles, or years, away.

"I remember when he and Father came back to us here at Westminster, after they'd been victorious at Barnet. I was six or so, and I'd made mother wash my hair and let me put on my best gown. As soon as he came in the door, I ran to him. But my brother Edward had been born while they were away, and Father just gave me a pat on the head as he walked right past me to see the new baby. I didn't matter to him anymore, once he had a male heir.

But Uncle Richard was right behind him, and saw me start to cry. He picked me up in his arms and whirled me around so that my skirts billowed, and he told me that I was the most beautiful princess in the whole world."

She sighed. "Being the youngest son, I think he knew what it was like to be passed over, and ignored."

There were so many things about Richard I would have loved to ask her. But what excuse could I have for my interest? She'd never asked me anything about my relationship with him; she must assume we had mainly communicated through the friar. At least I could listen to her talk about the uncle she obviously loved and respected. And any evidence of his kindness made it easier to justify my love for him, even knowing what he truly was.

I hoped she would continue talking about him, but instead she stood up.

"Let's go inside. I've a fitting for another black gown this afternoon. It appears we will all be in mourning for some time and I can't go about in this one day after day."

I started to follow her back inside the palace, where I knew I would be called on to give my opinion on the black silk versus the black damask for the next two hours, but all at once I couldn't stand the thought of being cooped up.

"Bess, do you care if I go out to the stables and visit with the horses?"

She stopped, and pouted. "I don't know why you want to spend so much time there. I really need your help in choosing the fabric for my gown."

I did my best to copy her pout, and it must have worked, because she said, "Oh all right, go and visit if you must. But don't go riding off anywhere. I want you to come back before my fitting is done so you can help me make my final decision."

"Thank you, Bess."

She turned back to me just as she reached the end of the path.

"I'm beginning to think you're in love with one of the grooms, or perhaps even the King's Master of Horse himself!" She gave me a wink. Sir William Broadbent was almost sixty.

My afternoon rides were the only privacy I had, and the only time I could let myself think of Richard, and of my former life. I'd been here now for more than six months. I'd grown accustomed to the inconveniences, the strange food, and the cumbersome clothing, but I was terrified of getting sick, or injured, and my lack of control over my future infuriated me. While out on my solitary horseback rides I'd faced a bitter truth: I might never get home.

As I neared the stables, I started to regret promising Bess that I wouldn't ride. Although in the twenty-first century, Westminster was just another part of London, in 1484 it was a separate village, a little world unto itself that was bordered on three sides by woodlands. There were beautiful clearings to ride across, and the cool spring sunshine made me long to be astride one of the gentle mares Richard kept stabled for the use of the ladies of his court. Just the smell of leather and hay and horse-flesh cheered me.

Rob, Richard's head groom, was sitting on a wooden stool just inside the door, and picking his black stumps of teeth with a piece of straw.

He stood up and grinned when he saw me.

"Good morrow, Mistress Lyons! Shall I be saddling Juno?"

I smiled back at him. He was kind to remember my favorite mare.

"No, thank you, Rob. I don't have time to ride today. I'll just visit with her, if you don't mind."

He gestured towards the long row of stalls.

"She's in the seventh down, and she'll be right glad to see you, the way you spoil her."

I wished I had an apple to give her, but fresh apples were only available in the fall. So I had to make do with stroking the mare's neck, which was still covered in her fluffy winter coat.

Rob followed me, chatty as usual.

"If it's peace and quiet you're seeking, it's a good thing you weren't here just an hour ago," he said.

I almost laughed. It appeared I was to have no peace and quiet now either.

"Oh, why's that?" I asked him, while I continued to pet the chestnut mare. I knew he would tell me anyway.

"The king came down here himself, and pulled White Surrey from his stall. He wouldn't let none of us saddle the beast, but did it all on his own. Ol' Broadbent a'most had a fit, he was so carked."

I gripped the wooden door of Juno's stall.

"Did he ride out alone?"

"He did, and he looked like the angel of death himself," he said.

"I don't suppose he told anyone where he was going," I inquired, but I already knew the answer.

He shook his head. "He wouldn't answer Sir William when he asked him."

My heart was beating so hard I felt sure Rob could hear it. I wanted to yank Juno out of her stall and jump on her back without waiting for a saddle, but I couldn't risk alerting him to what I was up to.

"Rob, I've changed my mind about riding. Will you saddle her up for me, please?"

"I'll be glad to, mistress. It's a fine day for a ride. Even the king thinks so." He laughed at his own joke.

I grabbed the mare's halter and held her while he strolled over to the tack room for a saddle. He carefully laid a blanket over the horse's back, then settled the saddle on top of it, whistling some cheerful ditty as he worked. His leisurely manner always amused me until today.

By the time he led her into the stable yard for me to mount, I could feel the sweat coming through the armpits of my gown.

"Do stay out of the king's way, Mistress Lyons," he admonished me. "He was right strong about no one following him. But St. James Park's a big place, a'course."

I already knew my plan was a long shot; I didn't need reminding. I wrapped my skirts around my legs and climbed into the saddle. Medieval women rode astride, and wore leggings made of leather or heavy cloth to protect them from the stirrup leathers. I wasn't wearing leggings under my skirts today, and my calves would be raw by the time I returned. But it didn't matter.

I left the yard at a walk. If Richard told his Master of Horse he didn't want to be followed, someone might try to stop me, and I didn't want to call attention to myself. He probably meant he didn't want the usual armed escort that accompanied him everywhere, but Sir William wouldn't make that distinction if he saw me leaving the stables.

I took a deep breath. There were two possible routes to the wood. The fastest way was through the north gate, which opened directly from the back of the palace grounds. My other option was the south gate, which also led out towards St. James Park, but to get to it, I would have to go through the main gateway out of the palace and into the crowded Westminster streets.

I turned the horse hard left and made for the north gate. I hadn't gone three strides when Sir William came out of the palace door nearest the stables.

"Good morrow, Mistress Lyons! Shouldn't you have an escort?"

I'd ridden out by myself dozens of times, and no one had said a word about it. Why today?

I tried to sound calm. "I'm not going far, sir. I didn't want to trouble anyone."

"Oh, it's no trouble. Rob can saddle one of the horses and accompany you. Where was it you were going?"

I'd learned that my complete set of even, twenty-first century teeth never failed to fascinate the medievals, so I smiled my widest smile. I winked in what I hoped was a conspiratorial manner.

"I'm off on an errand for the Lady Bess," I said. She asked me to hurry, and to be discreet about it."

He stared up at me. I could tell he didn't want to get into some debate about women's business.

After what felt like an age he shrugged his shoulders.

"As you wish, Mistress. But go out by the south gate. That will be faster for you."

Of course he assumed my business for Bess lay somewhere in town, not in St. John's Wood! I smiled at him again, and turned Juno towards the south gate. At least I could justify picking up a trot, since he thought I was in a hurry.

I nodded to the guards, who let me pass without question. They'd often seen me walking out with Bess, and sometimes Cecily, who both loved to stroll around the village and visit the shops. I usually enjoyed it too. The stalls around the square sold every type of goods imaginable, from fresh fish to fine silks. The Red Pale, the print shop owned by William Caxton, which was the first of its kind in England, especially fascinated me. Since the girls still didn't know that I could read, I pretended to admire the beautiful illustrations in the priceless leather-bound volumes.

But today the merchants hawking their wares, and the villagers and nobles calmly considering them, made me want to scream. For safety's sake, I couldn't pass them at a faster gait than a brisk walk, and even so, several goodwives gave me the dead eye for disturbing them.

I'd offended several medievals of both genders by the time I reached the gates. The two guards were men I'd never seen before, and I was terrified they would stop and question me, but although one of them gave me a disgusting leer, neither tried to prevent me from passing under the stone portal.

I kept Juno to a trot until I was well away from the gate, and then kicked her into a brisk canter. She responded with a burst of energy, and I thanked the friar again for his invaluable guidance. We'd resumed my riding lessons since I'd been with Bess at court, and I'd never been more grateful to him than at this moment.

I usually kept my solitary rides to a walk or an occasional slow trot, but today I needed to fly. Juno was a brave, intelligent little thing, and I would just have to trust her.

The wide meadow that lay outside the gate was beginning to show bits of green. Up ahead lay the wood, still winter-stark in places, but mostly thick with evergreens. I'd heard there were riding paths that led to an offshoot of the Thames, but I had no idea where they started.

I pulled Juno down to a trot. She resisted at first, tossing her head and pulling against my hands. But to my relief, after a moment she settled into the slower gait. As we drew closer to the woods, I realized that my plan was no plan at all.

I'd not thought past getting to St. John's Wood, but Richard could be anywhere in its hundreds of acres. And I had no idea if he'd even talk to me if I found him. He'd ignored me without fail since our only meeting, when Bess barged into his solar.

I stopped at the edge of the wood. I could always go back to the palace, put Juno in her stall, and make my excuses to Bess. She'd be furious that I'd disobeyed her request, but she'd get over it eventually.

What's wrong with you, Jayne? When did you turn into a coward? I checked my belt. After my second encounter with Sergeant Talbott, Brother Cynneth gave me a dirk, and told me to keep it with me at all times. The short, sharp knife fit into an etched leather holster that hung from my girdle. It was there today, if I needed it. I squared my shoulders and eased my horse into the woods.

CHAPTER 24

JAYNE: APRIL 21, 1484

I wandered along the edge of the wood until I found the first path. It was barely wide enough for two horses to ride abreast, and it seemed to lead nowhere. Juno pricked her ears and moved out without hesitating but I could tell she was nervous. At one point, she came to an abrupt halt, and refused my attempts to get her to move. I looked around to see what had spooked her and no more than thirty feet away a group of big does stood hiding in the trees, watching us. Then without warning, one of them took off and the others followed her. When they were out of sight, I could feel the mare relax and she finally responded to my kick.

We continued along the first path until it crossed with another. Both paths were hoof-marked, but I had no idea if the horses had passed this way today, or a week ago, so I decided to stay on my original pathway for a little longer, and after a while I heard the sound of rushing water. I clucked to Juno until she picked up a trot, and soon we came to a river bank.

I don't know why I thought I'd find him there. I supposed I pictured the place as soothing, and restful. I jumped down, and kept hold of Juno's reins while I walked to the edge of the bank.

The water rushed past me. The recent rains caused it to almost overflow its muddy banks. There was a depression leading down into the water, and I thought I could see fresh hoof marks in the mud. Someone, or ones, had crossed here. Maybe it was Richard. He would have to come back, wouldn't he? Or I could cross the river myself, and continue to search for him.

I looked at the water tumbling past, and I knew I couldn't do it. The mare was small, and my heavy skirts would soak up the water like a sponge. After more than an hour, I realized I couldn't stay out any longer. As it was, I would be lucky to get back before darkness fell. I'd been a fool. Bess would be angry, and worried, and it was all to no avail. Richard was probably back by now, holed up in his private chambers again. But maybe the ride had helped him even if I could not. As we headed back towards Westminster, Juno seemed out of sorts, and I had to kick her twice to get her to cross the other pathway again headed back towards Westminster.

I hadn't gone far when I realized something was wrong. When we left the river, Juno was walking out boldly, like a horse heading home to the stable. Now she was hesitant, and looked around at the rustle of every leaf. I ignored the signs until I couldn't anymore. We were lost.

Since I'd lied to everyone about my destination, no one would think to come looking for me here. I tried not to panic, but it was possible I could wander around St. John's Wood for days until some hunting party found me. That is, if some wild animal didn't find me first.

I was too overwhelmed to cry. Should I find one spot and stay in it, or keep moving and hope I was going in the right direction? Juno was fidgeting, and bobbing her head against the bit. I decided to keep walking.

Soon I heard the sound of the river again. I was moving in the wrong direction. I put my leg on my horse to turn her around, but she pulled her head in the other direction and moved sideways on the path.

"Come on, mare!" I said impatiently.

I put my shoulder back, and closed my legs around her body, like Brother Cynneth instructed me to do when a horse resisted. After a few more kicks I convinced her to turn away from the river, but as soon as I relaxed she whirled around again, threw up her head, and whinnied.

She'd always done as I asked with very little coaxing, but now I could feel a tension in her back, and jaw, that I'd never felt before. I was sure that if I tried to turn her back, she was going to leave me on my ass in the middle of the woods.

The friar told me never to dismount, that it showed the horse you were frightened. I didn't care. All I needed was to get hurt out here alone. I was about to jump down from her back and lead her in the other direction, when I heard another horse answer her call.

Oh, thank God! Another horse meant another human. She whinnied again, and this time I let her go in the direction she wanted to go. I relaxed my grip on the reins and she picked up a trot of her own accord.

Just as it occurred to me that the owner of the horse might not be the helpful sort, we rounded a corner and I saw the familiar shape of Surrey, Richard's big white charger, with its reins tied around an ash limb.

Richard was sitting on the wet ground, with his back against the trunk of a huge fallen oak. When he saw me, he pushed himself up, wiped his hand across his eyes and looked at me again, like he thought I might disappear. I jumped down from Juno's back and went to him.

His face looked pale and weary under a days-long growth of dark beard, and the crook in his right shoulder, usually undetectable unless he was naked, appeared inches higher than the left. He let out a low moan, put his arms around me, and rubbed his rough cheek against my face. His body, always tight and slender, felt painfully thin against mine, and instead of the clean, spicy smell I remembered, he reeked of sweat and damp leather. I held him as tightly as I knew how.

His chest began to heave, and I realized he was sobbing. He cried until his tears dampened my face, and my hair, and the raw, desperate noise of it made me close my eyes. I'd never heard anyone, man or woman, make such a hopeless sound.

I stroked his back until his sobs finally subsided. He eased me back away from him and stood taking deep, sucking breaths, like a runner after a sprint.

"Just over a week ago, I killed a stag in these woods," he said. "He looked at me with the eyes of a man, but I killed him anyway. I couldn't save him..."

"Richard, I love you. I don't care what you've done!"

"But I killed my nephew! I killed him, and God hasn't forgiven me! He took my Ned..."

I'd never hated religious superstition more than now.

"The world doesn't work that way..." I said. I stopped, and stared at his stricken face.

"What did you just say? You killed your nephew?"

He dropped his hands.

"Yes. Yes, Jayne! Don't tell me you didn't believe it anyway."

I shook my head. What did I believe, except what a toadying playwright told the world, more than a hundred years after the fact?

"Richard, I...I don't know what to think. But I know whatever you did, or didn't do, nothing will stop me from loving you."

He held his hand against his mouth, and closed his eyes. I thought for a moment he had started to cry again. But he wiped his nose against his sleeve and squared his shoulders.

"It's time you knew the truth."

He went to where Surrey and Juno stood, heads together, and took his cloak from where it was folded across his saddle and laid it over the fallen log.

"Sit," he told me.

I obeyed him, but I wanted to run. I'd cherished the thought that he might be innocent. After this, there would be no hope.

"One year ago," he began, "when my brother King Edward was on his deathbed, he made me Lord Protector of England. I was to care for both his family, and his realm, until his son Edward IV reached his eighteenth year. The child was only thirteen at the time, and so I had a long task ahead, and not one I relished. The queen had expected to be regent until her son was old enough to rule, and she and her Woodville kinfolk were determined to oppose me. But nevertheless, I left Middleham and escorted my nephew from his household at Ludlow Castle to London, and the royal apartments in the Tower, to await his coronation. His mother and I disliked each other and for years I'd stayed away from London except when Edward demanded my presence, so the boy and I had never been close. He was upset, and frightened by his father's unexpected death, and when I tried to comfort him, he would have none of it. So, to console him, we brought his younger brother, Richard, my namesake, to the Tower to join him.

My cousin Harry, Lord Buckingham, had accompanied us to the capital, and together we made plans for the boy to be crowned. But late one night, only days before the ceremony was to take place, an aged bishop named Stillington begged his way into my private chambers and cleared his conscience by confessing to me that he'd performed a binding marriage ceremony for my brother and a Lady Eleanor Butler. This marriage took place almost a year before Edward's marriage to the woman who called herself the queen. Therefore, Edward, Prince of Wales, and his brothers and sisters, were all of them born out of wedlock, and none of them fit to sit on the throne of England."

He paused, and took a deep breath.

"If I had been alone, I believe I would have thanked him and sent him on his way. But I wasn't. Buckingham was with me. And after Bishop Stillington left us, he told me bluntly that if I didn't take the throne, he would. How I wish to God that I'd let him! His claim to the throne was rivaled only by my own. But I knew that if Edward had been forced to make a choice, he would have wanted me to rule England, not Harry, who'd never been in Edward's confidence. So I called a meeting of the King's Council, and told them what the bishop had said. They were unanimous in their support of my kingship."

I nodded. Most of this I already knew, it was all of it well-documented history

– except the feelings of the man at the center of the story. Until now, no one knew how Richard, Duke of Gloucester, truly felt about accepting the crown.

"Go on," I said.

"Elizabeth was furious, and accused me of concocting the story of Edward's previous marriage so that I might steal what rightfully belonged to her son. She'd been queen for almost twenty years, and had bestowed many a favor during that time. A number of powerful nobles owed their titles and their incomes to her, and so she called upon them to oppose my kingship. Within weeks of my coronation, a group of her adherents made an attempt to remove the boys from the Tower, with the intent to use them as a rallying point for civil war. Buckingham, whom I'd made Constable of the Tower, succeeded in halting the attempted kidnapping, but he claimed that as long as the boys were alive, there would be those who disputed my right to the throne, and that for the duration of my reign, any noble who thought he might fare better with a child for a king would use them against me. And once my enemies had custody of the York princes, my own life, and my son's, would be the only obstacles in their way. And so I must kill them."

I gripped my skirts so he wouldn't see that my hands were shaking. I loved him, but he terrified me. What if, after it was too late, he regretted telling me?

"I refused. My brother had entrusted them into my care, and I'd loved him with all my heart. Nothing, not even fear for my own life, could make me betray his trust."

"Loyaute me lie," I murmured. "Then what happened to them? Did he kill them?"

He put his hand up, in that familiar gesture. "I will tell you. When I refused to do as he recommended, Buckingham left London and went to his castle in Wales. But not before telling me that I was too weak to be king, and that he'd made a mistake by supporting me. As you know, he launched a rebellion against me, the very one in which you lost your family."

So that was the reason for Buckingham's Rebellion!

"But I knew he was right about the boys. As long as they were there in the Tower, England would be plagued by the threat of civil war every time any policy I enacted displeased a powerful noble. So I did the only thing I could think of to do. I sent them to a place where no one would look for them."

I was giddy with relief. I put my hands to my temples.

He grabbed my wrists and held them.

"But Jayne, Edward is dead! I sent them away from the Tower in the dead of night, with only a small escort. They'd not gotten far outside the gates of London, on the Great North Road, when they were set upon by a gang of highwaymen. Horse thieves. They were taken by surprise, and three of them were killed in the ambush, leaving only two men to defend the boys. Sir James Tyrell was the only one of their escort to survive, and he saw what happened to Edward."

He stopped and put his head in his hands for a moment before he continued.

"When the younger of the two lads, Richard, tried to use his small dagger to stop them from taking his pony, the thieves pulled him from his saddle and began kicking him as he lay helpless on the ground. Edward drew his sword to defend his brother, and they set upon him, and cut his throat."

Soundless tears rolled down his face. I imagined that he'd cried like this more times than he could count.

"Richard! Buckingham would have killed them. Many men in your position would have killed them." I'd witnessed enough brutality since I'd been in the fifteenth century to know I was speaking the truth.

"But don't you see, Jayne? He was brave, and loyal. He would have made a fine king. I should never have let Buckingham convince me to take his throne. I should have found some way to see that he was crowned, even if I had to imprison Buckingham until the boy was anointed. But I didn't, and God has punished me for my ambition."

"But Richard, you didn't set out to be king. You didn't even want to be king!"

He looked at me and shook his head.

"What man on this Earth does not, in his naked heart, want to be king?"

He still held one of my hands in his. He looked away from me, stared out into the forest. We sat there together, without speaking, until just before dark, when Francis Lovell and his search party found us.

CHAPTER 25

JAYNE: AUGUST 24, 1484

*B*ess refused to ride a horse into London for the Saint Bartholomew's Fair, so she and Cecily and I traveled in a wagon pulled by two stout ponies. The Strand was crowded with all manner of persons, on foot or on horseback, and in wagons or litters, most headed from the village of Westminster to the first day of the three-day fair. I found it ironic that St. Bartholomew, an unfortunate martyr who'd been flayed alive in the first century for his Christian beliefs, was the patron saint of knives, and this was the traditional day that the farmers sharpened their scythes and other farm implements for the start of the upcoming harvest season. I wasn't sure that a fair would have grown up around this particular tradition, except that the saint was also the patron of bee-keepers, and honey. And honey means mead. St. Bartholomew's day was the day of the Blessing of the Mead, and I suspected that this was the reason for St. Bartholomew's Fair, which was held just outside the majestic Cathedral of St. Bartholomew, in a part of London called Smithfield.

A few of our fellow travelers appeared to have started imbibing the mead before the blessing. A group of four rustics staggered along beside us, and sang bawdy songs that made Cecily snigger, and Bess roll her eyes.

I laughed, and smiled, because last night Richard and I had engaged in at least one of the many acts they were praising. My body warmed at the memory, and I was glad that my legs were bare under my lightweight blue linen gown, and that I'd remembered to put my hair into a long braid before I covered it with a simple white veil. The late August day was bright, and windless, and for the sake of comfort even Bess forwent her usual summer silk.

As the Strand turned into Fleet Street, I could just make out Richard and his escort riding ahead. He wore a thin gold circlet around his head, in place of a crown, and his long dark hair fell down around his shoulders. I loved watching him, at dinner in the gallery where the court dined on informal occasions, or when our paths crossed during the day as he walked through the palace with his council. Yesterday, Bess and I had strolled down to the riverbank to enjoy the breeze off the water, just in time to see him hop into a barge, headed into London for a meeting at the Tower. He caught my eye before the rowers pushed away from the dock, and the flash of desire in his eyes told me to expect his servant at my door sometime before midnight.

The spring and summer had been so blissful that it was hard for me to remember the months of our separation. He traveled to his other castles at Nottingham, and Pontefract, and he and Anne had made a pilgrimage to Middleham to pray at the grave of their little Ned in late spring, but he lived at Westminster Palace the rest of the time, and when he did, we spent most of our nights together.

I tried to recall another time in my life when I'd been so happy and content. After Richard bared his soul to me in St. John's Wood, a painful burden had lifted from my heart. I was no longer in love with a man whom I suspected of a vile crime, but a kind man, who'd made a regrettable mistake.

And now my own conscience was clear. By revealing Henry Tudor's plans to use marriage with Bess to help him recruit an army to invade England, I'd saved Richard's life. Instead of dying at the hands of one of Tudor's Welsh pikemen a year from now, he would live to rule England. Tudor was still cooling his heels on the continent, with no plans to interfere with Richard's rule. Richard still grieved the death of his son; I felt sure he always would. But his duties as king distracted him from his sorrow, and I liked to think that our love also helped him cope with his loss.

"Where's our queen today?" asked Cecily. "I can't believe she's missing a chance to pray in public."

"Cecily! She prays for the soul of her son, and you well know it," said Bess. "I heard she isn't feeling well today."

"Maybe she's with child. Uncle Richard needs another heir, and quickly."

"She's not a good breeder," said Bess. "Her mother and sister weren't either, if you remember. Nan of Warwick had only the two girls, Anne and Isobel, and Isobel had only two children as well – one of them dead and the other a lackwit. And after the difficult time she had birthing poor Ned, Dr. Hobbys says Anne can't have any more children without risking her own life. So there's to be no future heir. It's a great misfortune for the king."

Cecily sniffed. "So I wonder what Uncle Richard does for cunny?"

Bess laughed. "I'm sure there's no shortage of ladies in our court that oblige him. After mass on Tuesday, Lady Stanley said she heard from the captain of the watch that his servants have been seen escorting women about the palace in the small hours. What do you think, Jayne? Have you heard any tales among the common folk?"

I felt myself go red. Could she be fishing for a confession? I often wondered how she could fail to be suspicious. I looked at her face. She was smart, and plenty shrewd, but I knew her well, and her bland expression wasn't an act.

Since we'd been at court, Bess treated me less like a friend, and more like a servant. I understood; she was no longer a princess, and it rankled. Her reference to "common people" was typical of her new attitude. I didn't dare point out that she was now considered a commoner herself.

"I've heard nothing, my lady. But then I spend most of my time with you," I said. I wanted to add, "Unless I'm with your Uncle," but kept the happy retort to myself. We'd gone to great effort to keep our relationship secret. I left his bed before dawn, and the same trusted servant escorted me to his chamber each time. The only time we spent together otherwise was in Bess' company. During the long summer evenings, he often asked her to walk with him in the gardens and naturally I would accompany them. He was careful not to give me too much of his attention, and made a great show of never cutting me a rose from the riotous bushes that grew there without first offering a bloom to Bess. He refused to embarrass Anne, whose obvious misery since the death of their son made us both determined not to add humiliation to her wretchedness.

My former jealousy of her had long since turned to sympathy. Richard told me they'd never been in love, but were cousins who grew up together, were fond of each other, and made a marriage of convenience. He hadn't made love with her since Ned's birth, and wouldn't risk her life now, even though he desperately needed another heir.

I wondered that Anne didn't use an herbal concoction like the one the friar prepared for me to prevent my getting pregnant. It had worked so far, and we'd certainly put it to the test. I wondered if her heart lay elsewhere. She had a kind word for everyone, but I saw her eyes linger on Francis Lovell longer than necessary, and the smiles she gave him were different from the mild expression she usually wore. I was sorry for her, but, I was glad she didn't love Richard in the same way that I did.

Richard and his party, which included Brother Cynneth, Francis Lovell, Jocky Norfolk, and John Milewater, who'd brought his wife to court with him for a few weeks before the harvest began, filed into the Cathedral just as our wagon pulled up at the entrance to the fair.

"Should we go in?" I asked Bess, who craned her neck after the royal party, probably thinking she should have been amongst them. I wanted to see the blessing, and maybe get another glimpse of Richard in the process.

She tossed her head, so that her long blond hair, which she'd left down in spite of the heat, swung over her shoulder.

"Let's go ahead to the fair. If Richard wants to see us, he'll come and find us."

Something about her tone made me uneasy, but I put it down to resentment of her diminished status. I knew better than to argue, so we walked under the archway of vines and flowers that had been erected on the green to mark the entrance to the fair.

The cocktail of aromas that assaulted my nostrils once would have made me ill. There were pens full of livestock for sale: sheep, goats, cows, and bulls, as well as dogs of every description from gigantic to terrier-sized, each with its own particular flavor of dung. And the food vendors walked amongst them, hawking everything from meat pies to apples covered in honey, which looked very much like the caramel apples from my own time. Instead of cringing, and holding my nose, I bought a candied apple for a few pence from the first vendor I saw, and without hesitation took a big, sweet bite.

The three of us wandered about at a leisurely pace, stopping frequently at the booths of the silk merchants to admire their lustrous yards of fabric imported from Brussels and Burgundy. Remembering the snowy days of our confinement in sanctuary, when I'd only had one change of clothes, I purchased a bolt of claret-colored wool to make up a winter dress. Richard gave Bess a generous allowance, out of which she shared a portion with me. I now had a lovely summer wardrobe, complete with several creamy white chemises made of fine soft lawn.

We had paused to laugh at a trained monkey that wore a diminutive gown and tiny hennin and danced like a court lady to the strumming of a lute, and I was about to ask permission to go look for a few yards of braid to decorate the claret wool, when the crowd parted for the king and his companions.

He raised Bess from her low curtsy and bowed over her hand and kissed her cheek.

"Good morrow, Cecily, and Mistress Lyons! Are you enjoying the fair? I see Mistress Lyons has made a purchase."

I had curtseyed as low as I dared. I carried my fabric in a bundle tied with string, and it affected my balance, and so the attempt wasn't my most graceful. When I looked up, I could see Richard was trying not to laugh.

He took the parcel from me and examined it.

"This will be most becoming, mistress," he said, before handing it back to me.

"Your Grace, do walk with us for awhile," said Bess.

"That would be delightful." He gave her his arm, and we joined their group.

"Hello, Jayne," said Brother Cynneth.

"How are you, friar? Did you help the bishop bless the mead?"

He laughed. "No, he didn't need my assistance, although I stood ready to help. This is one of my favorite saint's days," he said. "And I do think it's time we tried St. Bartholomew's favorite beverage."

We stopped in front of a booth where a rotund proprietor was selling the frothy sweet stuff. He bowed almost to the ground when he saw Richard.

"Please, Your Grace! Do accept a flagon of my finest."

He handed Richard a wooden cup filled with golden liquid, and Richard took a long swig.

"Delicious!" he said. "Pour up a serving for each of my companions, if you please."

The man scurried to do as Richard asked, and soon all of us had a serving. Richard forced the man to accept a gold sovereign for payment, which I knew was many times over the cost of the mead.

"God bless Your Grace," said the man, bowing again. "My good wife and I were right sorry to hear about your little one."

Richard's smile faded. Although he wore a black linen tunic in mourning for Ned, I knew he did his best not to dwell on his death. But he smiled again, a sad smile this time.

"I thank you, good sir."

"Your Grace, have you seen the horses sent down by my brothers at Jervalux?" asked the friar. He'd already drained one cup and was well into another. "I understand they were to be quite a selection of fine mounts."

I wanted to hug him. He loved Richard so well, and knew how to distract him.

"No, I've not seen them, but I would very much like to do so," said Richard. And so we told the mead seller goodbye and wandered in the direction Brother Cynneth indicated.

Everywhere the crowd parted before us, and we quickly reached a round pen that contained eight of the most beautiful horses I'd ever seen. The friar had told me all about Jervelux Abbey, the cloister in York that produced some of the finest horses, and horsemen, in England. He'd been trained there himself.

"There's a beauty!" Richard pointed towards a bright bay mare. She had a fine, delicate face and her ears sat perfectly on her dainty head.

"Uncle Richard, please buy her for me," said Bess. "So that I may come hunting with you!"

I looked at the friar with my mouth hanging open. Bess had never before mentioned any desire to ride, or even admired a horse, in my presence. The friar raised his eyebrows and shrugged his shoulders, but Richard smiled and patted her arm.

"Bess! Would you really like that? Johnnie says he has invited you more than once to come out with us."

She simpered at him. "Well, if I had a horse of my own that I knew would carry me safely, I would hunt."

"I didn't know you could ride," I said.

She gave me a withering look. "Father presented me with my first pony when I was but five."

Richard talked to the Franciscan brother about the horse, and he immediately made Bess a gift of it. One of the servants who'd been following us at a discreet distance came up to lead the animal away.

"You'll have to ride her a bit, and get used to her before you come out hunting," said Richard, as we watched the energetic little mare jigging on her lead rope.

"Oh, I will," said Bess. "You'll help me, won't you, friar?"

"But of course," replied Brother Cynneth.

We walked on, Bess chattering to Cecily about her new horse, and me dragging behind, staying close to the friar. The royal party rode beside our wagon on the way back to Westminster, but I found it hard to laugh at Lovell's jokes, or to meet Richard's eye. Somehow, the day was ruined.

CHAPTER 26

RICHARD: OCTOBER 1484

I held up the document up for the friends gathered in my privy chamber. It was resplendent with the impressive wax seal of the King of Scotland.

"Now there's a sight I thought never to witness!" said Brother Cynneth.

Jocky nodded. "This is a fine day, my lad. A fine day!"

The Scots had been harrying our borders since before my brother died. As his general, I'd fought them in his name, and even taken their capital, Edinburgh, and held it for a month in an attempt to subdue them. But this summer, diplomacy had won the day where force could not, and their king, James III, had at last agreed to my terms. And to seal our accord, one of my nieces, Anne of Suffolk, daughter of my sister, would wed the heir to the Scottish throne.

"You were wise to seal the treaty with a wedding," said Jockey. "Nothing holds an alliance together like blood, especially once they've bred themselves an heir."

I glanced over at Anne, where she sat reading by the fire. She seemed in better spirits today, and happy to share my triumph when I received the signed treaty from the Scottish Ambassador. I was afraid Jockey's comment might strike a wrong note, and upset her again, but she didn't seem to have heard. Her book lay open on her lap, and she gazed into the fire, oblivious to us all.

"Now it's time you found husbands for your other nieces." Jockey poured himself a cup of wine and sat down beside the friar.

"I've a likely candidate for Cecily, Lord Bolton's son Ralph. He's said he'll take her despite her bastardy if I'll settle the manors of Weston and Killington as part of her dowry," I said.

"That's fine, Your Grace, but it's Bess we must be concerned about," he said. "You well know that as long as she remains unwed, the Tudor will continue to try to find a way to wed her himself. Was only yesterday I saw Lady Stanley corner the poor girl after morning mass. She's not given up pressing that match on behalf of her wretched son, I promise you."

Lovell met my eye over Jockey's shoulder. He knew, as they all did, that I delayed finding Bess a husband so that she might remain at court, and Jayne with her.

"I'd like Bess to stay here at Westminster a bit longer," said Anne.

She spoke so rarely of late that we all turned to stare at her.

"I find her company cheers me, and the teas and possets she makes for me help me to breathe better than those foul-tasting concoctions of Dr. Hobby's." She put her hand over her mouth and suppressed a cough.

Dear Bess! Since Ned's death, she'd spent hours with Anne. No one else seemed to cheer her, and the girl knew more about herbs and physic than many a doctor. But Anne, always thin, looked fragile almost to breaking.

Jockey looked down at the floor. He would be saying no more about sending Bess from court until my wife's condition improved. I knew my companions felt the irony in her request, but Anne was my friend and helper in so many things that it almost seemed natural that she would be the one to insure my love remained by my side.

God's blood, but Jayne had been a godsend to me these last months since Ned's passing! I knew now that her love for me was true; she wanted nothing from me but my heart. And my confession to her had given me absolution that no priest and no prayers had provided. All at once, I felt I must see her. I called a servant to bring me my cloak.

"Gentlemen, I feel the need for fresh air. Let's take a turn around the courtyard before the sun begins to set."

I knew they wouldn't accompany me; they knew I didn't wish it. I walked through the crowded halls of Westminster to the small solar where Bess and her ladies would be plying their needles. I imagined Jayne, head down over her stitches, wild curls concealed beneath her veil. Her embroidery was atrocious, but her hands had other skills.

She and Bess rose to their feet and curtseyed as soon as the servant opened the door for me. Cecily was a beat behind, as usual. At first I blamed her attitude towards me on the vagaries of youth, but I realized now that she resented me, and probably always would. Once, I would have brooded over her behavior, and let my guilt over her brother's death make me cast the blame on myself, but since I unburdened my soul to Jayne, as we sat together on a fallen oak, her forgiveness was like a shield thrown up against such thoughts.

"Would you three like to walk in the courtyard with me? The weather's fine today, but John Milewater said the morrow will bring a cold rain with it."

"That would be lovely, Uncle. Fetch my cloak, Jayne," said Bess. Jayne nodded and smiled at me over her shoulder as she turned towards the door that connected the solar with Bess' chamber. Cecily sat back down on her stool and picked up her hoop.

"What are you working on so industriously, Cecily?"

"A prayer cushion," she answered, without looking up.

"And you, Bess?"

She rushed over to her chair and hid the piece of work she'd left there.

"You're not to see it, Your Grace. Not until it's finished."

How like my brother she looked, with her smiling blue eyes! There was little of her Woodville mother in her, but she was the very image of Edward at her age, with his features just softened to feminine form. He would be pleased by the woman she'd become.

"I'll not force you to show it to me now," I said. "But if you don't finish it soon I'll coax Jayne into telling me what it is."

Jayne returned, with two cloaks over her arm.

"Thank you," said Bess, taking one of them. "But as we're entertaining the Scots ambassador tonight, I need you to see to my lilac velvet now, Jayne. There's mud on the hem. When Uncle said it's to rain tomorrow I was reminded of it."

I spoke before I thought. "Oh, surely that can wait, Bess."

"I don't want us to rush our walk, Your Grace. And there's scarcely more than an hour before we must dress."

I got a glimpse of Jayne's despondent face before Bess took my arm. I couldn't insist she accompany us, but I hated to leave her unhappy. While I walked with Bess and listened to her chatter with half an ear, I considered Jayne's sad expression. Could it be just missing a walk with me that had her so downcast? No. She was lonely, with no one to talk to but Bess and Cecily. I seemed to remember a girl she'd befriended during our travels, a kitchen maid in Jocky's household. What had happened to her? I would find out.

The burly Scots ambassador took so much ale at dinner that I could scarce keep up with him. At last I could see Anne was fading, and after apologizing to him, I stood up and ended the dinner. We'd been at table three hours, but he still had much to say to me and so followed me up to my privy chamber where he proceeded to swallow another four flagons. It was after midnight when he staggered out of my door, so I considered leaving Jayne to her sleep. But I had a surprise for her, and, selfishly, I couldn't wait to share it.

As soon as Giles brought her to me, I took her in my arms, a sleepy fragrant bundle. I kissed her, and parted her cloak to put my hands around her slender waist.

"I saw you were disappointed today, when Bess made you stay behind," I said. "I was sorry, too. I only left my desk to see you, sweet Jayne."

I expected a smile, but she sniffed, and turned her face away from my lips.

"Are you crying?"

She sniffed again. "Not yet."

I took her chin in my fingers and forced her to look at me.

"This is not about a missed walk around the courtyard, is it? I know you're lonely. You've made no friends at court, have you? Friends of your own station, who will treat you as a friend and not a servant?"

Two great tears rolled out of her eyes and down her cheeks.

"No, I haven't any real friends, Richard, that's true, but that's not why..."

"Well, I have a grand surprise for you. Remember Rose, the serving wench of Jockey Norfolk's that you fancied so?"

"Sure I do, but she married one of the grooms at Dover Castle."

"Broadbent can always make use of another groom, so I've sent for him to serve in my stables. Lord Dunbarton was quite flattered, and of course your Rose is coming with him."

She wrapped her arms around me and laid her head against my chest. My cock stiffened so I tugged at the cord that held my robe around my waist, but she pulled away from me and sat down on my bed.

I'd left only two candles burning, so their flames, and the flickering fire, were the only light in the room. Had I somehow made a blunder?

"Jayne, is there something else the matter? Are you unhappy here, with me? When I had a choice, I always stayed away from court, so I understand. I won't keep you here if you don't wish it. You deserve better, I know..."

She jumped up and put her arms around me.

"No, it's nothing Richard. I am happy with you, more than you'll ever know. Please don't ever send me away."

I pushed her cloak off of her shoulders, scooped her up, and carried her back to the bed. She rubbed her soft face against my throat before I lay her down on the edge of the bed, and raised her chemise to expose her slender thighs, and the soft brush at their apex.

I ran my hands down the curve of her waist and hips, and I wanted to enter her and take my pleasure then and there, but I wanted more for her to know how much I needed her. So I parted her legs and kissed the tender flesh between them until she wrapped her fingers in my hair and arched her back. I felt her body pulse against my lips, and could wait no longer. I spent myself inside her after only one thrust.

We climbed under the coverlet together, and she snuggled under my arm. Her hair smelled of lavender, and I almost drifted off before I remembered her tears.

"Sweet, was there something you wanted to tell me tonight?"

"No, my darling," she said. "Let's go to sleep."

Giles announced himself and parted the bed curtains just before dawn.

CHAPTER 27

JAYNE: DECEMBER 25, 1484

Christmas Day

*E*vergreens and holly festooned every window, door, and archway of the Great Hall in Westminster Palace. A giant Yule log had been brought in and set aflame with great ceremony, and so many courtiers in bright Christmas finery gathered to watch, that for the first time, the vast space felt warm and cheerful.

The long u-shaped table was set with gleaming silver plate, which reflected the light of the candles. Richard sat enthroned at the middle of the high table, and the sapphires and rubies in his crown glowed in the light of the two magnificent candelabra that stood behind and on either side of his chair.

From my spot towards the end of the table, I saw that he glowed, too, with health and vitality. He looked happy, and proud, and I hoped he didn't know how painfully his vigor contrasted with the pitiful aspect of his poor queen.

She wore a stunning green satin gown, decorated with seed pearls, and a gigantic ruby suspended from a gold chain around her neck. On her head was a smaller version of the crown that looked so regal on

Richard, but her face was gaunt and shadowed beneath it, and her skinny neck looked about to break from its weight. There was no doubt in my mind that she was dying.

"Your master's sure to be without a queen afore much longer," Rose had predicted that afternoon, as she fastened my pale blue satin sleeves to the royal blue velvet of my bodice. She'd been with me at court for more than a month now, and had already made herself at home. She knew every tale and tidbit of gossip there was to be known in Westminster, about everyone from the great lords to the kitchen maids. So of course she knew that Anne was very sick, even though no one spoke of it aloud.

Even Richard was in denial. He'd given her a length of gorgeous red wool for a cloak, to encourage her to go out of the palace. She'd had the cloak made up, and trimmed in miniver, but she'd given it to Bess for Christmas instead of wearing it. Bess strolled the grounds with it wrapped around her, arm wound through Richard's, ever since Anne had given it to her twelve days ago. It lay across my chair for me to clean, the bottom of it dirty from snow where she'd walked out with him this morning.

"That one wants to be queen herself, or my name's not Rose Brannon," said Rose, talking around the pins she held in her mouth.

She was in the middle of attaching my tall gold hennin to my hair, and although I wanted to pull away from her, I didn't dare upset the delicate balance of the thing. I had to be satisfied with a rebuke.

"Rose, please quit saying that! Richard would never marry his niece. It's ridiculous, and disgusting. And besides, she's a bastard, remember? And a bastard can't be a queen, not in England or anywhere else."

God knows I'd heard enough about that issue while we'd been cooped up in sanctuary.

Rose took the last pin out of her mouth and wove it through the creamy silk veil to hold it in place at the point of the hennin and arranged it over my shoulders.

"He's married to his cousin now, id'n he? I'm only sayin' it 'cause I love you. If he does marry her, she won't put up with him having a leman, not like Anne done. You've done a mighty job of keepin' it secret, but that one won't give him time to lie with any other maid. I've seen how she looks at him."

I wanted to be angry with her, but how could I? She was telling the truth, at least about Bess. Bess seldom confided in me anymore. She just sat quietly working on her embroidery, a dreamy smile on her face. She worked for two months on Richard's Christmas present, a sash for his waist, embroidered with the white rose of York, the symbol of the house they shared.

I'd almost said something to him about it one night, weeks ago, but I couldn't bear to play the jealous woman, threatened by a younger, more beautiful specimen than herself. I continued to swallow my anger, and fear, and when I was with him it was easy to do. He sent Giles for me most nights, and on Christmas Eve when we were finally alone, he'd given me the most beautiful gift I'd ever received.

He'd known the pretense that I was unable to read was a constant source of irritation. So he'd commissioned Master Caxton to print me a copy of Le Mort d'Arthur, a novel about the Arthurian legend that would be a favorite of mine in my other life, five hundred years later. Not only did the coincidence make my head reel, but the book was illustrated with colorful drawings of Guinevere and the Knights of the Round Table as intricate and detailed as the examples I'd seen in the British Museum. He'd even inscribed it, "To J from D," using the first letter of his child-hood nickname in case it was discovered.

I loved him for it, but it was a risky thing to do. No woman of my status would possess such a thing unless it was a gift from someone rich. If Bess or Cecily ever found out that I had it, I would be hard-pressed to explain my secret benefactor – not to mention the fact that I could read. So I kept it wrapped in linen, under the clothes in my trunk, and the key in a locket that hung from a ribbon around my neck.

After receiving such a thoughtful, loving gift, how could I let him suspect that I was jealous of his niece without looking like an insecure, clinging fool? So every day I watched her watch him, her eyes full of adoration, and desire.

Rose interrupted my reverie. "Tom says there's talk about it every-where. Some say the reason he's tarried so about finding her a husband is a' cause he's saving her for himself. And they're both of 'em just waiting for the queen to die."

"Who says that?"

"None other than the Duke of Northumberland's squire. He says his master's right suspicious, and don't like the idea of Queen Anne being made to look the fool, and with his dead brother's own daughter, too."

I felt the blood drain from my face. Northumberland was one of the most powerful Northern lords, with thousands of men answerable to his command. His support was crucial to Richard's kingship. He and Richard were never close, but he was loyal to Richard because of Anne, who was born and bred in the North Country.

I wished there was someone else I could tell about Northumberland, someone who could share the information with him besides his jealous mistress. But the only one of Richard's friends I knew well enough to tell such a delicate thing was Brother Cynneth, and he'd gone to spend the holiday with his fellow Grey Friars in Leicester. Leicester, where my adventure began, in Richard's grave.

In that instant, I made up my mind. If he sent for me tonight, I would tell him what was being said. If he thought I was ridiculous and insecure, so be it. If his Northern allies decided to desert him, my feelings would be the least of his worries.

How I hated to be the bearer of such rotten tidings! Now, at the Christmas feast, I recalled my resolution, and when the servant held out a platter of roast swan for me to take a portion, I waved him away. My appetite was gone. The gossip about the Princes seemed to have died down, but this was potentially just as dangerous. Richard looked every inch the happy, confident king tonight, and I dreaded ruining his holiday, but I had to warn him.

After the desserts were served and eaten, I saw Anne lean in and whisper to him. He nodded, putting his hand on her arm, and they both stood up. The surprised courtiers followed protocol and stood up as well, dropping cakes out of their fingers and scrambling to set down cups of wine.

"Please finish your sweets!" said Richard. "Queen Anne is weary from our holiday revels, and would like to retire to her chamber. She has asked that we continue our celebration."

Francis Lovell gave Anne his arm and escorted her to the staircase that led to the second floor and the royal apartments. The courtiers murmured as they sat back down, and at a signal from Richard the minstrels struck up a lively number than drowned out their whispers. He took the hand of his sister, Lady Suffolk, and led her to the center of the floor for the first dance, and many of the nobles followed them. He went to Bess and took her hand for the second.

As they twirled and skipped together in the steps of a complicated quadrille that I'd never quite been able to master, they complemented each other with undeniable grace. Her golden blondeness shone with even more luster when she stood next to her dark-haired uncle, and when the steps of the dance called for him to pull her in close for a moment, she gazed up into his face with open adoration.

I was thinking how perfect and royal they both were, when my misery was interrupted by a titter from across the table. I looked away from them and for the first time, observed the people around me and their reaction to Richard and his niece instead of focusing on my own green-eyed assessment. Several of the ladies nodded together, and shared knowing smirks, and I thought I caught a wink or two amongst the men. I could read their minds. If she wanted him, wouldn't he want her? She was the most beautiful woman in the room.

I wanted to shout he loves me, not her! But they wouldn't have believed me, and as I watched them together, I almost doubted him myself.

Then, sometime in the early morning hours, Giles knocked on my door. He knew to wait until I slipped on my chemise and my cloak before I traveled across the courtyard and through the cold stone halls to the royal apartments. I wanted to see Richard, but thanks to Bess, I would have to spoil our time together with warnings, and accusations. Her dirty cloak was still flung over the chair beside my bed. I snatched it up and threw it over my shoulders.

The flicker of desire in his grey eyes disappeared like I'd doused the light of a candle.

"Are you telling me you think I'm swivving my niece, Jayne?

"No, I don't, but I'm telling you, that's what your courtiers are saying."

"And how do you know this? I had to send for Rose from Dover as a companion for you. Are you branching out into friendship with the court gossips?"

I had to go on, despite the pain behind my eyes where the tears were starting.

"Rose told me. She's..."

"Then I wish I'd never brought her here."

"Bess is in love with you, Richard. If you can't see it, you're the only one."

His black look frightened me, but just as suddenly, his expression softened and his shoulders relaxed.

"Jayne, you have nothing to fear from her, or anyone else. I promise you."

I gritted my teeth.

"This has nothing to do with jealousy."

He smiled.

"They're saying you plan to marry her, Richard. After Anne dies."

He took a step backwards and clenched his fist. I shrank back on the bed, but he turned his back on me. I could see his uneven shoulders rise and fall with every breath. The sight made me ache with tenderness for him; their disparity was more apparent every day.

"Why do you always doubt me?" he asked, without turning around. "You believed the sods who told you I'd murdered my nephews so that I could be king. Now this."

How to make him understand? A painful truth might help.

"I am jealous of her. There, I admit it. She's young, and prettier on her worst day than I am on my best. But that's between us. I'm trying to warn you because I'm scared for you. We both know the power of rumor, and you pay her a great deal of attention."

When he turned around, his eyes looked dull instead of angry.

"A great deal of the time I spend with her is because of you. I keep her at court, instead of finding her a husband and bestowing him with a manor house in Kent or Shropshire, because of you. And I'm kind to her because she's my brother's daughter, and God knows I wasn't kind enough to his sons."

I got up and went to him. I could see I'd done nothing with my conversation other than hurt his feelings at the expense of my own. My jealously was assuaged, but he still didn't see the danger he was in.

To my surprise, he put his arms around me.

"When I look at her, I see Edward," he said. "When I look at you, I see the woman I love."

I went to sleep happy despite my fears.

PART III

CHAPTER 28

RICHARD: JANUARY 5, 1485

FOOL'S DAY

*A*nne's blue eyes were glazed over with pain. I remembered the merry-eyed little girl who greeted me when I arrived at her father's castle when I was but twelve and she only nine. Although I wanted to cry, I couldn't let her see my distress, so I held her hand and forced back my tears.

"I wish I could be beside you at the revels tonight, Richard, but I cannot. This Christmas has been hard, in so many ways, and I'm tired. So tired."

"I understand. I do. And you'll be better by Easter. We'll have a grand celebration then."

She looked away from me, but she squeezed my hand. Her touch was like the flutter of a sparrow.

"I've never enjoyed Fool's Day much anyway. It's a poor excuse for poor behavior."

"But you must celebrate tonight. Your court expects it. Who have you declared the Lord of Misrule?"

"A fellow named Tom Brannon. He's a new groom, a fellow from

Dover Castle. He's not been here long enough to have too many favorites, or too many enemies."

She nodded. "Remember when we were children, and Edward came to Middleham on Fool's Day to pay us all a visit? He was only just crowned, not yet married, and still on happy terms with my father. He brought you a wolfhound pup."

"And Fergus is that hound's great-great grandson."

She smiled up at me, and for a moment she was herself again. "Do you recall Edward's guise?"

"How could I forget? Your father made a lovesick boy from the kennels the Lord of Misrule, and he ordered us all to dress as our heart's desire. Edward arrayed himself as a whore with silver-gilt hair and dugs the size of melons! He looked a great deal like his future queen, now I consider it!"

She laughed, for the first time in a week, but the laugh turned into a cough, and she held a handkerchief to her mouth, careful, lest I see the blood I knew was there.

I had to look away. I was ashamed of myself. I'd killed men in battle, more than I could count. Why was the sight of my dying wife more than I could bear?

When the spell of coughing ended, she lay back against the pillows, with her eyes closed. I was about to take my leave when she opened them and smiled again.

"I remember your costume," she said. "You were a knight, in full armor, helm to sabatons. And we all laughed at you for being so serious."

"Everyone laughed at me but you, Anne," I said.

She patted my hand. "Go be king, Richard. Your court is waiting on you."

Tom Brannon sat on my chair at the center of the high table. His red-and-yellow stockings fought with his purple-and-green tunic to win a prize for hideousness, and his paper crown sat upon his greasy head at a jaunty angle, whether from intention or sloppiness I couldn't tell. He leered at the crowd of courtiers in a parody of royal arrogance. I congratulated myself on choosing a perfect Lord of Misrule.

His first pronouncement came this morning, after prime, when he declared each guest at the Feast must wear a mask that represented his or her house. That set my court to scrambling, and the shopkeepers and milliners of Westminster to earn a month's worth of coin.

So now I sat at the end of the table, below the salt, with the face of a boar made of papier-mâché covering my own. Each of my nobles and their ladies wore their own sigils, made into some wearable masquerade. Even my Jayne had one, a lion's head complete with tawny mane. I teased her that I'd wasted my pennies when her own riotous curls would have done just as well. Tonight, the only crown in the room was on Brannon's head, and the high table was reserved for the squires and gamekeepers.

Our mock lord enjoyed the fine ale and wine from the palace buttery, and I watched him trade cup for flagon and back again until I was sure he'd not be awake to see the mummers he'd arranged for the evening's entertainment.

I'd had a generous share of the wine myself, by the time the mummers danced in, accompanied by flute and drum. I could see their talent forthwith; their music was deliberately discordant and disturbing, rather than melodious, as if their song was only just a note out of tune.

The foremost figure wore a tin crown, over a boar's head, similar to my own mask. But this boar's great tusks dripped bright red blood, which flew in gelatinous drops on the diners when he slung his head to the rhythm of the drum.

The boar was followed by a court of horrors. Lovell's dog was mad and slathering, my lawyer Catesby was a black cat with six-inch claws and Jockey Howard's white lion was old and grey. Even the friar was portrayed, wearing black instead of his usual pale cassock, with his cowl over his head and face, a grim reaper instead of a healer.

I had expected to be the brunt of the jest. The upside-down nature of the festival made the king the lowest of the low, and gave the world the right to cut japes and capers at his expense. In truth, I was relieved to see the boar to be vicious, but not disfigured. My shoulder pained me more every day. Sometimes even Jayne's gentle fingers couldn't soothe it, and I had feared its ugliness would be the focus of the entertainment.

But the figure's back was straight and his shoulders even, and he and his fellows danced a jerky dance in a circle around the musicians. The

Boar King waved his hand, and a servant brought two stools into the center of the room, one of which he sat upon. His macabre courtiers groveled on their stomachs before him, eliciting cheers and laughter from the crowd. Jockey, who sat across the hall from me, raised his glass in my direction.

The Boar King and his toadies turned to face the great doorway of the chamber, and a fifth mummer, a tiny creature no bigger than a child, walked into the mock court, struggling to support itself with a crooked walking stick, and wearing the moth-eaten head of a bear. A tiny tin crown sat on its pitiful head. The figure struggled to the second stool and sat down beside the boar.

The Bear and Ragged Staff. The symbols of Anne's father, Lord Warwick. I placed both palms on the white linen sanap that covered the table. I was prepared to be mocked, even maligned, but that they would be cruel enough to make a parody of Anne's illness never occurred to me.

Then another figure came through the doorway, this one as different from the last as it was possible to be. It wore a cloak made of cheap bright red cloth, and its head was a white rose.

As if in the perfect execution of a dance, every head in the room swiveled to look my way at the same moment. Under my mask, the sweat rolled down my cheeks and into the corners of my mouth, but I didn't move my hands from the table. As long as I could keep them still, perhaps no one would see my fury.

In contrast with the other caricatures, the figure in the red cloak moved with sinuous grace as it twirled and dipped in front of the Boar King. It swiveled its hips and arched its back, and he leaned forward to watch it with his hands on his knees, and his grunts could be heard over the sound of the lute. Then the dancer stopped and dropped to its knees in front of him. It threw off its cloak, and revealed huge dugs and a ragged mop of yellow hair.

The music stopped, and the only sounds in the Great Hall were the grunts and pants of the Boar King. He reached between his legs and fumbled at the laces of his hose, but the black-robed friar ran forward and gestured for him to wait. Then he went to the tiny queen and pulled her off of her throne.

But she fought him, and beat him with her staff until he backed away.

The Boar King leapt off of his throne and pushed her into the friar's arms. As the friar dragged the dead queen out of the room, the Boar King pulled the figure of the princess onto the throne the queen had just vacated. He pawed her bosom, and she slapped his face and snatched his crown off his head, putting it on her own, as the musicians played a crescendo. A deathly silence fell upon the chamber.

I could not vomit. I could not take Tom Brannon's filthy head and twist it from his neck, nor could I run a sword through the villain who put him up to this disgrace. So I pressed my palms into the table and stood up. When I broke the silence with my clapping, a collective sigh of relief rose from the assembled company. But I did not resume my seat, and as I left the chamber I heard benches scraping and skirts rustling as they struggled to follow. Among them was a crueler, and more creative, enemy than any man deserved.

I had always wondered why Catesby insisted on maintaining an office in the city, when I provided him with such a splendid chamber in the palace. The Lord knew that my lawyer had no time left for other clients. But as I wandered through the twisted warren of narrow streets to get to his door, I understood. I relied on him for much of my covert intelligence, and his network spread out from London all the way to the Continent. In this dark hole, his spies could come and go as they pleased, and it would be easy to spot anyone who followed. There was no reason to make this convoluted journey unless you had business with William Catesby.

I'd not heard from him in some days, not since I tasked him with finding out who put Tom Brannon up to that ghastly piece of mummery at the feast. I could summon him to my privy chamber, but I needed to get out of the palace; of late, it was more like a prison to me than ever. So, I refused my usual escort, and left Westminster plainly dressed, with only Giles by my side.

Two rogues in filthy, patched cloaks passed us in the lane, going in the other direction. The lane was so narrow that we were almost shoulder to shoulder with them as they went by. They only nodded at us. They didn't expect to see their king here.

When I knocked, he took a moment to give me leave to enter, and when I did, he rose from his desk like a jack-in-the-box, and knocked over a sheaf of documents he had stacked at his elbow.

"Your Grace! What has happened?"

"Nothing. Nothing more, that is. I hoped for news from you by now, and wanted to get out of that cesspit of a palace. Sit back down."

He gestured towards a stool in front of his desk.

"Then please sit you down as well, Your Grace. It won't do for me to sit while you remain standing."

This didn't bode well. He was always at his most obsequious when the news was bad.

He took a deep breath before beginning.

"I do have several pieces of intelligence, and I intended to report it to you this very afternoon. They confirm our suspicions regarding Stanley."

"Then that's good news!"

He shook his head.

"Tom Brannon is dead, killed in a brawl outside a tavern, by a man named Peter Mudd."

"I can't say I'll miss him. Were your people able to talk to him before he died?"

"No, but Peter Mudd is a blacksmith in the employ of none other than Sir Reginald Bray."

I was glad to be sitting down. Bray was one of Lord Stanley's most trusted retainers.

"So there's no doubt."

"But we can't accuse him. He'll just say he has no control over a broil between a groom and a blacksmith, especially one that doesn't work for him directly."

He was right.

"So were you able to discover anything else?"

He looked away from me.

"Catesby!"

"Very well, then. I was able to find out the genesis of the thing from more than one source. Besides the fact that you and your niece are much together, and her fondness for you quite apparent, it seems she was seen crossing the courtyard of the palace after midnight on Christmas, and was followed to your chambers."

I gaped at him.

"That never happened."

"They recognized the red cloak Anne gave her."

I pressed my cold fingers into my burning eyeballs.

"It wasn't her. It was Jayne."

"Why would she be wearing Bess' cloak?"

I got up, and tried to pace, but the room was so crowded with teetering stacks of law books, and piles of rolled parchments, that I soon sat down again.

"She was distressed that night, and tried to tell me that Bess was making a fool of herself, and me, with her behavior. I put it down to jealousy. And I did notice the cloak. I assumed it was a mistake. She was most unhappy."

"I won't remind you of my repeated warnings, Your Grace."

"Thank you for that, Catesby. Now please tell me you've no other wretchedness to impart."

I'd never seen him look so miserable.

"One more, by far the worst."

My throat, and chest, were already tight, but I sat up straighter on the stool.

"Go ahead."

"Two men just left here. They're just recently returned from France. It seems news of your disgrace has reached Henry Tudor, and he is overjoyed."

I snorted. "That's no surprise. I'm sure his dear mother sent him a message about the mummery while she was planning it."

"Yes, but he's made his way from Brittany to Paris, and is now the guest of King Louis, who has promised him ships, and money to hire mercenaries. The rumors have put you in a vulnerable position, and he believes that once he's on English soil, he can persuade at least some of the key nobles to rally to his side. My informants said that he is planning to invade England this summer."

I struggled to control my breathing.

"So it's back to that after all."

212 | ANNE-MARIE LACY

He sighed. I didn't envy him his position just now.

"I'm most sorry to convey such dreadful news, Your Grace," he said.

I was too shocked, and too dispirited, to do more than nod.

I took my leave of him soon after, and stood outside in the muddy street with my back against his door.

"Oh, Jayne, what have you done to me?"

I must have spoken aloud, because Giles looked at me with eyebrows raised. I didn't bother to explain.

In less than eight weeks, Anne was dead. The day her soul departed this world, the sky went black at noon, and the sun stayed hidden until the next morn. The Londoners said it was a sure sign from God that I was being punished for my sins, murder and incest being foremost among them. After the mummers did their dirty work, what had been a vile rumor became accepted as fact, and the news spread as fast as a good messenger can travel. Anne lay in state in the Abbey for three days, her small coffin a hideous reminder of the tiny actor who portrayed her on Fool's Day. Only hours after her funeral service, Lord Bolton of Scrope, one of the most powerful of her father's Northern lords, begged an audience.

"Your Grace," he said, and swept his hat from his head. He bowed low, but when he stood up his blue eyes were chilly.

"My most sincere condolences on the death of your sainted queen. May the good Lord rest her sweet soul."

"Thank you, Lord Bolton. We were close since our childhoods. She will be irreplaceable to me."

He cleared his throat. "I regret that I must speak to you on such an unpleasant topic at this time of your grief, but I feel I must, if only to forewarn you."

"Go ahead, sir. I am always willing to listen to one who has my welfare in mind."

Now that he had my permission, he seemed reluctant to begin. He looked about, as if he thought to find someone else in the room to say his piece for him. Just as the silence was becoming awkward, he found his voice.

"Incredible tales have made their way North, Your Grace. I have known you all your life, and believe you to be an honorable man. So I do not speak for myself in this, however, you must know that many of my neighbors, in Yorkshire and beyond, are very distressed."

I wondered how long it would take him to get to the story that disgusted us both.

"It is said abroad that you deceived Anne of Warwick, as she lay dying, with your niece, Elizabeth Grey, and that you plan to dishonor her memory by marrying the girl, and making her Queen of England."

"Lord Bolton, I assure you on my soul, that neither of those statements have any remnant of truth."

He stared at me for so long that I knew that despite his protestations of loyalty, he believed the tales himself.

"Why tell me this, if you do not accept my response?"

"I do, I do. But there are some who say that you are far from grief-stricken at the queen's passing, and that you may have even done something to hasten her demise."

I stood up from behind my desk, and he took a step backwards.

"Your Grace, it is my suggestion that you do not let this...situation... continue unchecked. You have more of your subjects that just me to convince. And with the rumors that the Tudor plans to invade this summer..."

As soon as he left, I called for John Howard and the rest of my councilors. I had an army to raise.

CHAPTER 29

JAYNE: JUNE 20, 1485

*T*he journey from Westminster to Sheriff Hutton Castle took our small party almost two weeks. Bess, Cecily, Johnnie, and I planned to make the small castle our home until after the invasion; Richard sent Brother Cynneth with us, but he would remain only until we were safely and comfortably lodged. The castle, which lay ten miles north of the city of York, belonged to Richard, and he thought it would be the safest place for the three of us.

Henry Tudor's fleet was rigging at Harfleur, on the coast of Burgundy, preparing to invade England before the end of the summer, so Richard and his household were headed to Nottingham, a central location from which he could rally his troops and plan his battle strategy.

Even now, three months later, I kept seeing the dull look in his eye, and the grim line of his lips, when he shared what Catesby had discovered. In one foolish instant, by an act driven by jealousy and pique, I had gone from Richard's savior to his betrayer.

It was so much worse than if he'd shouted at me, as I deserved. Instead, he sat on the edge of his bed with his head in his hands.

"Jayne, if you had but trusted me..." he said.

Ramifications of my childishness continued to beset him; support for Henry Tudor, which had practically ceased after Elizabeth and her daughters left sanctuary, had heightened again, to the point that his challenge to Richard's throne seemed inevitable.

I hadn't changed history after all.

The night before I left for Sheriff Hutton, Richard held me in his arms while I cried until my eyes were swollen shut, and his chest and shoulder were damp from my tears.

I tried to convince him one more time.

"Richard, please let me go with you to Nottingham. I'm so afraid for you..."

He pushed himself up in the pillows and took my chin in his fingers.

"Jayne, mayhap I was dismayed when I first heard of the Tudor's intentions, but don't you see, he's giving me a great boon? Once I've beaten my rival in battle, the whispers and rumors about my right to rule England will finally cease. I'll miss you, sweeting, but you'll be safe in Yorkshire, and it will only be a few months before we'll be back in each other's arms. Would you like to spend a fortnight at Middleham, after the battle? It lies only a day's ride north of Sheriff Hutton. We will go there before we return to London. I crave to show you my home, my real home, in the autumn, when the heather blooms..."

His grey eyes were bright, and full of confidence; he was far surer of himself as a soldier than as a king. But unless something changed, his enemy would land in Wales in August, and by the end of that month, Richard would die at Bosworth Field, and leave a legacy tainted by accusations of murder.

So all I could do was cry, and cling to his lean, hard body until finally he gently pushed me away so that he could sleep.

Our group left Westminster the next morning. Richard hugged Johnnie and Bess, and patted Cecily on the shoulder. He clasped Brother Cynneth's hand, but he could only nod at me. I had never felt the misery of our situation so desperately. He managed to look into my eyes for just a moment, and I had to be satisfied with that.

We traveled from Westminster through the crowded streets of London, under the wide stone arch of Bishopsgate, to the Great North Road. We were a mixed bag of moods and emotions. Bess was furious at being sent away to the country, despite Richard's assurances that Sheriff Hutton would pleasantly surprise her. He'd treated her with stiff formality since Fool's Day, and although she still hadn't taken me into her confidence, her dismal face told me all I needed to know.

Richard sent Sir John Milewater with eight of his household guard to accompany us, and he and his men were cheerful to the point of rowdiness.

"Here's to the Tudor!" Sir John raised his cup at dinner on the night we spent at a roadside inn near Olney. "May his ship land safely on our shores, that we might have the pleasure of killin' him!"

This brought cheers from our escort, and even the friar raised his cup, but later he sought me out.

"Jayne, are you just lonesome for the king, or is there aught else on your mind?"

"I'm just worried about him, friar."

"He's a fine general, and a clever swordsman, and he's won many a battle. He fought his first when he was only eighteen."

But would he survive this one to see his thirty-first birthday?

I looked into Brother Cynneth's kind face and almost told him the truth about myself, and what I knew about Richard's future. But why would he believe me? Sometimes I barely believed it myself. My former life felt long ago now, and my recollections of a Richard III who was nothing more than an ancestor with a bloody reputation felt like memories that belonged to some other person. The paradox allowed me to cling to the slim hope that somehow it would turn out differently this time.

As we made our way north, the terrain grew wilder and steeper, and the populated areas less frequent. The village of Sheriff Hutton was little more than two intersecting lanes, and the few villagers who had business there on the day we passed waved at us and doffed their caps. We traveled without fanfare, and they had no idea they were welcoming the former princess and her lady-in-waiting. After the cloying attention we received at Westminster, it was refreshing to be anonymous again.

The June morning was sunny, but cool, after the swelter of London, and it was not until we reached the castle that I pushed back the hood of my light wool cloak. Richard had let me take Juno with us, and she was restless today, as if she knew we were nearing the end of our journey. She'd danced around all morning, and when the castle came into view I thought she would pull the reins from my hands, but I held her back so that I could get a look at my summer home.

The whitewashed stone walls of Sheriff Hutton gleamed in the sunlight like they were made of pearl. It was a jewel of a castle, built in a perfect square with a tower at each corner, like an illustration from a fairy tale.

Johnnie pulled his little cob up beside Juno.

"We'll be happy here this summer, Jayne," he said, and reached out to take my hand. "I wanted to go with Father, but as he wouldn't let me, I can think of no one I'd rather be with than you."

My heart lightened, in spite of my worries.

"Thank you, Johnnie. Likewise."

We trotted under the arch at the Warden's Tower, which was decorated with the bright heraldic shields emblazoned with the white boar. We crossed over a drawbridge that spanned a narrow moat, and under another, lower archway into the inner bailey. The four towers were taller than they'd looked from a distance, at least four or five stories high, but the effect was still one of symmetry, and neatness. Sheriff Hutton came as close as a stone castle could to looking cozy.

Bess had ridden up beside me as we passed under the inner gateway.

'This might not be so bad, Bess. Let's ask the warden to show us the gardens," I said.

She didn't answer, so I turned away from my perusal of the courtyard to look at her face. She was staring, mouth open, at something over my shoulder. Before I could ask her what was wrong, Johnnie jumped down from his cob and ran across the courtyard to where another little boy, dressed in the clothes of a groom, stood in the walkway.

"Dickon!" he shouted.

The children grabbed each other and cavorted together, laughing and squealing.

I looked back at Bess. Her mouth was shut, but her face was as white as the castle walls.

"Who is that?"

"My younger brother," she said.

Richard of York, younger of the missing Princes, flew across the bailey yard to his sisters. Blond and blue-eyed, he was almost as pretty as Bess.

Cecily was already down from her horse and had him in her arms before Bess dismounted.

"Oh, Dickon, praise the Saints! Where's Edward?"

She looked over his shoulder.

"He was killed, Cecily. He died trying to protect me. We were attacked on our way here." He sobbed, and hugged her closer.

"But...why did you come here?"

"Uncle Richard sent us to stay here. He said we weren't safe in London."

One of Sir John's men had helped Bess from her horse, but she still stood leaning against its side as if she was afraid she might fall down. Dickon jumped out of Cecily's embrace and ran to wrap his arms around her waist.

She bent down to hold him, buried her face in his bright curls, and squeezed her eyes shut. Tears were streaming from their corners.

I walked to where the friar stood watching the York family.

"You knew all along, didn't you?"

"Yes. I believe I was the first to know of His Grace's decision to send the boys into hiding, after he discovered Buckingham planned to kill them. It was I who recommended this quiet place. And when did he tell you, my dear?"

"What? How did you know he told me at all?"

He grinned. "I've come to understand you, Jayne. For a long while, there was a shadow of doubt in your eyes when you looked at him, but the cloud lifted sometime this spring."

"Yes, when little Ned died, the day I found him in St. John's Wood, he told me he'd sent them away, and what happened to poor Edward. But he didn't tell me Dickon was here."

"He wanted to surprise you all."

"And he knew you wouldn't spoil it on the way. But I'm surprised Sir John didn't say something accidentally, especially as drunk as he was in Olney."

"He's far more canny than he seems, Jayne, and besides, his mind is on the upcoming battle."

THE MEDIEVALIST | 219

Johnnie came up and pulled the friar's arm.

"May I share Dickon's chamber with him, Brother Cynneth? We've much to say to one another!"

"I don't know what apartments the warden had planned for us, but the chambers won't be so numerous as they were at Westminster. I can't think why it should pose a problem."

Johnnie looked happier than he had since he was forced to leave his father's side. It was easy to forget he was only twelve.

When the warden led us up a wide stone staircase to our apartments, Cecily walked beside me.

"Mother knew," she said.

"What? When?" I couldn't believe Elizabeth's grief and fury over the fate of her sons had been feigned.

"Dickon said Uncle Richard let him write her a letter, to prove to her that he was alive, and unhurt. That's why she left sanctuary. That's why she decided to trust him."

Of course! The second document Elizabeth received, after Richard came to visit us in the abbot's house, must have been the letter from her only surviving son. Now I understood her bizarre behavior. She was dealing with the unexpected survival of one child, and the confirmation of the death of another.

As we reached the landing, Cecily sighed and shook her head. "Poor Uncle Richard. I hated him all this time, and he didn't deserve it."

"You, and more people than you could ever imagine," I said.

CHAPTER 30

JAYNE: JULY 26, 1485

SHERIFF HUTTON CASTLE

*J*ohnnie and Dickon carried the picnic basket between them. Rose had loaded it so full of ale, meat pasties, custards, and other treats that neither could manage it alone. Two stout servants had already positioned an archery butt on a flat spot in the meadow, and I carried a heavy woolen blanket for the York girls and me to sit on while we watched the boys shoot their arrows.

"We're going to roast like geese out here," complained Cecily, as she shaded her eyes with one hand, and held her linen skirts up with the other.

"I believe it was you who suggested we come out here with them," replied Bess.

"What else have we to do? I've sat on a bench in that garden until I'm sick of the sight of roses."

I spread the blanket out on a small rise above the makeshift archery range. The heather wasn't blooming yet, but the buds were set, and it reminded me of my last conversation with Richard. I'd thought of little else in the last few weeks, and after the friar left to join Richard at Nottingham, I had no one to talk to about him. Bess rarely mentioned him, but I knew she was upset that he hadn't written to her. On two occasions, a messenger brought letters to us all from Brother Cynneth, who'd passed on well-wishes from the king, but there'd been nothing directly from him, not to Bess, or to me.

I understood why he couldn't write to me. I still masqueraded as illiterate, and, what excuse could there be for the king writing to a lady's maid? But, like Bess, each time the messenger trotted into the courtyard, some foolish part of me hoped for a letter.

Rose came with us from London. Her pride when Tom was chosen as the Lord of Misrule changed to mortification after what he'd done to Richard and Bess, and she fought with him over it the afternoon before his murder. She grieved for him all the more because of how they parted. I worried about her; the lack of good-sized chambers in the small castle forced me to share a room with Bess and Cecily, and Rose was quartered with the servants, in one of the wooden buildings that lined the courtyard. She declined to join our picnic today, and I missed her company, but each week she appeared a little more cheerful, and I hoped soon she would be her jovial old self again.

The boys left the basket on the ground beside our blanket and ran down the hill to shoot their bows. I sat down on one corner, spread out my skirts, and held up my braid so that I could fan the back of my neck. It couldn't have been more than seventy degrees, but my body had grown used to the medieval cold.

Dickon shot first. His arrow landed in the first ring outside the bull's eye. He cheered, and Johnnie slapped him on the back before he took his turn. He hit the bull's eye dead on. His father had taught him well.

Dickon cheered as if the victory was his own, and Johnnie nocked another arrow. After a few more rounds, Dickon hit a bull's eye and they both yelled, "Huzzah!"

"Give us a cup of ale, Jayne," said Cecily.

I rose to my knees and dug into the basket for the cask and cups.

"Someone's approaching," said Bess. She stood up and pointed towards the road behind us, where three riders rode towards the castle at a steady canter. They were still too far away for us to see their livery, and they didn't carry a banner. But as they got closer, I saw grey robes flapping against one horse's side.

"It's Brother Cynneth!" I said. I stopped fishing in the basket, and stood up to wave.

He motioned to his escort to go on, and trotted up to us. He climbed down from his horse, and we all three ran to hug him.

"What a welcome!" He laughed. He dropped the reins and the horse stood like a statue where he left it; I'd never seen any equine disobey him. He took off his gloves and wiped his hand across his sweaty brow and back across his tonsure.

"Have some ale, Friar," said Bess.

He accepted a cup and downed it in one swallow.

"Whew! I can't remember so hot a summer," he said, and turned to watch the boys down in the vale, where they hadn't yet noticed his arrival.

"They're good company for one another, aren't they," I said.

"Yes, poor Dickon must have been quite lonely after Edward was killed," he replied, and we were all quiet for a moment.

"What news of our uncle?" asked Bess, at last.

Brother Cynneth tucked his robes around his legs and sat down beside us.

"He's just allowed Lord Norfolk to return south to Kent, to gather men and arms, and Lord Stanley is there with him, still pledging his full support."

"And did he send any message for...for any of us?" said Bess.

The friar reached into a leather pouch he had suspended from his belt.

"As a matter of fact, yes, he did."

He pulled out a slim roll of parchment and held it out to her.

Her face lit up. I'd grown used to her beauty, but happiness made her dazzling. I forgave myself my jealousy that he'd written to her, and not me.

"This is for you and Cecily," he said.

The smile left her face as quickly as it had appeared, and she took the letter and passed it to her sister.

"Why don't you read it to us, Cecily? Jayne might want to hear it too."

"'My dear nieces,'" Cecily read, "'I hope this missive finds you well, and that Sheriff Hutton is proving as comfortable as I hoped it would. My preparations are going exceedingly well. I do not yet know when, or where, Henry Tudor will land, but I have no doubt that he will do so before the summer is over. I welcome the chance to put an end to his threats once and for all, and as soon as I have dealt with him, I will make arrangements for your return to Westminster.

"'In the meantime, while mustering troops, I have had cause to speak with many loyal noblemen, and you will be glad to know that in the course of doing so, I have arranged excellent matches for you both.

"'Cecily is to marry Ralph, the heir of Lord Scrope of Bolton, and Bess, you will wed the Duke of Viseu, who is a close cousin of King Juan of Portugal. I hope you are both pleased; I will be proud to provide generous nuptials for each of you, or you may be married together if you so choose.

"'I also hope you were delighted to see your dear little brother. Please greet him for me, and tell him that together we will make plans for his future also. Loving regards, Uncle Richard.'"

All the blood left Bess' face, but her expression never changed. I could see her bosom rising and falling under the laces of her bodice.

"Well, sister," said Cecily. "You said he would find us husbands. You are to be Duchess of Visue, and I, Lady Scrope. Quite fine matches for a pair of bastards. I can't imagine how he did it."

"Nor I," said Bess.

"Oh, tales of your beauty have reached far and wide, my dears," said the Friar.

"Uncle Richard's gold is prettier, I'll wager," said Cecily.

Bess continued to stare straight ahead, and I wondered at her composure. I wanted to cry myself, and Richard hadn't just paid a vast sum of money to marry me off to someone else. Even if he'd dictated it to a scribe, he would have signed it himself, and I longed to run my fingers across the part of the document that his hands had touched. But, he hadn't even sent me a greeting

The boys spied the friar and ran up to see him, and Cecily put the letter in the pocket of her gown. Richard had written a short note to Johnnie as well, and he read it aloud to us, but again, he failed to mention me.

I tried to hide my disappointment, but I wasn't far from tears by the time we all headed back down the hill to the castle. I intentionally fell behind, to try to get hold of myself before anyone saw my brimming eyes. Brother Cynneth turned back and saw me, and waited for me to catch up to him.

"Jayne, have you confessed your sins to Father Robert a single time since you've been here?" he asked.

It was a strange question, but a valid one, since I had managed to avoid the castle cleric as much as possible.

"No, I don't guess I have," I said.

"Well you must confess to me, this very day, after vespers."

I found the idea of confession ridiculous, like so many of the medieval religious observances of which I was forced to partake, but now I was grateful for the custom. The confessional was the one place we were sure to be alone, and uninterrupted.

The afternoon wore on, with me counting the minutes until evening mass. We gathered in the small castle chapel just before sunset, and although I usually just went through the motions of prayer, tonight I begged anyone who was listening to give me guidance.

As soon as we rose to our feet, and the rest of the occupants filed out into the summer night, the friar went to take up his position behind the lattice screen of the confessional, and I sat down on the narrow seat and shut the door behind me.

"Bless me, Father, for I have sinned," I began, in case someone had lingered behind.

"Jayne, you are indeed a sinner, but I've given up seeking a confession from you," said Brother Cynneth. "However, I do have a message from the King's Grace."

I looked through the lattice; I could just make out his smile.

"What? Tell me!"

"He was concerned that you would be downcast when you heard Bess was to be married, and that you might fear that he would send you with her to her new home. He wanted me to assure you that after the battle you would return to his side, and remain there, as long as ever you wish it," he said.

This time I didn't try to stop the tears.

"I need to be with him right now, Friar! I'm so afraid I'll never see him again!"

He crossed himself. "Shush, child, don't even say such!"

"No, Brother Cynneth, you have to listen to me. We have to help him. You're going to have to believe me..."

"Calm yourself first. I'm sure I will believe you. I know you love him, as I do." He handed me a handkerchief through the slats of the confessional.

I took the folded linen and wiped my eyes and nose with it.

"When we met, you tried to get me to tell you where I found the silver boar, remember?"

"Yes!" he said. I could feel him leaning forward in the darkness.

"I found it in his grave!"

"I knew it...I knew it..." he murmured.

That was the last thing I expected to hear.

"How? Is that why you quit asking me about it?"

He opened the lattice door that separated us and I could see he was pale and sweating.

"How did you know where I found it?"

"Because I put it there," he said.

CHAPTER 31

JAYNE: JULY 26, 1485

"*I* was afraid to tell you. I thought you would accuse me of witchcraft, or treason, or both," I said.

"I can see you're no witch, but I admit I might have thought your mind was unhinged. That is, if I hadn't had the vision already myself. I have had seeings of the future, for good or ill, all of my life. Some have come to pass, others have served as warnings, and still others are mere impressions about the persons involved. But this vision disturbed me like no other I have had before or since. I was alone at my prayers in the chapel at Middleham, before Edward's death. We had consecrated the silver boar there, Richard and I, fifteen years earlier when he first adopted it as his sigil, the same day he adopted the motto "Loyalty Binds Me." I was looking at the stained glass images in the windows, and suddenly it was as if they disappeared, and were replaced with a scene of hideous carnage.

"I saw him dead, and thrown naked into an empty hole without a coffin or a shroud, or even the meanest ceremony or blessing other than my own. I stood there..."

He paused and took a ragged breath. He reached his hand out to me and I handed him back his handkerchief, and he rubbed his face with it before he continued.

"I stood there by his pauper's grave and looked down at his body. It was broken and twisted, and covered in bloody wounds that no one had troubled to cleanse. His hands were bound behind his back, like those of the lowest felon, and the back of his head was crushed..."

"Stop! Stop! I can't bear to hear it!" I cried.

I knew what happened to Richard at Bosworth was brutal, but now that I had touched and held him, now that I loved him, I couldn't stand to listen to such horrible details.

"I saw myself drop the silver boar into that pitiful hole where it landed beside him," said the friar. "Then the vision ended. So I don't know when it will happen, but I fear that it will."

The capon and peas we'd had at dinner earlier that evening threatened to reappear if I didn't get hold of myself. At least some parts of the mystery were clearer to me now. Brother Cynneth would have access to the chapel in Leicester and to Richard's grave because of his ecclesiastical association with the order of Grey Friars – the same order that took Richard's body for burial in after the Battle of Bosworth Field. So it was Cynneth who had put the boar there for me to find, over five hundred years later.

"That night in the camp when I saw the badge in James Talbott's hand," he continued, "and he said that you had stolen it, I knew that could not be true, for I'd seen it with my own eyes hanging round the king's neck when we knelt at our prayers the night before. But yet you had it in your possession, so I knew you were no ordinary wench."

I had been about to tell him all; that I had been born five hundred years after Richard's death, and found the boar at an archeological search for his lost grave. But his revelation about his psychic premonitions showed me an easier way that just might work.

"I too have the seeing, and I had a vision of his pauper's grave, but it must have been many years after his death, because the boar lay beside his bones."

"Oh, no, then it must come true, if we've both seen it," he murmured, and I knew he believed me, at least so far.

"I saw my own hand reach down into the dust to pick it up, and when the vision passed, I found I was holding it."

He gasped. "That cannot be!"

"But it happened. You said it first: there's no way I could have taken it from around his neck."

"But..."

I interrupted him. I couldn't explain boar's magic, when I didn't understand it myself. And right now it didn't matter.

"Friar, listen to me. I don't know how or why the boar ended up in my possession, but I have had other visions, visions that may help us save him if you will only believe me. If we do nothing, Richard will die in battle this summer. Lord Stanley will betray him, and send his troops onto the battlefield at the last minute, on Henry Tudor's side. And his legacy will be tainted forever by the rumor that he murdered his nephews. We have to find some way to stop him from fighting!"

"But how, Jayne? The Tudor is planning to invade; Richard has no choice but to defend his throne..."

"Why not? He doesn't really want to be king anyway." I envisioned some peaceful abdication, where Richard agreed to exile himself somewhere on the continent and me with him.

But Brother Cynneth shook his head. "You know him better than that. He would rather die than run from a fight."

My heart sank. He was right, of course.

"Well, you have to go back to him, tomorrow, and convince him to fight another time. Or send his navy to kill Tudor before he lands. Something. You have to help him!"

He bit his lip. "You know I will do whatever I can. I've loved him most of my life."

We walked back across the courtyard from the chapel together, and it occurred to me I'd forgotten to ask him one more question.

"Friar, why is the silver boar so special to Richard?"

"Ah. That is a long tale."

"Please tell me."

"Richard's father gave him the piece of silver as a gift, just before he was killed in battle on Christmas Eve. Richard was but eight, and for his own safety, his mother sent him, with only his ten-year-old brother George at his side, into exile in Burgundy. Storms beset them all through the voyage, and he was greensick and frightened, but he held on to the bit of silver for comfort. After he survived his exile to return to England,

and was sent to Middleham to study as a page, he took it with him. He was convinced that it was a talisman and that it had protected him in his father's place. He showed me the blank silver when we were boys, and years later when he was knighted, and needed a symbol for his household, he commission the finest silversmith in England to melt it down and form it into the shape of a boar. We consecrated it together in the chapel at Middleham. I had just taken my vows."

"But why a boar?"

"Because the boar is the fiercest of all creatures in the animal kingdom when defending its own," he said. "He held it over his heart and pledged always to care for those God saw fit to place under his protection."

The friar's story made my heart swell with love for Richard, and I felt better than I had since we heard the news that Henry Tudor was again planning to invade. Maybe there was still a chance for him to survive. Despite my confirmed agnosticism, I said a little prayer of thanks.

Brother Cynneth left the next morning before Matins, much to the surprise of every one but me. The hot summer days went on as before. The boys practiced with their swords and bows, and the girls and I watched them, or sat around in the garden listening to Cecily read aloud from one of the romances she'd brought with her from Westminster.

I looked every day for some word from the friar, but no messengers came to relieve my tension. On the first day of August, we celebrated Lammastide with the first fresh bread of the harvest, and afterwards, Sir Bartholomew Braden, the constable of the castle, gave us the best news we'd had in weeks.

"Ladies," he said, bowing towards Bess. "My daughters are leaving tomorrow to visit their maternal aunt, who is wife to the Lord Mayor of York. They will be gone some three weeks or more, and it occurred to me that during that time one of you might wish to lodge in their chamber. I know you have been quite cramped here after the luxury of Westminster Palace."

Bess lost no time in answering.

"Jayne, I think you will be glad to have your own chamber again, won't you?"

"Yes! But I would like to ask Rose to join me if I may."

230 | ANNE-MARIE LACY

She shrugged. "You may suit yourself."

Rose's face lit up when I told her we could share a room again, and I looked forward to the comfort of her cheerful presence. Her spirits had continued to improve, but I was glad we would have time to ourselves in case she needed to talk about Tom. And I could confess my worries about Richard's safety to her without fear of anyone overhearing us.

The Ladies Eleanor and Ursula Braden left Sheriff Hutton for York two days later, and as soon as they were out of the postern gate and headed south, Rose and I ran up to the chamber she currently shared with one of the kitchen maids and grabbed her small bundle of belongings.

As we crossed the courtyard back towards the main part of the castle, Bess and Cecily, and the boys, were still hanging about, deciding what to do with another long summer day.

"Can we help you two?" asked Cecily.

I shook my head and looked around for a servant. One of the grooms was just returning from accompanying Eleanor and Ursula to the outer gate, and I motioned him over.

"I'm sent to saddle a mount for Sir Bartholomew to take hunting, my lady," he said. "I'll be done in two shakes of a lamb's tail and I'll help you."

"We only need help with the one trunk," I said.

"We can move it for you," said Johnnie.

"Sure we can," said Dickon, and curled his biceps.

We all laughed, and trooped up the stairs to the tiny room we three had been sharing.

There was no wardrobe, only a few pegs along the walls to hang our gowns, so most of my things, including my heavy winter gowns and cloaks, were in the trunk, which was so full it no longer latched. The room was an obstacle course, what with the big bed, the gowns and chemises that were easily knocked off their pegs, and the sharp corners of our trunks, including two that belonged to Bess. I would be glad to be out of there.

I gathered my green linen dress and a dirty chemise from where I'd hung it last night. Bess and Cecily stood ready to rearrange their own things; I could see they were as anxious as I was to have the extra room.

"Here, pick up that end, said Dickon.

He'd already taken one of the rope handles and lifted the side of the trunk a few inches off the floor.

"All right," said Johnnie, moving past me to take up the other side.

"What in the name of heaven have you got in there, Mistress Lyons? Gold? Jewels?"

I laughed. "Not hardly."

I went to the door to hold it open for them, just as the handle Dickon was holding ripped out from where it was attached to the trunk. It fell on its corner, the top flew open and my gowns spilled out onto the floor. Johnnie reacted quickly, and twisted the side he still held in the opposite direction. But that only made matters worse.

The heaviest object the trunk contained came flying out. It was my copy of Le Morte d'Arthur that Richard gave me for Christmas.

I lunged for it but Bess was quicker.

"What are you doing with this? You can't read it. Is it yours, Cecily?"

I thought up a good lie. The elaborate, colorful illustrations would be my excuse. But I didn't get a chance to use it.

"Of course she can read," said Johnnie.

Bess gasped. I stepped forward to try to snatch the book away from her but she turned her back to me and opened it.

"To J from D, on the occasion of Christmas, 1485," she read.

She whirled around. Her face was red and twisted.

"Dickon! Richard, rather! It's been you all along!"

The boys were looking from one of us to the other, open-mouthed.

"Johnnie, take Dickon and go practice your archery, or go riding."

"But why…"

"Go!" I said.

Rose took each boy by an elbow and hustled them out the door.

"I knew it," said Bess. "It was you in my cloak, you that caused that horrible pageant, you that went to his chamber! You betrayed me!"

Cecily was shaking her head at me, but her face was sad rather than angry. Rose hovered at my shoulder, as if to protect me from Bess' venom. But I felt sure she wouldn't hurt me, except with words, at least some of which I deserved.

"It was never the same afterwards, with all the court watching us. He couldn't dance with me, or walk in the garden. He was too afraid of what people would say. And it was all because of you."

She glared at me, her beautiful face ugly for once.

"Everything I planned for, worked for, you ruined. I could have been queen..."

I wanted to slap her.

"Is that all you care about? Do you understand that those rumors harmed him far more than they did you? I do feel terrible about what happened, but because of what it's done to him, not to you."

She stepped back as if I'd done what I wanted to do.

"He loves me, Jayne."

"He loves you because you're his niece."

"No, Jayne. I've known him all my life, I believe I've been in love with him since I was little more than a babe, and the way he looks at me has changed over the years. He sees me as a woman, not just his brother's child."

"You're too closely related, you know that, and besides..."

"Besides, I'm a bastard? A king can do what he wants. My father married my mother for love; she was a commoner, and a widow with two sons. He can marry me, and I still believe that he will."

I wanted to say that her father was a popular king, who'd won his throne in battle, not one whom many thought to be a usurper, with his reputation already tarnished by rumors of treachery and murder. But I couldn't make myself say those words about Richard, even to her.

"The Church won't let him, Bess. You're too closely related."

"He can write to the Pope, and get a dispensation. He can ask the Holy Father to legitimize me, too. That's been done before as well."

"Bess, if you're legitimate, so is Dickon, and he would be the rightful King of England, not Richard."

"Get out of this room," she hissed.

I bent down to pick up my things.

"Now!"

"I'll get your gowns for you," said Rose. She glared at Bess.

"Give me my book," I demanded. She threw it towards the door, and it landed in the hallway, unharmed. I ran to pick it up, then crossed the landing to the room Rose and I would share.

The only other person who'd ever looked at me with such hatred was Sir James Talbott, Stanley's henchman and my would-be murderer. But this was far worse. I had once counted Bess as my friend.

I lay down on the bed to wait for Rose.

CHAPTER 32

RICHARD: AUGUST 5, 1485

NOTTINGHAM CASTLE

I thanked God for the breeze that blew across the battlements, since my position there would have been almost intolerable otherwise. As it was, the stagnant air of the inner bailey made it even hotter down below, and gave me an excuse for my constant pacing of the wall walk. Through the summer haze I could see the wide swath of green that was Sherwood Forest off to the east, but it was the western and eastern approaches that I watched closely. From there, some day soon, a messenger would come to tell me where the Tudor had landed.

I'd already had word that his ships had sailed from Harfleur on Lammas Day, so when I saw a small group of riders approaching from the north, I was surprised, and not a little disappointed. The bell would ring for dinner soon, and I would have to go into the Great Hall, and leave my pacing and watching for another day. But I stayed on the battlements long enough to recognize the bulky form of Brother Cynneth as he rode into the inner bailey and handed his reins to a groom.

I'd hated to see him leave for Sheriff Hutton. Few of my closest confidants remained at my side. Jockey was on his southern estates, recruiting men and assembling arms, as was John Milewater. After the friar left, I had only Francis Lovell as a bulwark between Stanley, and his son, Lord Strange, who'd accompanied us from Westminster, and me.

But although I'd missed Brother Cynneth's company, his return after a mere ten days could only bode some unpleasantness. Could Jayne be ill, or injured? I pictured Juno returning to the stable from the Vale of York, saddle empty. I rushed to the bastion and down the curving stone staircase to where he'd dismounted.

"Friar! Welcome back!"

I took his arm and walked him away from the grooms and pages who were scuttling about the busy courtyard.

"What brings you back so soon? Is aught amiss at Sheriff Hutton?" I said, as soon as we were clear of them.

"All is well there. You may calm yourself," he said.

I relaxed; I didn't realize I'd been holding my breath.

"Why didn't you stay longer? I thought you planned to be gone a fortnight or more."

"Oh, that will take a good deal of explaining, and more privacy than can be had in a castle courtyard. Isn't it almost time for dinner?"

I laughed. "Yes, and I sent an arrow through a roe buck just this morning in the forest, it's been roasting half the day."

"Give me leave to wash my face and change my robe, if I may, and we must closet ourselves alone after our meal."

"You've made me curious, friend. You give me your word that Jayne is thriving? She's not with child, is she?"

I couldn't wait until after dinner for such news.

But he shook his head.

"No, no. Richard, what I have to tell you is a strange tale, and not a happy one."

"Bones of the Saints! It seems I'll have no good news until I'm told the Tudor has landed!"

The look on his face startled me.

"What do you know? Tell me now, Cynneth."

"Do let's wait. I am tired from my journey, and need to rest a bit."

"Oh, all right," I said. But I was curious almost beyond tolerance.

I tried to enjoy my dinner, and the minstrel the Castellan had so thoughtfully provided for my entertainment, but I couldn't forget about

Cynneth's cryptic tone, and dismal countenance. He sat below the salt, as always, but I saw him wave away several courses. He was indeed distressed.

As soon as I could without rudeness retire to my apartments, I headed for the stairs and to my privy chamber. I knew he would follow me.

I poured a cup of wine from the vessel on my desk and sat down to drink it. With Lord Stanley seated on my right during dinner, I'd needed to keep my wits clear. Now I had a feeling of great foreboding about the news Brother Cynneth brought back with him from Sheriff Hutton, and I downed the first cup in two swallows.

He didn't make me wait. The servant ushered him in before I could pour another.

"Out with it," I said.

He sat down on one of the stools in front of me.

"Your Grace, I will start not at the beginning, but at the conclusion of the tale. You must find a way to delay, or avoid, the battle with the Tudor."

"What? You must have ridden like a demon to get back here this speedily, and just to repeat Jayne's cautions? You surprise me."

"I wish that's all it was. Richard, she has the vision, as I do, and we've both seen disaster."

He stood up and went to lean against the window.

"I wasn't sure before. It was just before Edward's death, and...I thought...I hoped...perhaps there was some mistake. I suppose I didn't want to believe it. But now that I know Jayne saw it too..."

My head suddenly ached, and I poured another cup of wine.

"May I?" he asked. I nodded and passed him a cup.

"Richard, I've warned you before, and you were later glad you paid me heed," he said.

It was true. The first time was when we were boys at Middleham, and he'd warned me not to go into the village, to the market fair, with the other pages. I'd hated to indulge him; there had been peddlers there hawking everything from sweetmeats to horses, and I'd been dying to escape the confinement of the castle. But his troubled face had convinced me. When the others had returned, half of them had been sick with the fever, and half of those had died in a week's time. And there'd been other warnings, over the years...

"What did you see, Cynneth? And did Jayne see the same thing?"

Why hadn't she confided in me herself? I started to anger, until I remembered her tears.

He looked away from me.

"We did see the same thing, and..."

"Tell me!"

"We are both convinced that Stanley will betray you, and that you will die in the battle."

I crossed myself.

"I can't listen to this. You are both worried about me, and I love you for it. But you well know I cannot run from my sworn enemy. What shall I do, stay here like a craven in this great fortress until he lays siege to it? And I know Stanley for the slippery weasel that he is, but I have no choice in that regard. He has too many men for me to openly challenge his loyalty. That would only assure his defection. As it is, he knows the Tudor is an untried boy, who can't beat me in the field. That's why he's here with me now."

The friar sat back down and laid his palms upon my desk.

"Couldn't you let Jockey Howard lead the army? He has a host of loyal men, and you could still plan the strategy yourself. No one would think the worse of you."

"No! Don't you see this is my one chance to win my people back again?"

A knock sounded on the door and a servant bowed his way into the room. "Lord Lovell wishes to enter."

'Tell him to come," I said, before turning back to Brother Cynneth.

"I will remember what you've told me, and I will heed you as best I can. But I won't run, and I won't let someone else win for me."

Lovell came in, and we spoke no more of visions or seeings or death that night. But it was long after Compline before I slept.

I awoke next morning to a heavy rain, but instead of quenching the heat, it made the ancient citadel only that much damper. So we went out hunting anyway, and brought back a half-dozen rabbits for the table. Brother Cynneth joined Lovell, the Stanleys, and I, and I was thankful he'd shed his dismal expression from the night before and replaced it with his usual benign countenance.

The next day, a messenger arrived from London with a dispatch case full of documents for my perusal and signature, and I worked at my desk until late afternoon. I was about to resume my station on the battlements when the servant announced Lord Stanley.

He bowed low, as always.

"My liege," he said. "What news from the capital?"

"The Lord Mayor prepares to defend London from the Tudor if necessary, although I've assured him I'll never let the wastrel get that far."

"Ah, the Tudor! Do we know if he has reached our shores?"

He knew the answer, but I humored him.

"No. I will be sure to share that information with you as soon as I have it myself."

"That is what I would like to speak to you about. It has been months since I've been home to my estates. Indeed, I've not left your side since the coronation, and after much consideration, I believe that I could better serve you there than here."

"How so?"

"The mustering and equipping of soldiers cannot be done so well from a distance, my lord. Lord Norfolk left for Kent some weeks ago to see to his own men. I ask leave to do the same. I will join you whenever, and wherever, you choose to rendezvous."

I'd allowed Jockey to go home to prepare for battle weeks ago. But him I trusted to return. Stanley's shrewd face disappeared and I saw Jayne's tears, and heard the friar's warning, and my hands shook so that I was forced to hide them beneath my desk. How could I refuse him?

"I understand your concerns," I said, my voice even. "But surely you can allow your son to return in your stead. It will be a fine chance for him to prove his leadership."

He paused. "I am flattered by your confidence in him, but I fear this is a matter of too great importance to leave to an untried boy."

"Like the Tudor?"

H laughed. "Like the Tudor, indeed. Old age and treachery shall win the day, Your Grace! Old age and treachery!"

I wished for a breeze from the open window, and praise the Saints, I felt a soft gust across my face. With it, a godsend of an idea.

"I grant you leave to return to Latham, and I trust your efforts there on my behalf will go well."

He smiled, and began bowing his way out of my chamber.

"Just a moment, Lord Stanley. I do have one request."

"I am yours to command, Your Grace."

"I would like Lord Strange to remain here, at my side. You have made clear that you don't need him at Latham, and his presence here gives me comfort."

How gratifying to see the blood drain from his arrogant face!

"It's true, Lord Strange cannot be left to organize our efforts on his own, but nevertheless, I need his help. My estates are vast, Your Grace, and the soldiers I can bring to the field on your behalf number in the thousands."

"I understand, and your son's attendance at my side will serve to remind me of that important fact."

We stared at one another. Finally he bowed again.

"I will tell Lord Strange to cease his preparations for our journey north, and that he will be remaining here at Nottingham."

I nodded. "Very good. Thank you for indulging me."

As soon as he left the room I sent for Brother Cynneth.

A week later, as I paced the wall walk, I saw a lone messenger galloping through Sherwood Forest. I watched as he cantered up the long hill to the outer gates, and crossed the wide lawns of the outer bailey to the inner gate without slowing his horse. I felt his urgency in my bones, and I could taste the very sweat that he wiped from his tired brow.

I forced myself to wait on the battlement until he ran up the steps and knelt at my feet. He handed me parchment, but he panted out his message before I could unroll it.

"Your Grace, Henry Tudor has landed in Wales, at Milford Haven."

I sent Francis home to Lovell Minster to gather his retainers, and sent messengers to Jocky Norfolk and Lord Stanley that Tudor would be marching inland from the east.

In a few weeks, it would all be over, and I could fetch Jayne from Sheriff Hutton, and take her with me to Middleham. The heather would be in bloom, just as I'd promised her.

My waiting had ended at last.

CHAPTER 33

JAYNE: AUGUST 10, 1485

SHERIFF HUTTON CASTLE

*I*n the days following Bess' discovery of my relationship with Richard, the atmosphere at Sheriff Hutton was tense, to say the least. After a few miserable encounters in the Great Hall, and the garden, we each carved out our areas of operation. Rose and I spent time with the boys, riding out across the vale, or watching them practice their archery, while Bess claimed the garden as her domain. She and Cecily dined in the Great Hall with Sir Bartholomew and his wife, and Rose brought a tray to my room each evening.

Messengers came and went several times, and I assumed Bess discussed my perfidy with her mother. Now that they knew I could read, did they connect the dots between their plan to marry Bess to Henry Tudor, and Richard's sudden appearance at their door, all those months ago? If so, I knew they hated me all the more.

I could have cared less; my fears for Richard made everything else unimportant. If he listened to the friar's warning, and found some way to avoid engaging in battle with Henry Tudor, maybe there was a chance he would survive. If not, he had only a few weeks to live. I had to go to Nottingham Castle, and see him myself.

Rose insisted on accompanying me. I wanted to ask Sir Bartholomew for an escort, but what if he decided to prevent me from leaving? I couldn't take the risk. We'd rested at Nottingham on our way to Sheriff Hutton, and I hoped that between us we could remember our way. I recalled the major stops – York, Doncaster, Blyth – and I now rode well enough to make good time. We each packed a change of clothes in a tiny bundle, and planned to head out the next day, under the pretense of going on a morning ride across the vale.

That afternoon, we sat in the sun watching Dickon and Johnnie fight with their wooden swords in the grassy center of the inner bailey. I usually enjoyed seeing them spar together, but today I could hardly focus. My stomach was in knots, and Richard's handsome, doomed face swam before my eyes. I counted the minutes until sundown, but I knew I wouldn't sleep that night.

Suddenly, Johnnie lowered his wooden practice sword and put a hand to his forehead.

"Do you confess I've bested you?" said Dickon. His hero-worship of the older boy didn't alter his competitive streak.

Johnnie dropped his sword on the ground beside his feet, and put a hand out to grip Dickon's shoulder.

"No, I...I'm dizzy, Dickon. I don't know what's wrong with me..."

I jumped up from my seat on the grass and ran to him.

I put my hand on his head – he was hot, and sweating, but they'd been playing in the August sun for over an hour.

"Let's go inside and get you cool," I said. "You'll feel better in a minute."

I hoped I sounded more confident that I felt. His face was fish-white under his tan.

Rose and I helped him into the relative cool of the hall, where the wide windows on each side were thrown open to create a cross-breeze, and Dickon followed us, quiet for once.

"I'm greensick, Jayne," Johnnie said, just before he threw up his lunch in the clean rushes Lady Bartholomew's servants had spread on the floor that morning.

"Let's get him upstairs," said Rose, and we supported him between us up the curving stone staircase to the room he shared with Dickon.

"I'm sorry you're ill, Johnnie," said Dickon. "Do you think you ate too much at lunch today?"

"I don't know. I just felt tired, and my head began to swim." He pressed his hands against his eyes. "I must lie down," he said.

We helped him out of his tunic and he lay back on the bed in his linen shirtsleeves and hose. I pulled off his short leather boots and sat down on the edge of the bed. He looked so like Richard that I wanted to cry, but I forced a smile onto my face as I held his hand.

Rose ran to fetch cool water and a cloth.

"Dickon, why don't you go back outside and shoot your bow for awhile? Maybe Johnnie will feel like joining you later," I said.

He sat down beside me on the bed.

"I'd rather stay here with Johnnie, until he feels better."

Johnnie's forehead was still burning to the touch, and he continued to sweat through his thin linen shirt. Whatever he had could easily be contagious.

"Dickon, the best thing you can do for Johnnie right now is let him rest. Go out to the garden, and find your sisters. You haven't spent any time with them today."

His pretty mouth turned down at the corners, but he shrugged his shoulders and eased out of the room without arguing. In a moment, Rose returned with a wooden basin and a rag.

I held the damp cool cloth to Johnnie's head, and wiped his pale cheeks with it.

He reached up and clasped my hand.

"You'll stay with me, won't you, Jayne?"

Rose and I locked eyes. Our clothes were packed, and she'd chosen a horse to ride alongside Juno in the morning. But Richard's son needed me, and besides, I'd grown to love Johnnie for himself and could never refuse him.

"Of course I will," I said.

Rose ran to find the castle physician, Dr. Allred. I'd seen him wandering about, robes flapping, a tall skinny man with a narrow white face that contrasted sharply with his name.

She returned with him in just a few minutes, and ugly as he was, I wanted to hug him.

He felt Johnnie's forehead, just as I had done, and made him stick out his tongue. Johnnie described his sick stomach and aching bones. His dark blond curls were damp with sweat.

"I will get a basin, and my scalpel. The bad humors of the blood are causing the fever, and must be released."

I almost screamed.

"We'll wait about that, Dr. Allred," I said instead. "If he isn't better in a few days, I will send for you again."

He towered over me.

"This boy may die while you are waiting, Mistress Lyons. And how do you have the authority to speak for his father, the king?"

I pulled out the only weapon I had, besides the dirk the friar had given me, and I would have used that if necessary.

"I am the king's mistress. That's my authority."

He mouth dropped open and his eyebrows flew up.

"I thank you for your diagnosis, and as I said, I will send Rose for you again if I think it's necessary."

I could tell he didn't know whether to believe me or not, but he left the room in a huff.

"You don't think it would help to let him bleed me? I'm not afraid." Johnnie's voice was weak.

"No! We will find someone or something else to help you, I promise."

I would have to swallow my pride. I had to get him well, or at least on the mend, before I could go to his father. And his father's days might be numbered.

"Rose, stay here with him while I go get Bess," I said.

"You can't mean it! She'll not even speak to you!"

"I have to try," I said. "She's better with herbs and medicines than anyone I know except Brother Cynneth."

I suspected Rose was right. Bess was probably too furious with Richard, and me, to help his child. But to my surprise, I found her in the garden, smiling and humming while she made a circlet of flowers. The black hostility that had fairly emanated from her being had disappeared.

"Well, Jayne, where have you been keeping yourself?"

I was speechless for a moment. I'd planned to beg her forgiveness, but now it seemed that would be unnecessary. I launched into my request.

"Johnnie is very sick. He has a fever, and can't keep food in his stomach. I know you can help him. Please, will you come with me, if only for Dickon's sake? It will be hard on him to lose another companion."

I thought I was being clever, but she gave me an odd look that I couldn't interpret. But she got up and followed me, without forcing me to beg any further.

When we got to Johnnie's room, she leaned down and put a gentle hand against his cheek.

"I'll make you a tincture with rosemary and yarrow to help you sweat out the sickness, and another of mint for your stomach. You must do as Jayne says, and drink your broth. But even so, you'll be abed for a few days, at least. Keep him under a light cover, Jayne, and keep his brow cool."

She stood up and surveyed the room. The only window faced the wild meadow, three stories down.

She pushed the casements back as far as they would go.

"I'm glad this doesn't open onto that fusty courtyard," she said. "Keep it open."

When she came back with the medicines, she actually smiled at me, for the first time in a week.

After I helped him drink the tincture, Johnnie turned over on his side and rested quietly until dinner, but he refused to drink the broth that Rose brought up for him. That night, a servant made me a pallet on the floor beside his bed and set up a similar arrangement for Rose and Dickon in our room. She insisted that Dickon have the bed; she never stopped thinking of him as a little prince.

I tossed about on the horsehair mattress. I'd grown used to sleeping nude and was hot and uncomfortable in my gown. I tried not to disturb Johnnie's fitful sleep. What if I couldn't leave him to see Richard, before it was too late? It was a two-day ride to Nottingham. But I knew he would want me to stay with his only living son. I could never face him, or myself, if I let Johnnie die.

The next day he was about the same, although I did persuade him to

246 | ANNE-MARIE LACY

sip a little of the venison broth the cook made especially for him, and that night he slept much more quietly.

The day following that, his color was better, and his cheek felt cooler to my touch, so I asked Rose to go get Bess to have another look at him.

She took his hand and wiped his tangled hair from his brow.

"I believe the worst is past," she said.

I felt I'd been holding my breath for three days.

"Bess, I'm so grateful to you," I said.

"Oh, nonsense. I'd nothing else to do here. And from the time I was a small child, my grandmother taught me 'most every use of herbs, and flowers. She said I had a talent for it."

"You do! I remember how you helped poor Anne," I said.

She smiled her beautiful smile. "Yes, it was a pity there was no saving her."

She left a few minutes later, and I took her place on the edge of Johnnie's bed.

He held out his hand. It felt warm, but not blistering hot as it had done only a day ago.

"I'm so glad you're better," I said.

"Me too. I was scared, Jayne. I wondered if I'd ever see Father again. Thank you so much for staying with me."

I looked away. I couldn't let him see how worried I was that neither of us would see Richard alive again. I had to get to Nottingham.

"I'll bet you're no longer contagious. I think Dickon can move back in with you now."

He tugged on my hand.

"Please stay just this one more night!"

I sighed. "Okay, but just tonight, Johnnie. You'll be getting better every day now."

I told Rose to plan to leave for Nottingham at daylight the next morning. We'd have to bribe a groom to help us with the horses, but I had a purse full of money Richard gave me for the journey when we left Westminster for Sheriff Hutton, and I only used a little of it.

The Great Hall was filled with guests celebrating Lady Bartholomew's birthday, and even the servants were joining in the party.

I begged off, using Johnnie as my excuse, and ate part of a loaf of crusty bread and a slice of cheese in my room.

As soon as it finally got dark outside, I went to Johnnie's room to settle in for another night on the pallet. He was already sleeping, so I left one candle burning in case he woke up and needed me. I unbuckled the girdle at my waist, and set my dirk and leather purse down beside it, and lay down on the floor for my last night at Sheriff Hutton. I was so tired that not even the cumbersome weight of my gown or the discomfort of the thin mattress could keep me awake.

I slept soundly until I heard Johnnie's stifled scream.

At first I thought I was dreaming, so I lay still, and opened my eyes.

"You're Old Dick's bastard brat!" Sir James Talbott whispered, as I recognized his hateful voice. "Where's the Prince? Where's Richard of York? Tell me or I'll kill you!"

Johnnie sputtered and gasped. "I'll tell you nothing, James Talbott!"

No, Johnnie! Now he knows you recognize him!

God bless his brave heart, he must remember Talbott from when we first met, two years ago in Richard's tent.

"You will tell me, or you'll draw your last breath! The world can always do with one less bastard."

I thought Johnnie would call for me, but he didn't. My heart was bursting, but I kept my body still while I reached behind me for my dirk.

I heard a muffled croak. Talbott must be strangling him, just as he'd tried to strangle me after he took the silver boar.

My fingers found the knife and I held my breath while I worked it out of its leather sheath. I jumped to my feet. Talbott was on top of Johnnie, huge hands around the boy's throat.

I jumped on his back and drove my dirk in up to its hilt. It sliced through woven fabric of his tunic, and into the meat beneath it. He muffled a roar, and let go of Johnnie's throat, but I yanked the knife out and thrust it in again before he slung me off.

I landed on the floor at the end of the bed, and my head hit the wall on the opposite side of the small room. I pushed myself up and tried to stand, but Talbott was on top of me before I could get to my feet. My hand was empty.

He pressed his thumbs against my windpipe. I struggled against the weight of his body, but his knees held my skirts to the floor, and I could barely move. He put his mouth close to my ear, and I smelled his sour breath.

"You bitch! Do you know what you cost me? Stanley said I'd shamed him before his enemy! He..."

His whisper changed to a rasp, and he exhaled warm blood across the side of my face and into my hair.

His grip on my throat relaxed, and his body collapsed on mine. I tried to push him off of me, but he was dead weight now, and my arms were pinned beneath his shoulders.

"Help me, Johnnie!" I said, but he was already out of bed and pulling Talbott by his feet. As soon as my arms were free I pushed myself up and jumped out from under him.

Johnnie threw his arms around me.

"Oh, Jayne, you killed him! I'm so glad! He was after Dickon!"

I closed my eyes and held him tight. Then I took his arms.

"Johnnie, we have to get out of here. Now! Are you strong enough to ride?"

He sat back on the bed. "Yes," he said. But he was pale again, and beads of sweat dotted his upper lip.

"Stay here, and lie back down for a moment while I get Rose and Dickon. We have to take him with us."

I stepped past Talbott's body and eased open the door he'd shut behind him.

Rose and Dickon were both fast asleep. I shook her shoulder, and she looked up at me and opened her mouth. I slapped my hand over her lips before she could scream.

"Rose, Talbott tried to kill Johnnie, but he was really here for Dickon. We have to leave here tonight, and take them with us."

She sat up and brushed her hair back.

"What? What's happened? You're bleeding!"

"It's Talbott's blood, not mine! He came in Johnnie's room, looking for Dickon. I stabbed him with my dirk. He's dead, but we can't leave without taking the boys. Stanley will send someone else."

She ran to Dickon to wake him.

"Get him ready and I'll go see to Johnnie. He'll have to ride with me on Juno, he's still too weak to ride by himself."

"You've got to wipe the blood out of your hair," she said. "Here."

She pulled the sheet off her pallet and handed it to me.

I rubbed my hair and face with it as I ran across the hallway to Johnnie. He was sitting on the edge of the bed, supporting himself on his arms, but wearing his tunic and boots.

"Push him out of the window," he said.

"What?"

"There's a ten-foot drop, more if you count the hillside. And there's nothing but meadow below. No one will find it for days."

"You're a genius, Johnnie," I said.

He smiled a weak smile, and started to push himself up.

"No, let's wait for Rose and Dickon. You've got to save your strength. We've got a long ride ahead."

"Where are we going?"

"To your father, at Nottingham."

He smiled again, as Rose and a bewildered-looking Dickon tiptoed into the room.

"Who's that?" asked Dickon, pointing at Talbott's body.

Johnnie sat up. "Dickon, you've got to be quiet, and do whatever Jayne says. That man tried to kill me, and Jayne, and he wanted to kill you. We're going to my father."

Dickon nodded, eyes wide. Thank God he worshiped Johnnie. I wasn't sure he would have followed me and Rose otherwise.

"Rose, help me. You too, Dickon. We've got to get him out the window."

I slipped my hands under his arms and tried to lift his shoulders, but I couldn't raise him but a couple of feet off the floor. Rose had to get on one side of him, and me the other, before we could drag him to the open window.

Together we raised him up and propped him against the wall beneath the casement. The window sill was just level with the top of his hip.

"Rose and I are going to grab his feet," I said to Dickon. "You push his shoulders. Be careful!"

Rose and I each grabbed a heavy leather boot and the three of us strained and heaved, until the body toppled headfirst out the window. In the murky dawn we could barely see it after it rolled down the hill.

I took a deep breath. "Let's get out of here."

We tiptoed into the hallway, and down the stairs into the courtyard. The torches in metal brackets that were meant to light the walkways were nearly gone out, but the daylight was spreading fast. We cut across the bailey to the stables.

Johnnie sat on a wooden stool by the door while Dickon, Rose, and I pulled the horses from their stalls and ran to the tack room for our saddles.

Juno stood with her hindquarters towards the door, asleep with her head down.

"Come on, girl," I whispered as I slipped the halter over her ears.

She shook her head and I let her stretch before I pulled her out into the hallway of the barn.

Dickon was faster than we were, and I fumbled with Juno's bridle with clumsy, nervous fingers until he ran up to help me.

Johnnie crawled up behind my saddle and wrapped his arms around my waist. We walked out across the bailey towards the inner gate. I'd thought of a lie while we were tacking up, and I hoped the guard wasn't too bright, or too conscientious, to believe it.

He was slumped against the postern, fast asleep, but the iron gate was locked. We would have to wake him.

Dickon jumped down and shook him by the shoulder.

He jumped, and wiped his eyes.

"What's this? What do you want, sonny? It's the middle of the night!"

"No, it's not," said Dickon. "These ladies want to see the sun rise over the vale. Will you let us out? We won't be long."

He made a face, and shrugged his shoulders. "Sure."

He took an iron key from a ring at his belt and stuck it in the massive padlock. "Enjoy yourselves," he said, and rolled his eyes.

It was already hot, and sticky, and the armpits of my gown were already soaked. We trotted across the wide outer bailey to the outer gate, our last obstacle before the open road.

But this gatekeeper was awake. Before Dickon could dismount and repeat the lie that had worked so well on the other guard, the man walked up to Juno and put his hand on her bridle. He looked at me, and then at Johnnie.

"Where are you taking this boy?"

I smiled at him, and did my best "medieval maiden."

"Good morn, sir. He's been ill; he's just better today. He asked if he might see the sun rise over the vale. We thought it might cheer him."

He stared at me, his face hard as the stone gate he guarded.

"I'm not to let anyone out before sunrise," he said.

"But if we wait, the beauty of it will be spoiled for him."

I reached in my pouch, the one Richard had so generously filled, and pulled out a gold coin. It was more than a month's salary.

He snatched it as if he was afraid I would change my mind.

"Go ahead," he said. He let go of Juno's bridle and went to unlock the gate.

"Fool," he mumbled under his breath.

We walked slowly under the archway like we were headed out to picnic. The gate clanged shut behind us, and another man's voice rang out as he shouted to the gatekeeper.

We kicked our horses into a canter, then a gallop. Johnnie tightened his grip on my waist.

"You gonna be okay back there?" I asked over my shoulder.

"I pray so," he said, and laid his cheek against my back.

I gave Juno another kick, and we headed for the Great North Road.

CHAPTER 34

JAYNE: AUGUST 15, 1485

YORK

here were still several hours of summer daylight left, when we walked our horses through the magnificent Micklegate that led through the ancient stone wall surrounding the city of York. Rose and I had originally planned to try to make it to the village of Towton, at least ten miles further, but Johnnie was still so weak that we'd had to stop often for him to rest, and now he was so tired I was afraid he would fall from the saddle. We trotted across the bridge that spanned the River Ouse and into the city center. The narrow cobbled streets were packed with people of all sorts. The laborers in worsteds jostled rich merchants in bright velvets and priests in wool cassocks, all made temporarily equal by their common mission to get their business concluded before night-fall. York was Richard's favorite city, and any other time, I would have been fascinated by the spectacle, but today I only wanted to find a safe, clean place for Johnnie to rest, and to get all of us fed. We hadn't had time to pack any provisions before our flight from Sheriff Hutton, and none of us had eaten since last night.

Dickon had been silent for so long that I finally asked him if he were feeling sick also.

He trotted up close to me. Tears ran down his face.

"This journey puts me in mind of the ride from the Tower to Sheriff Hutton, when Edward was slaughtered. What if we're attacked? This time we're only women, and boys. And Johnnie's too weak to use his sword."

Johnnie's sword hung from his belt, but Dickon was right. I doubted if he could even raise it.

"We aren't going to be traveling at night, and we aren't traveling nearly as far," I said. "We should be to Nottingham in just a day or two."

I smiled at him, and forced the last of my optimism into my voice. Unless Johnnie's condition improved, we would have a hard time making it to the castle in that amount of time. And if he got worse...

I wouldn't think about it.

"We'll be all right, Dickon," said Johnnie. "Jayne will take care of us. She's already killed Stanley's strongest henchman today."

Dickon nodded, eyes wide. But the fact that I'd killed a man was yet another thought I didn't want to dwell on.

When we reached the shadow of the Gothic spires of York Minster, I spotted a charming half-timbered building whose upper stories hung out over the street. The wooden sign hanging over the wide doorway was decorated with a drawing of a star. I decided to take it for a good omen. I was becoming more medieval by the day.

"We'll stop here," I said.

"I'll fetch a groom to help us," said Dickon, while Rose went inside to find the innkeeper.

I'd chosen well. The Starre was as tidy as could be, and I hoped its proximity to the cathedral ensured it was safe as well. However, the main taproom was crowded with a loud group of merchants, and poor Johnnie's white face told me he needed peace and quiet where he could rest as soon as possible. So he and Dickon went up to the room they would share, and Rose, helped by a coin from my purse, persuaded a serving girl to bring them up a tray.

Rose and I elbowed our way to a corner, as far away from the other patrons as possible, and ordered meat pies and ale. A smiling boy in a crisp white apron brought us a jug and two wooden cups, and filled them both to the rim with the frothy golden stuff.

As soon as he bustled off we knocked our cups together and drank. Rose downed hers without stopping for breath.

"I don't think I've ever been so frightened in all my days," she confided.

"Yes, you have. Remember that night in the rain, when we were captured by Stanley's men? You were pretty scared then, too."

She made a wry face. "Aye, I was, now that you remind me. Talbott was there that night as well."

She crossed herself.

"Praise the Saints, he won't bother anyone any more."

I finished my cup of ale and poured another.

"Rose, how do you think Stanley knew where to find Dickon? Richard has managed to keep his whereabouts a secret for almost two years. Do you think someone at the castle betrayed him?"

She sat silent a moment.

"Well, there's gossip at any castle, even one so remote as that one. And Stanley has the coin to tempt even the truest afterling to turn traitor. But I've been considerin' it all day, while we were ridin', and I've got me own ideas."

"Well, don't torture me!"

"On the day you moved me out of the servant's quarters, the day the Princess Bess found your book, do you remember what you said to her about the little Prince?"

I'd long since given up correcting her about the York children, and I didn't remember what I'd said that day, so I just shook my head.

"You told her that if she wasn't born on the wrong side of the blanket, he wasn't neither."

I'd been furious at the time, but now I remembered.

"And if he was legitimate, he would be the rightful heir to the throne."

She nodded. "So your Richard couldn't make her a queen, even if he wanted to…"

"And neither can Henry Tudor, as long as Dickon is alive," I said.

We stared at each other.

"And him such a darling child, and her own brother too," said Rose.

I barely heard her.

I should have figured it out myself. Bess sitting beside Lady Stanley, Henry Tudor's mother, almost every day at mass in the chapel at Westminster...the messengers to and fro from Sheriff Hutton...and Bess' sudden changes from depression to anger to cheerfulness...

It all made sense.

"What will we do with the boy? We can't protect him from Stanley for long, I'll warrant," said Rose.

"We just have to get him to Richard. He'll find him someplace safe," I said. I hoped I sounded more confident than I felt. Historically, Dickon's fate was one of the mysteries of Richard's life. Would Stanley succeed in killing him? Not if I could continue to protect him.

The boy set the meat pies we'd ordered down in front of us. I thought my disgust with Bess, and my fears for Dickon, had taken my appetite, but the crusts were perfectly brown around the edges, and the smell of cinnamon made my mouth water. My stomach reminded me that I hadn't eaten since last night, so I cut into the pie, and tender meat and raisins spilled out onto my wooden trencher. I ate every bite.

As soon as I was finished, the adrenaline that had fueled my body since before dawn abruptly ran out. I had to get away from the noise, and the funk generated by so many unwashed bodies at the close of a long summer day.

As soon as Rose swallowed the last cup of our ale, we made our way back out to the door that led to the second floor, and our room. I was almost too tired to take off my gown, but I couldn't bear to sleep in it another night. I hung it on a peg and slipped under the clean, fragrant sheets, where I slept until the first light of dawn crept in our window.

*W*e were on the road early the next morning, but not before I watched Johnnie eat a breakfast of hot bread and sausages. I worried that such a large meal would make him sick, but he climbed aboard Juno without complaint. We only stopped once to rest before noon, when we sat on the roadside and devoured the lunch the innkeeper had packed for us. We passed through the village of Towton without stopping, and by late afternoon I was certain we would make it to Doncaster before dark.

"Are you okay to go a little bit farther, Johnnie?"

I felt him take a deep breath.

"I think so," he said. "I've been so much better today, but now I'm growing weary."

"We'll be in Doncaster soon, I think, but if we pass a village or any place to sleep before then, we'll stop there, okay?"

"Yes, Jayne, I'll make it," he said, and laid his head on my shoulder.

I knew he couldn't understand my urgency. Since we'd left Sheriff Hutton behind, we'd encountered dozens of other travelers; farmers carrying produce into the market at York, merchants with loads of goods headed south, and lone men on horseback, who nodded at us and went on their way. There was no sign that anyone followed us. I couldn't tell him that his father was in danger, and that every minute that passed brought him closer to his last battle.

We made it into Doncaster just as darkness fell. It was a far smaller town than York, and the inn we slept in wasn't nearly as tidy as The Starre, nor did it feel as safe. In the morning, Johnnie said that he felt well enough to ride on his own, but there were several rough characters lounging about the stables, and I was afraid to risk revealing my full purse by buying a horse.

So we went on riding double on Juno, and made it to the village of Blyth by late afternoon. We were so close to Nottingham that I was dying to press on, but there was no way to make it to the castle before dark, so we spent one more night on the road. I rousted everyone out of bed before the cock crowed, and we were back on the Great North Road, headed south for Nottingham, by the time it was fully light.

I had to warn Richard, to stop him from fighting if I could, but also I wanted to be with him again, to sleep beside him and wake up in the morning to his desire. At Sheriff Hutton I'd dreamed of his mouth, and his hands, and my body had ached for his touch. When I caught my first sight of Nottingham, high on its promontory, just a few miles in the distance, I kicked Juno into a canter.

"Hurray!" cried Johnnie, and took his hands from around my waist to clap them.

But as close as it had looked to our eager eyes, Nottingham was still over an hour away. When our tired horses finally reached the huge grey fortress, I closed my eyes and wished with all my soul that I would be able to persuade Richard to stay there.

We approached the three-story gatehouse at a canter. We pulled up sharp; soldiers stood ready on the battlements above us, the iron gates were lowered, and the drawbridge over the moat was locked tight behind it.

A gatekeeper in a gleaming breastplate and metal helm looked down at us before gesturing over his shoulder, and, with a clang, the portcullis started its clattering ascent.

At last, after almost three months of longing for him, only a drawbridge separated me from Richard.

Johnnie hugged me. "It will be grand to see Father again. I've missed him."

"Me too, Johnnie. Me too."

As soon as the portcullis was high enough for us to clear its iron spikes, I clucked to Juno and we trotted under it and over the drawbridge. The inner gate was already open.

"A'most looks like we're expected!" said Rose.

We were halfway across the moat when I heard the portcullis clang shut behind us.

I pulled Juno to a halt and Rose and Dickon stopped behind me.

"What's wrong?" said Dickon. "Go ahead, Jayne!"

A group of soldiers had gathered just inside the inner gate, and now they jogged under the stone archway and onto the drawbridge. One of them grabbed Juno's bridle before raising his helm.

"Jayne Lyons?"

I nodded.

"We've orders from Sir Bartholomew Braden to take you into custody."

I sat up taller in the saddle, and hoped he didn't notice the cold sweat I felt break out on my face.

I tried to keep my voice even. "We're here to see King Richard. I'm bringing his son, John of Gloucester, to his father."

"The king left Nottingham yesterday," he said.

"Where did he go? I have to get to him!"

"That's none of your affair."

As if she sensed my dismay, Juno pulled backwards, away from the man's hand.

"Let go of my horse's head! I'll go with you. just tell me where the king has gone."

"His Grace and his household left here before dawn yesterday."

Thank God I wasn't the fainting type, but the bile rose in my throat. He must be headed to Leicester. The Battle of Bosworth Field was only days away.

CHAPTER 35

RICHARD: AUGUST 19, 1485

LEICESTER

*J*ohn Kendall's drawn face and sagging shoulders told me the trip from London to Leicester at such a pace had fair worn him out. But he smiled as he handed me the casket which housed my silver boar; I'd confided in him by messenger that I wanted it to wear in the battle, and he'd ridden over a hundred miles to bring it to me himself.

"Thank you, John," I said. "I can't tell you what this means to me. Please take some ale, and have a lie down. I can see you're tired, and well you should be, after riding all night."

"Thank you, Your Grace, but I'll be fine. With your permission, I'd like to remain here and assist you in your preparations."

"Well, do sit down, at least," I said, and indicated one of the stools that the innkeeper had brought to the chamber.

We'd left Nottingham the yesterday morning, riding in square battle, with wings of cavalry spread out on either side, my household in the vanguard, and the baggage in the middle. A force of northern lords, gentry, and commons brought up the rear. My men-at-arms and I crossed the bridge over the River Soar and through the gates of the city last night, just before sunset, and I'd commandeered a private dining room in the upper story of The White Boar for a makeshift office.

Jockey Howard met me with his troops from East Anglia, and now they, along with my other captains and their retainers, were quartered throughout the city and in the fields beyond. I planned to stay here until my scurriers brought news of the Tudor's movements. The last I'd heard, he'd left Litchfield headed east towards the village of Tamworth, some twenty miles away. He was marching right towards me, but there was still a chance he might swing south and make for London, and from here I could move easily in either direction.

"Unless the Tudor makes for London, I'd like you to stay here during the battle, John. I've decided I'll return to Leicester before I go north again."

He accepted a cup of ale from my manservant and sat down with it. "I plan to fight at your side, Your Grace."

An awkward silence engulfed the room. I didn't dare look at my men.

"How long has it been since you've donned armor, Kendall?" said Francis Lovell, at last.

Kendall squared his shoulders. "It's been a number of years, but my place is by King Richard's side."

"He has need of your support in other ways, too. No need to take a useless risk," said Jockey.

"I assure you I've wielded a sword before, Lord Norfolk, so I'll not be useless, however I choose to serve the king.'

"Well spoken!" I said. "I will be proud to have you amongst my knights."

I glared at Jockey and Lovell; Kendall's loyalty touched my heart, and I'd not see him embarrassed further. But I would ask Brother Cynneth to say a prayer for his especial safety.

Cynneth was even now at his devotions, in the chapel of his brother Grey Friars not far from the inn. As I'd hoped, he'd been mollified by my decision to force Stanley to leave his son in my custody, and although the friar had spent more time than usual in prayer, he'd left off his talk of visions and portents.

We'd spoken no more about Jayne's fears, but even during the daylight hours, as I arranged for billets for my men, and assigned them places in the ranks, she was never far from my mind. And at night, my dreams of her were exquisite torture that left me throbbing with unful-filled desire. How I would love to have her kisses send me into battle, but the knowledge that she was safe at Sheriff Hutton gave me peace despite my loneliness.

After another cup of ale, Kendall agreed to go to his chamber to rest, and he'd not been long away before another dusty traveler begged admittance.

Sir Robert Brackenbury doffed a crumpled hat and bowed low.

"I've a large contingent from London, Your Grace," he said.

"Good man," exclaimed Jocky, and Lovell, in unison worthy of a choir.

It felt good to laugh.

"You've been a fine Constable of the Tower, Sir Robert," I said. "My faith in you has never wavered."

Our eyes met; I knew he recalled the night he'd helped Tyrell smuggle Edward's sons out of the Tower in the blackest hours of the night. He'd mourned the death of the elder, and rejoiced in the survival of the younger, almost as much as I had.

After making a full report, he left to find food and drink, and rest.

"So what are our numbers now?" asked Jockey.

"About four thousand," I said.

"And the Tudor?"

"Quite a bit fewer, it seems. My scurriers tell me he hasn't picked up many supporters on his march through the countryside."

"I'll bet his asshole is tighter than a cat's right now!" said Lovell.

We laughed again, but this time Jockey didn't join in.

"Are you counting the men Stanley can bring in that four thousand?" he asked.

"I am."

He looked away.

"I still have his son, remember?"

"I suppose he could make another," he said.

I'd still not heard a word from my old enemy.

"The day is young, and Tudor still miles away," I assured him.

But when the innkeeper brought in our lunch of roast goose in a rich murrey sauce, I had to force myself to eat a respectable portion, if only to hide my anxiety. I was headed for the privy soon after, and when I returned to my desk a trembling messenger awaited me. On his left shoulder was a badge in the shape of an eagle's claw: the livery of Lord Thomas Stanley.

He bowed so low his head almost touched the floor, before regarding me as if he would rather be anywhere else.

"I hope you are well, Your Grace," he said.

"I'm as well as can be expected, as I am sorely missing your master."

He swallowed.

"Lord Stanley asks your forgiveness for his delay, but he has been ill with the sweating-sickness. He is bringing near a thousand men, and is marching towards Leicester now."

"Did he deign to give me a time at which to expect his arrival?'

He twisted his cap in his hands, and looked at his feet. "He did not, Your Grace."

"Very well. Go and find a place to rest from your journey."

I turned to my squire.

"Bring me Lord Strange. He's under guard somewhere in this inn."

"What are you going to do?" asked Lovell.

"You'll see."

Lord Strange's narrow face so much resembled that of his disloyal father that it was all I could do to look at it.

"Send word to your father than I command him to rendezvous with me no later than tomorrow noon. I will give you the loan of my swiftest messenger," I said.

The coward was trembling. "Is that all I am to say, Your Grace?"

"No. Tell him that if he doesn't appear, the next command I send him will be pinioned on your severed head."

I believe he would have fallen to his knees if not for the two strong guards who escorted him from the room.

"Will you do it?" asked Jocky.

I sighed. "I don't know."

$\mathcal{F}$rancis and I left the hot confines of the White Boar soon after, him headed to check on his men and me to seek out Brother Cynneth, and the cool air of the Grey Friars chapel.

The smiles and bows of the townspeople cheered me. I'd stopped here over a year ago, on my way to battle against Buckingham, and it seemed they remembered me fondly. It was Saturday, and the market square was crowded with merchants. A man selling sweetmeats pressed a sack of sugared figs into my hand.

"May God speed you to victory, Your Grace," he said.

I thanked him, and nibbled on them as I crossed the square to the priory. I found Cynneth kneeling in the chapel nave, eyes shut and hands clasped. I dropped to my knees beside him, and looked up at the plaster statute of the Holy Mother above the altar.

Her head tilted gently sideways, and her smile was compassionate, but her eyes were hard. Did the artist fail at his task, or did he depict the true nature of one who must choose life or death for her supplicants? Was Henry Tudor on his knees at this same instant, begging her for victory? She could not help us both.

"You aren't praying," said the friar.

"I've prayed to crush the Tudor until I'm weary of my own beseeching."

He looked at my face, and then at my cap, which I'd placed next to my knee. His face blanched and he crossed himself.

"What?" I asked him, then I remembered I'd pinned my silver boar into the velvet.

"I thought you'd left your badge behind, in London."

"I did, but I asked Kendall to bring it to me. He rode all night to get it here before the battle."

He hung his head, and I saw a drop of water fall from his eye and splash the stone floor.

"Are you crying, Cynneth?"

"Take the boar off of your hat," he said.

I loosened the silver clasp from the back of my sigil and held it in my hand. Even in the dim light of the chapel it gleamed like a star in God's firmament. It had never been so beautiful.

"If you had another request for Our Father, besides winning in the field of battle, what would it be?"

I took a moment before I replied, but only to find the right words, for I knew the answer in my heart.

"I would pray that someday, the people of England will know me for the man I am, and not for the man that others have made me out to be."

He put his hand over mine, and we prayed together until the bells rang for Nones.

On my way back to the inn, a young man in plain livery ran up beside me and pulled off his cap. I recognized him as one of the many scouts I'd sent out into the countryside.

"Beg pardon, Your Grace, but I've news of the Tudor! He makes his camp for the night at Atherstone!"

At last, my enemy and I were less than ten miles apart.

I gave the man generous praise, and a sovereign, and went to give the order to my captains. We would march at dawn.

CHAPTER 36

JAYNE: AUGUST 21, 1485

NOTTINGHAM CASTLE

The guards hauled all four of us to a large chamber that served as an office for the constable of Nottingham Castle. Richard had probably been in this room many times, maybe as recently as yesterday, and the idea distracted me despite our desperate circumstances. His presence hung in the air like a ghost, and I could hear his voice, and see his dark face silhouetted against the colorful tapestries. Sir Bartholomew, who'd been standing by the open casement window, turned and faced me. His usually benign face wore an expression of cold disappointment.

He looked both boys up and down before he spoke to me.

"Mistress Lyons, you have caused me a great deal of difficulty. The king placed these two boys, as well as yourself, in my care. What possible reason could you have for removing them from my custody? Do you charge me with mistreating them, or you?"

Could it be he didn't know about Talbott? He and his men must have left Sheriff Hutton before anyone spotted the body! Relief flooded my body, and I snuck a grateful look at Rose for helping me clean up Talbott's blood.

"No, we aren't accusing you of anything. You've been very kind to us,"

I said. "But I received a message from the king requesting that I bring the boys to him at Leicester."

"Why wouldn't he have sent a message to me, if he wanted the boys moved from Sheriff Hutton?"

"I don't know. I only know he wants them."

"This is absurd. Show me this letter."

"I'm afraid I left it behind. We were in such a hurry..."

He shook his head. "I don't believe you."

How to convince him to let me go? I had only one card to play.

"Didn't the constable tell you the king is headed to Leicester?"

"Yes, but..."

"I haven't seen the constable. How would I know where the king was headed, if he hadn't told me himself?"

Sir Bartholomew looked down, and I could see the wheels turning. If he didn't buy it, my chance to help Richard, and Dickon, would slip from my grasp.

"The king will be angry with us both if we don't do as he asked," I said. "Take me to him yourself, if you don't believe me."

I held my breath until he nodded.

We slowed our horses to a trot when we reached the High Street of the City of Leicester. I'd tried to convince Sir Bartholomew to leave Nottingham immediately, but he claimed it was too dangerous for the boys to travel at night. Now it was late Sunday afternoon, and no one had to tell me that Richard was already gone. The shops were shuttered and the streets bare and devoid of the excitement and energy the presence of the king always generated. The torn grey remains of white roses littered the cobbles; he had passed here, and the people had welcomed him, or told him goodbye, but he wasn't here anymore. I pulled Juno down to a walk.

An iron fist gripped my heart. How could I stop him now? He must have already marched his men into the field, and taken up his position against Henry Tudor's army. But I couldn't give up, not while we were both still breathing.

"You've sent me on a fool's errand, Mistress Lyons," said Sir Bartholomew.

"No, I haven't. Where is the priory of the Grey Friars?"

"Do you think the king is there?'

"He could be," I said. Lying was the least of my worries.

We reached the front door of the chapel at sunset, just as the bells rang for Vespers. Several monks in grey habits were making their way from various parts of the priory, but I didn't see Brother Cynneth among them. I jumped down from my horse, and handed my reins to Rose.

"Have you seen a friar named Brother Cynneth?" I asked the first monk I reached.

"I believe he is at prayer in the chapel, but..."

I didn't wait for him to go on. I pulled open the heavy wooden door and stepped into the chapel. The cool air hit my face, and it took my eyes a moment to adjust to the dim light, but when they did, I looked up to the nave and saw the familiar bulk of the friar kneeling in front of the altar.

I ran down the middle of the aisle, dodging the other monks until I reached him. He looked up at me, his face tear-stained.

"Brother Cynneth! I have to talk to you! Where's Richard?"

"He's gone out to Redmore Plain, to face the Tudor. I'm afraid all my attempts to dissuade him were unsuccessful."

I grabbed his plump arm and tried to pull him to his feet.

"There's nothing more we can do," he said.

"Yes, there is! I have Dickon and Johnnie here with me. Stanley sent James Talbott to Sheriff Hutton to kill Dickon. Talbott made a mistake and tried to kill Johnnie instead. Sir Bartholomew is outside, too; he almost stopped me from bringing them to you."

He looked behind me as if he thought Talbott would burst into the church any moment.

"Where is he?"

"I killed him with the dirk you gave me."

He stared at me, eyes wide. He nodded. "Good," he said.

We ignored the astonished looks on the faces of the other monks as we rushed back down the aisle and out into the courtyard.

Sir Bartholomew was headed towards us.

"Good day to you, Brother Cynneth," he said. "I apologize for this intrusion."

"Where are the two lads?" asked the friar. "It is the king's wish that they remain here with me until after the battle. Many thanks to you and your men for providing them safe escort. The king will be most pleased."

The old knight's shoulders had been up around his ears, but now he relaxed and smiled.

"You are quite welcome, friar. I know you have the king's confidence, if anyone does," he said, and nodded as if he'd expected that answer all along. I applauded the friar for his quick thinking.

"Let me offer you and your men some refreshment, and a cool place in which to rest yourselves."

After Brother Cynneth handed Sir Bartholomew and his knights off to another monk, we rushed to where Rose and the boys stood beside their horses.

"Friar!" said Dickon, and ran to wrap his arms around Brother Cynneth's wide waist. "Where's our uncle? A man tried to kill us!"

"Hello, lad! I thank the Saints you are safe." He stroked the boy's golden head. "And you, dear Johnnie," he said.

"Friar, I've got to talk to you, and I know these boys are hungry."

He stopped a young novice who was crossing the courtyard, and sent the boys and Rose with him towards the kitchens.

He hurried me down one of the walkways and into a small room furnished with a cot and a table.

"This is my chamber while I am here at the priory," he said. "No one will disturb us here."

I recounted everything, from Johnnie's sickness, to Bess' betrayal, to my interception at Nottingham by Sir Bartholomew. He listened, rarely interrupting except to try to slow me down.

"And so," I said, after I told him about our frantic gallop from Nottingham to Leicester this morning, "we have to find a way to protect Dickon, or Stanley will keep trying until he kills him."

He sighed, and pursed his lips.

"I have only one solution for Dickon's future, and I thought to put the idea to His Grace after the battle," he said. "But now..."

"But now we can't wait for that. What is it?"

"No one would ever think to look for Dickon here," he said.

"You mean in Leicester? Who could he stay with that Stanley couldn't threaten, or bribe?"

"Me," he said. "We've novices his age, and younger, who dedicate their lives to serving our Lord. I doubt Stanley would look for him here, and once Dickon has taken Holy Orders, he would no longer be eligible to be king. Even if Stanley found him, he would have no need to kill him."

The beauty of it astounded me.

"But do you think Dickon will agree to it?"

"I do. I think he's been so frightened by what happened to his brother, and what almost happened to him, that he will be relieved to finally be safe."

"Friar, I've got to get to Richard. I might never find his camp on my own. Please take me to him!"

He turned away from me.

"I said my goodbyes to him this morning, and thought to remain on my knees in the chapel until after the battle..."

"Please, Brother Cynneth! I haven't given up!"

I pulled at the rough grey wool of his sleeve.

"The road goes straight out of the City, and you'll not be able to miss the camp," he said.

I'd been in Leicester less than two hours when I trotted back out under the western gate of the city. Brother Cynneth had fed Juno and rubbed her down himself, and the game little mare felt eager as ever beneath me. We picked up a canter over the wide stone bridge that spanned the River Soar.

In five hundred years, the bridge and the gate would still be standing. I had seen them myself, and admired them with the eyes of a tourist. Now all that mattered was that I was following Richard on the same road that carried him out of Leicester towards Bosworth Field just this morning. The battle would take place on Monday, August 22. Tomorrow.

But it was too dark to gallop. If I lamed the mare, I'd never get there on foot, so I forced myself to slow down to a trot. The grass was flattened and dotted with piles of horse dung on either side of the road for as far as I could see by the moonlight. So many marching feet, and prancing hooves, headed out to fight for their king. Knights, archers, pikemen, billmen. How many would be alive this time tomorrow?

I shivered despite the warmth of the August evening. The ghosts of those who would die in the morning were already haunting me, Richard's chief among them. What would my life be like without him? I'd long since despaired of ever getting home again. Home to me, now, was with Richard. I had to stop him from fighting.

But I remembered the friar's last words before we'd parted.

"Jayne, will you make me a promise?" he said.

"Of course. Anything."

"Don't send him into battle with tears, and dire warnings. If you see you can't dissuade him...don't do as I did."

I didn't answer him. I planned to beg Richard not to fight, on my knees if necessary.

"Promise me, Jayne. That's not what he needs."

What could I do?

"I promise," I said.

It was almost two hours before I heard the sounds of the camp. At first it was just a dull roar in the distance, but soon I could make out the shouts of the men and the neighs of their horses, and the clanging of metal as the soldiers arranged their armor and the cooks unpacked their pots and pans. The light from their torches and cook fires spread out in all directions, like the universe.

I headed across the plain towards the lights, not daring to go faster than a walk. The closer I got to the camp, the more it looked like the one I'd landed in on my first night in the fifteenth century, and I remembered the pain of Talbott's fingers around my throat. I felt sweat soaking the armpits of my gown, and trickling between my shoulder blades. But he was dead, and I was no longer a lost, confused girl.

At first the two guards at the edge of the camp looked so surprised by the sight of a woman approaching the camp that I thought they weren't going to stop me. Then a man in a padded canvas jacket and a visorless helmet strode up to take Juno's bridle. He wore a long dagger at his waist, and carried a long wooden staff with a vicious-looking metal blade attached to the end.

"What do you, lady? You're not safe here."

How different my reception was this time! Even though my gown was travel-stained, the long skirts that draped over Juno's saddle were made of fine linen, and costly braid decorated the hem and the edges of my sleeves. To my relief, even by torchlight he must have seen I was no prostitute. And he wore a badge with a lion on his shoulder – the livery of Jockey Howard.

"Is this Sir John Howard's camp?"

"It is."

"I have an urgent message for him. Please take me to him!"

"Lord Norfolk is preparing for battle on the morrow. Your message must wait."

By now a small crowd of soldiers blocked my path, and the billman tightened his grip on my horse's bridle.

"My message regards Lord Stanley," I said.

They each took a step back, and looked at each other.

"Lord Norfolk will want to hear it, I promise you."

The billman let go of my horse and shrugged his shoulders. "Are you one of His Grace's spies?"

I smiled down at him. "I am," I said.

He led me through the camp, past staring soldiers, many already in their shirtsleeves for the night. Soon we came to a tent that was larger than any of the others, The canvas flaps stood open, but it was guarded by two men wearing bright yellow and red tunics, and holding gleaming axes.

"What's this?" asked one of them.

"Is Lord Norfolk inside? I must see him!"

I jumped down from Juno and handed the billman the reins.

"Jockey!" I shouted.

"Ho, there, lady!" said the guard. They stepped in front of me and barred the entrance.

"You've got to let me in," I said, just as Jocky came out and motioned them aside.

"Jayne! I knew I heard your voice!"

He grabbed me in a bear hug, and I nestled my face against his shoulder. He grabbed my arms and looked down into my face.

"I thought you were at Sheriff Hutton!" he said. "You must know you have no business here!"

"Please take me to Richard. Please! I have to see him before the battle!"

"I and the rest of his captains just left him for the night, and he told us he wanted to be alone."

He hesitated, then he grinned. "But he'll be glad to see you."

*W*e crossed the distance between the two camps on horseback. By the time we reached Richard's tent, I was used to the astonished stares of his knights. When they saw Jockey, his guards stepped aside, and as soon as my feet hit the ground I ran under the canvas flaps.

Dozens of candles illuminated a huge desk covered with maps, and filled the air with the smell of tallow, just like the first time I saw him. He was standing with his back to me, and his dark curls shone against the white linen of his shirt.

"Richard!" I cried.

He whirled around, and I was in his arms.

"Jayne, what in God's name?"

"I know I'm not supposed to be here, but had to see you! Please don't trust Stanley! He's not going to help you!"

He held me close and stroked my hair, then took my hand and led me out of the tent.

"Look on that hill."

He pointed to our right. "Do you see those hundreds of torches?"

"Yes."

"That's Lord Stanley's camp. There are two thousand men there, ready to fight for me tomorrow. Now, do you see the other side? That's his brother, Sir William's, camp. He has brought almost that number."

"I've Stanley's son in my custody, where he will stay until after the battle. Stanley wouldn't dare betray me! So you see, I took your warnings to heart."

We walked back inside, where his breast plate and greaves, helm and gauntlets, stood gleaming and ready in the corner. Surely Stanley wouldn't forfeit the life of his own son! Could it be that I'd managed to save Richard, as well as Dickon? It felt much too good to be true.

He dismissed his squires, and sat me down on a long wooden chest that rested beside the desk.

"Now, how did you get here from Sheriff Hutton?" he said. "Tell me you didn't travel alone."

"No, Rose came with me, along with Johnnie and Dickon. I left them in Leicester."

The smile left his face and his grey eyes darkened.

"You took Dickon from Sheriff Hutton? Why would you do such a thing? Where are they now?"

"They're both fine. They're with Brother Cynneth. Richard, Stanley sent James Talbott to Sheriff Hutton..."

For the second time that day, I recounted the tale of how I'd killed a man. I didn't relate my suspicions about Bess, because Richard would only blame himself. But I told everything else the way it had happened, and I watched the expression on Richard's mobile face change from dismay, to amazement, and finally to tenderness.

"You are the bravest woman I've ever known," he said. He went to a table in a corner of the tent, and came back with a small silver box in his hand, a box I recognized immediately.

He opened it, and there, on its bed of midnight blue velvet, lay the silver boar.

But I didn't want it anymore. Tears ran down through the dust on my cheeks.

"I can't take it. It's too important to you."

"I planned to wear it tomorrow, but I want you to have it. You saved the life of my son, and my nephew! You've proved your loyalty to me more than once. And I want to prove mine to you."

He knelt beside me and placed the box in my hand.

"After the battle, no more hiding. This was the first sigil I had made, when I was a just a boy and chose the boar for my symbol. I want you to wear it on your gown, or on a chain around your neck. I want the whole world to see it, and know you're mine. I love you, Jayne."

He stood up, and went to get a pewter bowl and a piece of cloth. He dipped the cloth in the tepid water, and he took my chin in his rough brown hand and began to wash the dirt and tears off my face. His touch was thorough, but gentle, and to my horror I started crying again.

"What's wrong?" he asked me. "I thought my gift would make you happy."

I shook my head, and wiped my eyes. I smelled the warm, musky clove scent of his living body. How could I explain to him that the simple routine acts of his breathing, and the blood pumping through his veins, were miracles to me, miracles that might have only hours until they ended forever?

He dropped the cloth he'd been holding and pulled me over onto his lap. I kissed the firm line of his jaw, and the curve of his throat, and rubbed my face against the coarse stubble, not caring if his whiskers scratched a raw spot on my cheek. I wanted to be marked by him, to feel the living fact of his existence in every way possible.

I put my hand under his shirt and touched his bare skin. Scars from other battles marred the smoothness, and the tears threatened to spill from my eyes again, but I blinked them away. Nothing would cloud my vision tonight. I untied the laces of his hose, and when he was naked, he pulled me to him.

"Wait," I said. "Let me look at you."

He smiled, and I could see he didn't understand. But he let me run my hands over his crooked shoulder, across his chest and down his waist and hips. If only I could memorize every detail of his flesh!

At last he grew impatient. He slipped his arm behind my knees and scooped me off my feet, and carried me to a dim corner of the tent to lay me down on the narrow camp bed where he would spend his last night.

He lowered his face to mine and kissed me again, and the familiar taste of his mouth aroused me in spite of my aching heart. After both our bodies were spent, I laid my head against his chest and listened to the beating of his heart. My eyes ached from holding back the tears. The silver boar belonged to me now, and if what I believed about its magic was true, all I had to do was take it in my hand, and I would be back in my old life. But for the rest of my days, I would listen to the world condemn the man I loved, a man I knew to be innocent.

He took my hand in his.

"You have to leave now, Jayne. I must attack him before dawn."

I gripped him tighter than ever, but the friar was right. I couldn't stop him.

"Will you do one thing for me before I leave? It may seem foolish, but..."

He listened to my request with a furrowed brow; for a moment I thought he would refuse. But he threw on his hose, and shirt, and went to his desk to get parchment and a quill.

CHAPTER 37

RICHARD: AUGUST 22, 1485

BOSWORTH FIELD

Jayne's request baffled me, but I saw no reason not to grant it. She watched me sign the order, and pour the wax and emboss it with my seal, as if her life depended upon it.

The squire I'd appointed to ride back to town with her brought her horse to the front of my tent. I held her tight, and inhaled the sweetness of her skin. A grey light was breaking in the east, and in just a few hours, the battle smell of blood and death would fill my nostrils. But for a moment, there was only her.

Then the sounds of clanking harness, the twanging of bowstrings and the stomping and neighing of horses told me my camp was waking.

"You have to go, my love. My captains will be here soon."

She held on to me as if I hadn't spoken.

I unwound her arms from around my body as gently as I could, and looked for the leather pouch I'd tied to her waist.

"You have my gift, and my heart. Now please go and wait for me in Leicester. I'll come to you there, I promise."

I lifted her onto her horse myself. She was crying again, silent tears that contorted her lovely face.

Then she smiled, and reached for my hand.

"I love you, Richard Plantagenet," she said.

I told the squire to protect her with his life and slapped her horse on the rump. She turned and waved goodbye again before they were lost from sight among the tents of my soldiers. In the west, lights were just flickering in the Tudor's camp.

I was forcing myself to swallow a crust of bread when Francis Lovell came into the tent.

"Am I dreaming, or did I just see Jayne ride out of the camp?" he said.

"You did."

He grinned. "You sent for her, then?"

"No, she just appeared. I thought I was dreaming myself for a moment."

"She's a jewel, Richard. Not many women are so loyal, or so brave."

Her tear-stained face floated before my eyes. How I longed to make her smile again!

"What are you thinking?" asked Francis.

"Thinking about how my brother married for love," I said.

He laughed and slapped me on the shoulder.

By the time my squire buckled me into my armor, the rest of my captains had gathered. All except Stanley.

"What's he playing at?" mused Jockey. "You ought to flay that son of his alive."

"He's waiting to see how the hounds run," said Francis.

"Then we must reach our quarry first," I said.

We gathered around my desk to look at the map one last time. Jockey and his son would lead my vanguard, and my household knights and I would follow close behind.

"We'll march through Sutton Cheney to Ambien Hill," I said. "From there we can see the camps of both Stanleys, and Tudor's as well."

Jockey and my other captains rode back to their detachments, leaving only my household knights, and my faithful secretary John Kendall, awkward but proud in his old-fashioned armor.

Our squires had our horses waiting. Surrey jigged and pulled so that it took two men to hold him. I stroked his silky white neck, and he calmed long enough for me to get a foot in the stirrup. I bent down from the saddle, and one of my officers placed my crown around my helm.

"Are you sure that's wise?" asked Catesby, ever my lawyer.

Before I could answer, a red-faced soldier cantered up.

"Lord Norfolk is ready to march, sir," he said.

I looked around for a squire. "Ride to Lord Stanley's camp and tell him that if he values the life of his son, he will meet me on Ambien Hill."

We made our way down from the camp and turned west towards the village of Sutton Cheney. I stopped my men just on the other side, to give my foot soldiers a rest. After they'd had time for a swallow of ale, I gave the signal and we moved forward again.

Jockey's vanguard proceeded up and over the hill with the Howard banner of the silver lion leading the way. The long column of my own men stood waiting, each detachment marked by the livery and banners of its leader. I gave the order to march, and we moved out into the cool August morning just as dawn reddened the sky. I had a sharp sword and a game horse, my bravest men beside me, and my enemy in front of me. My heart lifted.

I was disposing my division on the hill top, and had just ordered a group of mounted archers and men-at-arms to ride ahead of us up along the ridge to the crest, when the messenger I'd sent to Stanley's camp approached us at a gallop.

He stopped in front of me, jumped down from his horse and removed his helm.

His breath came in gusts.

"Your Grace, Lord Stanley says he's not disposed to come to you right now," he said, his voice shaky.

The world went silent. So Stanley would have his revenge at last. I knew he'd never forgiven me for Johnnie, and that he never would, but his frank betrayal left me stunned.

The messenger was looking down at his mailed feet.

"What else did he say, man? I'll not punish you for it."

"He said to remind you that it's easy to make a son."

Lovell brought his charger as close to Surrey as the two stallions would allow.

"You know what this does to our numbers," he said.

I knew. "And however goes Lord Thomas, so goes Sir William," I said.

The Stanleys between them had over three thousand men. We were now badly outnumbered, and with a Stanley brother and his army on either side of Jocky's men like pincers.

The trumpets of the Pretender rang out, and a bedlam of commands in Welsh, French, and English rose on the air. Jockey's archers let fly their arrows, and were in turn raked by the arrows of Tudor's hired mercenaries. The lines of men ebbed and flowed like a sea of axes, swords, and spears. The most pressure was in the middle of the lines, which soon bent inwards and began to thin, but by the Saints, they held their ground! I watched as Jockey and his son showed themselves worthy of the silver lion on their shields.

But a flurry of fighting men formed a cluster around them. They hacked with their swords on first one side, then the other. I gasped when the standard bearing the silver lion went down. My oldest and truest friend...

"Lord Norfolk is killed!" yelled a squire.

A lone horseman caught my eye as he galloped across the plain away from where Jockey lay, towards the enemy. I watched him stop and make obeisance in front of a mounted knight, close beside the banner bearing a red dragon. Tudor! The messenger must be telling him that my greatest ally was down.

Jockey's men began to scatter, even as Stanley's began to move towards my position.

"Your Grace," said Catesby, "We must seek safety while yet we can! One battle is not all..."

Henry Tudor sat safely out of the fray, surrounded by some twenty-five men. The villain who'd smeared my name, and threatened all I held dear, lay only yards away. How I longed to look him in the eye! If I could strike him a mortal blow, his rebels would have nothing to fight for; it would be over, and England would be at peace.

I rose in my stirrups.

"I ride to seek Henry Tudor, and engage him man to man! I must cross the front of Lord Stanley's army to reach him, so I'll not order you to follow. Who is with me?"

The cheer that rose from the lips of my household knights sent my heart into my throat.

The morning breeze caught my standard as the knight who carried it rode up to my side. The white boar blazed against the red of the pennant, and I thought of Jayne. The silver badge I'd given her would provide for her the rest of her days if God willed that I should not.

A squire put my battle-axe in my hand. I looked back at my friends, who'd been loyal to me, and given me good service, at peace and at war. Francis Lovell, Rob Percy, John Milewater, Robert Brackenbury, William Catesby, John Kendall, and the dozens behind them. Now they sat ready, swords and axes bristling, to ride down the hill at my side. I loved them all.

I motioned to the trumpeter, and the thrilling sound of the battle call of the Plantagenets filled the air, the same notes that sent my mighty brother and me into combat at Barnet, and Towton. One more look at the Tudor, slouching on his horse while men died all around him, before I lowered my visor.

"Your Grace, at least take off your crown!" said a voice from somewhere in the back.

"I will live, or die, King of England," I said, and gave the signal to charge.

CHAPTER 38

JAYNE: AUGUST 22, 1485

BOSWORTH FIELD

"*B*ut my lady, I've the strictest orders to take you straight to Leicester! You heard King Richard!"

I felt for the man. First his king sent him away from the battle to escort a woman, and now she insisted on disobeying him. But no one would stop me from seeing Richard one more time.

I left him sputtering behind me, and cantered Juno to the top of the rise.

I looked down on Richard's camp. I'd seen it before: the sea of tents, with their colorful banners, and the glinting armor of the knights was identical to the vision I'd had that day in the trench when I first touched the boar. I closed my eyes against the dizziness that overtook me, grabbed a handful of Juno's mane to steady myself in the saddle, and looked again.

Richard's tent, where we'd been together last night, was near the middle of the camp, under the double banner of the white boar, and the royal lions and lilies of England. Was that Richard's dark head next to the massive form of White Surrey? Yes! It was him. He took the reins, and swung into the saddle. The sun gleamed on the gold crown around his helm.

No! I kicked Juno and we ran back towards the camp. The squire took off after me, and he must have been a better horseman, on a faster horse, because he was beside me in an instant. He grabbed Juno's bridle in his glove and whirled his horse in front of her nose.

"Mistress Lyons! I mean no disrespect! But I will follow the king's orders!"

"He's wearing his crown!" I was wailing now, I didn't care what the man thought. "They'll kill him!"

He stared at me, and I could have sworn there were tears in his eyes, too.

"You must let him fight his battle, my lady."

I looked past him down into the camp. The soldiers in their narrow columns had moved off towards the west, and all that I could see of Richard was the banner with its white boar.

"You can let go of her bridle," I said. "I'll go with you."

We walked back to the old Roman road and headed for Leicester.

*T*he battle was a dull roar behind us, that rose and fell with the wind. The clash of an axe against Richard's head, and his screams of pain and fury, were somewhere in that din, and I had to get away from the sound. I kicked Juno into a gallop, and we ran so fast that the squire could barely keep us with us, but when silence fell, it was more horrific than the noise. We crossed Bow Bridge into the gates of the city in less than two hours.

I found the friar in the chapel, kneeling in almost the same spot he'd occupied the day before. Before I got to his side, I stopped in the cool peace and prayed to go back to yesterday, when my last night with Richard was still ahead of me. I closed my eyes, and heard the steady beating of his heart, and felt his warm flesh beneath my hand. For just a moment, we breathed together.

But when I opened my eyes, Brother Cynneth was looking up at me with swollen lids, and for Richard's sake, I tried to push my misery aside. I fell on my knees beside him.

"You couldn't stop him," he said.

"No, no, I tried, but..."

He took my hand, and the pain on his face mirrored my own.

I pulled the parchment, and the silver casket, out of my pouch.

"He gave you his sigil," he said.

"Yes, and I'm giving it to you. Along with this."

I unfolded the parchment and handed it to him.

"You have to make me a promise."

He nodded as I explained, and when I finished, his face had almost returned to its usual peaceful expression.

"I will do as you ask, but now you must go."

"I want to wait. I want to see him one last time."

"No, Jayne! I told you before how horrible he looked, in my vision. If you see him that way, that's how you will always remember him. He wouldn't wish it."

"But maybe I shouldn't leave at all. What about the boys? What about Johnnie? He needs me."

"Johnnie is almost a man grown. He will fight his father's battle here for the rest of his life, and you will only alienate him by trying to protect him. And you must fight Richard's battle in the future, where it can still be won."

The old oaken door of the chapel swung back on its hinges and the squire Richard has sent with me to Leicester ran to us.

"The king is dead! He's dead, and his crown is on the Tudor's head!"

The young man's shoulders shook with his sobs.

Brother Cynneth stood up and put an arm around his shoulders.

"I must go to John of Gloucester. Would you come with me?"

He nodded, and wiped his nose on his sleeve.

When they reached the door, the friar turned back to me.

"Jayne, you know what you must do."

When the door was shut behind them, I knelt back down on the stone floor and opened the casket. I folded the parchment and placed it inside the lid. A stray shaft of sunlight came through the stained glass window behind the altar, and the boar shone like Richard's eyes.

I took a deep breath, and reached out my hand.

CHAPTER 39

JAYNE: AUGUST 2012

"*H*ey! Are you all right? What happened?"

I wasn't all right. I was sick, and dizzy. I put a clammy hand to my head. Above me, a figure of a man was silhouetted in the sunlight.

I closed my eyes until my stomach quit heaving.

"Hey!" he called again. "Let me help you."

I opened my eyes again. I was in a hole of some sort. I almost panicked before I remembered.

"We have to be careful we don't disturb the body," he said. "Do you think you can climb out if I give you my hand?"

"Yes, just give me a minute," I said. I looked down at my feet.

It took a moment for my eyes to adjust, but when they did, I saw it there, just as before, lying next to the bones of his crooked shoulder.

"I think I found something!" I said.

CHAPTER 40

JAYNE: OCTOBER 6, 2017

YALE UNIVERSITY

"*A*nd so that's how one of history's greatest cold cases was finally solved," I said.

A girl in the back raised her hand.

"How do we know Richard really wrote the order?" she asked. "I mean, could someone else have just put the document there later?"

"Forensics, my dear. The parchment has been dated to the last half of the fifteenth century, and the signature is an exact match with proven examples of Richard's autograph."

Another student raised his hand.

"Where is the document now, Professor Lyons? Can we see it?"

"If you're willing to cross the pond, you can. It's on display in the British Museum. There was a heated debate about where it should be exhibited. Some people thought it should stay in Leicester, where Richard was re-interred in 2015. But the Museum is a more central location."

"Which did you favor?"

"The British Museum. The more folks who see it, the better. Next?"

"Have you got the contents of the letter memorized?"

I laughed. The original was pictured on the screen behind me but I didn't need to turn around to recite it.

"*I*, Richard Plantagenet, King of England, hereby place my nephew, the bastard son of King Edward IV formerly known as Richard of York, into the care of Brother Cynneth Beauchamp and the Franciscan Order of the Grey Friars in the Priory of the City of Leicester. It is my wish and intent that his life be dedicated to the service of our Lord, and in particular to the supplications for the soul of his elder brother, the bastard son of Edward IV, formerly known as King Edward V, who was killed by highwaymen on the Great North Road between London and Sheriff Hutton Castle. I hereby grant the sum of 100 marks sterling per annum to said Priory from the revenues of our lordship of Middleham for the upkeep and maintenance of Richard, and for daily prayer for the soul of Edward."

By the King

22 August 1485

At Bosworth Field

"So one of the princes was still alive when Richard died," said the first girl.

"Yes, and as you probably already know, the remains of the eldest prince were found at the ruins of Sheriff Hutton, and positively identified last year using DNA," I said.

"Everyone who thought he killed the Princes in the Tower was wrong, including Shakespeare," said the man next to her.

"Especially Shakespeare," I said.

They laughed.

"If there are no more questions, we'll start next time with his birth and early childhood. See you on Wednesday!"

They stood up and began packing up laptops and notebooks.

I turned off my MacBook and shoved it into its case. I was already nearly late to pick up my son. I pictured his grey eyes and head full of dark curls and grabbed up my purse.

"Professor Lyons?"

It was the girl from the back who'd raised her hand first.

"I'm Becky," she said, and held out her hand.

I rearranged my belongings and shook it.

"I'm glad to meet you, but I'm afraid I'm in a hurry to pick up my little boy."

"Can I walk out with you?"

"Sure. Come on."

She followed me out into the hallway of the History Building and fell into step beside me.

"I heard you were there at the dig, the day they found the silver box with the letter inside it," she said. "That must have been an incredible experience."

"It was. I can honestly say it changed my life."

"Did you have any idea that it would be so fantastic?"

"Not a clue. I was just a volunteer. I'd overheard some other students talking about it in a pub the night before," I said.

"Well, I just wanted to tell you how much I'm looking forward to your class. You seem so passionate about your subject. I envy you. I hope someday I find something I can love like that."

I smiled at her. "I hope you do, too."

We'd reached the parking lot.

"How old is your son?"

"Dickon will be four this spring."

"And you named him after Richard III?"

"I named him for his father."

"Oh, cool! Well, goodbye; it was great meeting you. Can't wait 'til Wednesday!"

"Same here!" I said.

THE END

Thank you for reading! For more about Anne-Marie Lacy find her across social media.

Facebook: www.facebook.com/annemarie.lacy

Pinterest: www.pinterest.com/annemarielacy64/

Please sign up for the City Owl Press newsletter for chances to win special subscriber-only contests and giveaways as well as receiving information on upcoming releases and special excerpts.

All reviews are **welcome** and **appreciated**. Please consider leaving one on your favorite social media and book buying sites.

For books in the world of romance and speculative fiction that embody Innovation, Creativity, and Affordability, check out City Owl Press at www.cityowlpress.com.

ACKNOWLEDGMENTS

Thank you with all my heart to my early readers, who encouraged me without fail through three years of researching and writing, and rewriting, THE MEDIEVALIST.

Theresa Menefee, Brenda Buschmann, and Heather Pemberton-Levy, you supported and inspired me. I was privileged to meet distinguished author John Crowley at the Yale Writers Conference in 2014, and I am forever in his debt for forcing me to acknowledge the weaknesses in the first manuscript. Lawrence Christon, you convinced me it would all be worth it in the end.

To my husband, Allen Lacy, who cheerfully listened to every word read aloud: you are a saint, even by medieval standards.

And to Yelena Casale and Tina Moss of City Owl Press, I appreciate your faith in The Medievalist more than you will ever know. Strong women, empowering other women – that's what it's all about.

ABOUT THE AUTHOR

ANNE-MARIE LACY is an attorney and amateur historian who loves both reading and writing about magical experiences. She lives in a small town in north Alabama with her husband Allen and an Irish Wolfhound named Devon.

Facebook: www.facebook.com/annemarie.lacy

Pinterest: www.pinterest.com/annemarielacy64/

ABOUT THE PUBLISHER

City Owl Press is a cutting edge indie publishing company, bringing the world of romance and speculative fiction to discerning readers.

www.cityowlpress.com